The Girl in the Photograph

KATE RIORDAN

PENGUIN BOOKS

PENGUIN BOOKS

Published by the Penguin Group
Penguin Books Ltd, 80 Strand, London WC2R ORL, England
Penguin Group (USA) Inc., 375 Hudson Street, New York, New York 10014, USA
Penguin Group (Canada), 90 Eglinton Avenue East, Suite 700, Toronto, Ontario, Canada M4P 2Y3
(a division of Pearson Penguin Canada Inc.)
Penguin Ireland, 25 St Stephen's Green, Dublin 2, Ireland (a division of Penguin Books Ltd)
Penguin Group (Australia), 707 Collins Street, Melbourne, Victoria 3008,
Australia (a division of Pearson Australia Group Pty Ltd)
Penguin Books India Pvt Ltd, 11 Community Centre,
Panchsheel Park, New Delhi – 110 017, India
Penguin Group (NZ), 67 Apollo Drive, Rosedale, Auckland 0632, New Zealand
(a division of Pearson New Zealand Ltd)
Penguin Books (South Africa) (Pty) Ltd, Block D, Rosebank Office Park, 181 Jan Smuts Avenue,
Parktown North, Gauteng 2193, South Africa

Penguin Books Ltd, Registered Offices: 80 Strand, London WC2R ORL, England

www.penguin.com

First published 2015

001

Copyright © Kate Riordan, 2015
All rights reserved

The moral right of the author has been asserted

Typeset in 12.5/14.75 pt Garamond MT Std by Palimpsest Book Production Ltd,
Falkirk, Stirlingshire
Printed in Great Britain by Clays Ltd, St Ives plc

B FORMAT ISBN: 978–1–405–91742–1
TRADE PAPERBACK ISBN: 978–0–718–17928–1

www.greenpenguin.co.uk

For my four parents, for their love and belief

Prologue: Alice

Midsummer, 1936

Fiercombe is a place of secrets. They fret among the uppermost branches of the beech trees and brood at the cold bottom of the stream that cleaves the valley in two. The past has seeped into the soil here, like spilt blood. If you listen closely enough you can almost hear what's gone before, particularly on the stillest days. Sometimes the very air seems to hum with anticipation. At other times it's as though a collective breath has been drawn in and held. It waits, or so it seems to me.

The word 'combe' means valley in some of England's south-westerly counties but the roots of 'fier' are more obscure. At first I thought it was a reference to a past inferno, or perhaps a hint of one to come. It seemed just the sort of place that would dramatically burn to the ground one night; I could imagine too easily the glow of it from the escarpment high above, smoke staining the air, the spit and pop of ancient, husk-dry timbers as the flames licked faster. But I was quite wrong: in Old English it means 'wooded hill', aptly describing the dense and disorderly ranks of hanging beech that leer and loom as you descend steeply towards the old manor house.

Things you would never accept in everyday life – strange happenings, presences and atmospheres, inexplicable lurches of time – are commonplace at Fiercombe. They have become commonplace to me. I have never grown accustomed to the darkness of night here, though. The blackness is total, like a suffocating blanket that steals over you the instant the light is turned out. When open eyes have nothing to focus on, no bar of light under the door, no chink of moonshine through heavy curtains, they strain to catch sight of something, anything. During those early nights here, my eyes would flick from where I knew the windows were to the door and back, until exhaustion turned the walls to a liquid that rose up me in oily waves.

Like a blind person, my other senses grew quickly acute for the lack of visual distraction. Even in the dead of night, when the house finally slept, I was convinced I could hear it breathe, somewhere at the very edges of my hearing, beneath the whisperings and scratchings I thought I could discern. Even in the day, when nothing looked out of the ordinary, I would still find my skin prickling with the vibrations of the place, something instinctive and animal in me knowing that things had been knocked out of balance, that something had gone awry.

I have been here a little over three years now, since the late spring of 1933. When I arrived from London I was not quite six months' pregnant by a man I wasn't married to. A man married to someone else. If it hadn't been for him and my own foolishness, and the subsequent horror and shame of my parents, then I would never have come to Fiercombe at all. What a strange thought that is now, after all that has happened.

When I think back to the time before I came here, it feels like someone else's life, read in a book. It's difficult for me to recapture how I truly felt about things then; how I went about my normal routine of working, the evening meal with my parents, going to the lido or the pictures with my friend Dora, and daydreaming about the man I thought I was in love with. I see now that I wasn't very grown-up.

I came just as spring was softening and deepening into languid summer. It was a beautiful summer – more beautiful than any I've known before or since – though I was still glad to put it behind me when autumn finally arrived. Too glad, perhaps. There were rifts in the valley that remained unhealed as the leaves began to turn but I was too busy forging my own new beginning to acknowledge them. The signs and clues were there; I simply chose not to heed them. I have let three years of contented life in the present chase away the unresolved past, just as the morning sun does the nightmare. Today's confession has changed all that and I can no longer turn away. They deserve better. They always did.

Alice

Four years earlier

In the summer of 1932 I had never heard of a place called Fiercombe. I was still living an ordinary sort of life then. A life that someone else, looking in, would probably have thought rather dull. That was certainly how I viewed it, though I was reluctant to admit that at the time, even to myself. After all, admitting it also meant facing the likelihood that nothing more interesting awaited me on the horizon.

It wasn't until after I left school that I began to feel a creeping sort of restlessness. I had got a full scholarship to the local grammar and I had liked it there – not just for the solace of its rituals and order but for its pervading sense of purposeful preparation. Preparation for what was to come after: the tantalizing, unknowable future. What shape that would take I had no idea. Much of its allure lay in its very amorphousness, the vague sense of expectation that edges closest on those perfect summer evenings of which England never seems to have enough. Evenings gilded with twilight, the perfumed air brimming with promise. Yet the mornings after those evenings always seemed to go on in the normal way – the world shrunk to a familiar room again, consoling but uninspiring, the walls near enough to touch.

Quite suddenly, or so it felt, school was long behind

me and I was a woman of twenty-two. Still nothing of any note had happened to me. I remained at home with my parents, I had a job that I could have done perfectly adequately in my sleep, and there was no sense that whatever I had blithely expected to lift me clear of the mundane was any nearer. If anything, it seemed to have retreated.

My mother was no less frustrated by my lack of progress – though for rather different reasons. I was a good-looking girl, she told me somewhat grudgingly, so why did I never mention any gentlemen friends? Why was I not engaged, or even courting? After the milestone of my twenty-second birthday had passed, she aired those anxieties with ever-increasing frequency, her expression at once baleful and triumphant.

Triumphant, I suppose, because she had never really wanted me to go to the grammar school, believing that girls with too many brains were fatally unattractive to prospective husbands. Though the shortage of men after the Great War had been the crisis of an older generation, there lingered a sense of urgency for unmarried girls, at least in my mother's mind. She also professed not to see the point of school beyond the legal leaving age of fourteen. Anything after that was for boys, and girls with plain faces, she said. After all, no woman could keep her job after her wedding anyway.

For the time being, my own job – one I knew I was fortunate to have when so many had no work – contributed to the household budget, an aspect of it that even my mother couldn't criticize. Each morning I took a bus south to Finsbury Park, where I caught the Piccadilly line to Russell Square. Just off the square was the office where

I was the junior of two typists to a Mr Marshall, a minor publisher of weighty academic books. I had a smart suit I had saved to buy rather than make, and two handbags between which I transferred the gold-plated compact my aunt had bought me one Christmas.

On my first day I had felt rather sophisticated as I walked to the bus stop, the pinch of my new court shoes a grown-up and therefore pleasurable kind of discomfort. A few years on from that hopeful morning and I still occasionally felt a vestige of that early pride – it was just that sometimes, particularly during the afternoons, which were so quiet I could hear the ponderous tick of the clock mounted on the wall, I couldn't help wondering when my life – my real life – would begin.

I had never had any sort of serious attachment to a man. Perhaps the closest I'd come was a boy at school, whom I'd let kiss me a few times. At the grammar, some of the lessons were mixed and David had been in my French class. He'd thought he was in love with me during the last summer we spent there and, during those drowsy afternoons, when the high windows were opened and the smell of cut grass made us long for the bell, he would stare at me across the room. His gaze made my skin tingle warmly, and left me conscious of how I sat, how my hair was arranged, and what facial expression I wore. But the truth of it was not love, or probably even lust. What I liked was the way he felt about me, and I'm sure he was more in love with the sudden intensity of his feelings than he was with the girl in the next row.

Now many of my friends – David Gardiner too, in all probability – were married or engaged, or at the very least courting, yet I had failed to meet anyone. Dora, who was forever trying to persuade me out to meet a friend of whichever man she was currently interested in, teased me gently for being so fussy. My mother, being my mother, was rather more direct.

'You'll be left on the shelf if you don't get a move on,' she said one Saturday, when I had been made to accompany her shopping on our local high street in a north London suburb. 'I've said it before and no doubt I'll say it again, but if you spent less time reading and more time out and about in the fresh air or going to dances, you'd give yourself a better chance.'

I remember we were in the chemist's shop, which was hushed except for my mother's voice and the bell that trilled whenever the door opened. The air smelt of floral talc and carbolic soap, and faintly bitter from the medicines and tonics that were measured and weighed out of sight.

We had an argument then – about lipstick of all the ridiculous things: she wanted me to buy a brighter shade than I could imagine myself wearing. That led to other topics of discord and by the time we were walking home, past the new cafe that had just opened opposite Woolworths, we had returned to the subject of my job and her conviction that I would never meet anyone if I remained in it.

'Why don't you try for work in there?' she said, nodding towards a girl behind the cafe's plate glass, pert in her smart uniform with its starched white collar.

Shifting the bags I was carrying to my other hand, I couldn't rouse myself to reply.

'I know you're a typist in an office in town, and that's all very fancy,' my mother continued, 'but May Butler's daughter Lillian met her husband when she was waitressing and look at her now, with a house in Finchley and a little one on the way.'

Lillian had left school at fourteen and eventually got a job as a Nippy in a Lyons Corner House on the Strand. According to my mother, Lillian had been admired half a dozen times a day by her male customers, solitary men in suits who'd come in for a plate of chops or some tea and toast. Eventually, apparently without much ado, she had married one of them.

'I don't want to be a waitress,' I said wearily.

'You shouldn't turn your nose up at it – you don't earn much more than the ones in the nice places do.'

'Yes, but I –'

'Oh, I know you think you're meant for better things but it hasn't happened yet, has it? And it won't while you're stuck up there with old Mr Marshall.'

What she could not possibly have known was that only a week after that desultory wander around the shops I would at last meet a man I actually desired, someone who would bring the world to life for me, at least for a time. In fact, the circumstances that would throw us together were already in train: an appointment made, a crucial hour already approaching. For it was in Mr Marshall's office – the obscure, dusty office my mother believed had already sealed my spinsterhood – that everything was about to change for me.

As if to further dramatize this episode, to darken the line that marked before and after, he arrived towards the end of a particularly silent, stultifying day. I remember that he was a little out of breath after climbing the stairs to our small office. A late summer shower was flooding the pavements outside and he brought with him the smell of damp wool and cologne as he came noisily through the door. Mr Marshall heard it crash back on its hinges and came rushing out of his tiny room to greet the new arrival, whom he had obviously been expecting. They made a curious pair: Mr Marshall, an inch shorter than me and probably half a stone lighter, only came up to his visitor's chest.

'Who was that?' I said to Miss Cunningham, after they had gone out to lunch, Mr Marshall not having thought to introduce us. Miss Cunningham was the senior typist and didn't like me very much, perhaps because she knew I didn't aspire to her job.

'Mr Elton? He's too old and too married for you to concern yourself with,' she replied crisply.

After I had made her a cup of tea she relented, unable to resist demonstrating that she knew more than I did.

'He's the new accountant, if you must know. The old one's retired and now we've got him. Bit too sure of himself, if you ask me.' She sniffed and went back to her work.

They didn't return from lunch for two hours, and when they did, Mr Marshall was uncharacteristically flushed, eyes glazed behind his spectacles. Miss Cunningham got up and pointedly opened a window, though I couldn't smell any alcohol on them; only the rain and the new accountant's cologne.

While she was at the window he crossed the room towards me and I saw that his eyes were the same shade

9

of deep brown as his hair. He didn't have a single feature that stood out as exceptional but they combined in such a way as to make him handsome.

'Pleased to meet you,' he said, his voice low and unhurried. 'I'm James Elton.' He shook my hand. His was warm and dry. 'I've met the lovely Miss Cunningham, of course, but you are?'

'Alice,' I said, more bluntly than I'd meant to because I was thinking about my hand being cold. I was forever cold in that office, regardless of the season. 'Alice Eveleigh.'

When I left work a couple of hours later he was waiting for me in the cafe that I had to pass to reach the Underground. I spotted him before he saw me: sitting up at the window on a stool that looked silly and feminine beneath him. If he hadn't glanced up from his paper at that moment, and raised his hand with a smile, I would certainly have walked on. It would never have occurred to me to tap on the window.

Of course, I didn't know then that he'd been waiting for me; he didn't tell me that until later. Instead, he smiled his easy smile and, when I hesitated, gestured for me to come in and join him. We had some tea and he tried to persuade me to order a slice of sponge cake. We talked about this and that: London, the weather, of course, and what I thought of my job in Mr Marshall's quiet office. I said, rather primly, that I was very grateful to have it and he grimaced, which made us both laugh.

That was the beginning. Shared pots of tea became habitual until one fog-bound autumn evening he appeared out of the shadows as I left the office for the day and suggested that we had dinner together. It was too filthy a night for a paltry cup of tea, he said. Perhaps we might try this little restaurant he had discovered down a nearby back-street.

Afterwards, on the way to the Underground, he stopped and pulled me towards him. I would like to say I resisted but I simply couldn't. In truth, my face was already tilted up towards him before his lips touched mine. You find that once something like that has happened, it's very hard to go back to how it was before.

He was almost fifteen years older than me. When I was eight or nine, a schoolgirl with pale brown hair cut to the jaw, he was a newly minted accountant. Each morning he took the Metropolitan line into the City, his briefcase unscuffed, his newness such that he had not yet earned a regular seat on the carriage he always boarded.

His wife, when she came along, was a suitable, pretty girl called Marjorie. His domineering mother apparently approved; she and Marjorie's mother played bridge together, I think. He once mentioned in passing that Marjorie was an excellent tennis player, which I found both intimidating and fascinating.

When I met him he was thirty-six, already eleven unimaginable years into his unhappy union. He once said that you would imagine time spent like that would crawl by – the inverse of it flying when you are enjoying yourself. But in fact those years, packed tight with obligation – the tennis doubles and dinner parties and whist drives – had been compressed.

Once, when I think he must have been rather drunk, he confided that Marjorie didn't like the physical side of marriage much. He was desperately unhappy, he told me, time and time again. They had made a terrible mistake when they got married; they had never really loved each other; the whole thing had been engineered by their mothers.

After that first kiss, I went around in a fug of guilt and excitement. I didn't confide in anyone, not even Dora. I knew that, despite all her casually knowledgeable talk of men, she had never gone beyond a certain point and would never dream of doing so with a married man. You simply didn't, and the boys we had grown up with knew it as well as we did.

When I wasn't with him I thought about him constantly, indulging myself in the delicious agony of it all and mooning about, like a girl in a sentimental song. Precisely like that, in fact: it was around that time that Dora bought a gramophone record of Noël Coward's new song, 'Mad About The Boy', and played it endlessly. Every day I felt queasy as I walked past the cafe on my way home from work – in case he was there, waiting, and in case he never was again.

He didn't appear for three weeks after the kiss and I felt eaten away by misery. When I finally saw him in the cafe one evening, head bent over his newspaper, it was as though the whole world – the sour breath of London's air, the hollow clip of women's heels and the rumble of the Piccadilly line's trains far below – ceased to be. I knew that nothing would have persuaded me to keep walking. I had been a nice, bookish sort of girl, and now I was someone different. I felt as though my life was out of my hands. It was like an attack of vertigo.

I only went to bed with him once, at a hotel. Of course,

that's all that's required, as anyone with their wits about them knows. Although it didn't occur to me then, I'm fairly sure I wasn't the first woman with whom he had been involved since his marriage. No doubt there had been dalliances, illicit kisses stolen, rooms booked for a couple of hours, even. He once took me to a nightclub tucked down an obscure lane behind Oxford Street that was so suitable for the job – with its shadowy corners, unobtrusive waiters and melancholy jazz music – that he must have discovered it in the course of some other liaison. I don't think I'd have minded that, though, even if I had realized it at the time. I think his attraction lay in his worldliness and how truly grown-up he seemed, so different from my own despised girlishness.

It was Dora who guessed the truth; I suppose I wasn't facing what was obvious at all. It was April by then and the weather had abruptly turned into something that felt like summer. One Sunday she rang the doorbell. I hadn't seen her in weeks, just as I hadn't seen James – who had disappeared without a word after our visit to the hotel. I stood at the top of the stairs and heard my mother asking her in. When she called me I went down reluctantly, knowing I looked pale and that my hair needed washing.

'Dora's come to see you,' said my mother. 'She thought you might go to the lido together.'

I smiled wanly at Dora. 'I don't think I will, if you don't mind. I don't feel very well.'

'You don't feel well because you're either at work in that office or cooped up in here,' retorted my mother. 'Go and get your things. Dora's come specially to see you. Where are your manners?'

I found I did feel a bit better out in the air. The lido was thronged with people; it was the first really warm day of the year and every last deckchair had been taken. Dora was lean in her bathing suit – mine felt tight and uncomfortable even though I'd been eating little. Before anyone could look at me I jumped into the unheated water, the shock of it dissolving the lead weight of my misery for a blissful few seconds.

After we'd swum, Dora wanted a drink. With our towels wrapped around ourselves we wandered into the relative gloom of the cafeteria. It was almost empty: everyone was sitting outside on the viewing terrace. I can't think why anyone would have wanted hot food on a day like that but they were frying something in the kitchen, the cloying smell of stale oil wafting through a hatch. I had hardly eaten that day but what little I'd had came up into my mouth. The thought of swallowing it made me retch again and I heaved into my cupped hands.

'Oh,' I said, and began to cry.

Dora took me to the ladies' lavatories and washed my face and hands for me, as if I was a child.

We looked at each other in the mirror. Her face was sharp and rosy; I was pallid and blurry-looking next to her, my brown hair lank on my shoulders.

'Please tell me you're not, Alice,' she said. 'Not you.'

'Not what?' I said, but, as I spoke, I knew.

'How long?' she said.

'I don't know it's that. I miss a month here and there. I always have.' My voice sounded desperate even to myself. 'Besides, it was only once.'

Dora simply stared at me. I tried to think of another

excuse but instead hung my head, the tears silently dripping off my nose and into the basin. A woman about my mother's age came out of the furthest cubicle and washed her hands next to me. In the mirror I saw her eyes flick over to my left hand, her lip curling with disapproval when she saw it was bare. She bustled out with her hands still wet.

'Will you get rid of it?' Dora said softly.

My stomach churned with fear at the decisions that had materialized from nowhere but now lay ahead, inescapable. 'It's against the law,' I whispered.

'I know that. People do, though.'

'I can't bear to think about it. I wish I could just lock myself in my room and never come out.'

'Why on earth did you let him?'

'He's getting a divorce. He said he wanted to marry me.'

'Oh, Alice.'

'What?' I said. 'What do you know of it? You're quite content to go to the pictures with a different man each week and you don't care about any of them. I suppose one day you'll just marry whichever of them happens to be taken with you at the time. I'm not like that. James and I love each other.'

Dora dried her hands on the roller towel. 'Have it your way, then. You obviously don't need my shoulder to cry on.'

She pulled open the door and looked back at me. 'I think you've been a perfect fool,' she said. 'I don't understand you, Alice, not any more.'

After she'd gone, I stood for a time, looking at myself in the mirror. I couldn't quite make myself believe what now seemed glaringly obvious.

When I got outside, Dora had gone, my clothes and shoes left in a neat pile. Feeling limp and dazed, I sat down and stayed there in the spring sunshine for an hour or more, watching the mothers and their children in the shallow end of the pool. The sound of the nearby fountain was soothing and I think I must have dozed for a while. When I woke, there was a wonderful second before I remembered the awful, incomprehensible fix I had got myself into. I sat up and tried to hug my knees close to myself, noticing with a shudder that it was now uncomfortable to do so. I stared down into the turquoise depths of the lido's perfectly oval pool until my vision swam with tears, which I blinked surreptitiously into my towel before any well-meaning person asked me what could be wrong on such a lovely day.

Of course, there was no conceivable way I could become a mother out of wedlock. Not just because I was woefully unprepared for it but because it would ruin my reputation. Needless to say, my parents would be mortified. I had been allowed to stay on at school because I had been good at my books. That would count for nothing now. I would lose my job and the wages that had made my parents' lives more comfortable. I had always been such a sensible girl. At the grammar, our teachers had told Dora's parents that I was an excellent influence on their more impetuous daughter, who hadn't got a scholarship like me and whose bank clerk father paid fees to keep her there.

Yet Dora would never have got herself into such a terrible mess. Impetuous she might have been, but she was never naïve. When she told me some of the romantic nonsense men had whispered to her, while sliding an arm around her shoulders at the Empire on a Saturday night, she always rolled her eyes. She knew what they were about while I, despite my cleverness, was as innocent as a child. I cast my mind back to all that James had said to me and understood why I had never told Dora about it. Somewhere in me, I had known she would laugh at me for being so easily taken in.

On my way home, while I still felt some semblance of resolve, I decided to do what I knew had to be done. I wasn't sure the pregnancy counted yet; I was barely three months gone and I hadn't felt a thing, apart from the sickness. There were medicines you could take but I didn't know exactly what or how much to ask for. If I went into a chemist's and asked for quinine or pennyroyal – both of them sounding like relics of evidence from a Victorian poisoning – wouldn't they guess what it was for?

In the end I bought a small bottle of cheap gin, telling the disinterested girl who took the money that it was for my father, and that evening ran myself a scalding bath. I was terrified my mother would smell the alcohol fumes on the steam so stuffed the gap under the door with a towel. As the water slowly cooled and the gin swirled into my blood I grew so dizzy and sleepy that I almost fainted. I couldn't even do that right, I thought, as I finally sat up and pulled out the plug. I'd nearly drowned myself instead of finishing what had scarcely begun inside me. I woke up the next morning with a nauseous, clamping headache, a furred mouth and a feeling of acute misery, but there was no blood.

I somehow endured a week at the office but the long, empty hours of the next Sunday undid me. Saying I was going out for some fresh air, I made the familiar journey to Dora's house.

'I'm sorry I called you a fool,' she said, once we were safely in her bedroom.

'No, you were right,' I said. 'I've been completely stupid.'

She sat up against her pillows. 'Have you thought about what you're going to do?'

I swallowed. 'I bought some gin but it didn't work. All I managed to do was nearly faint.'

'You do look awful,' she said, with her usual frankness. 'I'll have to tell Mother you've got a cold.'

'I was going to go to the chemist's,' I continued desperately, 'but I didn't know what to ask for. Then I thought of bumping myself down the stairs but I can't very well do that when my mother and father are in, can I?'

Dora stifled a giggle of hysteria. 'I'm sorry, Alice. I always laugh when I shouldn't, you know I do. The whole thing is just so awful. I can't really believe it yet.'

I sat down on the end of the bed and put my head in my hands.

'I've heard that Beecham's powders can work if you take enough of them,' she said. 'And washing soda, though I can't think how anyone would be able to force that down.'

'I think it's too late for all that. Perhaps if I'd done it weeks ago but now . . . I feel like it's taken hold, somehow. I don't think anything would work except . . .'

Dora sighed and covered my hand with hers. 'I think it's the only way. You can't possibly go ahead and have it.'

'No.'

We sat in silence for a few minutes until Dora spoke quietly. 'I know where you might go, I've been thinking about it. I heard Mother talking about someone once, when she thought I was upstairs. Remember she was a nurse before she married Father? Well, there was a midwife she knew then. They weren't friends or anything but she knew her. Anyway, it turns out that she does them in her kitchen. She lives in one of those streets the other side of the green, beyond the Empire. I know where it is because Mother said it was two doors up from the sweet shop on the corner. She said what a disgrace it was, all those innocent children walking past a house like that. We could easily go there one evening and no one would ever know. She charges two guineas – I'm sure that's what Mother said.'

'What do they do to it to get it out?' My voice was a whisper.

'I don't really know. I think they give you something to make it sort of come away, and then it's just like having your monthlies, only heavier.'

I nodded slowly because there was nothing else for it.

A few evenings later, Dora and I stood at a drab-coloured door. The woman who let us in was short and squat, her enormous, shelf-like bust emphasized by a dark apron.

'Don't just stand on the step, then,' she said, ushering us into a dingy hallway that smelt of boiled vegetables and something sharper.

After closing the door briskly, the evening sun shut out with a bang, she gestured for us to follow her towards the back of the house. Once in the kitchen, she looked at us enquiringly. When I didn't say anything, Dora spoke up.

'We've come … Well, we've come for my friend,' she gestured at me, 'because she needs …'

'I can guess why you're here,' said the woman, bluntly. 'I like to take payment first.'

'We were told it would be two guineas.' I could hear the tremor in Dora's voice.

The woman nodded. 'That's right.'

I took the money from my purse and put it into her outstretched hand. She transferred it deftly to the front pocket of her apron.

'Now then, lovey, how far gone are you?' she said, the endearment at odds with the situation.

'About three months,' I whispered.

'Not as late as some,' she replied. 'What have you tried already?'

I stared at her blankly and Dora broke in: 'She had some gin and a hot bath.'

'When it's taken, a bit of drink and warm water won't shift it,' the woman said. She pointed to a narrow table in the corner of the room. 'Take your underclothes off and get up on there. We'll soon have it done.'

I must have looked frightened because her face softened a shade. 'I've been a midwife for thirty years,' she said. 'I know what I'm about. You'll be right as rain in a few days. You've just got to think of it like we're bringing your monthlies on because they're late.'

I removed my shoes, stockings and knickers and folded them neatly on top of my handbag. I clambered up on to the table awkwardly, with Dora helping me, but kept my skirt pulled down and my legs together. Dora's hand on my arm was clammy.

I looked around the room, noticing a tray of congealed dripping on the side. Once I had, I thought I could smell it and it made my stomach turn. Through a smeary window I could see part of a yard, the door of an outhouse and a sagging line of washing.

Dora gave my arm a hesitant pat, then went to stand by the door. I knew how much she wanted to run back to her pretty bedroom, where she could lose herself in her magazines about Joan Crawford and Greta Garbo, the new vanishing cream and the latest permanent wave. I would have given anything to do that myself.

The woman unscrewed a jar, the contents of which she poked at with a spoon.

'What's in there?' said Dora.

'Slippery elm and a bit of pennyroyal,' she replied, without looking up.

'Do I drink it?' I said stupidly.

She laughed mirthlessly. 'You're an innocent one, that's for sure. Why would I have you undress for that? No, we put this up there to bring it on.'

I glanced at Dora but her gaze was fixed on the jar. 'Does it always work?' I said.

'It opens you up so I can have a proper look.' She unwrapped a metal knitting needle from a piece of cloth. 'You've nothing to worry about. I'll heat this up so it's sterilized.'

The needle was identical to those my mother had at home; I could picture a pair of them stuck in a ball of wool next to the wireless.

I scrambled down from the table and began dressing before I consciously decided to. Dora didn't move to stop me. The woman pulled out the needle she'd laid in the grate and clattered it down next to the dripping tray.

'Now then, don't get yourself all worked up. It'll be over before you know it. You don't want this baby, do you?'

I shook my head. 'But I don't want this either,' I said breathlessly. I felt as if I would collapse if I didn't leave that kitchen.

'Please yourself,' said the woman, crossing her arms across her chest as she watched me fumble with my shoes.

'Alice, are you sure?' said Dora. 'You can't afford anything else. A private doctor would be twenty times as much.'

'Let's go. Please, Dora.'

'Here,' said the woman, her hand in her apron pocket. 'I'll keep a guinea for my trouble, but you can have the rest back. God knows you're going to need it more than me in six months' time.'

The truth of the matter was not that I couldn't bear to have an abortion; it was that in the moment, I was more viscerally afraid of letting that woman put a dirty knitting needle inside me than I was of having a baby. Because, however hard I tried, I simply couldn't imagine that at all; the notion of it was as ungraspable as wet soap on porcelain.

When I got home, I caught sight of my face in the hall mirror. It was the colour of chalk. My mother was alone in the kitchen, washing the best china. She looked up when I came in, studying me for a moment before turning back to the sink. 'Are you going to tell me what's wrong with you?' she said, as she continued with the plates, the water steaming hot, her hands already puce. The clean china squeaked as she lifted each piece out of the bowl and placed it in the rack.

I leant against the cupboards, which hadn't altered since I was a baby, toddling around and getting under her feet. I got the biscuit barrel out for something to do and the action of easing off the stiff metal lid was so familiar that I nearly cried.

'What do you mean?' I said feebly.

Always sharp, she looked over her shoulder at me. 'Tell me the truth, Alice. I'm your mother. You've been acting peculiar for weeks now.'

The tears came then and I couldn't stop them, though I was at least silent about it, biting the inside of my cheek so that I didn't sob. They ran down my cheeks and began to soak into the collar of my blouse.

Without moving from the sink, she sighed. 'It's a man, isn't it?'

'Yes,' I managed to get out. 'But it's ended now.'

'So you've had your heart broken. Well, men will disappoint. Doesn't he want to marry you?'

'He can't.'

At that she turned. 'What do you mean he can't? I hope he doesn't think he's too good for you. Where does he live?'

I shook my head and she stared at me for a long moment.

'What, then?' she said but, as she did, I saw the possibility enter her mind. I watched her features seem to harden and narrow.

'Oh, so it's like that, is it?'

I looked down at the lino that was always sticky underfoot, however hard it was scrubbed.

'Answer me, girl! Is he married?'

'Yes, but he said —'

'He said what? That she was mad? That she had run away to sea? What nonsense did he have you believe?'

My voice was barely more than a whisper. 'He said that they had never been happy, that they would get a divorce.'

My mother tutted in disgust. 'And it never occurred to you that he would say that? I thought you were supposed to be the clever one.'

I wiped my face with the back of my hand.

'I did not bring you up to gad about with other people's husbands. You've never shown any interest in a man before — I was convinced you'd be a spinster all your life. And now this. The only thing to be thankful for is that he's thrown you over now, before things could get any worse.'

She dried her hands and leant back against the sink, arms crossed. 'I hope you've at least had the sense to keep this to yourself,' she continued, after a pause. 'That Dora's flighty enough to tell her mother. I can see *her* face now, pretending sympathy, when I next see her on the high street.'

'Dora won't say anything.'

My mother sniffed. 'We'll see.'

I took a breath. 'Mother, I won't be seeing him again but —'

'There should be no buts about it. You've had a narrow escape, by the sound of it. It's her I feel sorry for, the wife. Someone should tell her.'

My legs were trembling with the effort of not running

from the room. 'Mother, please listen. It was only once but I think . . . I feel awful every morning. My waistbands are tighter, though I haven't been eating much and –'

She went white with shock and put her hand back, blindly clutching at the sink's edge for support. 'You're not . . . ?'

I looked down, my heart beating wildly in my chest.

'Alice!' Her voice was jagged. 'Tell me. Are you pregnant?'

I swallowed, then forced myself to look up. 'I don't know.' I paused. 'Yes, I'm almost certain of it.'

'How long?' She was too horrified to shout.

'I – well, I –'

'Have you felt the quickening yet?'

I stared at her, confused.

'The quickening. That's when you know. You feel it inside, I can't explain it. You might be too early for it yet. It comes around three months.'

'I haven't felt anything like that. Just the sickness.'

'Some people think it doesn't count until you feel it. You must know how long it's been unless you're lying about it only happening the once.' She looked me straight in the eye.

'I'm not lying about that. It's three months,' I said quietly.

'Well, that's that, then. At three months it's taken. You can't do away with it that late and, besides, I've always thought that was a wicked thing to do. No, you'll go through with it now. And when it's born, you'll give it up.'

We stood in silence for a few minutes. I wondered what James was doing right at that moment to the north-west, where London seeped into the countryside. I wondered if he'd had dinner yet, cooked and served by his wife. I wondered whether I had crossed his mind at all.

'Go to your room now, Alice. I don't want to look at you. I need to think about this and to speak to your father.'

Little more was said until just over a week later. I spent the intervening days in a state of numbness, scarcely able to think coherently about the baby or what my mother would eventually say. In the end, my fate was announced after dinner, in the room with the display cabinet full of ugly china figurines and the gilt-framed print of Constable's *Hay Wain* above the mantelpiece. I suppose it was the only time the three of us were together.

'We've made up our minds, your father and I,' she began, after we'd eaten in near-silence. This was it, I thought. The next part of my life – perhaps all of it – would come down to this conversation.

As my mother began to speak, I glanced at my father but he was looking down at the tablecloth. His face was grey and thin with worry and shock, skin stretched too tautly over fine bones. She must have told him while I was out at work.

It was always stuffy in the front room. Next door, Mrs Davies was running a bath for her two young children. I could hear the water sluicing through the pipes in the walls. Unable to sit still, I picked with my nail at the faceted glass of the vinegar bottle until my mother pointedly moved it out of my reach.

'Now listen carefully, my girl,' she said. 'I wrote to Edith Jelphs last week. It's all arranged.'

'Edith Jelphs?' My mind cast around to place the name.

The memory came to me in a rush: an afternoon so bright that the curtains in my parents' bedroom had been pulled across and were lifting inwards on a soft breeze. My mother, mellowed by the weather, had let me look through her tin box of mementoes while she changed the sheets. I remembered being struck for the first time that she wasn't the sort of person who kept anything for its own sake and wondered why she had saved the contents of the tin.

'She's the girl in the photograph,' I said now.

'What photograph?'

'The one of you as a girl in Painswick.'

Though she seemed utterly at home in London, my mother had grown up in rural Gloucestershire. I had gone there with her as a child.

'Trust you to remember that,' she said. 'Yes, I'd forgotten I had that. She's housekeeper at Fiercombe, has been for years.'

'Fiercombe?'

'Have you not heard of it? And you, with your nose forever stuck in a book. It's an estate not far from Painswick. She went there as a maid when she was young and never left.'

'What's all this got to do with me, Mother?'

I think I knew then, but wanted to hear how she said it.

'It's all arranged,' she said again, her face implacable. 'You'll go when you start to really show. Edith was very good about it, wrote as soon as she could to say that you might, and to think we haven't spoken all these years. The family live abroad most of the year so you won't see them. She told them about your situation and it looks like someone's taken pity on you. You'll get bed and board in

27

exchange for some light duties to pay your way. A bit of dusting, mending, that sort of thing.'

I remained silent. My father gazed absently out of the window. His foot was jiggling under the table; I could feel the movement through the floor. I knew he was desperate for the conversation to be over so he could go back out to his beloved garden and be wrapped in the undemanding cover of dusk. 'And what if I don't want to go?' I said, a childish stubbornness briefly surfacing.

'You'll go, all right. You've made your father ill with worry. Look at him.' She stood and reached over the table to grip my chin. 'I said, look at him. He's been so proud of you, doing well at the grammar and then getting your job, and this is what you do. No husband of your own so you get yourself into trouble with someone else's. Besides, what choice do you have? It's either Fiercombe or a mother-and-baby home in some godforsaken place. And who's going to pay for that, I'd like to know? No, you'll go to Gloucestershire until it's born.'

She sat down again and smoothed her skirt over her lap, a thoughtful expression on her face. 'I trust Edith Jelphs. I knew her as a child. This is for the best, and after all we've done for you, Alice, it's the least you can do.'

I glanced at my father and his eyes met mine briefly. They were full of sadness but there was something else there I had never seen. I suppose it was disappointment.

I swallowed the sob that rose in my throat as he got wearily to his feet and went out, closing the door quietly behind him.

My mother waited until his steps had died away. 'Alice, I know you think I'm too hard on you, that I've always been hard on you, but look what you've done – not just to yourself but to me and your father. There's many who would have disowned a daughter for this but we haven't so you'll do as we say. It's that or you'll be destitute.'

I knew she was right.

'You're best off at Fiercombe,' she continued. 'I've told Edith Jelphs that you were a newlywed who had only just found out she was expecting when her husband got himself killed. Knocked down by a motor-car on his way to work.'

Despite the roiling anxiety in my stomach, I almost laughed. 'You said what?'

'You heard me. She and the family would never have agreed to it if they'd known the truth. I said in my letter that you'd had a dreadful shock and that the doctor had said you must get away from London – for your own health, as well as the baby's. That your nerves might never recover unless you had some peace and quiet in a new place that had none of the old associations.'

She looked satisfied with the story she'd woven for me and I found myself almost admiring her inventiveness. I would arrive in Gloucestershire as a grieving widow rather than a fallen woman while she played the role of concerned mother from a distance – someone following doctor's orders for the good of her daughter's fragile health, not to mention her future grandchild's. It was perfect. She had even dug out my grandmother's narrow wedding band.

'Don't you lose that now,' she said, as I slipped it on, already feeling like a fraud. I shook my hand and found the ring fitted as though it had been made for me. 'You'll keep to that story if you know what's good for you,' she continued. 'This way, no one will talk behind your back or give you dirty looks for being in your condition and on your own – not like they would here, where they know there was never any husband, knocked over or otherwise. Your father couldn't have borne that sort of talk about you. You won't even have to do much around the house, by the sound of it. Edith said there was a maid who came in most mornings and that you could "recuperate properly" until the baby came.'

'When am I to go?' I felt unbelievably tired.

'Like I said, when you start to show. When you can't work any more. Another month or so, if you're like I was.'

'I'm not like you, though.'

'You're in no position to speak to me like that, young lady. I don't know if you realize the fix you've got yourself into. If you don't go, there's nowhere for you but the workhouse and let's see how far your grammar-school education gets you there. Don't think other girls like you haven't ended up there without a penny to their name. Sure as eggs, they have.'

She got up and reached for the cruet set. Her rings clinked against it as she picked it up, along with the butter dish and the teapot.

'Get the door for me, will you?' she said.

Mr Marshall, to my great surprise, seemed to notice me for the first time when I told him I had to leave my position in order to look after my sick mother. He wrote me an excellent reference and said my mother was lucky to have such a good daughter. It was more than I deserved or expected. I'm not sure if Miss Cunningham believed my story but, thankfully, she chose to remain silent on the matter. When I thought of all the lies my mother and I had crafted between us – her illness, my dead husband – I felt quite ill myself, but what other choice was there? None, as far as I could see.

The weeks leading to the day of my departure felt like an age. One afternoon during my last week at work I felt desperate enough to go and see James at his office, having dug out the address when Miss Cunningham went for lunch. I had the deluded idea that if I told him about the baby he would make everything all right. In the event, I knew from the moment I saw him that he would be horrified and left without saying a word about the pregnancy.

I finished work three weeks before I was due to leave; I was beginning to show too much to risk staying there any longer. After that, time dragged unbearably, with nothing to occupy my mind but my memories of James, the enormous mistake I had made and dread that I was soon to be exiled to a place where I knew no one. Dora came round when she could but her job at the local department store meant I was alone with my mother most of the time. I hadn't spent so many consecutive hours in her company for years, and the cloud of tight-lipped disapproval that seemed to hover around her turned the house into something like a prison. As if to rub salt in my wounds, I dreamt of James most nights – happy, serene dreams that were shattered on waking: contentment turned to misery. I became adept at crying silently into my pillow so my parents wouldn't hear.

On my last afternoon, I went to the local library in

order to escape the house. I hadn't been there since I was a schoolgirl, when Dora would have been in tow and protesting at the Goody Two Shoes worthiness of it. I had always liked the hushed atmosphere, though, and wished I'd visited more often.

It was almost empty by the time I got there, with nothing to be heard but the murmurings of an unseen conversation, the thud of books being stamped and the whispering of the trees that crowded at the tall Victorian windows.

I wandered around until I found myself in the history section. Idly scanning the names of kings, queens and fallen dynasties I hadn't thought of since studying for matriculation, my eye was snagged by a huge tome entitled *England's Manors and Mansion Houses*. I heaved it out and sat down on some steps abandoned by one of the librarians.

It had been printed in 1912 and had been taken out only half a dozen times since. Turning to the index at the back, I ran quickly through the lists of halls, abbeys and courts until I found it. There was only a single page reference, as if the author had felt it should be included but was unable to dredge up much about it. I leafed through the pages, missing the right one twice, until finally there it was: just a couple of paragraphs tacked on the end of a chapter about another, better known, house in the same part of the county.

Of course the English seat of the Fitzmorris family is not the only estate in the vicinity. Just a few miles to the west in the neighbouring valley, hidden to all but the most prying eyes, is the Fiercombe estate.

A place of uncertain origin and mixed fortunes, it has lately shunned attention, withdrawing quietly into the deepest recesses of the silent valley as if to blot out painful memories and to sink, gratefully, into a healing slumber. The trees that cloak and obscure the valley floor so well are a rare remnant of an ancient wood much reduced elsewhere but surviving here even as the people who own it come and go.

The estate's golden era ended as the last century dwindled away. It had enjoyed a brief flicker of local fame under the stewardship of the sixth baronet, Edward Stanton, and his wife Elizabeth, a renowned beauty, but those halcyon days turned out to be few indeed. Today, the springtime rambler is not encouraged to walk the paths that meander through the trees and bluebells towards a manor house completed when another Elizabeth was on the throne and now all but forgotten.

Elizabeth. That was the first time I saw her name. What did I think, if anything? I'm sure I traced the letters with my finger; perhaps I even whispered it under my breath, the hiss of the second syllable, the sigh of the last. But that was all. My interest in her and the estate's history was fleeting then – a faint glimmer of intrigue that glowed, then dimmed, though not before it had lodged itself at the back of my mind, ready to be brought out later. There, in the library close to home, close to everything that was familiar, she was not yet able to drown out the clamour of my own thoughts. It was later that she would come alive to me, when I was in the place that had once been hers.

I looked up from the book to see that it had started to rain outside, heavy gouts spattering the glass unevenly as the wind flung it about. My eyes went back to the stark black type on the page. Fiercombe. Tomorrow I would be there, among those ancient trees. I put my hand to my stomach and felt again the now-familiar jolt of disbelief and fear.

The day I was due to depart London for the west dawned mild and bright, a pink blush colouring the sky. I didn't need to leave for Paddington until after nine but I woke at five and was unable to get back to sleep, staring instead at the faded roses of my bedroom wallpaper, my insides tightly strung with nerves.

When it was finally time to go, my mother announced that I didn't need both of them to accompany me to the station and that she would stay behind. At the door, she pulled me back inside so none of the neighbours would hear her. 'Mind you don't get yourself into any more trouble,' she said, as she squeezed my arm. She was unwilling to show me any other sign of affection but her face was drawn and her eyes were puffy. 'You don't know how fortunate you are to be going there.'

She bent to straighten the hem of the light summer coat I had bought with the last of my wages, the generous cut almost successful in hiding my altered figure.

'Write and tell us how you find it,' she said. 'You know I won't be able to come until you're ready to have it, don't you? We can't possibly afford the expense of a visit before then.'

I tried to think about how things would be for me beyond the labour and the giving away of the baby in London's anonymous heart, but found I couldn't. It seemed as remote to me as hearing about something that would happen to someone else, many years from now.

Once we reached Paddington, I insisted that my father

34

didn't wait for the train to leave. He had said barely a word to me on the journey from home and I didn't think I could stand the tension between us a moment longer. The panic that for weeks had risen inside me whenever I thought about going away, nasty spurts of fear that only sleep could temporarily quell, had actually eased a little now I was on my way. I knew I would feel better still once I was alone.

'Please don't wait,' I said again, when he seemed reluctant to move. 'It won't go for almost half an hour yet.'

'Well, if you're sure,' he said, and considered me properly for the first time in weeks.

I glanced away because I thought I would cry if I didn't. My father had always made me feel quietly adored and I didn't seem to have ruined that entirely. He pulled me towards him briefly, then patted me awkwardly on the back. 'Take good care of yourself, won't you?' he said, and when I looked up from searching in my handbag for a handkerchief he had done as I asked, just as he always had, and vanished into the mêlée of the station concourse.

My hand was trembling as I pulled the door of the second-class carriage shut behind me and took a seat. After what seemed an age the whistle was blown, the last door was slammed and the train started to move off down the platform. I had unthinkingly chosen a seat facing backwards and, as we picked up speed and pulled away from the station's grimy bulk, I experienced the unnerving sensation of watching my hitherto life recede into nothing.

As we gathered speed across the metal tangle of tracks that erupted out of Paddington, I reflected on how strange it felt to be making a journey I had last done as a little girl. My mother had grown up just five miles north of the valley that shields Fiercombe Manor from the rest of the world, so this was a journey she had done many more times than I, clattering back towards the easy green fields of her girlhood.

She had left for London to work in service when she was sixteen. My father, a groundsman whom she had met a few years later, was a Londoner who didn't understand the appeal of the open countryside. On the contrary, he had found the silence and emptiness oppressive on his sole visit to meet my mother's family. It was too dark to sleep, he said, and never went again.

By the time I was born – a good way into the marriage – a pattern had already been established: my mother visited Painswick once each summer while my father stayed at home. In my earliest years I went with her, but at some point that had changed, my mother deciding there was no sense in taking a child on a long, stuffy train journey. After that I went to my father's sister in Archway instead.

My own memories of Gloucestershire soon narrowed to a few crystalline images: my grandmother's dresser with its ranks of blue willow-pattern plates; a morning when I was allowed to eat slice after slice of buttered toast because my mother wasn't there to say I was greedy; being wrenched through a late summer field by a dog that was stronger than me. After I had stopped going to stay, my Gloucestershire relatives seemed content enough with a new studio photograph of me every so often. There was apparently no thought of them coming to London. After my grandparents died, within months of each other when I was ten, we seemed to lose touch with the rest of them. Now I was returning, though I could never have predicted the reason for it.

The first leg of the journey passed quickly. I was hungry – I was always hungry by then – so I made my way to the buffet car and treated myself to a round of ham sandwiches, which I washed down with lemonade. I hadn't experienced any strange cravings, only the urge to eat lots of red meat and anything sugary. My mother had a sweet tooth and bought herself a weekly quarter of pear drops but I wasn't usually very partial. Now, however, I drank the glass bottle of lemonade as if it was water and went back to the counter to buy an iced bun. The man who took my money nodded his approval. 'I like to see a lady enjoy her food,' he said.

I smiled but put a defensive arm across my stomach, though I knew I didn't show much in my new coat.

I changed trains at Swindon and, though it was hardly the countryside, I fancied the air smelt different from the fresh-cut-grass scent of London's parks. It was earthier, with a hint of fresh manure that I found I quite liked. The branch-line train was rickety and slow, stopping so regularly that it never gathered any real pace. Unlike the deep cuttings of brick the Victorians had built to bury London's railway tracks from the terraces above, here we trundled through on high, the rails snaking along the ridges of lush valleys.

Finally we came to a jerky standstill at Stonehouse, where I'd been told to get off. The small platform soon cleared of people, with no one left looking for me, so I made my way out to the front of the station. A single, battered van idled there, its driver sound asleep, and a couple of boys were sitting on the kerb next to their bicycles, which they had flung down carelessly.

I had been wondering what on earth I was to do when a clopping sound made the boys look up. I followed their gaze. A horse pulling an open carriage was approaching in unhurried fashion. A weather-beaten man, wearing a flat cap low over his forehead, was holding the reins. As he turned into the station forecourt I realized with a start that he had come for me. The boys, also realizing this, grinned in my direction. I wondered bewilderedly what else awaited me.

The driver introduced himself simply as 'Ruck' before swinging my case into the footwell and helping me up on to the narrow seat. Behind us the carriage's seats were covered with sacking and strewn with an assortment of tools but it would have been quite grand when it was new.

We processed silently through a series of small villages, the iron-shod hoofs of the horse muffled by the earth road. The honey-coloured hamlets, where the cottages invariably cleaved towards an exquisite church, were even more picturesque than postcards and packets of fudge had given me to imagine – and much more so than I had noticed as a tiny girl. After Paddington's tired terraces, grubby streets and draughty terminus, it was almost obscenely pretty.

I knew nothing of the local topography then, still accustomed as I was to an orderly kind of nature, bound within the tidy perimeters of London's sprawling suburbs, the bright squares of lawn and plump hedges tended by office men after hours. I found out later that these villages, so sturdily set among the lanes and luxuriant pastures, are in fact balanced on a narrow ridge that runs between two deep valleys. This up-thrust of land marks the place where the Berkeley Vale meets the Cotswold escarpment. Beneath the rich, loamy soil two distinctly different types of bedrock have fused together; evidence of some ancient geological cataclysm of which there is no sign on the surface.

About an hour passed before we began our descent into the narrower and deeper of the two valleys, the very last of the Cotswolds' combes to the west. As the land fell away I reached for the handle of my case to stop it tumbling off into the dirt, and braced my knees against the front of the carriage. My other arm lay protectively across my lap. I saw Ruck's eyes flicker over me as I moved and wondered if there was a smirk on his weather-cracked lips.

'Won't be long now,' he said, his voice loud in air that had grown stiller yet. 'Though you won't find a deeper bottom in these parts.'

I blushed at the last words, feeling foolish for doing so. Later I discovered that he wasn't really making fun of me; that 'bottom', like 'combe', is a local word for valley. Or perhaps he was being sly, knowing I would be ignorant about such things and ill at ease in a strange place.

As we descended deeper, the light changed, turning ever more green and fractured as we passed beneath the thickening canopy of leaves.

'What trees are these?' I said a little shakily, to prove I wasn't bothered by the previous comment. He looked right at me then and, despite the diminished light, I could see the broken veins that fanned out across his cheeks from his nose.

'Beeches they is,' he said gruffly. 'There's bluebells here in spring, acres of 'em spread out through the trees as far as the eye can see. Like a carpet, they says. Folk come to look at 'em, folk from Stroud, sometimes Chelt'nham.

You've missed 'em this year. You're not too late for the glow-worms, though. You'll see them come dusk in July if you look hard enough. Some summers bring 'undreds of 'em to the loneliest corners of the Great Mead.'

I gripped the seat with my hand as we hit a deep rut in the lane, gritting my teeth as I imagined the baby being jostled about dangerously. Perhaps that would be no bad thing; I could go home to London if . . . I forced away the thought and glanced at Ruck to see if he'd noticed my discomfort. Perhaps he had because the pace slowed a little.

'There's not many that comes this way,' he said, as he pulled on the reins. 'It's the one public road in the valley but it's hard to find. There's folk who've lived round here all their lives what don't know about it or else don't bother with it. Too easy to get lost. Too many tracks off to the side that don't lead nowhere.

'O' course in the winter it's impassable. Or, rather, you can get down it easy enough – if it's icy, you'll be in the Great Mead wrong way up before you knows it – but you won't get out again. In high summer it cracks like a dried-up riverbed. Times in between it floods. Once you're down there, you stays.'

'Don't the family mind it?' I said. 'It must be terribly inconvenient.' I heard my voice, like a stranger's, in the unmoving air and it sounded shrill and affected. I felt the heat rise again in my cheeks.

'The Stantons? They's growed used to it, I s'pose,' he said. 'Or the maister has. Sir Charles. He were born to living in the country. Lady Stanton don't like it much, her think it too quiet. It's she what makes sure they're overseas most of the year now.'

40

'They don't ever spend the summers here?'

Ruck shook his head. 'Hardly the winters neither. It's France they goes to.' He drew out the *a* in France to a long 'aah'.

'Apart from a couple o' days last Christmas they haven't been back for nearly two year now. Down south to the French resorts they goes. Her was promised that by the maister, that when the younger boy were grown they didn't have to spend another summer here.'

'But why? I'm sure the winters can be hard but the summers must be glorious.'

He shook his head again. 'Her can't abide 'em since . . . Well, there were a bad summer here. Since then her's got notions about things. Sleeps bad. Flits around, she does, with this look on her face. The melan-cholic, they calls it. O' course, some of us are kept too busy to have it.'

He laughed then, a dry, creaking sound that made me shudder slightly, though it was harmless enough. By the time he'd recovered we were approaching a fork in the lane, no doubt one of the many that deceived the unwary.

'I'll take you the slow way down to the manor,' he said, his gruff manner resumed. 'You'll get a good look at it then.'

He pulled the horse off to the left, on to a path that was yet more pitted and overhung with beeches, their lowest limbs pressing in towards us as though they hadn't been cut back for a long time. It seemed as though dusk had already fallen under those heavy boughs, the light leached out of the day, although my wristwatch told me it was only half past two. I tapped the small circle of glass and the long hand jumped as though it had stopped some minutes back.

Instead of the steep path that had been leading us directly towards the valley floor, we now seemed to be weaving our way down a gently looping course. I allowed my legs to relax but kept hold of my case as the turns were sharp. The trees to our right soon grew sparser, the sunlight breaking through bravely to light up the brambles and tinge the ferns sepia.

'Keep your eye out,' said Ruck. 'Any second now you'll see 'er to your left.'

Slowing the horse as we turned another corner, he gestured off to the left, where the trees were thinner still. I sat up straighter as I caught the first glimpse, a flash of soft, sunlit gold among the dun-coloured bark of the beeches.

'Is that it?' I said softly, as if speaking too loudly would make it disappear altogether.

'That's the manor,' he replied, as triumphant as if it was his own. 'You'll get a better look if you hang on there. Keep looking now.'

He was right. At the next bend the trees had been cleared, presumably deliberately, to reveal and frame a three-gabled house made of the same stone as the cottages high up on the ridge. After the dim light of the wood it seemed even more golden than those more modest dwellings, its stone warmed by sunrays that had managed to reach over the steep valley walls and drench it.

The manor, I realized, was not very large. It made some of the grander houses I'd seen on postcards seem overblown by comparison. The glowering woods encroaching upon its north side made it look smaller still; a noble house in miniature. I was glad of this: where the wild valley was intimidating, the manor, reposing quietly in the sunshine, seemed welcoming.

Ruck looked over at me, clearly wanting some kind of response.

'It's a beautiful house,' I said truthfully. 'Much more beautiful than many of the more famous ones.'

He seemed satisfied with that. 'It's older than most of 'em too,' he said, as we negotiated another hairpin bend in the road. 'The gables were all built separate, you know. There's two hundred year between the eastern and western ends.'

'It's Elizabethan, isn't it?' I ventured, half remembering the small footnote I'd found in the library about it. 'The period it was completed in, I mean.'

'I don' know about that, miss. Five hundred year or more some of it's stood. That's all I know.'

When I think back to that memory, that first glimpse of Fiercombe Manor and the valley it seemed almost entombed in, I cannot recall any sense of unease. Beyond the mild embarrassment of being in close proximity to a stranger and the constant state of anxiety I was in about the baby, I felt almost grateful to be away from London and the chilly disapproval of my mother. I think I even felt a glimmer of something approaching enthusiasm at the thought of exploring the place, of it becoming known to me, its secret corners commonplace, and of seeing it as late spring eased into summer. It seems amazing in the light of what happened but I can't say I felt any foreboding about the valley at all. All the trepidation swirling around inside me was bound up in how convincingly I would be able to lie to Mrs Jelphs and what would happen to me after I returned to London, once the baby had been born and taken away, and I had to begin again.

After a time the ground began to level off: we had reached the valley floor.

'Not long now,' he said.

We rounded another corner and, quite suddenly, we were free of the woods and out into the sunshine. There wasn't a breath of wind so deep in the valley and I wondered vaguely if I would find it uncomfortable when I was bigger, and summer had come. It was as I was thinking this, absentmindedly stroking my stomach as I had taken to doing whenever I wasn't otherwise occupied, that I saw the graveyard and the tiny church in the far corner of it. Though I tried to cover it, the sight made me start.

Ruck nodded towards it. 'Only Mrs Jelphs ever uses the chapel now. There was a time when more came, when people was still here. They rang the bells then.'

'I assumed the nearest village was the one at the top of the valley,' I said. 'Stanwick, was it? Is there another?'

'Fiercombe had its own village of sorts. It weren't just the Stantons, you know. In the last century there was forty or more folk what worked the land or were in the house, or were family to those who did.'

I looked across the graveyard and the stones that punctuated the uneven ground, some of them listing dangerously, others sinking into the earth as though it were quicksand. He was right, of course: they couldn't all have been from one family. In the middle stood a tree, its slender trunk gnarled and twisted but its branches hidden by a profusion of pink blossom. Barely a petal littered the grass beneath, so undisturbed was the air.

'What happened to them all?' I asked.

He paused before answering. 'Fortunes come and go. When the big house went there wasn't any work to be had. Where they might have gone to Stroud or Painswick fifty year before, there was hardly no wool trade left to take 'em. In a few short years they was gone, as if they had never been here at all. The present family came here as the new century began but it were never the same. Now there's just a few of us what's left.'

'But where did they all live?' I pressed on. My glimpses of the place had not revealed any signs of a village, even an abandoned one. The valley felt entirely empty to me.

'You'll see if you go for a wander. There's a few cottages left, mostly tumbledown. A couple burnt to the ground. Others there's nothing left but the foundations and the weeds have hidden them well enough. Nettles high as your chest there now.'

We had by now passed the chapel and its lonely graveyard and I leant forward in expectation of my first proper look at the manor. Up close it was no less golden, the stone not only reflecting the late spring sunlight but apparently exuding a rich glow of its own. The age of the building and the hard winters it must have endured had softened every edge so that there was not a straight line to be seen. From timber to roof tile to window ledge, all was slightly askew, sloping, buckling or otherwise returning to the haphazard laws of Nature.

We came to a halt at the eastern end of the house. Ruck did not help me but he did take my case and wait for me while I clambered down awkwardly, clearing his throat and looking the other way in a manner that made me like him more. He led the way through a small but lovely kitchen garden that seemed very well tended. It was wonderfully fragrant, and even my city-deadened senses told me that mint, rosemary and sage all grew there. Behind tall ranks of hollyhocks, heavy ivy clung to the garden's walls and snaked up and around towards what I guessed was the intended front of the house. I decided that I would see it for myself, once I'd had a wash and changed my clothes. I lingered for a moment in the garden and, despite everything, felt something like anticipation swell in me. Behind the show-off perfume of the flowers you could smell something subtler: the first intimations of summer.

I looked back up at the valley walls, so steep that they might have been built for the very purpose of concealing my shame from the rest of the world. All this was to be my home for the coming months yet I had no idea what those months would bring. I wondered if I would be unhappy and lonely here, or whether Mrs Jelphs would guess what trouble I had really got myself into in London and send me back. A picture of James, as vivid as if he were standing in the little garden, flashed across my mind but, with all my strength, I pushed it away. Taking a shaky breath, I turned to the ancient door and pushed it open, telling myself it was going to be a single summer, that was all; a summer in limbo in the deepest countryside. I could never have imagined all that would happen in those few short months and how, by the end of them, my life would have altered irrevocably and for ever.

Elizabeth

1898

The weather had turned out beautifully for the summer party. Elizabeth had privately believed that it would, knowing that the rain they had woken up to would simply clear the humidity that had infected the valley with an irritable lassitude all week. At noon it had ceased altogether, the clouds rolling back like a curtain lifting on a stage.

At half past twelve Edith brought some tea into the morning room, her face pink with excitement and relief. 'Oh, my lady, have you seen it's stopped? If it stays like this the grass will have time to dry out too. We've been praying downstairs and it looks like He's listened to us.'

Elizabeth smiled at her lady's maid, who still seemed younger than her years; at twenty-one Edith was only three years younger than herself. 'Edith, what did I say to you when you brought me my tray this morning?'

The maid smiled sheepishly. 'You said it would be fine by the afternoon. And you were right too, almost to the minute. I just couldn't see it stopping.'

Any relief Elizabeth felt about the evening's celebration being able to take place in the garden, as planned, was for other people's sakes. Not only the servants, who hadn't arranged a large occasion for some years, but her husband Edward, who had been as excited as a child about the

47

preparations. Since they had sent out the invitations a month ago, he had come to her almost every day with a fresh list of things that needed buying or making or doing. Usually buying: she shuddered to think how much it was all going to cost.

'When will you be wanting to dress, my lady?' said Edith. 'The first guests aren't due till seven but you know Colonel Waters always arrives early when he comes to dinner.'

'What about six o'clock?'

Edith looked scandalized. 'It will take more than an hour to dress your hair, never mind the rest of it!'

'Half past five, then. It's not as though you'll be lacing me into my usual corsets.'

She placed a careful hand on the enormous, almost comical, mound of her stomach, which was even larger than the swell Isabel had made almost five years earlier. In these last weeks, the child had moved up to rest against her lungs, making her breathless when she climbed the stairs or walked too fast. It was a strange sensation, akin to nervousness, and worse today.

'Has he or she been kicking again this morning?' Edith had been following the baby's progress almost as intently as Edward, who was convinced his future heir was inside. Who was apparently convinced that she would not lose this baby.

Elizabeth shook her head. 'No. He or she knows I've got quite enough to think about today without that to distract me and has been wonderfully still for me all morning.'

After a paltry lunch – she hadn't wanted to put out Mrs Wentworth, the cook, who was understandably preoccupied with the coming evening's menu – Elizabeth wandered outside to the gardens. In truth, there was little for her to do today: her part would come later, when the guests had arrived. At the thought, a jangle of apprehension went through her. Of the eighty-six invitations sent out they had not received a single apology or excuse, which was surely unheard of. Elizabeth knew they were all too intrigued not to attend the first major gathering at Stanton House of all the county's families since just before Isabel's birth. Of course there had been polite invitations to tea, hunt meets and dinner parties for the most trusted and discreet friends, but nothing on such a grand scale.

The gardens were glorious. The morning's rain had been closer to a vapour and not a single bloom had been bruised. The last of it, fairy-sized jewels of moisture caught between petals and blades of grass, glittered in the sun. Elizabeth closed her eyes and exhaled deeply, letting the tranquillity of the garden slow her racing heart.

'It smells wonderful, doesn't it? We couldn't have asked for better timing with that blasted rain.'

She was jolted out of her reverie. Her husband stood before her, his pale blue eyes bright with anticipation. Under the clean-washed sky she could clearly see the lines around them and between his brows. They seemed out of place on his face, whose fine features must have best suited boyhood and were already fading and coarsening. He would be forty in the autumn.

'But if it wasn't for the rain, it wouldn't look and smell as it does out here,' she said.

To her surprise he took her face in his hands and kissed

her gently on the lips. She could feel the dome of her stomach between them, like a barrier. He was rarely so affectionate with her now and the embrace felt oddly intrusive. 'You're right, of course,' he said. 'You even predicted it would stop at noon and, look, it has.'

'I'm glad,' she said, as convincingly as she could. 'It will be so much nicer to hold the party outside, and on Midsummer's Eve too. Have you been for a walk?'

'Yes. I went to watch them erect the marquee. They were getting grass stains on it and I kept saying they ought to be careful until Harding made it clear I would be better occupied elsewhere.'

He laughed, and she remembered that she liked him best when he was poking fun at himself. It happened so infrequently that she had almost forgotten it.

He pulled one of her curls free from its pin and wound it around his finger. 'Look at it light up in the sunshine,' he said softly. 'There are real embers there among the brown.'

He smiled down at her and she cursed herself for being unable to meet his eye, to savour the love while it flowed. Instead, she found herself comparing the smile to the way he had looked at her when she had been brought so low in the weeks after their daughter's birth. And the way he had been unable to look at her at all after the miscarriage that had followed almost two years later. It had been a boy. What she had never told him was that there had been another miscarriage, too – a child who had slipped away almost before she had known he was there. It had been too early to tell but she was sure it had been another boy. That had been just last year.

As they stood together in the glorious garden, she

realized that, to a stranger, she and Edward must look like a picture of connubial bliss. She glanced away as he continued to gaze at her, pretending coyness because she didn't want him to see the bitterness that seeped into her thoughts on the odd occasions that he showed her tenderness. It was easier when they were as friends. It was easier in front of the servants.

She turned to walk towards the house and made herself reach back with her hand so that he would follow.

'I've been as far as old Fiercombe Manor,' he continued, oblivious to any change in her. It always amazed her that he never seemed to guess her thoughts, overhear the surge and babble when too many crowded in at once. 'The yew trees are quite monstrous now and as high as the roof. They've even dislodged some of the tiles up there. Perhaps the whole lot should go. We could build a guest cottage there. That part of the valley gets the sun for the longest.'

She stopped and turned to him, dread sluicing through her. She was careful to keep her voice low, her tone calm, so that it wouldn't alarm him. 'Really, Edward, no. You can't demolish the manor. It's been there for centuries. Besides, you know Isabel loves it. She and I walk there often – we had a picnic just last week on that side of the Great Mead, close to the summerhouse by the stream. It's idyllic.'

It was true, but what she had chosen not to mention was that she also went there by herself, that the warped beams and soft stone of the old manor, crumbling and rotting in places, had become a sort of sanctuary to her. By the water there, in the manor's weed-sown Tudor garden and in the pretty little summerhouse, she could breathe. It was only when she returned and the grey, uncompromising lines of Stanton House came into view that she felt the bands tighten around her chest again.

Edward walked on and she followed, her size and breathlessness making her awkward. His face had taken on the expression it always did when she mentioned their daughter. She could never decide precisely what it was – a fierce blend of impatience, guilt and love was the closest she had got to untangling it. She suspected that she inspired the same slightly pained look when someone asked him about her.

'I suppose my little brother would never forgive me if I knocked the old house down either,' said Edward, more thoughtfully. 'He's forever eulogizing about its craftsmanship when he's here – the wall hangings, the chapel and even the Tudor garden, where those wretched yews are planted. All of you are hopelessly sentimental.'

He inspected his hands, which were one of his best features, strong and smooth-skinned. They were one of the things she had first noticed about him. He flexed them and the tiny golden hairs on their backs caught the sun. Such a lot of power is held there, she thought. Power to raze an ancient house. Power to do with your wife as you see fit.

'No, he wouldn't forgive you and rightly so,' she said lightly. 'It was built over hundreds of years by your ancestors. You were born there and so was your father. Can't you feel any . . . protectiveness or loyalty towards it now it's a poor, neglected thing?'

Her voice shook a little but he seemed not to notice.

Instead a look of genuine incomprehension crossed his face. He sighed with impatience.

'It's shabby and cramped, built piecemeal with no logic or uniformity of style. I designed for you and Isabel a far superior house. Stanton House has forty rooms to Fiercombe Manor's twenty. It's built with the finest granite I could find. An earthquake wouldn't bring it down.'

She swallowed the words that rose unbidden in her throat. *You didn't build it for Isabel and me. You built it for you. You and your Stanton son. The son I still haven't given you after six years of marriage.*

They started up the steps from the sunken garden that had been laid out and planted at great expense six years earlier – the appropriate finishing touch to the grand house that had been completed just a year before she had come to the valley as a new bride. The garden was beautiful, there was no question of that, but, like the house, it seemed incongruous in its Gloucestershire setting – which, of course, it was, having been copied from a famous garden overlooking Lake Garda in Italy. Edward had blanched when he received the bill for the work but when she had asked to see it he had told her it was none of her concern: it was his estate and his inheritance to do with as he pleased. She had chosen not to remind him of the money she had brought with her to the marriage, the sum settled on her by a childless uncle who had always favoured her. After all, he would only have responded that her money was best looked after by her husband, just as she herself was.

Edward was too busy thinking about the evening ahead to say more. The pitifully forlorn manor house had dropped cleanly out of his thoughts. When she looked at his profile she could almost see his brain working, half of it cataloguing what still needed to be done while the other half played out scenes of how it would be when the music had started up and the guests were assembled and approving.

She wondered if he remembered the last comparable occasion they had held here in Fiercombe valley. How could he not? Of course, it hadn't been significant in itself. In those days, the early, still hopeful days of their marriage, they had hosted many parties and balls. It was the events that followed that had retrospectively gilded the last one: an enchanted night when it had felt as if everything was to come. In fact, it had turned out to be something of an ending – at least for her.

A cry intruded into their thoughts. Isabel had spotted her mother's hat from the terrace and was flying across the lawn where the marquee had now gone up. When she noticed her father she stopped and coloured. Father and daughter were always awkward and diffident with each other and Elizabeth didn't know how to mend it, or even where exactly the roots of this discord lay.

As usual, she covered the unease with chatter and fuss, straightening the sailor hat that Isabel hated wearing and refastening her hair ribbon. She had inherited Edward's hair, slippery and silky, the colour of sunbleached wheat, so different from Elizabeth's dark, abundant waves that seemed to double in thickness whenever rain threatened. She was glad of this: she hoped it meant her daughter was like her father in ways deeper than the merely physical, that she would share his pragmatic grasp of the world, his unflinching conviction in everything he did.

They crossed the lawn together and Elizabeth wondered how they appeared to the various indoor servants and under-gardeners who were securing the marquee, placing tables and putting up a miniature gazebo for the string quartet that was due at four. She knew she was considered a beauty, with her mass of dark hair and large eyes of peridot green, flecked with the same gold as the old manor's stones. And Edward was still handsome, though this was as much conveyed by the confidence that emanated from him as his actual features.

Isabel had not just inherited her father's hair but his pale blue eyes. Indeed, to look at her there was very little to discern of Elizabeth. The servants apparently agreed: she had once gone downstairs to tell Mrs Wentworth that Edward would be staying on at his London club for another few days and overheard one of the kitchen maids say to someone unidentified (she did not think it could have been Edith and hoped it had not been), 'There is nothing of the mother in that girl at all. But perhaps it's a blessing. Better to lose out on those big green eyes than be saddled with the rest of it.'

Elizabeth knew, though, with a flicker of fear whenever she allowed herself to think of it, that Isabel was like she had been as a girl. Her child already knew that each thing had its shadow, even at midday. She saw the world aslant, and in that she was her mother's daughter.

Last spring, Edward had taken Isabel to see the lambing at the farm on the far side of the estate, close to Ruin Wood. Elizabeth had noticed that he was frustrated when they returned after only half an hour so she had kissed a white-faced Isabel and told her she could go and help in the kitchen, always a coveted treat.

'Did something happen?' she asked, when she and Edward were alone.

'It was the damnedest thing,' he replied, shaking his head. 'She wasn't interested in the lambs, not even the older ones who'd been cleaned up and were running around as pretty as clouds. She kept asking about the ewes, saying it must hurt them dreadfully and why did we make them do it. I had to take her out – the men might have heard her.'

Edward had gone to London the next day, as he always did when something difficult occurred. He had never experienced anything complicated before his marriage, having enjoyed a simple childhood in the valley with parents who had been captivated by their elder son. His younger brother, too, idolized Edward just as Elizabeth had when she had first met him. It was hard to believe that that had been little more than six years ago.

She had been born in Bristol, the only child of a moderately wealthy merchant and his wife; the uncle who had left her a settlement had been the real success of the family. The three of them had been content enough in their tall, narrow house that teetered on the edge of the Avon Gorge, though. Sometimes she yearned for the ribbon of water that had glinted far below her window. It was probably why she felt most like herself by the stream close to the old manor. Her gentle parents were both dead now, a fact she couldn't yet comprehend, though her father had been gone for two years, her mother for four. She preferred to think of them as though they were still there, some thirty miles to the south-west.

It was her uncle who had made the introduction to Edward, at least indirectly. Until his death he had lived in some style in a house near Cirencester – Elizabeth and her parents had been regular guests there. At one gathering, a Christmas ball, Edward, back in the county permanently after completion of the great house that he had set about building soon after his father's death, had also been a guest.

In retrospect, and though she knew he had fallen deeply in love with her, she understood that it had also been the perfect moment for Edward to find a wife. He had already enjoyed a great deal of freedom in London by the time his father had died, two years before Elizabeth had met him. His inheritance of the Fiercombe estate, and the enforced responsibility that came with it, coincided with his growing certainty that the bachelor lifestyle, though still alluring in its way, would eventually bore him; even self-indulgence became monotonous, given time. While he would never entirely forgo the glitter of the capital, its thrust and energy, its clubs and diversions, he was increasingly drawn to an image of himself as a gentleman of substance, no longer the callow carouser throwing his father's money at a last game of hazard.

He envisaged his London friends coming to stay and leaving impressed and envious by what he had achieved: a model wife and children, irreproachable servants and a fashionable home. He tackled the latter first, immediately appointing an architect to build an entirely new house of much grander proportions in a different part of the valley:

Stanton House. His intentions had been good, if a little shallow: he had wished to rouse that provincial corner of Gloucestershire from its slumbers and introduce it to the latest styles in design and architecture. He had been seduced by the notion of using impregnable granite to shelter the family he would create around him. He was thirty-three to Elizabeth's eighteen when they met, but a very young thirty-three. The old manor he had grown up in — returned to after his father's funeral on a bleak November day — had seemed gloomy and impractical in contrast to the new house that was forming in his mind.

Elizabeth understood what had driven his desire for the new in place of the old but from her first day in the valley she had felt an aversion to Stanton House. Of course, she had hidden it from her new husband and had continued to do so ever since. Though her life before her marriage seemed like a thousand years ago, she remembered the day of her arrival as a new bride with startling clarity. She hadn't visited Fiercombe beforehand: Edward had wanted the place to be a surprise, a gift to his new wife.

The weather was pleasant enough in Bristol on the morning after their autumn wedding. A little overcast, perhaps, but nothing like the heavy skies and torrential rain that enveloped them as they travelled north into deepest Gloucestershire. The rain coursed down the windows of the carriage, which grew steadily more opaque with their expelled breath. Eventually, they left the principal roads and passed through the village of Stanwick, its waterlogged green deserted, then turned down what Edward informed her was Fiery Lane.

The new carriage's springs creaked in protest at the punishing gradient of the weaving path that took them into the valley. After a few minutes of being thrown around, the wheels jarring against loose stones or sliding abruptly into flooded ruts in the earth road, Elizabeth began to feel queasy. She reached up to wipe off some of the condensation on the window, using a corner of the travelling rug that Edward had tucked securely around her legs earlier. It made little difference: she could distinguish nothing but the indistinct outlines of tree trunks and, above, the gnarled fingers of leafless branches reaching out to one another.

'We'll soon be there, my darling,' Edward said, a slight edge to his voice. He was angry about the rain; Elizabeth already understood him well enough to know that. Edward was a man who wanted things to be perfect, or at least to conform to his own often uncompromising ideals. He had envisaged his wife's first glimpse of her new home as a crisp scene of sunshine and dazzling frost, not under lowering clouds and through sheeting rain. In so many ways he was still the hale and handsome little boy whose sense of entitlement had been instilled in him by his doting, less charismatic parents, the child who had, on his fifth birthday or so the family lore went, raged at the sky for remaining stubbornly grey.

'I hope this infernal weather won't last,' he continued now, irritably. 'You can't begin to appreciate the house's position and true effect, not when it's sunk in mist. It was designed so that the valley walls would frame it, you see, a natural backdrop.'

Elizabeth smiled at him encouragingly, although she

had heard the words before. With a visible effort, he smiled back.

As the ground levelled off, she suddenly spied a glimpse of warm colour among all the grey and dun. 'What is that place, Edward?' She twisted around in her seat to see it better: a house of pale yellow stone surrounded by dark green thickets of holly and yew that stood, like sentinels, planted to protect and conceal something mysterious. It reminded her of a fairytale she'd loved as a girl. 'It's just like an enchanted place, where a princess might have slept for a hundred years,' she cried, delighted.

Edward smiled indulgently, as he still had then at her more charming flights of fancy. 'It's just the old manor,' he chided her. 'I've told you about it many times. As you well know, I lived there most of my life.'

'Of course you told me about it. You just didn't tell me how lovely it is.'

'I'm not sure I've ever thought of it as lovely. Perhaps that's why,' he said dismissively.

Soon after they had passed it, the path swung around in a wide arc to the right and Elizabeth could see the manor properly, from its best angle: the three asymmetrical gables and the box hedges that marked out a small formal garden at their feet.

'I've never seen anything like it,' she said. 'It's –'

'It's a pleasant spot for a picnic and no more,' Edward interrupted, a hint of impatience in his voice. 'Do try to save some excitement for Stanton House, won't you?'

After a few minutes the carriage slowed as its wheels met the resistance of the freshly raked gravel drive. Edward's new house appeared quite suddenly out of the misty shroud of rain then, like the stern of an enormous ship: a great grey galleon anchored in the choppy waters of the carriage-sweep. The numerous windows, reflecting the densely wooded slopes of the valley, were dark, like empty eye sockets. Elizabeth shivered slightly and, glancing down into her lap, saw that she was clutching the wool of the travelling rug so tightly that her knuckles shone white.

'What do you think of it?' Edward said, close to her ear, startling her. 'You are to be mistress of all this.' He gestured towards the great house.

She faltered then, knowing that she couldn't possibly tell the truth: that her first impression of Stanton House was that it squatted menacingly at the end of its drive, seeming to glower at her. Instead she told herself that it was merely the effect of the inclement weather and, with some effort, turned to him with a bright smile. He looked back at her with such hope and expectation that she understood why his parents had found him so irresistible as a boy.

'Goodness, Edward. What a house you have built,' she said. 'I'm sorry if I seem a little stunned but I am. I didn't expect it to be so very . . . grand.'

He absorbed her words as she looked on apprehensively. Eventually, tentatively, he began to smile and, because she loved him, because she wanted to please him more than anyone else, she reached out to clasp his hand. 'It's a wonderful, elegant house, and I can't wait to come to know it,' she said firmly, and was rewarded by Edward's widening smile and the genuine pride and pleasure that lit blue eyes the colour of forget-me-nots.

Six years on, as the house was polished, swept and garlanded for a great occasion, little had changed. She was now in the habit of tiptoeing around her husband, of dressing up unpalatable truths in flattery or avoiding them altogether. When he fled the valley in a temper, she never alluded to it on his return. When Isabel clung and cried, she hid her from him. When he knocked on her bedroom door after a period of physical estrangement, she was careful to avoid both the tearful relief and cold resentment she truly felt, and instead went to him as she had at the beginning, giving the best impression she could muster of simple passion. *But he also deceives himself,* Elizabeth thought as the three of them — husband, wife and daughter — stepped inside Stanton House's cavernous hallway. *Not only has he never realized how much the local people resent this misguided indulgence of a house, but he has never understood that I have come to view it as a prison.*

Alice

By the time I had pushed open the door leading from the kitchen garden into the manor, Ruck had gone through with my case and was nowhere to be seen. There was no entrance hall. I was standing in a room that, after the brightness of the day, seemed dark and low-ceilinged. The enormous hearth at the far end was quite black with what must have been centuries' worth of accumulated soot. I walked over and had put out a finger to touch it when a figure appeared in the darkened doorway to my left and made me jump. As my eyes adjusted fully to the gloom I saw that it was not Ruck but a woman in her fifties, dressed in black except for her starched white collar. She stepped forward then and took my hands, though she didn't smile. Her skin felt powdery and soft, like a pair of kid gloves.

'Mrs Jelphs?' I stammered.

She nodded. 'We're glad to have you here at Fiercombe, though I'm sorry it's under such tragic circumstances, Mrs . . . I don't think your mother mentioned your married name.'

I stared at her for a long moment, until I grasped that she was referring to my fictitiously deceased husband. My mind cast about desperately for a plausible surname but all I could think of was Elton. 'Oh, no. I mean, thank you. And, please, please, call me Alice.'

'Yes, of course, if that's easier for you. I suppose those kinds of motoring accidents have grown quite common in a great city like London but that doesn't make it any less dreadful.'

'No.' I looked at my feet. I felt horribly dishonest lying to someone who seemed kind. I wondered what had happened to her husband and felt awful at the thought that she might have been genuinely widowed.

'We won't talk of it, if it upsets you. I can't pretend to understand exactly how you must feel because I never married – we housekeepers are always referred to as "Mrs",' she said softly, as though she had read my mind. I shifted uncomfortably from foot to foot. 'Well, I hope that you will find some peace here. I think it was a very sensible idea of the doctor to prescribe a new setting for you after all that's happened. I'm so glad your mother remembered me and thought I might be able to help. She said that you must earn your keep but, in truth, and with the family so rarely here, there is not a great deal to do. What you need is quiet, a place for your mind to heal itself while your body is busy growing your child.' She smiled for the first time.

I nodded, not quite trusting myself to speak. It seemed that Mrs Jelphs believed my story implicitly.

'Is she keeping well, your mother? I still picture her in my mind as the girl I knew from the village where we grew up, when she was still Maggie Litten. It's been so many years. A whole lifetime ago.'

'She is quite well, thank you. She sends her regards to you, of course.'

'You'll be wanting some tea,' she said, and turned to

the hearth, her movements deft and economical as she worked.

She had about her a scent of lavender and talcum that reminded me unexpectedly of my mother's mother, my Gloucestershire grandmother. At this thought I felt tears prickle alarmingly behind my eyes and inhaled audibly so I didn't cry. She turned at the sound and saw my face almost crumple, I felt sure, but she didn't say anything, merely crossing the room to a sideboard where a tray had already been laid with cups and saucers and slices of bread and butter. I had been so afraid that she would be hard like my mother but she wasn't, only contained.

When the tea leaves had been measured and spooned into the pot and the steaming water poured over them, she picked up the tray and led the way through the doorway from which she had surprised me. The corridor was narrow and without windows, which accounted for the lack of light. Under my feet, which I could hardly see, I felt the floor fall away slightly only to rise and almost trip me. It seemed that the manor's resistance to straight lines and perpendicular angles extended inside, lending the oak boards a drunken camber.

When we had passed half a dozen closed doors in the same dark wood that rippled beneath me, the passage widened and eventually opened out into a large hall. This was the formal entrance to the house; I supposed the kitchen garden led to the service, and servants', entrance. After the confinement of the corridor, the hall felt enormous and chilly. It soared to the full height of the building and contained a staircase that was intimidating rather than elegant, its newel post as tall as a man and the carved balusters deeply stained but unpolished.

Mrs Jelphs paused with her tray and nodded towards the wide turn in the staircase, above which hung a huge gilt-framed oil. 'That's the third baronet,' she said. 'He was said to be an alchemist, or at least that's what was believed locally. The current baronet is not a direct descendant of his. That's often the way with these families. It only takes a childless marriage, or a premature death . . .' she paused here, I assumed out of respect for my loss '. . . and the line dies out.'

I hesitated at the foot of the stairs, peering up at the painting, while Mrs Jelphs made off down another dim passage. Decades, probably centuries, of grime had turned the background of the portrait to mud, so that the long-dead baronet's pale hands seemed to loom out of the folds of his dark cloak and the canvas, while his shadowy face floated grotesquely above the white froth of a lace ruff. There was something about the picture I didn't like, some echo of the man in it that made my skin crawl, and I knew that I would always rush past it, never looking up to meet those hooded eyes. Turning away from it, I hurried to catch Mrs Jelphs, her long, old-fashioned skirt whisking around the corner out of sight.

The little room she had chosen for us was the room in which I came to feel most at ease during that first summer at Fiercombe. The mullioned windows were wide for its size, and some gardener, or perhaps Mrs Jelphs herself, had made sure the ivy that grew on the walls outside was kept trained back to allow as much light in as possible. Dusty-pink tea roses and the odd stray festoon of honeysuckle peeped in regardless and on clear days, such as that first afternoon, their shadows danced with the sunbeams on the pale, unpapered walls.

Mrs Jelphs gestured for me to sit down. She herself sat with her back to the window, the sunlight no doubt warm on her. Now I could see her properly, I could recognize something of the girl in the photograph I had once seen.

'These are a few of the girls I grew up with,' my mother had said that day in her bedroom. We were sitting on her and my father's bed, the tin of old letters and photographs between us on the eiderdown. 'Mary Woodward. Sarah . . . something, I can't think now. Rosie Hewer. And Edith Jelphs. We would have been fifteen, though perhaps Edith and Rosie were only fourteen. I was one of the older ones. That was the last summer I spent at home before I went up to London.'

The picture had been taken by a travelling photographer, which explained why the girls' expressions seemed shy or, as in my mother's case, guarded. Other than her, Edith Jelphs was the most composed of the five, her face quite closed. They were positioned to the left in the picture, the photographer apparently keen to capture Painswick's famous churchyard in the background. Though slightly blurred, the dark, sculpted yew trees stood out in stark contrast to the girls' pale dresses and pinafores.

I looked as closely as I dared at the same woman, now some forty years older. Her skin had not sagged but thinned in the intervening years, its surface delicately creased, like the tissue paper you'd find wrapped around an old wedding dress. Her eyes when she looked up to hand me my tea were still sharp, and of a blue so dark they would look black in artificial light.

My mother had rarely talked at length about her childhood, or the people she had known. She would open up briefly, as she had on the day she'd got out the tin, but then the shutters would come down and she wouldn't be pressed.

'Enough of that nonsense,' I remember her saying, as she bustled over to the wardrobe to replace the tin. 'There's no point dwelling on what's passed. Those days are long gone.'

In the small, sunlit parlour at Fiercombe, Mrs Jelphs looked at me over her teacup. 'Your mother didn't say much in her letters about your plans once the baby's arrived,' she said.

I swallowed a sip of tea while my mind raced. I needed to answer convincingly now, so that I wouldn't need to be asked again. 'After the birth I will go back to London,' I said slowly.

Mrs Jelphs nodded encouragingly.

'I'll move back into my parents' house and my mother will help me bring up the baby. When it's old enough to be left, I will try to get a job like my old one. I don't know if she said but my father is a groundsman – for a couple of local schools and the cricket club – which doesn't bring in as much money as it used to.'

Once I'd started, I found that the lies came quite easily. 'My husband's house – our house – has been let to someone else. It was only small but I couldn't possibly have afforded to live there on my own, and now that . . .' I gulped some tea, feeling quite disgusted at myself but knowing it was necessary.

'You need not talk about it any longer,' Mrs Jelphs said gently. 'It must be very difficult for you. Please don't worry yourself about having the baby here. Nearer the time I will look out some things you can use – a crib and so forth. There's a good midwife in the village – in Stanwick, I mean. I thought perhaps you might like to meet her in the next few weeks. She doesn't stand for any nonsense, I've heard, but has been delivering babies for thirty years or more. You'll be in good hands when your time comes.'

I nodded meekly, whispered a thank-you and did my best to blot out a sudden and vivid recollection of the abortionist's grubby kitchen.

'How long have you been here, Mrs Jelphs?' I said eventually.

She took a careful sip before answering. 'I came here as a maid when I was eighteen. Before that I worked in two other houses, both in Cheltenham.'

'It must have made quite a change,' I said, 'coming here after being in a town. It's so quiet.'

She would have shrugged if she had not been such a correct sort of person. 'You grow accustomed to it,' she said, looking down into her cup. 'Besides, it wasn't as quiet then as it is now. There were a decent number of staff here, working in the grounds as well as in the house.'

'Ruck said something about the people going away, and that there was no wool trade left for them.'

She looked up sharply. 'That began much earlier,' she said finally. 'This house – the old manor – like many of the surrounding towns was gradually extended as the local wool trade became richer. That easy wealth declined very quickly when the great mills of the north were built. For a time this valley was kept quite insulated from the poverty everywhere else, as more and more money was poured in by the current baronet's older brother, Sir Edward. There seemed to be no end to the spending that went on in the valley then but –' She stopped, her cup suspended in mid-air, and I tried to remember if Edward was the baronet mentioned in the library book. 'Well, anyone's luck can change. Things come to an end. As you can see for your-self, this is hardly the great estate it once was. Far from it. But Sir Charles, who inherited it as the new century began, would never sell the place. He grew up here and, unlike his elder brother, remained fond of this old manor house. I think he would live here still, if it wasn't for Lady Stan-ton. She prefers to be abroad, and that's understandable. I am kept on throughout the year to make sure that the place is clean and aired, and to open up the house prop-erly on the odd occasions when the family need to come back on estate business.'

Taking a last sip of tea, she stood, holding her back as she did so. I saw a flash of pain cross her features but in an instant her face had resumed its inscrutable expres-sion.

'I've got to get on now but you finish your tea and do have some bread and butter. Remember, you're eating for two now. I'll come back in half an hour and show you to your room. Ruck has already taken your case up – you shouldn't be lifting anything too heavy. Tomorrow I'll go through the first of the tasks I would like you to do for me while you're here.'

'Oh, yes,' I said hurriedly. 'I wouldn't expect to stay here and do nothing in return. I'm perfectly well enough to do most things. I'm just a bit more awkward than I used to be.'

'Nevertheless, you won't be doing anything strenuous. We have a maid who does the scrubbing and blacking in the kitchen but there are plenty of other things you can help with.'

With a quick smile, she turned and left and, though I strained to catch them, there were no retreating footsteps to be heard. It was as if she had been immediately swallowed by the rest of the house.

I took my time over the bread and butter and filled my teacup twice more. It reminded me of all the pots of tea James and I had shared and the last in particular. He hadn't wanted to be seen with me at his office and so had bundled me off to a Lyons Corner House up the road. I had almost managed a wry smile when I saw it, remembering what my mother had said about Lillian Butler in her starched uniform, catching the eye of the man who was now her husband.

James hadn't said much, caught between anger that I had sought him out and anxiety that someone he knew would see us there, which meant he startled every time the door opened. He had missed me too, though. I knew that from the way he could hardly meet my eye; I think he knew he would soften if he did.

'I have looked in at the cafe every night for weeks but you're never there,' I said in a whisper. 'If I hadn't come, would we ever have seen each other again? I don't think so.'

He looked out of the window and sighed. 'I'm not sure. I thought it was best that we probably didn't. Listen here,

Alice, I did this for your sake. I've made my bed with my marriage, but you – you've got everything ahead of you. I would be getting in the way of that.'

I swallowed a bitter laugh at the idea that I had everything ahead of me. How little he understood. That was the first time I found myself hating him, just a little. 'Why did you say you were going to get a divorce if you weren't? Was it because you knew I wouldn't go to bed with you otherwise?'

'Look, I meant everything I said in the moment. I did care for you, a great deal. I still do. But I think we got rather carried away.' He dropped his voice. 'After – well, after that night at the hotel, I sat on the train home, and the further I got from London, the less I could believe I had done it. I mean, it was lovely. You are lovely, and if I could turn back the clock a decade or so, I would find you and marry you.'

'Ten years ago I was just a child,' I said.

'Well, quite,' he said heavily, pressing his thumb and forefinger to his brow in the way he always did when he was troubled. It had become a familiar gesture and I had grown to love it. I understood then that I would probably never see it again.

I got to my feet carefully, making sure my coat covered my thickened waist. 'Goodbye, then,' I said stiffly. 'Thank you for the tea.'

He scrambled to get up and in doing so knocked over his cup.

'Are you going already?' he said, surprised. 'I've – well, I've missed you, Alice.'

I looked at him for a long moment. More than anything

I wanted to sit down again and tell him everything, but I knew for certain that he would no longer be looking at me with the first glimmers of renewed interest if I did. I needed for the sake of my pride, what little of it remained, to leave it there, with him having wished that I'd stayed. I leant over and gave him a quick kiss on the cheek, quite like the dignified wife I would never be to him. He put his fingers to the place my lips had touched.

I didn't look back as I walked to the door. I knew that he was staring after me, though, for what that was worth.

In the small parlour of Fiercombe Manor my tea had gone cold. I glanced over at the gilt carriage clock on the mantel – no longer trusting my own wristwatch – thinking it would nearly be time for Mrs Jelphs's return. In fact, barely twenty minutes had crawled by.

Determined not to think any more about James, I went over to the window and perched on the wooden seat beneath it. The old walls were thick, as thick as the seat's depth, and chilly to the touch. They would keep the manor warm in winter and cool in summer.

Outside, all seemed quiet through the glass. Almost everything was still, too – everything but the gently bobbing roses and the beech trees at the top of the valley. I could see an upright rank of them, high on the ridge, their branches in jagged silhouette against the sky. They seemed braced against a wind that was unfelt on the valley floor and, as I watched, hard white clouds massed behind them to cover the blue I had thought would see out the day.

I went to tuck a loose strand of hair behind my ear and realized I still had my hat and coat on. Alone in the small parlour I blushed, wondering what Mrs Jelphs must have thought of me. I was not usually so gauche. At the same time, I wondered why she had not said anything, why she had not shown me where I might hang them or made light of it: 'Are you not planning on staying long then, Alice?' Then I remembered that she had also had the tact not to ask me too many uncomfortable questions.

I turned and looked around the rest of the room, hoping to see a book or magazine. Even an old newspaper would have done. There was no reading matter but something else drew my eye. It was a wooden case that took up most of a small side table placed next to the chair Mrs Jelphs had sat in.

It was a sewing box, I saw, as I lifted the lid, its underside lined with padded satin the colour of forget-me-nots and studded with an assortment of needles and pins. It had been costly, made from a rich, polished oak, the lid intricately inlaid with three other types of wood: cherrywood, perhaps, ebony and something the colour of pale brandy. A complicated pattern of diamonds and squares, like the parquet floor of a grand ballroom, flanked a central panel of dulled brass. On this, tangled among the curling tendrils and exotic flowers engraved into its surface, I could make out a florid letter E. Edith Jelphs – was it hers? It seemed too ornate, too expensive. It was a lady's sewing box, surely.

I tipped the lid up so it caught more light from the window, and saw something else, half buried in the knots and twists of foliage: words in looping script. It took me a moment to understand why I was having such trouble deciphering them: they were in Latin. *Post tenebras, lux.* My schoolgirl Latin told me the first and last words immediately.

The middle one took longer, but in the end I had it: 'After darkness, light'. It was a strange sort of inscription, neither romantic nor pious.

I had seen something like it before – belonging to Dora's mother and her mother before her – though that little box of plain oak had not been nearly so grand. It was the padded satin underside of the lid that chimed in my memory. I lifted it again and ran my fingertips along the braille of the pinheads, my mind's eye seeing Dora and me that day years before, the pair of us crouching over the treasure, heads together.

'There's a secret compartment Mother showed me once,' Dora had said, in a whisper because we were not supposed to be in her parents' bedroom going through their private things. 'Do you want to see it?'

Her fingers had fumbled at a small rounded nub of brass that I would have assumed was part of the lid's hinge, if I had noticed it at all. When she managed to press it in with her thumb, the satin had seemed to shift forwards half an inch. Triumphantly, she had got her fingers behind it at the top and pulled it away so I could see the narrow recess behind. Inside, her mother had kept her wedding certificate and Dora's birth certificate.

Despite the superiority of the box I was looking at now, the small brass button was identical. My finger hovered over it as I glanced guiltily towards the door. Of course it was bad manners to look but, even as I thought it, I was pushing the button. Just as before, it sprang open at the top, this time to reveal a slip of paper, folded once, and something else, which I brought out: a dried flower. As careful as I was, a petal fell and disintegrated when I tried to pick it up. Putting the withered bloom back before I could do any more damage, I drew out the piece of paper. It was a short note written in an old-fashioned hand and signed at the end with a single, flamboyant initial.

My dear Edith,

A little note to tell you that I have gone for a walk to my usual place. I know you fret when I go on one of my wanderings to the other side of the valley but I promise I will be back before anyone else misses me and, for you, I will be particularly careful (no paddling about on the slippery stones in the stream!). I simply had to go – the morning is so beautiful, the valley laid out before me so invitingly when I looked out of the window, that I couldn't wait another minute. Besides – and though I am afraid to set this down in case I tempt Fate and it returns – the sickness hasn't come this morning. Perhaps it has gone altogether and I will be able to eat a little breakfast when I am back. Will you beg Mrs Wentworth to keep a little scrap for me? You know she will do it for you even if she does not wish to do it for her mistress! If she makes a face tell her that I must keep my strength up, as my husband never tires of reminding us all …

And if the first of the wild roses are out I will pick you one, for I know they are your favourites.

E

So there were two Es – Edith and someone who had been her mistress. Perhaps it had been her box once and she had passed it on to Mrs Jelphs for her service. That made more sense. One phrase in the note had struck me and I read it again: 'the sickness hasn't come this morning'. Had she been ill or – and I wasn't sure if my own condition was making me see things that weren't there – was it morning sickness and she had been expecting a child?

Ever since that awful day at the lido, I felt as though mothers – expectant or otherwise – were everywhere I turned. Of course I knew they had always been there; it was just that in my predicament they had taken on a new and frightening significance. Now here was another, or so I suspected. What had she been like, this woman who must have been so different from me in all ways but one? She had had a husband, a cook and a maid who cared where she was and what she was eating.

As I clicked the satin platform into place, the note tucked safely inside once again, I remembered the entry I'd read in the library the day before, about the renowned beauty who had shared her name with a queen. Perhaps the E – on the lid of the box and in the note – stood for Elizabeth. Someone who had once occupied this valley, as I would, had once used this box and written that note, had gone for walks and known this house. Possibly – just possibly – she had expected a child here too, as I now did. And, just like that, she came to life for me – this Elizabeth I still knew so little about. It wasn't only because I thought I might be about to experience something she had in the same place, but because she made me feel a little less alone.

I was still thinking about her, my fingertip tracing the box's engraved lid, when something – a pale flash, nothing more substantial – made me look up to the doorway. Mrs Jelphs had left the door ajar but I could see nothing through the gap into the passage except the vague lines and shadows of the wood panelling. I replayed the brief glimpse in my head but it dissolved even as I tried to examine it, like the white-tipped crest of a wave that looks for a moment like the face of someone drowning. I dismissed it and returned to the window-seat to wait out the remaining minutes of solitude. It was peaceful enough, though I still found myself occasionally glancing back towards the door.

Mrs Jelphs reappeared precisely when she had said she would. Now carrying my coat and hat I followed her meekly down the passage towards the main hallway. I couldn't resist a glance over my shoulder, but there was nothing glimmering palely in the murk, only the outline of firmly closed doors stretching away down the manor's length. I was tired; I was expecting a baby; my eyes had obviously been playing tricks on me.

'There are other stairs as well as these,' Mrs Jelphs said, as we climbed the broad treads of the grand staircase. 'They're closer to your room but I wouldn't use them. They're in the oldest part of the house and they're steep and far narrower than these. There's not much light there. The yew pylons see to that.'

It was the first time I had come across that description and I was too shy to ask what she meant by it. I was to find out soon enough anyway, when we arrived at the room that was to be mine. One of its two windows was almost obscured by a single column of yew – there were four altogether – and it reached higher yet than that, almost as high as the steeply pitched roof. If I had opened the old casement and reached out I could have brushed its dense, dark foliage.

'They haven't been cut for years,' said Mrs Jelphs. 'Ruck is too old to clamber up there and I'm not sure it's worth the expense of getting anyone else in to see to them. The family think not. Even in my time here they have never been tended as carefully as they were when the sixth baronet lived here as a small boy. Then the yew parlour was kept as neat as could be, each one no taller than eight foot. It's called a parlour, you see. A yew parlour. I don't know precisely why but I think it must be because the trees are so dense that when you're in among them it's like being shut up inside.'

'I don't think I've ever seen so much yew outside a graveyard,' I said.

Mrs Jelphs didn't answer but continued to stare out of the window at the monstrous shrub.

After she had left me alone, I made a timid inspection of the room, easing warped drawers open as quietly as I could and setting down the ornaments I picked up exactly where they had been. Every surface had been dusted but the air smelt musty and old, and a little of mothballs. It was foolish but I was behaving as though someone was stationed outside the door, listening.

The room was situated at the corner of the house and therefore had windows on two sides. It was sparsely furnished but what there was looked expensive, if rather careworn. A large wardrobe squatted in one corner. Made of polished mahogany, a slightly foxed mirror was set into the door. My face looked drawn in it and I wondered if its reflection was true. Inside there were half a dozen coat hangers that clicked forlornly when I opened the door. Other than a Victorian dresser topped with an old-fashioned jug and bowl, there wasn't another stick of furniture in the room.

Save the bed, of course, and a pair of matching tables that flanked it. It was far bigger and higher than the one I was used to and I had to clamber awkwardly to get on to it, my swelling stomach getting in the way. I lay down on my back and felt myself sink deeply into the old mattress. Above, there was a canopy with heavy, wine-red curtains that were tied back. I reached up to shake one out. The fabric was a thick brocade with a faded pattern I could just make out, of fruit trees and strange figures picked out in gold thread.

Something tickled my hand and I jumped, dropping the curtain so it swung down, sending up more dust. A large moth, desiccated except for its plump furry body, had landed on the back of my hand. Its wings flapped open and shut slowly as I held my hand as far from my face as I could. Eventually it flew away, flitting around the loose curtain until it disappeared above the canopy. I shuddered and rubbed at my hand, though there was nothing there.

With the curtain down on one side, it was gloomy on the bed. Even the air felt more solid behind the dense weave of the fabric. I couldn't imagine why anyone would ever want to sleep with the curtains pulled: it would be like a slow suffocation. I told myself I was being silly then – getting jittery about a moth when I had no real fear of them. It was an old house, after all. The only surprise was that the brocade had survived so long. I tied the curtain back, kneeling up on the lumpy mattress to manage it, and started humming something tuneless, deliberately making a noise in the silence, ignoring my heart beating hard in my chest. The baby shifted inside me and I wondered if he could sense my nervousness. I say he: he became a boy to me from my first hours at Fiercombe.

It was the smaller side-facing window that supplied the room with most of its light; the enormous yews grew only at the front of the house. I crossed to it and opened the casement as wide as its swollen hinges would allow. The air outside was balm after the stuffy room. Leaning out I could see a long way towards the west, the only direction in which the steep sides of the valley flattened out a little. The sunsets from there would be spectacular.

Beyond a quaint stone building a little way off and the formal garden, with its square beds and box hedge, I had an uninterrupted view of the valley floor. A great meadow rolled away into the distance. I knew that close up it was probably dotted with weeds and clusters of garish dandelions but from the window it was a flawless carpet of soft green. As I watched, a figure came into view on the far side, a dog off to his side, running in and out of view in the long grass. It was Ruck. He wasn't tall or particularly broad but he carried a shotgun easily on his shoulder. He didn't look up or around him as he walked and I thought that his surroundings must have grown so familiar that they were now invisible to him. He paused at the top corner of the meadow and I heard a low whistle. The dog, which had lingered behind, came careering up at the call and scrambled through the gate leading to the next field.

I felt oddly shy for watching him and closed the casement softly, though he couldn't possibly have heard me. Turning back to face my new room, I heard a soft but insistent ticking. It was coming from a clock I hadn't registered before, though it squatted in the centre of the mantelpiece, an ugly thing of gilt. In the silence the ticking seemed loud and I didn't understand how I could have missed it. Though I immediately dismissed it as fanciful, I had the idea that I hadn't heard it before because it had only then started up. I peered at the face from where I was, feeling strangely reluctant to approach it. The hands told me it was a quarter to six, which I knew was impossible. I turned over my wrist. My own watch had stopped again. I tapped it but there was not even a flicker of movement.

After I had unpacked my suitcase and pushed it to the back of the wardrobe I felt ready to go and look outside. I found my way back to the main staircase with no trouble, though I kept my eyes on my feet going down so I didn't have to look at the painting of the alchemist baronet. I thought I would leave by the front door this time, but when I turned the heavy iron handle and pulled, it didn't budge. Perhaps everyone used the other.

The kitchen was deserted, all trace of my tea tray tidied away. I found myself creeping through on tiptoe anyway, and it was a relief to be outside in the fragrant air of the kitchen garden. I went round to the front of the house only to be greeted by the looming yews as soon as I turned the corner. They seemed to leach some of the warm afternoon light away, their foliage almost black against the golden stone of the house. Sinister now, in the middle of the afternoon, I thought about the shadows they'd cast after nightfall if the moon was out. My scalp prickled.

A sudden noise made me start. An upstairs casement

was protesting loudly as it was scraped open. Mrs Jelphs's pale face appeared above me.

'You're looking at the garden,' she said, her voice carrying in the quiet of the yew parlour. 'It's such a shame you can't see the gardens that used to be here.'

I wasn't sure what she meant but her closed expression stopped me asking. She spoke again after a pause. 'There'll be a light supper in the Red Room at seven. I'll join you. There are some things I must tell you about the house, where you can go in the grounds and so forth. You won't find it easily so come to the kitchen and I'll take you there.'

She withdrew without waiting for me to reply and the casement was dragged shut. I realized then that it was my own room she'd been speaking to me from. I had shut the door behind me so she must have knocked, received no answer and gone in anyway. I wanted to go back and check it immediately, though I don't know what I expected to find. Even if Mrs Jelphs had gone through my things, she was hardly careless enough to leave behind any clue that she had. Perhaps she had gone in to make sure I had everything I needed – enough coat-hangers and so forth – but the uncomfortable image of her fingering my slightly shabby possessions persisted. I wondered with a lurch if she had somehow detected my poking around in her sewing box and if her presence in my room was therefore a warning for me to mind my own business if I wanted to be left alone myself.

I spent the next half-hour wandering aimlessly around the small formal garden, inspecting the shrubs and flowers with an interest I feigned because I felt I might be watched from the house. It was too bright an afternoon for any lamps to have been put on inside so each window was dark and blank, telling me nothing.

The garden was formed of a series of terraces, the stone steps cracked and sown with moss and weeds. A bench had been placed on the uppermost terrace and I sat down gingerly, expecting the wood to be rotten. It creaked but held, and I looked up to my first proper view of the house's main façade.

The trio of gables were all slightly different, and I remembered Ruck saying they had been built at different times, a century between each. At first glance I'd thought the house very beautiful, its age-softened lines and golden stone lovely. But as I continued to look, I found I could soon see only its faults and oddities. The lack of symmetry in the gables and chimneys, the sagging roof and a small round window just below it in the oldest part of the house knocked the whole building out of kilter. There was an air of disharmony about it and, once I'd noticed it, I wasn't sure I could find my way back to being charmed. But when I looked again, it had returned to its former benign beauty.

I gave in soon after that and returned to my room. As I'd thought, there was no sign that Mrs Jelphs or anyone else had been there. I had more or less stuffed my underwear into the drawer at the bottom of the wardrobe and nobody had tidied it or the stockings that lay as tangled as I had left them. My diary, which I had kept sporadically since I was a small girl, was next to the bed, just where I'd placed it. There was no way of telling if it had been read but fortunately it was quite a new one I'd started only a couple of weeks before. Beyond my frustration with my mother, there was little that could possibly have been of interest to Mrs Jelphs. I had found I couldn't write in it about James: it was still too painful. I was doing my best to put him out of my mind altogether and, after reliving our last meeting in the small parlour, I was determined not to indulge myself again for the rest of the day.

Still, new diary or not, I didn't much like the thought of my privacy being trespassed upon. I went to the door but there was no lock, not that I was convinced I would have had the nerve to ask for the key if there had been. A strange thought crept into my mind then, almost as if someone had placed it there: *I might not be able to lock anyone out but at least that means no one can lock me in.* Tutting aloud – I was rarely given to melodrama – I climbed up on to the bed and lay down on my back, breathing a long sigh of relief as my weight sank into the mattress.

I must have dozed for a while, because when I sat up and looked out of the windows, the shadows from the trees high on the escarpment had lengthened and now loomed across the meadow. The clock on the mantel was still ticking but I knew it showed the wrong time and decided to find another. The last thing I wanted to do was be late for supper with Mrs Jelphs. I knew there was a grandfather clock in the hallway but when I got to it the pendulum was still, the hands stuck at precisely three o'clock. I sensed, with no way of confirming it, that it had stopped at three in the morning, not the afternoon. A shiver of unease rippled over my skin and I rubbed my bare arms, feeling the goose-bumps rise. No longer minding that I might be early and in the way, I set off for the kitchen.

Supper in the Red Room that first night was sombre, though the food was delicious: a few slices of lamb with mint sauce, fine green beans and potatoes that had been piped to form perfect golden peaks. Apparently much of it had come from the estate and we managed to stay on this topic for most of the meal, though I didn't much care about last year's carrot yield (which was paltry). Mrs Jelphs's portions were not large. She picked at her food and I felt embarrassed for wolfing mine.

It was fast growing dark in the valley and candles had been lit in preparation. Even an old oil lamp had been brought in to squat at one end of the table. The electricity supply, temperamental at the best of times at Fiercombe, didn't work at all in the Red Room. It was aptly named. The walls were painted a deep crimson while the windows were hung with curtains in a deeper shade still. The effect, especially in candlelight, was Gothic – the shadows cast by each flame a dramatic spike, the shadows under Mrs Jelphs's eyes like soot smudges.

She had by now cleared the table of its condiments and serving dishes and produced the pudding. I had been hoping for something stodgy, a schoolboy's jam roly-poly with custard; something that would fill me up and warm me through. With the sun gone, I wished I'd put my cardigan back on. There were no radiators at Fiercombe, needless to say.

A bowl of tinned pears was placed in front of me. I

added as much cream as I could, without looking greedy, and watched it marble with the sweetened juice.

'Has the house always relied on the estate for its food?' I said idly, thinking of the starched white sheets of my bed upstairs.

Mrs Jelphs inclined her head. 'I keep up the herb garden, and a couple of gardeners come in to tend the formal garden now and then, though not the yews, which they claim are too large a job for what they're paid. Ruck looks after the vegetable patch and keeps an eye on the game birds in the woods. The vegetables we don't eat or preserve are taken to Stanwick and Painswick and sold. The current baronet – Sir Charles – used to bring a shooting party during the pheasant season in September but then the habit was broken. The grounds and formal gardens are open to the public during summer, on Thursday mornings. Very few come, though, I'm afraid.'

'Are they not allowed in the house?'

'Some have asked, especially those with an interest in the Arts and Crafts movement. Americans occasionally. They expect something quite different, I think. They are rather put out when I have to tell them that the house is closed, private. Fewer and fewer come each year.'

'I suppose it's rather out of the way.'

Mrs Jelphs was looking off into the middle distance. 'Yes. Fiercombe is well hidden. The nearest main road is three miles away and that's as the crow flies.'

'You said not many come. Do you think that's the only reason why?'

What else had it said in the library book? Something about visitors not being encouraged, I thought. Reading it had given me the sense that the place had turned its back on the world.

'We have never advertised the gardens,' Mrs Jelphs said, after a pause. 'Any interest in Fiercombe tends to be limited to those who know a great deal about the kind of restoration work that was done here at the turn of the century, and those who wish to see our formal garden. It's one of the earliest of its kind in England. But you've seen the yew pylons. While we do our best, it's hardly a showpiece. And the few Arts and Crafts people who still come, hoping that the house and chapel might be open to visitors, are turned away disappointed.'

'So, a day in August attracts, what, fifty?'

Mrs Jelphs laughed thinly. 'Oh, no, my dear. We would be amazed to see fifty in a whole summer. Those who do come are all my age or older, and they remember hearing about the place in childhood. Today's youngsters aren't interested in gardens.'

I felt a spark of interest light again. 'What would they have heard? What was it like when you first came here?'

Mrs Jelphs didn't answer but looked down into her bowl, where half her pears lay untouched in a dribble of cream. When she looked up, her smile didn't reach her eyes. 'Why don't you finish my pears?' she said. 'I hope you won't stand on ceremony.'

I held out my bowl. She spooned them into it, then poured the rest of the cream over them.

It was obvious that she had changed the subject and I wondered why. Not wanting the conversation to dry up, I plunged in with a question I might not have asked so directly otherwise.

'I found a lovely old sewing box in the little room we had tea in this afternoon. Is it yours?'

She took so long to answer that I began to fear she had seen me reading the note after all.

'It's mine now,' she said eventually. She didn't look up but folded and then refolded her napkin, smoothing the linen with hands that weren't quite steady.

'It's just that I thought the E might stand for Elizabeth, rather than your name.'

Her head snapped up. 'What do you know of any Elizabeth?' she said, and her voice was quite changed: cold but something else too. I realized it was fear.

'I'm sorry, I didn't mean to . . . Well, it was nothing, really – just something I read in a library book.'

'Saying what? Even books in libraries can be economical with the truth.' She hadn't raised her voice but her tone was like iron.

'Really, it was just a note . . . a footnote,' I stammered, anxious that I had offended her and that I would give away I had read more than just a dry old library book. 'It said that she was a renowned beauty.'

Mrs Jelphs's face changed as I watched it. It was hard to read – not only because I had just met her and because the dim light cast strange shadows, but because so many emotions flitted across it in quick succession. 'Well, that at least is true.' She seemed to be speaking to herself more than me, the words barely audible. 'I rarely talk of it. The past, that is. Talking cannot bring it back. Perhaps people would be surprised, looking at me here,' she gestured at the candelabra and ornate china, 'but I've no love of old things just for the sake of them. If I could choose to, I'd have a nice new kitchen, with clean lino on the floor and a gas oven. Hot running water out of new pipes. Heating in my bedroom for the winter mornings.' She looked down at her hands. 'Everything in the valley was new once, when I first came here. We had the best of everything.'

I didn't dare speak or move, not even to nod in encouragement. If I did, I knew she would stop; I didn't think she was aware any longer that I was there.

'Mrs Wentworth, the cook, liked things done the old way but she was bought every sort of new-fangled implement and machine, whether she wanted to use them or not. Of course, I was hardly in the kitchens myself, except if there was a party, when we all had to wait on the guests. I was a lady's maid. In Cheltenham I had been first a kitchen maid and then a tweeny, with some duties upstairs. I had been very good at my lessons when I was young and dreamt of being a schoolteacher but we were too poor for me to stay on. So I went into service.

'In those days it was fashionable to have a lady's maid who was fairly accomplished, who knew the fashions from Paris and how to dress hair in the latest styles. Indeed, some of the most coveted maids were French. Not many ladies would have taken on a simple village girl with only a few years' experience of upstairs work – and it didn't make me very popular with the rest of the staff, not at first.

'But I was an excellent seamstress and I found I had a knack for dressing hair too. She had beautiful hair.

Conker-brown, but conkers when they're freshly fallen, before they dull. It was so thick, so heavy, that I had to use a hundred pins to keep it up when she dressed for dinner. I always thought it was a shame she couldn't wear it down as a girl would, running like a river down her back.'

Mrs Jelphs fell silent then, staring into the candlelight, lost in the past.

'Are there any pictures of her, of Elizabeth?' I said softly, knowing I risked breaking the spell. 'Any photographs?'

'Not any more, no.' Her voice was curt again.

There was a long silence and my spoon scraped loudly on the china as I ate the last of the pears. Mrs Jelphs was quite still in the chair opposite mine, her thoughts held fast by days long gone. I thought about how I'd run my finger over the flowing script of the E on the sewing box. Perhaps the last person to have done that was Elizabeth herself, an infinitesimal trace of her still there.

'Will you tell me about her?' I had spoken as softly as before but I still made the housekeeper flinch.

She remained silent for so long that I thought she wouldn't speak at all. Her eyes, now fixed on mine, grew blank and so fathomless that I had to look away. Perhaps it was the antiquated lighting but she seemed to have aged a decade. I was about to apologize for prying when she finally spoke, her voice measured and almost without expression.

'I'm afraid you'll have to excuse me,' she said. 'I'm feeling rather tired. I'm not as young as I was and it's really time I cleared away. I've got things to be getting on with before bed.'

I nodded, oddly ashamed that I'd questioned her at all and worried that I'd ruined things between us already.

She stood and clattered the dessert bowls on top of each other. I offered to help but was politely rebuffed. Left in the silence of the Red Room, the tapers hissing and flickering in the draught from the open door, I thought about what she had said – or, rather, what she hadn't – about her first mistress at Fiercombe. It was obvious that the present Lady Stanton had done little to supplant her in Mrs Jelphs's affections. In the housekeeper's heart, she remained the young lady's maid who had waited on Elizabeth Stanton.

Elizabeth. Her name was already capable of sending a frisson through me. One thing I was certain of was that something had happened to her, something out of the ordinary. A scandal, perhaps. She had taken a lover in the village, or she had run away from her life in the valley, boarding a liner to a new life in America. Or perhaps she had died tragically young. Perhaps it wasn't pregnancy she had alluded to in her note; perhaps she had been ill. I wondered about tuberculosis: all those consumptive women who'd gone uncomplainingly to their graves in the Victorian novels I'd read – delicately coughing into handkerchiefs spotted with blood and watching their flesh melt from their bones.

Had she been struck down by consumption, was that it? Or was it something more dramatic? Could she have been killed in a terrible accident – a fire in her bedroom or a carriage overturned by horses that had taken fright? My mind ran on until it got to murder, a vision of strong hands around a narrow neck setting me on edge in the gloomy room.

'Would you like some tea?' Mrs Jelphs had returned.

I would dearly have loved some but I shook my head, not wanting to put her out any more. Shame flooded me again, as if she had heard my sensational speculation.

I wished her goodnight and climbed the stairs to my room. There was scarcely any light in the hallway and the stained oak swallowed most of what little there was. As I passed the alchemist's portrait I kept my eyes down, yet in my peripheral vision I could still see his pale ruff and hands, disembodied and suspended in the gloom.

I don't remember falling asleep that first night. I had thought it would be difficult in a strange place but I must have dropped headlong into it, more tired than I had known. The baby was still and that probably had a great deal to do with it. When I woke in the smallest hours of the night, I was immediately wide awake, my body alert like an animal's, my mouth dry. My eyes scanned the gloom but the darkness was complete, the heavy curtains absorbing any glimmer of moonlight there might have been outside.

The air was heavy, thick and chilly, and an image of cold cream in a glass jar came into my mind. I put my hand out for the bedside lamp, pushing it through the dense atmosphere and feeling my skin cool. My fingers fumbled for the switch. I was torn between turning it on and being afraid of . . . I didn't know. Making contact with something lurking there in the dark, perhaps. What might be there I didn't want to think about.

It seemed to take an age to find the switch, my eyes scanning for movement all the time, and when I did I pulled the whole thing over, the crash horrifying in the smothering silence. The lamp had rolled off the table so I untangled myself from the layers of sheets and blankets and put my feet to the floor before I could think too much about it. Even before I tried it I knew the bulb would be broken. Pointlessly I held it up to my ear and shook it, hearing the tiny vibration of the coiled filament inside, tinging mournfully, useless inside the thin glass.

Then something – I can only describe it as a sort of charge in the air – made me look up. I stood still, my ears straining. A creak, just discernible, made me turn towards the door. Where I hadn't been able to see anything, even make out the shapes of the furniture, I could now see its faint outline. It was old and warped, the gap between it and the bare floorboards a good few inches. This void now shone with a bar of dim light that seemed to roll and alter even as I watched it.

Instinctively I held my breath but there were no more creaks, and in the lull I realized the sound of breathing hadn't stopped. In and out, soft and steady, far slower than the beating of my heart, it went on, while my own breath was still held, my chest tight with it. Still holding the broken lamp I stood for what felt like an unbearable length of time, my eyes fixed on the wavering, undulating light that was seeping under the door. The breathing had grown softer but was still there, just out of time with my own, which I couldn't hold any longer. I didn't think I could move until I suddenly did, putting the lamp down on the bed, then walking slowly towards the door and the light, as though not of my own volition but someone else's. I watched my hand, just visible in the strange glow, reach out for the door handle, which turned easily.

The corridor was empty and now completely dark in both directions. I made myself tiptoe out into it, my heart thumping painfully. It was utterly silent and, for a fleeting second, I thought of home and wished for the city's comforting hum, the explicable creaks of near neighbours. While there was nothing to see or hear, I thought I could detect the faintest trace of scent on the air. It was vaguely floral, a trail of something more delicate than the wood, polish and dust of the house. But when I inhaled again it had gone, if it had ever been there at all. I ran my hand along the wall to find a light switch, my fingers fumbling, but there was only the dark oak panelling's tongue and groove.

I remembered a candlestick I had seen then, tucked away at the back of the wardrobe's shelf above the hanging rail. I closed the bedroom door as silently as I could and made my way over to that great slab of mahogany, instinctively creeping as carefully as a cat. I told myself I mustn't wake Mrs Jelphs, whose room was sure to be close by. In truth, I felt as though I had to be quiet so that I didn't further alert something else to my presence.

I reached up to where I had seen the candlestick, and the smooth metal felt unnaturally cold as my hand closed around it. Just as I remembered I had no matches, the base knocked against something small and light.

It took a few tries before a match took properly. My hands were shaking and the box was slightly pulpy with damp. The candle's wick lit quickly, sending eerie shadows darting around the room and making the curtains and tapestries look as though they were moving. As I watched they seemed to settle, as though an invisible hand had stilled them.

I carried the candlestick to the bedside table, my hand cupped around the precious flame. Even so, the melting wax that pooled around the wick was disturbed and hissed in protest. I stopped and the flame wavered before lengthening again. When I'd put it safely down I clambered back into bed and looked around, wondering which item of furniture was light enough to move in front of the door. There was nothing I would be able to shift easily, especially the wardrobe with the mirror I didn't want to look into. Even the dresser on its rusty castors would make a dreadful racket if I dragged it across the boards. It was a childish impulse I felt a little ashamed of so I pulled the blankets over my cold legs and leant back against the wooden headboard.

It was then that I remembered something from my childhood that I hadn't thought of in years. A week in a damp old house on the south coast that had belonged to a great-aunt of my father's. We had gone there because she was dying. The room I was sleeping in was high up in the eaves of the house, furnished with two narrow beds and painted a dismal watery green. Badly painted too: you could see the rough strokes of a cheap brush dragged in different directions. One night I had woken disoriented from a nightmare, all the more confused because the dream had been set in the same room. In it, I had been compelled to turn over and look at the bed across from mine. Though it was empty, the still-clean sheets were moving, rhythmically swelling and deflating by an invisible force; phantom lungs. I could hear the breathing too.

I'd forgotten it until now. I took up my diary and set to work writing a list in the back, just as I'd always done as a child when I was afraid at night. As many Christian names beginning with each letter of the alphabet as I could think of – though I hesitated to write 'Edith' and 'Elizabeth' when I reached E. When I ran out of those I would list English monarchs followed by counties and their principal towns.

Every fibre of my body was listening out for more sounds and strange scents, even as another part of my brain sorted through its cache of names, but there was only the profound silence of the deep countryside and the cloying smell of liquid wax. I wondered how long the candle would last and prayed that dawn would come before it burnt out.

Elizabeth

The house, after the intensifying light and heat of the garden, felt as cool as a church. Edward made off towards his study without a goodbye, his mind trained once again on the numerous tasks he had to complete before the coming evening. Isabel had also gone, darting up the stairs to the nursery.

Elizabeth stood alone in the hallway and allowed the chill of the tiles to penetrate her thin-soled shoes. She unpinned her hat and tossed it on to a nearby chair, fighting the familiar twinge of guilt at the thought of one of the servants finding it and having to put it away for her. She had tried to be considerate when she first arrived in the valley, used to her parents' house and the small staff she had grown up with: a cook and three maids who were almost family to her. At Stanton House, these small kindnesses had earned her only bemusement and, from a few, contempt. *That's not how things are done here*, Edward had taken her aside to tell her one day. *You are embarrassing them*, his blunt words surely causing her much deeper shame than she had inflicted on any parlourmaid or footman.

This was one of the reasons she had engaged Edith as her maid. She had told the girl it was because she had looked so presentable at the Painswick fair but it wasn't really that. It was because she seemed kind. Elizabeth had seen her standing with a group of girls by the old iron stocks. While the rest of them had laughed at some poor boy who had tripped and made a fool of himself, Edith had stood slightly apart, dreamy-eyed and serious, more comfortable on the periphery. Elizabeth knew that some people thought a French maid better, more fashionable, but she didn't care. Edith was her ally, perhaps the only one in the valley, apart from her small daughter.

With a last glance at her abandoned hat, Elizabeth crossed the hall and climbed the stairs slowly, deciding at the top to go not towards her own rooms but in the other direction, to where Isabel would be. Some combination of this sudden decision and the medicinal smell of the passage in the nursery wing suddenly reminded her of ... She didn't know what. She stopped and shook her head slightly, as if to loosen the memory. The not-quite-remembering was a peculiar sensation and she had experienced it before – when ordinary rooms and unremarkable corners of the grounds abruptly reared up at her, the same yet altered, like a familiar face lit from a new angle, and darkly hinting at past associations she could not connect to her own memories.

The same thing had happened only a few days before, when she had been walking in the gardens. The day's blustery winds had died down as abruptly as the dusk had been overtaken by night and she knew she must hurry, or Edward would know she had been out in the dark and view it as eccentric. Even so, she had stopped short by the steps that led down to the lake, where the waters lay like a bolt of dark silk that had been shaken out but had now settled, the last ripples smoothed away. The thought entered her mind quite clearly: *It was colder when I was here before.* But when she reached back through her memory to

99

find out when and what *before* had been, she might as well have been grasping at smoke.

It was no good: she simply couldn't attach any extraordinary significance to either the lake or the passage that she now continued along towards the nursery door. It stood ajar and, tiptoeing closer, she could hear her daughter's high, clear voice, like silver bells. She was talking to herself, Elizabeth realized, the nursery-maid, no doubt, gossiping downstairs in the bowels of the house.

Putting her eye to the crack in the door, she could see a slice of her child, a creamy arm and then a flash of bright hair as she moved about. She was kneeling on the hearth-rug with an old peg doll she had never much liked in her hand. At her feet were an old tin soldier that had once belonged to her father and the tiny velveteen hare that Elizabeth had sewn for her last winter, straining her eyes over it in the gloomy drawing room, where the dark green wallpaper absorbed most of the gaslight.

Elizabeth leant closer so she might catch all the words. Isabel was talking as though she were the doll, the tiny red dress moving up and down like a warning flag. Elizabeth almost laughed aloud and clapped her hand over her mouth to stifle the noise, remembering how she had been lost in similar games at Isabel's age.

'If you don't stop being such a naughty girl, you will make her ill again,' Isabel was almost chanting, as she banged the doll down on the rug in the same rhythm. 'And then she will be sent away for ever so long.'

Despite the day's heat, which was beginning to creep up the stairs to the upper floors in the house, Elizabeth went cold.

'If you're not a good girl, he will come,' the little girl continued, her voice oddly expressionless. 'The magician will come again and he'll lock her in her room where you can't see her.'

Elizabeth couldn't bear to hear any more. Forcing herself to smile, she bustled noisily into the nursery surprising Isabel out of one reality and into another.

'Mama!' The little girl ran to her, the doll forgotten on the floor.

'What were you doing just now, my darling?' Elizabeth asked, before she could stop herself.

'Playing with my doll,' said Isabel, the omission making Elizabeth want to weep. She had tried before to replace the nursery-maid, whom she had never liked, but Edward wouldn't hear of it: the girl had come with an excellent character from a rather grand acquaintance in London and he couldn't be seen to contradict their regard for her.

The little girl wanted a story read to her then, so Elizabeth dragged the low wing chair over to the open window. Outside she could see that her husband had been drawn back outside and was now among the men on the lawn, his fair hair glinting under the high sun. She had only reached the bottom of the second page when she felt Isabel, who had curled herself around the mound of the baby, slacken in her arms, asleep. Elizabeth allowed her own eyes to close and the book of fairy tales dropped to the floor. Then she remembered what she had overheard and her eyes opened wide again.

She had long feared that Isabel, always so alert, had seen and heard too much in her short life. However, the strange performance she had just enacted on the nursery floor was surely proof of that. Guilt flooded her and she found her free hand going to her stomach and the baby on whom so much rested. What would she do if . . . But she wouldn't allow herself to think about that, not now, when there was so much else to think of.

Of course, the spiteful nursery-maid was only a symptom of a larger problem. Things would be different if only she and Edward could navigate their way back to how it had been when they were first married. No, she had not warmed to Stanton House and, no, she had not found some of the servants easy to contend with, but things had been simpler in those early days. What had made it bearable then was that, whatever she had thought of the house and whatever the servants had thought of their new mistress, Edward had not yet found fault in her: the hairline cracks in her nature were not yet visible to him.

Indeed, their first year in the valley had generally been content, especially once she had been able to tell him, shy but full of pride, that she was with child, having conceived just a few months after the wedding. The child turned out to be Isabel. While she was not a boy, she had been blessed with beauty enough for that not to matter: a pink and white girl who was the image of Edward and his brother Charles at the same age. *We have all the time in the world for more children*, Edward had said. 'Boys' was what he had meant by 'more children', of course.

But before Isabel, before the wedding, what of then? What of the first time they had met, at the Christmas ball held by her uncle? She tried to think back but the memory that came was a later one, inspired by the sun streaming through the window and warming her back. It had been hot that day, too.

It was the last day of June – the June after the Christmas ball – and just a month before Edward would propose, though she hadn't known that then. They were gathered in her uncle's garden, not just her and Edward but ten or twelve guests, her parents among them. As it was such an exceptionally beautiful day, tea had been served under a huge, spreading cedar, though its feathery boughs were no match for the blazing sun.

She had set down this episode in the diary she kept hidden in the summerhouse by the old manor, describing the languid heat that had turned her to liquid, the intimacy of Edward watching her eat and drink, the combined embarrassment and thrill of knowing his eyes remained on her as she licked her sugar-dusted lips.

She hadn't written down the perfect, naked truth of it in the diary – some horror of it being read by someone else, one of the servants finding it, perhaps. Not that she was always so cautious – there were other times in the summerhouse when she had to let the words flow out of her as they came, for fear that if she didn't she would go out of her mind. Then she wrote in pencil, the soft lead so much easier than ink to cross out or erase altogether.

Her marriage's progression from desire to discord must have been slow and incremental, a creeping rot setting in by degrees, for there was no evident turning point in the diary. Perhaps it was the fate of all diaries, never to be accurate or objective. She hadn't just blushed when she recorded the tea party, she had also omitted what she couldn't bear other eyes to see. When her marriage had begun to unravel, she had started omitting things for her own sake, when she read the entry at a later date in a vulnerably hopeful mood.

Instances that reflected poorly on Edward were often excluded, as were some of those that reflected badly on herself – times when she had been made to feel tiresome or foolish. And, if she was entirely honest with herself, those omissions had been necessary from the beginning.

In her first months of carrying Isabel, for instance, she, Edward and a friend, who was visiting from London, had set off for a walk in the beech woods that encircled the valley. It was early spring and the bluebells were suddenly, miraculously, out, their perfume clean and quenching, the haze of violet-blue intense and cool against muted bark and leaf. She had woken that morning in a bright, rather frenetic mood, and on the walk had been chattering about the room the baby would occupy and the kind of nursery-maid they would employ, deliberately making the friend laugh. Edward, she knew, found these displays of overt charm rather taxing. Next to other, more demure, women she seemed unfeminine; with a man she seemed flirtatious.

When the three of them came across a baby bird that had fallen from a nest, Elizabeth's high spirits vanished. It was still alive but had suffered a great gash in its neck, its tiny beak opening and closing soundlessly in what looked like agony. Elizabeth knelt and swept the mangled body on to her lap, dirt and blood staining the pale stuff of her gown.

'The poor thing has fallen out of the nest,' she cried, tears already trickling down her cheeks.

'If it's the weakest, it might well have been pushed,' said the friend, who had knelt beside her. 'The parents probably don't have enough food to go round. Unfortunately there's nothing we can do for it, Lady Stanton.'

'Darling, he's right,' said Edward, and Elizabeth heard the strain in his voice, though he was battling to be gentle. 'Come now, you're spoiling your dress.' He put his hands under her elbow and tried to raise her to her feet.

'Get off me, Edward!' she cried. 'Can't you see it's in terrible pain? Would you have me drop it and go back to the house for tea without a backward glance?'

He let her arm drop as if it had burnt him and glanced at his friend, who looked away. Later, when they were alone again, he spoke harshly to her, in the jagged undertone he had taken to using in case the servants were close by.

'What a scene you made in the woods today. There was no call for you to become so . . . shrill. It was just a dead bird. Your dress is ruined and Browning goes back to London in the belief that I have an hysteric for a wife.'

It was just a dead bird. His words had brought a forgotten episode from her childhood flooding back. She was a small girl of eight or nine, and a pigeon had flown into her high bedroom window with a sickening thud. It had dropped to the small front garden below and she had run pell-mell down the stairs to find it, her mind busy with torn-up handkerchiefs and pencils for bandages and splints. She found the bird splayed on the front steps, its neck broken, eyes dull. The blood that clotted in the exposed fan of its pearl-grey feathers was shockingly thick and red. Her father had found her there more than an hour later, tear-stained and still cradling the pigeon in her arms, oblivious to the chill that was turning her lips blue. He had carried her inside as though she had been the one to fall broken to the ground, not the bird.

In the nursery, Isabel stirred in her sleep and opened her eyes to look up at her mother. In the dazzling light from the window Elizabeth noticed for the first time that the colour of her daughter's left eye was slightly different from that of the right, a driftwood sliver of gold in the sea of blue. She didn't think it had been there before and instinctively hoped Edward wouldn't notice.

What had Isabel said, when she was speaking as the battered little peg doll? *The magician will come again.* Of course he hadn't been a magician – Elizabeth couldn't fathom where Isabel had got that from. Perhaps it was his black stovepipe hat, or the large leather bag he carried, as polished as his shoes and as waxed as his thin moustache. She could still remember the scratch of its hairs on the skin of her palm as she turned away from him. She could also remember, with horrible clarity, his cool, damp hands: the skin as soft as hers but the bones underneath capable of gripping like iron vices. She hadn't written about that in her diary, either.

Alice

I woke late the following morning, having slept far better than I expected after the episode with the broken lamp. My diary lay open by my side, my writing cramped and smudged, the lists of names sloping drunkenly. I had fallen asleep sitting up and rubbed my neck, which was sore from its awkward position. In the pale gold of the morning light, the room was far less forbidding – even the monstrous wardrobe seemed to have retreated and shrunk, the bulk that had squatted so menacingly in the shadows of the previous evening now revealed as mere furniture. I had obviously dreamt most of it, the un-familiarity of a new setting manifesting itself vividly in my sleep.

Feeling a little foolish, I went to the casement and flung it open. It moved easily and the air outside had already softened, with no trace of dawn's damp coolness. There would be no clouding over today. The midday sun would be hot and almost fierce, the late afternoon languorous and sticky. I dressed quickly, putting on a loose cotton blouse and a comfortable skirt that sat neatly over my small bump. Or so I hoped: my reflection in the ward-robe's mirror looked decent enough. The skirt almost concealed my thickened middle, the physical change I liked least.

With a rush I remembered the candle and glanced back

at the bedside table so fast that I cricked my stiff neck. Even through the hot pain, I felt a chill creep through me. The candle remained tall, hardly more used than when I last remembered checking its progress. I couldn't remember blowing it out so I supposed it had been extinguished by a draught. I smiled ruefully at myself in the mirror as I brushed my hair. I could almost hear my mother saying, 'Alice always did have the most overactive imagination and she certainly doesn't get it from me.'

I went down to the Red Room for breakfast but it was deserted, with no sign that Mrs Jelphs and I had spent the previous evening there. Only a slight darkening on the walls where the flames of the candles leapt indicated that the room was used at all. I headed for the kitchen and found it warm and full of good smells. A round-faced girl of sixteen or seventeen straightened up from scrubbing the flagstones and smiled at me.

'Hello,' she said, her small round eyes bright like brown glass buttons. 'I wondered when you were going to come down.'

'Is it very late?' I said, smiling sheepishly. 'I didn't sleep too well or I'd have been up earlier.'

She smiled back warmly. 'Oh, no. I meant I wanted to meet you. Anyway, it's only just gone half past eight.'

'I suppose you've been up since the crack of dawn,' I said.

'Near enough,' the girl replied. 'I don't mind it so much now it's almost summer, though. It's harder in the winter, when it's so dark. Now, do you want some tea? I was just about to put the kettle on for myself. I'll tell you what, I'll do you some eggs if you like. Seeing as it's your first day.

How do you like them? I do good scrambled. I put a bit of butter in for flavour.' She smiled again, cheeks red from her exertions with the scrubbing brush.

I wasn't usually hungry in the mornings, especially since the pregnancy, but I found then that I was ravenous. Perhaps it was the country air. 'I'd love some scrambled egg, thank you, though I don't think you should do it for me.'

'Don't be daft. It's either that or scrubbing the floor. Besides, this way you'll know where everything is for when you get your own tomorrow.' She smiled broadly at me, then went over to the bread bin. 'Do you want a slice of toast? I usually have one with a cup of tea in half an hour but I fancy it now. Mrs Jelphs won't mind. Go on, you sit down.'

I hadn't noticed it before but a small table was pushed against the wall, its leaves lowered so it took up as little space as possible. The legs were ornate with wooden scrollwork and I thought it must have found its way there from a grander room. I sat at one end, facing my new friend. 'What's your name? I'm afraid Mrs Jelphs didn't tell me yesterday.'

'Oh, she wouldn't think to! I come in the mornings mostly, to keep the house clean and swept. I'm needed at home in the afternoons. I help my ma round the house and I take in a bit of sewing too. We live up in Stanwick. I still haven't said who I am, have I? My name's Nan.'

I put out my hand but she wouldn't shake it until she had wiped hers on her apron. 'I'm Alice,' I said. 'I'll be here until . . .' I coloured. 'I'll be here for the rest of the summer.'

'I'm glad. It'll be nice to have someone young here and you can tell me all about London. I've always wanted to go and see the sights, not just the castles and what-have-you. All those cafes and picture palaces and grand restaurants. I've never set foot outside Gloucestershire. Oh.' She clapped her hand over her mouth. 'I'm sorry. Listen to me going on like that when you've come here to get away from the terrible time you've had.'

I smiled weakly, trying not to think about London's cafes and their inevitable associations. 'Please, you mustn't worry.'

She nodded, embarrassed, then turned back to the bread. She cut two thick slices and, after a minute or two, her smile was back. 'My ma said she saw Ruck off to fetch you in the carriage yesterday. She was walking to the post office when she saw him. He won't drive a motor-car – says they'd never get up the hills here if there was even a spot of rain.' She laughed, showing gappy white teeth. 'I did feel sorry for you having him turning up in that sorry old carriage.'

'It was a bit of a surprise,' I said, smiling but mortified that my arrival had been telegraphed through the village.

'So, when are you due?' she said, as she expertly beat eggs and milk in a bowl with a fork.

I blushed again at her directness and, noticing it, she was contrite once more. 'I'm always saying the wrong thing, I am. I should mind my own business. It's just that . . . well, it's just that I love babies. I had a little brother who come along late. He wasn't expected – my ma thought she was too old to have any more – and he died after a week.'

'I'm so sorry.'

'It was two summers ago. I loved him, even though he was with us for no time at all. He had these tiny perfect fingernails – that's what I remember most. At the bottom of each one was a little curved . . . I don't know what it's called.'

'Like a new moon,' I said.

'Yes, just like that.'

'This baby isn't due for a few months yet. It was arranged that I should come here to have it because my mother came from a place nearby. She knew Mrs Jelphs as a girl.' I didn't trust myself to say much more.

'So you're going to bring the baby up on your own, when it comes?' Nan's eyes were wide and full of sympathy.

'Well, my mother will help,' I said quickly, though the reality – the orphanage – would be quite different. My lies felt as remote to me as the truth.

'Well, I think that's really brave. I do,' said Nan, solemnly. She turned to stir the egg mixture over the heat. 'I'm sure you'll do a grand job of it.'

Just then Mrs Jelphs came in through the door leading to the kitchen garden.

'I hope you're not chattering on to Alice now,' she said, looking between us.

'No, Mrs Jelphs. I'm just doing some eggs and toast for her as it's her first day. She would have been up earlier but she didn't sleep too well.'

Mrs Jelphs looked at me anxiously. 'I'm sorry to hear that. It's important you get your rest for the baby. You mustn't over-exert yourself or . . .' She paused. 'Was the bed not comfortable? I know the mattresses in the manor should really be replaced – some of them date from well before my days in the valley.'

'Oh, no,' I said, relieved that she had lost her sharpness of the previous evening. 'It wasn't that. I was just restless. It's being in a new place, I suppose, and I'm not used to the quiet of the countryside. I must take after my father – he's a Londoner through-and-through, and when he came to this part of the world, he couldn't sleep either.'

Mrs Jelphs and Nan exchanged a look.

'I hope you weren't disturbed by my padding about,' I said, desperate not to have the housekeeper think I was a nuisance. 'Anyone sleeping near me would have had a pretty fitful night's sleep themselves. I even broke a light-bulb being clumsy.'

Mrs Jelphs shook her head. 'I didn't hear anything. Of course, I sleep at the other end of the house and the walls are very thick. The way the manor was built, over many years, means that it's peculiarly laid out inside. It's not a very large house, as these things go, but sometimes, even now, I have to remind myself which corridor leads to the staircase and which takes you off on a wild-goose chase past rooms that are closed up now.'

I felt the hairs rise on my arms as I picked up the cup of tea Nan had made me, imagining those abandoned rooms, their dust sheets and cobwebs, the air lying dormant and heavy, undisturbed for years. And then my mind moved back to the time before, when the rooms were lived in, the windows flung open and the floorboards creaking under the weight of people now long gone – the husband in front of a fire, the cook in her kitchen and Elizabeth . . .

Nan bustling over to me brought me back to the present. She set down a plate of fluffy yellow eggs and thickly sliced toast. 'There you are,' she said brightly. 'Tuck into that. It'll set you up for the day.'

I picked up my fork but a hazy image of what I'd been thinking about before lingered on in my mind.

'Do you mind sleeping here alone?' I said to Mrs Jelphs. 'I'm not sure . . . Well, I've only ever lived in my parents' house and that was built less than thirty years ago. It's just that I've never stayed in a place like this, where so many people have lived out their lives.'

Mrs Jelphs looked perplexed. 'I thought you were living with your husband?'

I swallowed a mouthful of egg without chewing in my haste to correct my mistake. 'Oh, yes, I did, but that wasn't for very long, and it was quite a new house too. It's just that it feels a little like a dream to me now.'

'I'm sorry, of course it must. Such a dreadful thing.'

Her expression was full of sympathy. I cast my eyes down to my plate. 'But in answer to your question, my dear, no, I don't mind it. It's true that some houses – houses like this one – have an atmosphere about them. They seem to hold the past in their walls somehow. But that is not something I've ever found frightening. On the contrary, I like to keep the past close to me.' Her face took on its faraway look. 'Besides,' she said, coming back to herself, 'I am not entirely alone in the valley at night. Ruck has a cottage further down Fiery Lane, on the edge of Ruin Wood.'

I thought of him walking across the meadow with his dog.

'Now,' said Mrs Jelphs, with a brightness that wasn't reflected in her eyes, 'I'll leave you to get on with your breakfast. When you're ready I'll show you around. I'll be in the garden.' She brought a large iron key out of her pocket. 'We can start with the chapel. It's very beautiful and not many get to see it. I thought you might like to go there sometimes, if you feel the need to. It's a very peaceful place.'

When she'd gone, I talked to Nan about this and that while I ate – what she thought of the village she'd lived in all her life, her older sisters and cousins, her uncle, who was gardener on another estate a couple of valleys away. She came and sat opposite me at the table, a mug of tea between her hands.

Now I had eaten something and my disturbed night had receded, I'd regained something of the previous day's anticipation. I had underestimated what a relief it would be to escape my mother's tight-lipped disapproval – I suppose I'd got used to living in its shadow during the weeks before I left. I pictured the kitchen at home, which never got the sun. Here, the contrast seemed symbolic: the brightness slanted in from the kitchen garden as distinct shafts of gold.

'It's nice what you were saying before, to Mrs Jelphs,' said Nan, interrupting my thoughts. 'About all the people living out their lives here. I never thought of it like that.'

'You can feel the past in some places, like it's just out of reach and that if you listen hard enough . . .'

'You don't mean ghosts, do you?' Nan's eyes were wide.

I laughed. 'No, not ghosts. I don't believe in them. No, it's something a bit quieter than that.'

She looked relieved. 'Oh, good. If I ever hear a ghost story, I'm jumping out of my skin for weeks afterwards. I don't believe in them either, but then it gets dark and I'm not so sure. Shall I tell you a story about this place?'

I hoped it would feature Elizabeth Stanton and that, if it did, I would find out more. My image of her remained tantalizingly blurred. Her hair, which Mrs Jelphs had mentioned, was the only thing I could see clearly: her long, dark river of hair. I nodded eagerly at Nan who leant forward, eyes sparkling.

'The oldest part of the house was built during the Wars of the Roses. Did you do them at school?'

A pair of stylized roses opened up in my mind, red and white: the Houses of Lancaster and York. It wasn't a period I knew well and it was much too early for Elizabeth. Feeling slightly disappointed but not wanting Nan to see it, I nodded again.

'Margaret of Anjou led the Lancastrians,' said Nan. 'She was French. I don't know how a Frenchwoman got herself mixed up in it but she did and her son fought for them too. On the way to the battle of Tewkesbury it's said that she stayed here a night or two, in the manor, when it was half the size it is now. She didn't know it then, while she was here, but the Yorkists would win and her son, the Prince of Wales, would be killed in the battle. He was her only son and it broke her heart.

'The thing I like best is that she's supposed to return about this time each year. She walks the corridor upstairs in the oldest part of the house, dressed in her fur-trimmed gown.'

Despite not believing a word of the haunting part, I

shuddered. I felt it again: the weight of the past pressing around me, almost tangible.

'What was the year?' I said. 'I never was very good at dates. It must have been the late 1400s.'

'1471,' said Nan, proudly. 'That and 1066 are the only ones I can ever remember.'

I smiled. 'So I suppose I should be rather alarmed, then. I haven't timed my arrival very well, have I?'

'Well, I've never seen anything,' said Nan, reluctantly, 'and I've been on my own upstairs in that part of the house plenty of times. Mind you, it's said you don't always see her.'

'Let me guess,' I said. 'You suddenly feel cold?'

'No, it's not that. They say that you know when she's been there because there's a smell of flowers in the air.'

At those words I felt my stomach tauten, just a little, before I dismissed the coincidence. Last night's episode was nothing but a combination of the heightened senses of pregnancy and the vivid imagination I'd had since I was a little girl. But then I remembered how Mrs Jelphs's lavender scent had made me think of my grandmother the day before and I wondered . . . Could it have been her prowling the corridors at night, making sure I was where I should be? It wasn't just the past that seemed to crowd in on me: something about Mrs Jelphs weighed on me too. She had gone into my room the day before, which had unsettled me, but it was also her manner towards me – one minute solicitous, the next closed and rather cold. The latter I could understand in someone who was naturally reserved – I was an interloper in her quiet domain – but the former, those occasional bursts of intense scrutiny, unnerved me. Her sense of responsibility to my mother wasn't enough to explain them.

Nan glanced towards the door, then leant closer towards me, her apron front soaking up a spill of tea on the table. 'I tell you who you ought to talk to if you're interested in the past,' she said. 'Mr Morton is a historian in the village. He's got books, ever so many. My mother does for him each week, dusts and takes his washing, and she says she's never seen anything like it. Stacked to the ceiling in some rooms, they are. She says that one of these days she's going to knock a pile of them over and no one will ever find her.'

Before I could ask where in the village he lived, Mrs Jelphs came in with a trug of cut flowers. Nan jumped to her feet.

'Are the pair of you still talking?' she said, a mild reproof in her tone. She raised her eyebrows, then gestured towards the flowers. 'I saw these and thought they would brighten the place up. They'll only die on the stem otherwise. Nan, if you could find some vases for them?' She looked at me. 'I can take you around now if you're ready.'

I scraped back my chair. It was probably no bad thing that I had to leave the kitchen and Nan. I knew I would have been tempted to prise out of her anything she might know about the valley's more recent past, and it would have been awful if Mrs Jelphs had overheard any mention of Elizabeth. I already knew it was important to tread carefully with her there, which ironically made me all the more intrigued about her one-time mistress. Mr Morton was another matter.

'It's well worth seeing, the chapel,' said Mrs Jelphs, as we threaded our way through the Tudor garden. 'It has some very unusual interior features. Not quite what you'd expect in such a remote little place.'

The yew pylons towered over us and I put out a hand to feel the springy foliage, as I'd imagined doing from my bedroom window the previous afternoon.

'I'll take you along the stream. It's prettier that way.'

Elizabeth had mentioned a stream in her note; there was a good chance it was the same one. I felt the fingertip brush of the past again and something else, too – a tiny alteration in the valley's atmosphere, as though it had heard my thoughts and was now listening more attentively.

We passed close to what looked to me like a miniature house of three floors and I wondered if it was the building I'd spotted from my bedroom. Up close, it was smaller than the most diminutive cottage but there was nothing rustic about the carved stone flourishes around the windows and the intricate sundial of blue and gold that had been set into the stone above the door's lintel. This strange dwelling – if that was what it was – teetered right on the edge of the stream, where the water ran clear and fast, the smooth pebbles at the bottom easily visible. I knew it would be bone cold.

'What's that place, Mrs Jelphs?' I called ahead to her.

'It's always been referred to as a summerhouse, though it seems rather too ornate for that. No one is sure what its original purpose was. One theory is that the estate accounts were dealt with there, the tenants going there each month rather than to the manor. It seems plausible.'

She paused to look at the diminutive building. 'It was also something of a refuge,' she said softly.

'To whom?' I asked.

As though I hadn't spoken she pointed to the stream that rushed on below us. 'It runs west down the valley towards the long barrow. Be careful: it doesn't look deep but the current is strong.' She continued to pick her way neatly through the mulch close to the bank.

At that moment, I remembered once reading the phrase 'steeped in history' and liking it. It might have been in a guidebook about Bath; that seemed likely enough. Just as I had said to Nan, I loved the idea of a place being saturated by the past, as though some essence of the years it had witnessed seeped out of its ancient stones.

A friend from school had once invited me to stay at her grandparents' house during the summer holidays. They lived in a sprawling red-brick rectory in Hampshire. There wasn't much money left and they had worn their shabby gentility lightly – the black-and-white photos of Oxford Blues from the last century hanging in dusty frames, the grand piano's lid scratched and strewn with piles of sheet music that betrayed generations of accomplished playing. On the day I arrived they had been opening the cellar from the outside. For reasons that weren't clear, it had been bricked up in the 1870s. As the smallest there I was lowered down through the gap first. Perhaps half a century of damp, stagnant air hit me, like a melancholy wave. I reached out to touch a glass medicine bottle half full of brackish liquid on a shelf. The person who had placed it there was probably dead and I held on to it tightly.

'Are you still alive?' my friend's older brother shouted

down to me. I looked up at him and nodded, shielding my eyes against the bright sunshine, in the present. I fell in love with the family and their house in that moment. For the rest of the week I even wondered if I might fall in love with the brother, too.

I had the same feeling, intensified many times over, at Fiercombe. The place was alive with the past. People had been here for thousands of years – here, in this remote valley. From the Saxons to Margaret of Anjou's Lancastrians, massed on the ridge before the march to Tewkesbury: they had been here and perhaps still were, in some sense. There was nothing but the sound of the water below us but the air crackled and vibrated as if some remnant of their presence echoed down the centuries, an empty valley crowded with ghosts.

The oldest parts of the chapel had been built with the manor but it had been extended in the mid-nineteenth century. According to Mrs Jelphs, who sounded as if she was reciting by heart from a book, the stained glass and elaborate tiling were a little-known but superlative example of the early Arts and Crafts style. Birds, flowers and vines were intricately entwined, creating an overall impression that was much more pagan than Christian. The theme of nature continued throughout the building, which was hewn from the same golden stone as the manor, and whose bare surface had been painted with stylized leaves in silver, green and gold. The air was completely still. I felt as though I was disturbing each slumbering molecule as I wandered around.

I am not religious but I have always loved churches, especially those with coloured glass, cut and leaded, the light streaming through. One summer my parents had had the idea to spend a day in Oxford and we had visited the cathedral of Christ Church, probably out of duty. Outside it was hot, the streets thronged with day-trippers determinedly enjoying their escape from routine. In contrast, the interior of the church was dark, cool and almost empty. My mother's court shoes clacked loudly on the smooth, worn tiles of the aisle and I moved away from her and my father, feeling that trio of adolescent emotions: humiliation, fury and guilt. Outside, stout white clouds were jostled along by a high wind not felt on the ground, revealing and then covering the sun again and again.

It came out just as I approached the largest window, making the glass sing. Shards of colour, dusky pink, amber and chartreuse green, lit the dark tiles and my own white T-bar shoes. I was thirteen and thought I was too old for them but there, just for a few minutes, I found I didn't mind and waggled them about, the colours bright against the pale leather. So many moments in childhood are forgotten, even those we think we recognize as significant at the time. That one stayed with me, the glass finding its way into my heart, like the little boy in Hans Christian Andersen's story about the Snow Queen. Except that my glass – that rainbow-coloured Pre-Raphaelite glass – warmed me right through.

Lost in that recollection I had almost forgotten Mrs Jelphs was there until she spoke. 'As I said earlier, you're welcome to come here, if you ever wish to. But I must ask you to lock up carefully. I'll show you where I hang the key when we go back to the manor.'

'I wouldn't have thought there was much risk of any-one stealing anything round here,' I said lightly.

Mrs Jelphs remained serious. 'It seems very cautious to you, perhaps, but the Stantons are particular about keep-ing the chapel locked. The pews, altar furniture and the rest are not worth a great deal but the wall decorations, the tiles and, of course, the glass are unique.' She gestured at a small stained-glass window off to the side that I hadn't noticed. It depicted a dark-haired woman in a long, pale green dress. Branches laden with golden fruit twisted over her, while brambles tangled around her bare feet.

'This was made in the early 1890s. That makes it one of the newer pieces in here. I think it's the most beautiful, though.'

I went closer to study it. Even my untutored eye could see that it was very fine work. Over the pieces of coloured glass, extra detail had been etched in, giving it greater depth and shadow. While her dark brown hair rippled out around her, as if she was under water, one tendril had been cut so it appeared to blow across her face, leaving only part of her mouth and a small nose showing.

I took a breath. 'Is this supposed to be …?'

Mrs Jelphs didn't reply.

We stood there, looking up, while the air grew stuffier, the smell of dust, prayer books and warm stone heady. I found myself rocking slightly on my feet as though I was on the edge of sleep. Blinking a few times, I forced myself to wake up.

It was then that Mrs Jelphs began to speak again, her voice far away. 'It was thought by some to be rather shock-ing. Elemental, it was called, and in a church too.' With a visible effort, she straightened her shoulders and smiled determinedly. 'I like to come and spend a few quiet moments here during the week and I always come on Sunday evenings – I find it more peaceful than the morning service up in Stanwick.'

I realized that something in the air had shifted, a veil of sadness lifted away.

'We really must get on now,' she said, her hand on my arm. 'I have things to do and they won't keep all day.'

We went back outside and the fresh air tasted delicious. 'It's going to be a beautiful day,' I said.

'Yes, I think you're right,' said Mrs Jelphs. 'Perhaps we're in for a settled spell.'

We made our way back, this time going through the little graveyard to reach a gate that would take us round the back of the manor instead of through the iron squeeze-belly stile and along the stream to the front. I wanted to stop and read the stones' inscriptions that hadn't been obscured by ivy or weathering, but Mrs Jelphs held the gate open for me in such a way that I didn't feel I could linger.

'The rhododendrons are late this year,' she said, as we walked. 'They were once as famous as the bluebells but they've been allowed to run rather wild.'

The bushes of dark, glossy leaves grew impressively high and dense on both sides, taller than the hedgerows I'd seen on the journey from the station. It was only at the very top that they grew unchecked, the very highest boughs reaching out towards each other in a bid to blot out the sky. 'If they keep growing as they are, you'll have a tunnel of green by the end of the summer,' I said.

'I'll have to talk to Ruck about cutting them back,' she said evenly.

We were both blinded in the gloom of the kitchen after the bright morning and I think we shared the embarrassment of being helpless in the dark with a virtual stranger. Nan had evidently gone for the day. When our eyes had adjusted, Mrs Jelphs beckoned for me to follow her out into the corridor. Cut into the oak panelling just above eye-level was a hidden cupboard. She showed me how to slide my fingers behind the wood in just the right place so that the catch released and the door swung back.

'Always put the key back here when you've finished with it,' she said solemnly. 'Some keys I always keep with me but the rest are here.'

The chapel's key was the largest, but perhaps a dozen others hung there, each on its own hook. Some were ornate and finely wrought; all looked old. Above each one was a tiny label written in a meticulously neat copperplate hand. The ink was the same faded sepia I'd once seen on a cache of Victorian postcards my mother and I had found in the attic of an old neighbour who had died. I had found them poignant, their authors – as well as their recipients – probably dead, the eagerly proffered anecdotes and brave endearments now orphaned and meaningless. My mother thought I was being morbid. 'Trust you to think of that, Alice,' she'd said, when I'd foolishly tried to explain.

Despite its embellishment, the handwriting above each key was easy to read. One label in particular snagged my eye. 'Nursery', it read. Without thinking, I reached out with my forefinger to trace the word, my other hand resting against my stomach. Before I could, however, Mrs Jelphs shut the cupboard door smartly.

'I'm afraid we'll have to resume our tour another day. Time has got away from me again. There's a job I would like you to start today.'

I nodded as enthusiastically as I could. I didn't want her to think that because I'd had an office job in London I felt myself to be above such things.

'I didn't imagine you'd want to be cooped up in the Red Room,' she said, as she set off down the passage, motioning for me to follow her. I almost tripped on a loose floorboard but managed to save myself.

'Mind how you go,' she called, from where she was waiting in the hall. In the weak light that filtered under the heavy front door, she looked like a subject from one of the oil paintings that studded the walls above the panelling; the planes of her pale face and the outline of her clothes were lit from one side, but the rest of her was shadowed.

'I'm fine. I just caught my foot,' I said.

'Still, you must take care,' she said, her eyes flicking down to my stomach. Again, I felt that intensity emanating from her. Finally she moved on and I followed, instinctively turning my face away from the alchemist as I passed the stairs.

In the small parlour she had cleared everything from the low table and spread it with newspaper. Various velvet-lined boxes had been opened, revealing rows of tarnished cutlery.

'It's hardly used and I keep the boxes shut but it still gets in,' Mrs Jelphs said ruefully, as she inspected a long-handled jam spoon.

'What gets in?' I said stupidly.

'The air, of course.'

'Oh, I see. Yes, it's the oxygen that blackens it.'

'No doubt. I would like you to polish it up, please. It shouldn't be left too long. There's baking soda. I don't hold with any of those fancy new polishes – they're not as good. Mix it into a paste with a little water and apply it generously. Where the tarnish is bad you might leave it on for a time. While it's taking, you can rinse off the other pieces in the kitchen – there's a tray here – nice and hot now. Then use this dry cloth to buff it all up. Silver's soft so please be careful you don't dent it. It's Regency and worth a lot of money. It was a wedding gift. Every piece was engraved, even the teaspoons and cake forks.'

She turned over the jam spoon and pointed out a small, highly ornate 'S', like you might see among the curlicues of a grand old iron gate.

'S for Stanton, you see. I remember when these were always in use. They weren't just kept for best, either. Sir Edward insisted that everything worth little or out of fashion was thrown away.'

I wondered if she would say more but she just slotted the spoon back into its box. 'I'll leave you to it then, shall I?'

After Nan's breakfast, I didn't feel the need to stop for lunch, and by the time I felt I'd done enough for my first day, the sun had moved round to the west and was pouring in through the mullioned windows, lighting the silver so it gleamed and betrayed every stray fingerprint. I tidied everything away, then went to the kitchen to wash my hands. My knees were stiff from kneeling up at the low table, even though Mrs Jelphs had provided me with a gardening pad to cushion them. I thought it would be nice to loosen them up, and that after I had written a letter to Dora, I would walk back to the chapel. I could have another look inside, this time with no one to rush me.

In my room I fetched some sheets of writing paper and propped myself up on the bed, leaning on my diary for support. I couldn't find my pen so made do with a stub of pencil I'd found at the bottom of my handbag.

Fiercombe Manor
Nr Stanwick
Gloucestershire

Dear Dora,

I told you I would write — I hope you remember your promise to write back! Please don't forget, will you?

It is my second evening here now and I am getting on quite well. I don't think you would like it here very much — you would say it was far too old and creaky, not to mention <u>empty</u>. There is scarcely a soul for miles; that is, apart from me, Mrs Jelphs the housekeeper, who knew Mother, and an old retainer called Ruck, who came to pick me up from the station yesterday — in a carriage of all things! It had seen better days — better decades, I should think. There were some boys watching as I clambered up into it and they thought it highly amusing.

Mrs Jelphs is quite different from what I expected. In fact, she seems quite kind, and today she showed me the chapel, which is very beautiful. The whole place is ancient, the house centuries old. In a way, although everything still feels strange here, I also feel like I've been here for years. Perhaps this pregnancy is addling my mind …

You'll be glad to know that my story — or, rather, my mother's story — has been believed. I hate lying, especially when Mrs Jelphs and the girl who comes to clean, Nan, have been so good about it, but what else can I do? It's not as if they would look at me the same way if they knew the truth. In a couple of weeks I'll probably half believe it myself. I hope so — I nearly slipped up this morning.

Anyway, all in all, I feel a little better to be away from London. I miss you, of course, and I don't know what I would have done without you these past weeks, but I can't pretend it isn't a relief to be away from Mother. Father too — I just felt so awful whenever I looked at him. So, in that sense, things are rather easier here at Fiercombe.

I'm trying not to think too much about James. Sometimes I seem to be able to banish him to the back of my mind, but then something will set me off and I want to sit down and cry. More than anything, I really do just want to forget about him — like you said I must. I know to my bones that I will never see him again but I suppose it's become a bad habit to think of him. After all, the James in my head was the only part of him I suppose I ever really had. So please don't get impatient reading this, Dora, I am trying my best.

I must go now, I've got to wash and change for dinner yet. I've been polishing silver all day and I feel filthy. The baby has been still — how strange it is to write of a baby, strange and frightening, but I won't think about that now.

Talking of strange, though, and before I really must go, I had a dreadful night. I thought I heard a noise, though, of course, it was nothing. I must have been half asleep because I even imagined I heard breathing. Quite ridiculous, really. I suppose it might be all the strain I've been under. Anyway, I hope I sleep better tonight. I'm sure you would say this old place is crammed with *ghosts but it isn't, at least not in the way you would mean. There's an atmosphere, though, as if something of what's gone before is still here, like an echo or a reflection in a dark pool. Now I will go – I can almost hear you laughing at that last line: 'Poor old Alice, her imagination has run away with her again.'*

Now, don't forget your promise – I expect a letter within a week. I want to know all about the department store and who you're going to the pictures with, so don't leave anything out.

Your old friend,
Alice

I put down my pencil and sealed the envelope carefully, in case Mrs Jelphs thought to read what was inside. Thinking of it winging its way to London, aboard a mail train that used the same tracks my train had, I felt a wave of misery and something like homesickness eddy through me. It was all the more forceful because it took me by surprise: I had so far felt quite removed from home. Pulling my sleeve down over my hand, I blotted away the tears that blurred the still unfamiliar room around me and took a shaky breath. My muscles were still sore and I knew I'd feel better once I got outside, where thoughts of my uncertain future would retreat again – or so I hoped.

The key hung where Mrs Jelphs had left it that morning and I put my hand in to get it down. I must have knocked the smaller key to the nursery because it began to swing freely on its hook. As I put out my hand to still it, I felt a strong urge to fetch it down and slip it into my pocket. I shut the door quickly: I could hardly go sneaking around in rooms I had no reason to be in, especially as I had only just arrived.

Just then a sound made me stop and look over my shoulder, back up the passageway that seemed, by some optical illusion, to narrow more dramatically than it should. It was like looking through a telescope the wrong way. There was nothing there, of course – but something made me open the cupboard door a crack to look at the nursery key again. It was still swinging, just slightly.

I was glad to get outside, where I took the back way to the chapel so I wouldn't slip in the boggy ground by the stream. Now that I looked more closely I could see that the rhododendron bushes were pregnant with tightly furled buds, each the size of a child's fist. They looked as though they might burst open at any moment.

I thought I would save my inspection of the graves for another time and went straight down the path to the impenetrable-looking chapel door. The lock was stiff but, after some coaxing, I got it to turn and stepped back into the air, which was cooler than it was outside. I made my way up the aisle and sat down with relief on the front pew. In the air above me a whirl of dust motes glittered, the sun's alchemy turning each into a speck of gold.

Despite the tranquillity of the chapel, my fears were not much less potent. Mixed with the terror that now always lurked inside me, a dark twin to the burgeoning child, there was also disbelief. In many ways, I still couldn't comprehend what had happened to me. The very fact of it continued to shock me, even then. The worst moments were those treacherous seconds after waking each morning, when I would be hurled from the last remnants of sleep into a wide-eyed, lurching anxiety.

There was a day, not too far in the future, when everything would change for ever, and I was powerless to alter that. I was utterly past any point of no return. Without any conscious effort from me, my body was getting on with growing another person inside it and I still hadn't come to terms with the strangeness of that. That women did such a thing every day offered no crumb of comfort. In fact, when I let myself think about it, I felt entirely alone.

In the soporific atmosphere of the chapel, I forced myself to breathe out slowly. Eventually the hot wave of panic subsided and I opened my eyes. Something caught my gaze under a pew against the far wall. I got up, forgetting my worries, and went over. Crouching awkwardly, I reached under and brought out a brightly embroidered kneeler. The others in the chapel were muted colours, dark greens and burgundies, but this one featured a stylized golden sun against a cornflower blue background. Bringing it out had dislodged something much smaller and I reached for it.

It was a soft toy rabbit made from plush or velveteen. Only about four inches long, it would have fitted snugly into the hand of a small child. I had no idea how long it had been there, forgotten in the sunny chapel, but it looked new, the nap of the material unclogged with dust. It was a delicate thing, each eye a tiny black bead. Looking at it more closely I saw the long hind legs and realized it wasn't a rabbit but a hare. I stroked it, then went to put it back but instead slipped it into the pocket of my skirt. It was like the urge I'd had with the nursery key, except this time I couldn't resist. Perhaps it belonged to one of the village children. I would ask Mrs Jelphs over dinner.

I made more effort with my appearance for my second meal in the Red Room. Once I was dressed, I leant out of the westward-facing window in my room and inhaled deeply. What I smelt was early summer in England distilled – a heady blend of damp moss, sun-warmed stone and honeysuckle. From one of the holly bushes growing close to the summerhouse a woodpigeon cooed and fussed.

Mrs Jelphs was waiting for me when I got downstairs. 'I really must do something about my watch,' I said. 'I'm sorry if I'm late but it keeps stopping.'

'Nothing seems to keep time very well down in the valley,' she said. 'You're not late, my dear. You must be hungry – you didn't even stop for lunch.'

'I hope you didn't make anything for me. It's just that after Nan's breakfast I was so full and –'

'You're not to worry. No one was inconvenienced. However, you should eat regularly, for the baby.'

She peered at me intently until I nodded meekly. I had the sense that she was trying to look inside me and it made me uneasy. Really, she had been nothing but courteous since my arrival and yet . . . I couldn't rid myself of the feeling that I had somehow disturbed the careful rhythms of the place, Mrs Jelphs's rhythms. I couldn't articulate it any better than that.

'I'll make myself a sandwich tomorrow, I promise,' I said. 'Nan didn't get round to showing me where everything is today but I can ask her then.'

'Apart from Fridays, Nan is gone by lunchtime so you'll have to catch her in the morning. She comes here early most days to build the fires, air the rooms and so on. On Fridays she dusts. There are other jobs she can't fit in so I have to find time for them. You will be a help.'

She smiled gently and I felt better.

'Now, I'm afraid I got rather distracted during last night's dinner. I had some things I needed to tell you about the estate and instead I must have bored you with stories of the past.'

'I loved hearing about all of it, about when you were a young maid. Like I said to Nan, I love stories from the past.'

'I suspect you're quite different from your mother in that.'

'She thinks I'm too romantic, that I have a tendency to be morbid. I don't mean to sound critical of her but she's completely unsentimental. No nonsense. Sometimes I think I would be better off if I were more like her.'

She nodded thoughtfully. 'I suppose it's different living in a city like London, but it's impossible to spend most of your life somewhere like Fiercombe and not be caught up in the past. Things change more slowly here, and when they do, people are more reluctant to let the old ways go. I'm wedded to this life and would probably be lost if everything was changed and new.'

Like the previous evening, Mrs Jelphs had prepared a delicate-looking meal. There was a green salad in shallow bowls of porcelain so thin you could see through them, a poached white fish and new potatoes. I was even hungrier than I had been the night before but I made myself politely sip some water before buttering a bread roll.

'Have you had a chance to explore any further than the chapel yet?' said Mrs Jelphs. 'I really ought to show you some of the wider estate but my back stops me walking too far, I'm afraid. Perhaps you would like Ruck to show you the extent of the place, so you can take some gentle exercise when you're not helping me here.'

I couldn't think of anything more awkward than a solitary walk with the taciturn Ruck. 'I'm fine really, Mrs Jelphs. It's a good idea but I like wandering by myself. Tomorrow I mean to get up earlier and go for a walk before I begin my jobs for the day. If I'm going to be eating so well here I'll need the exercise.'

'Well, if that's what you'd prefer. There are fairly flat paths through the beech woods that you could begin with. The boundaries of Fiercombe's land are all wooded so you shouldn't find yourself wandering further than is sensible. Just make sure you let me know if you plan to go off by yourself. Will you do that?' She looked up at me and it was there again, the intensity of expression that the subject matter didn't seem to warrant.

I nodded slowly, which seemed to satisfy her.

She attempted a smile. 'If you had come to us a little earlier in the season you could have seen the bluebells.'

'Ruck mentioned them,' I said eagerly, glad that the mood had lightened again. 'He said that people come from all over just to see them.'

'That's right, though not nearly so many as in the old days, as I said last night. There are a couple of steep, quite overgrown paths they use that start up in the village. It's private land here, you see, and we keep very limited opening hours for the garden. But we turn a blind eye during bluebell season – it has always been something of a tradition for people round here. As long as they don't trample them, I can't see that it does any harm. Sir Charles doesn't . . . well, he would prefer they didn't come, but he's here so rarely that it's a case of out of sight, out of mind.'

I watched her hands as she distractedly folded and unfolded her napkin. When she spoke again her voice had taken on a slight tremor.

'Now, there is one thing I must warn you about. I should have told you straight away – I've been rather remiss in not doing so. It's the old glasshouse – it's quite ruined and you mustn't go near it. It's a way off from here, in the eastern part of the valley. The path that you will have come down on yesterday with Ruck continues beyond where you turned off by the kitchen garden. If you stay on it, through the woods and past a couple of empty cottages, you'll reach it. The glasshouse.'

She fell silent for so long that I became aware of the sound of my own chewing and swallowed a mouthful of bread embarrassingly noisily. In the end I spoke just to break the quiet.

'Why was it built so far from the house?'

'It wasn't,' she replied, her tone curt. As if realizing this, she softened her expression. 'I'm sorry, my dear. It's my age – I find myself remembering things from long ago more clearly than the present.'

I was confused. 'Please don't apologize. You must have so many memories stored up and all of this one valley. Anyone would get lost in it sometimes. But I still don't understand. It sounds as though the glasshouse is quite a long way off but you said it wasn't built far from the house. Is that right?'

Mrs Jelphs frowned. 'Do you remember I told you that everything was new when I first came to the valley?'

I nodded, leaning forward in my seat. I sensed that, despite her obvious reluctance, she was at last going to reveal something of substance and I couldn't hide my interest.

She sighed. 'Well, the next generation – the present baronet, Sir Charles – hadn't long married when the title passed to him. He and . . . the new Lady Stanton were the first to live in this house for some years. It was the beginning of the new century.'

'Oh,' I said, puzzled. 'So the manor had been closed up?'

'If it had been left empty for a few more hard winters it would have been a ruin. However, Sir Charles was very fond of it – he had grown up here, of course – so he decided to restore it as far as funds would allow. In truth, he didn't have much choice. By then there was no other house on the land to live in.'

'I'm sorry, Mrs Jelphs, you must think I'm terribly stupid but I don't understand. Where did the previous baronet – Sir Edward – live, if Fiercombe was almost a ruin?'

She was looking off into the distance again. It was to become a familiar sight that summer. I waited quietly, suspecting that too many interruptions would bring the conversation to a close.

'It really was in a terrible way,' she said finally. 'The yews had been allowed to grow even higher than they are today;

they were by some feet taller than the roof. I'm afraid Sir Edward used the manor as nothing more than a picturesque picnic spot. The Victorians had so many fads and fashions and one was to picnic beside a pretty ruin. The yews must have spoilt the vista somewhat but it was quite the thing, I believe, to let an old house like this – still old even then, of course – go to rack and ruin, especially if you could afford to build a new one somewhere else on your land. Any sentimentality Sir Edward might have felt towards the home he'd grown up in was easily outweighed by his preference for all things new and innovative. He wasn't a man who dwelt on the past.'

She lapsed into silence again, a long minute passing before she resumed.

'So, Fiercombe Manor was almost lost, but then Sir Charles inherited the title from Sir Edward, who had never shown any interest in the manor. More than that, he didn't even like –'

'But didn't Sir Edward and Elizabeth have any children?' I broke in without thinking. 'Surely they would have inherited? Or –'

But Mrs Jelphs had continued to speak over me, her tone bright but brittle. 'Now Sir Charles, as he became after his elder brother's death, thought quite differently about this old house. He was on the fringes of a particular set who wanted to preserve the simpler traditions of craftsmanship that the factories had been in danger of wiping out. This was the Arts and Crafts style of decoration that you saw in the chapel, and which he had loved as a boy.

'He had become an acquaintance of Ashbee, who, if

you have heard of him, moved his guild of craftsmen from London to Chipping Campden in the northern Cotswolds around that time. This was 1901 or 1902, the very first years of this century anyway.

'Ashbee, or someone from that group, came here around that time and, as Thomas would probably say, "went into raptures" about the manor and its magical setting. All its faults – its asymmetry, its derelict garden and sagging roof – they overlooked. All they saw was the craftsmanship that had gone into it over the centuries. Not only outside but in – it's not much known but Fiercombe has some of the finest examples of early wall hangings anywhere. Despite the state of the roof the house had remained surprisingly dry inside. The chapel they loved too, of course.

'So, what money could be raised over the next few years was spent – and there was very little in the family coffers by then. In truth, there is not an enormous amount now. Sir Charles has always lived quite frugally. But Fiercombe Manor was patched up and became a family home again. Despite Nan's and my efforts, though, it's becoming a little more threadbare each year Sir Charles stays away.'

Her fingers were worrying her napkin again. 'It's a house that needs a family, with children running and laughing in the dark passages and the stiff old casements open to the fresh air.'

I frowned, rather puzzled. 'May I ask how old Sir Charles is? And his sons? Ruck mentioned yesterday something about them.'

Mrs Jelphs's hand fluttered to the high collar at her throat. 'Oh, no, you have misunderstood. There are no boys now. He . . . Well, Thomas is . . .' She tailed off.

I was unable to disentangle all the strands.

'I know Sir Charles and Lady Stanton live in France now,' I said slowly. 'Your letter to my mother said they lived abroad and Ruck mentioned France. He told me Lady Stanton had been promised they would live there when the boys were older. I had forgotten: I suppose I got them all muddled in my head. You mentioned a Thomas . . .'

She smiled tentatively. 'Thomas is the younger son. He's about your age now – no, a few years older, I would say. I've lost sight of the years myself.' She let go of her crumpled napkin and spread her hands. 'Anyway, the estate, what there was of it, passed to Sir Charles as the new century began. They lived a quiet sort of life, the life of an ordinary family. There is a little money – as I say, Sir Charles has always been very prudent – but they have lived a life far removed from the years that went before.

'In my first days as lady's maid here, almost every week brought a different set of people. The valley is so steep that it's like an amphitheatre and you could hear the chatter, glasses clinking and the band, as clearly as if you'd been right in among the guests.'

As Mrs Jelphs talked on her accent slipped and blurred a little. She spoke in very correct, clipped tones usually, with no sign of the village roots I knew she had through the connection with my mother. Immersed in her memories of when she was only twenty or so, she regained her old voice and the soft, loose Gloucestershire vowels that became more pronounced in my mother when she'd had too much sherry at Christmas.

'Mrs Wentworth was always happy to find me a job if I

went down to the kitchens on nights like that so, if I wasn't serving, I would slip away to the other side of the Great Mead. There was a place there, slightly higher and opposite where the house once stood, where I could see them all in the distance. I couldn't really make out their faces but I could hear them well enough.'

That was when everything clicked into place in my mind. 'So you mean there was another house in those days?'

She gazed at me blankly, as though she had forgotten I was there. 'Oh, yes, of course. I thought I'd said.'

Pausing, she seemed undecided whether to continue. I kept quiet and eventually, with a sigh, she did.

'Stanton House, as it was called, was built at enormous expense late in the last century, a great square house of almost forty rooms. It stood at the eastern end of the valley facing the west, where the valley flattens out. It was built from hard grey granite, quite different from the local limestone, which didn't make the building of it any cheaper, of course. Each of those blocks had to be brought here by horse and cart.'

'I had no idea,' I said, vowing to explore the estate properly first thing in the morning to see what else was secreted among the beeches and meadows. 'Ruck mentioned a big house but I thought he meant the manor. I wish I'd gone for a proper look around earlier now.'

'It's hardly worth it. There's very little to see. You'd have to know exactly where you were looking even to find the foundations.'

'But how can a great mansion have just gone like that?'

Mrs Jelphs shook her head. 'I believe there is only a

single photograph left to prove that Stanton House ever stood. I saw it once in an old book that is probably out of print now. It was strange to see it again.'

I remembered Nan's words about Mr Morton, the historian with all the books. Perhaps he had a copy.

'It was thought to be quite an ugly house,' continued Mrs Jelphs. 'Those who worked on the estate – and there were still a good number of them then – as well as those from up the hill in Stanwick all hated it when it was first built. It had every modern convenience inside and the garden was laid out in the Italian style by a famous designer who brought in marble statues. There was even an ornamental lake dug, with a great fountain installed.'

She stopped abruptly and I heard her swallow. She was fighting with her emotions, I could tell.

'It was the grandest house I'd ever been in,' she said softly, the tremor returned to her voice. 'There were large houses in Cheltenham but there was something about the setting here, the steep sides of the valley a backdrop, that made Stanton House particularly imposing.'

'But what happened to it?' I said, as gently as I could. 'I still don't see how a house like that can have disappeared off the face of the earth.'

'It didn't disappear. It was sold off.' Her voice was flat.

'But the building itself?'

'That was sold too. When the assets of an estate are stripped, they don't just get rid of every piece of furniture. The copper from the roof, the imported statues and Mediterranean plants – those that had survived the winters – the oak panelling from the billiards room, the books from the library and the shelves that had been hand-built to hold them, the metal from the gas generator, even those great blocks of grey stone. All of it was sold. The silverware you have been polishing, for instance, was bought back by Sir Charles much later on.

'The auctioneers made a neat job of it, like meat picked clean off a bone. Apart from the walls of the old kitchen garden and the glasshouse, there's nothing left. It was pure chance that the valuers didn't bother to look inside the old manor. They took one glance at the roof and the yews towering above it and wrote it off as a ruin, worth nothing.'

'But the other house. What a waste. Of money and time and . . .'

'Sir Charles was Edward Stanton's younger brother, by ten or fifteen years. I have said he is a prudent man and that made him very different from his brother. He has done a good job of paying off the great debts that Sir Edward amassed.'

'He must have died quite young,' I said. 'Sir Edward, I mean.'

'Yes,' she said. 'He was not much more than forty.'

I wanted to ask what had happened to him, but Mrs Jelphs's bleak expression stopped me. I knew it would probably curtail the evening's conversation but, more than that, I also wanted Mrs Jelphs to like me, to approve of me even as my own mother didn't. As intrigued as I was by whatever had gone so wrong all those years before, I didn't want to trample on the memories of the woman who had taken me in. All in all, steering the conversation back to Sir Charles seemed safer territory.

'Ruck seemed to say that it was the present Lady

Stanton who wanted to go and live in France. I just wondered, if Sir Charles went to so much trouble to restore the manor, why would he ever consent to leave it?'

'He loved Fiercombe once – it was his boyhood home, as I think I've said – but I don't think his wife ever shared that. I remember very clearly their arrival. I had been one of the few servants from the Stanton House days to stay on after it was demolished. One by one, the estate cottages became empty until Ruck and I were the only ones left.'

She stopped to sip at her glass of water and I realized how tired she looked, a trick of the dim light making her skin thin and sag as I watched.

'That's when I became housekeeper. Well, as much of a housekeeper as anyone can be with one house razed to the ground and the other falling into ruin. I lived in one of the estate cottages and stayed there until Sir Charles began to restore the manor. He very kindly kept me on after his brother's death and I've been here ever since. If someone had told me on the day I arrived at Stanton House what would become of it, I would not have believed them. It was so large, so . . . permanent. But I suppose nothing ever is, not really.'

'And Lady Stanton – Sir Charles's Lady Stanton, I mean – she just never took to the valley?'

Mrs Jelphs avoided my eye when she answered. 'It wasn't that she disliked it. But it was only a few years after the big house had been demolished and, well, there had been some foolish talk that the valley was tainted . . .'

She stopped and got to her feet, lifting my empty plate and her almost untouched one, shaking her head when I tried to help. When she returned from the kitchen she was holding a pie fresh from the oven, the crisp pastry lid a deep golden colour. She cut me a large slice. 'Do you take custard?' she asked. Her tone of artificial brightness was back.

'Yes, please. But the house' – I couldn't help but press her a little more – 'it can't even have been that old when it was knocked down. How could things change so quickly?'

From Mrs Jelphs's expression I saw that her mood had changed when she left the room.

'That's right,' she said briskly. 'It was quick. Stanton House stood for less than ten years. Now, I still haven't got to the point with all my rambling. We began by talking about the glasshouse.'

I leant forward expectantly again.

'The glasshouse that once belonged to Stanton House is still standing, but only just. Many of the panes have been smashed over the years, some simply falling out of their frames as they warp and weather. Others look secure enough but aren't, and the slightest disturbance will bring them down. On no account must you go inside – quite apart from cutting your feet to ribbons you could bring the whole lot down on top of yourself. I have tried to tell Sir Charles that it must be pulled down but . . .'

Even in the dim light Mrs Jelphs was pale, paler than she had been five minutes before. As she cut herself a slice of the pie, her hand shook. She put down the knife. 'I don't want you going there, Alice. Is that understood? It's strictly forbidden.'

I nodded meekly, though my mind was full of the story she had just told me. The valley, now cloaked in the darkness of night, was around us, witness to all that had happened. A single word came back to me as Mrs Jelphs and I began clearing the table together. *Tainted*. It seemed to leach out across my mind, rusty, like old blood.

I went up to bed soon after and, feeling something brush against my leg, I remembered the little hare. I had completely forgotten to ask about it. With a start I realized what else I'd forgotten: for the whole time Mrs Jelphs had been talking I hadn't thought once about James. In fact, my whole life in London – for all the city's bustle and press of people – seemed little more than an inconsequential blur. The valley and the people who had lived there were weaving their enchantment around me already.

Elizabeth

It was just as she was thinking that she must go down and welcome their guests that the gilt clock on the mantelpiece began to strike seven, the sound like long fingernails plucking at a fork's tines. She remained sitting at her dressing-table, her reflection staring back at her in triplicate. Edith had been and gone: she had fastened the dozens of tiny pearl buttons at the back of the new dress and pinned up her mistress's hair. Elizabeth turned to view it from the side and saw that her maid had done an excellent job. It shone deeply, and each coil was perfectly pinned so it would neither make her scalp ache nor slip from its mooring halfway through the evening.

'Sir Edward will fall in love with you all over again tonight,' Edith had said, when she finished.

'Is that all it requires?' Elizabeth had replied sharply. 'A new way of putting up my hair and a silk dress?'

Edith's face had fallen and Elizabeth thought for a horrible moment that the girl might cry. To rescue the situation, she had forced a laugh. 'Dear Edith, I'm just teasing. You've worked a miracle with this unruly hair of mine and I can't wait to show Edward.'

Edith had smiled tentatively and by the time she had left to go downstairs her eyes were dry and lit with excitement once more.

In truth, it was hard for Elizabeth to gauge what her

husband would think of her at these events: she always felt as though she were walking a high wire. That was one of the reasons she dreaded them.

Last year she had attended a formal party at another, larger, estate in the north of the county. The reason she had relented and accompanied Edward – as well as his brother – now eluded her. Possibly she had hoped it would grant her exemption from the next few such gatherings.

It wasn't far into the evening when things had begun to sour. She had been dancing with Charles, having assumed that partnering her brother-in-law would avoid rousing the jealousy she had always inspired in Edward.

In Charles she had discovered a very different character. He was neither as handsome nor as mercurial in temper as Edward – who called him 'the plodder' in private – but Elizabeth found him soothing. Charles was content in his own skin. Given the choice he would always prefer to be outdoors, walking, or making a brass rubbing in the chapel, but the social whirl did not perturb him. He was always himself, wherever he was. His older brother, in contrast, might reveal half a dozen different faces on a night like this. It all depended on whether he was talking to a pretty girl, a man who owned a more important estate or Elizabeth herself.

The curious thing about Edward was not that he could be as charming as he was arrogant and intolerant when he chose – his parents had bequeathed him all those characteristics. No, it was that their worship of him, along with his fine figure and privileged position, had made him neither content nor assured. Elizabeth sometimes wondered whether it was London that had shaken his sense of himself: its sea of men more wealthy, brilliant and extra-ordinary causing him to despise his own rural backwater. If not London, then what? A natural propensity to dissatisfaction?

She had thought it was safe to dance with Charles – that this surely wouldn't cause offence – but when she glanced at her husband she saw he was looking directly at her over the head of their hostess, who was futilely trying to engage him in conversation. He wanted Elizabeth to go to him, she knew, but that night she chose not to. Instead – because she was damned if she did and damned if she didn't – she recklessly accepted dance after dance with anyone who asked her.

It was airless in the ballroom. In order to create a romantic effect, mountains of candles had been lit, great clusters on every surface and in the chandeliers high above. Despite the January chill outside, their collective heat was almost overpowering and had turned the tall arched windows blind with condensation. The room reeked of sweat and scorched wax: she could see the sheen on the faces around her, could feel her own hair curling tighter in the humidity. Late in the night, when she hadn't exchanged a word with Edward for hours, one of the chandelier candles had dripped on to her bare shoulder. She flinched as it landed, a pinprick of pain before the wax set as a pale disc only a shade or two lighter than her own skin. The man she had been dancing with, whose name she hadn't absorbed, unthinkingly reached out to touch it, only drawing back his hand at the last moment. She didn't need to look over to the drinks table to confirm that Edward had witnessed the near intimacy.

On the way home, the carriage hurtling along alarmingly fast, he had kept up a ceaseless flow of conversation with Charles that deliberately excluded her, despite the latter's attempts to bring her in. Brought up by parents who had always sought her opinions and her approval, who simply enjoyed admiring their blossoming daughter, it was disconcerting to be rendered invisible. It was not a sensation she had grown inured to over the years with Edward, either. She stared out of the window at bare winter fields brushed silver by the moon and thought she could not feel lonelier if she were pushed out of the carriage and abandoned to them.

That time it was an endless three days before he deigned to speak properly to her again and she was initially so suffused with relief that she let the injustice of it melt away. Something was always left behind after these banishments, though, and it was rather like hardened wax – another drop setting each time she found herself exiled. She finally understood that he derived some perverse pleasure from striding away or looking impassively on as she tried to make amends.

After the relief had come anger that time, and she realized it had been there all along, lying dormant. That was a revelation: like being lifted high on the crest of a boiling wave. Never again would she follow him about the house, begging for scraps of affection, beseeching him, 'But what have I done?' In the early days, their reconciliations had made her passionate. Once she learnt to match his coldness with her own, it was disquieting how quickly her ardour for him had ebbed away.

In her bedroom, the larger of the clock's hands showed

it was now ten past the hour. By the sound of it, more than a few of their guests had already arrived. She couldn't help but think of them as circling vultures out there on the pristine lawn. The first glimpse they had of her would be the worst, when their beady eyes would drink her in thirstily, searching for signs of damage. She wished Charles had been able to attend, his presence in the valley always a benign solace. She should go now: if she hesitated much longer Edward would notice and be alert to the possibility that her health was failing again; that she was failing again.

There was no one to watch her descend the staircase and for that she was grateful. They were all in the garden, where the sky's blue was fading to palest primrose. There were no stars yet, only a wafer-thin sliver of moon, suspended by an invisible silken thread. She almost tripped on the last stair: the bulk of the baby had altered her centre of gravity. Her heeled shoe landed too heavily on the tiles of the enormous hallway but no one was there to hear it. She had drunk two eye-watering gulps of brandy from the decanter in the library before she dressed, for courage. Edward rarely went in there and was unlikely to catch her; its bound volumes were principally for show.

When she stepped out on the terrace, placing her feet more carefully now, the scene was so like the one she had imagined for weeks that she experienced the cool detachment of a dream and her nerves receded. At least forty people were there already and she could tell from the murmur of sounds coming from the house behind her that more were arriving, greeting each other on the carriage sweep, taking their time to cross the threshold because the whole evening was ahead of them.

She noticed Edward a beat before he saw her. He was talking to a woman who might have been his sister in colouring, though her cheeks and lips were subtly pinker than was natural. Perhaps this was how Isabel would look when she was a woman, but then Elizabeth drew closer and saw that the woman's face was harder, more ambitious, than sensitive Isabel's could ever be.

'My darling wife, we were just talking about you,' called Edward, slightly too loudly. 'Come and meet Adelaide March. Her father owns Clayford Park, near Hereford. Do you remember I went to shoot there once, when you weren't well? When Isabel was tiny?'

She was stunned that he had mentioned that time so casually, and to a stranger, and found she couldn't think of anything to say. It didn't seem to matter. Edward reached out a pale gold hand and pulled her gently towards him.

'We have only another few weeks to wait,' he said to Adelaide. 'Doesn't his mother look wonderful?' He gazed at Elizabeth with an adoration that felt almost violent. 'We are all hoping he's as beautiful as his mama.'

'Or as handsome as his papa,' said Adelaide, her voice light and fluid, like mercury. She was eighteen at most, a slender thing of narrow hips and small, high breasts. She was too young to hide her desire for a husband like Edward, or perhaps Edward himself, her china-blue eyes glassy with it – and with the champagne that she now splashed on her glove.

Edith came past at that moment, carrying a silver tray

crammed with crystal saucers that tinkled and chimed against each other melodically. 'You haven't a drink, my lady,' she said to Elizabeth.

'Thank you, Edith.' She took a glass that was only half full, unsure whether this was for Edward's benefit or her own.

Edith moved smartly away, even though Edward and Adelaide both needed new drinks. Elizabeth smiled at Edith's ramrod back as it disappeared into the marquee. *She understands much more than I realize*, she thought. 'Well,' she said, after her first sip of the champagne, dry and delicious, 'I must leave you in my husband's capable hands, Miss March. I should mingle with our other guests – it wouldn't do to spend the whole evening with the man I see every day. Edward, perhaps one of the maids can do something about Miss March's glove. It's stained with champagne.'

As the younger girl coloured, Elizabeth walked away with deliberate confidence and made for the colonel, who was their nearest neighbour. He lived at the top of the valley, his sprawling Georgian rectory Stanwick village's largest house. He pretended deafness and bluffness but his mind was needle-sharp and he had always been kind to Elizabeth. When he spotted her, his face lit up. 'Good Lord, Lady Stanton, you look splendid tonight. No. Resplendent is a better word. I haven't seen you look so well since . . . Actually, I haven't seen you look so well ever. Isn't she a sight to behold, Mrs Bell?'

Mrs Bell, whose husband owned one of the last large cloth mills in Stroud, turned at his voice. She was larger than Elizabeth remembered, her enormous bosom seemingly in danger of being pricked and deflated by the beetle-shaped brooch she had pinned there. Her eyes widened when she saw who was standing there.

'Lady Stanton, it's wonderful to see you so well, and for Stanton House to be hosting a proper celebration once more. We feared we had seen the last of them. Of course, it's understandable, given the circumstances . . .'

She tailed off and the colonel looked down into his glass. He cleared his throat pointedly but Mrs Bell soldiered on.

'Of course, we have seen you occasionally at other events but, as I have kept saying to Mr Bell, you couldn't be considered quite recovered until you were hostess at one of Stanton House's parties.'

She stopped to take a breath and beamed at Elizabeth, the colonel and the others who had drawn closer as they noticed to whom Mrs Bell's words were addressed.

'Thank you for your concern,' Elizabeth replied, and there was a short silence that felt just like the sensation on the stairs, when she had momentarily lost her balance. Six or seven faces stared expectantly at her, and in their expressions she thought she could read a mixture of genuine concern, glee and inquisitiveness shot through with scorn. Further off, two young men she knew only slightly – William Somebody and Hugh Morton, down from Cheltenham, she thought – were looking at her in quite a different way, with the very opposite of pity. Hugh nodded and smiled warmly, and she found she had regained her footing.

'As you can see,' she said, raising her voice, 'I am perfectly well. I do not know what you have all heard. Perhaps that Edward lets me out only occasionally and otherwise keeps me locked in the attic, like the first Mrs Rochester.' She smiled wickedly and glanced towards William and Hugh again, who were still watching her with frank admiration. 'Don't believe everything you hear, Mrs Bell,' she said, the merest hint of admonishment making the older woman drop her eyes. 'Most of it is servants' gossip, and who can blame them in this beautiful but rather uneventful corner of the countryside? If I have brightened someone's day with lurid stories of my descent into madness, my hair a tangled bird's nest, my nails torn and ragged, no one in the house able to get a full night's rest for my tortured screams, then I am glad.' She held out her hand, which was gloveless and delicate, the skin as white as lilies, the nails shaped like almonds. Someone put a fresh glass into it.

'To my apparent health,' she said, 'and to all of you for coming to bear witness to it.'

As they drank she put her arm through the colonel's and led him away from the small crowd that had gathered. She was trembling.

'What a woman you are,' he said quietly. 'That's held their tongues.'

On the far side of the lawn she could see that Edward was still talking to Adelaide, who had grown more flushed and was now pulling at his sleeve as she talked up at him. Elizabeth squeezed the colonel's arm. 'Edward will be furious when he hears I've made an exhibition of myself.'

'Let me talk to Sir Edward. I'll head him off at the pass. You've been exceptionally brave, not just now but since the last time we were all gathered here. The trouble with your husband is that he thought you were perfect. You are, of course, far more interesting than perfect but he doesn't understand that yet. What he did, he believed he did for the best – at least, I think so. We are often hardest on the people we love most. It's fear that makes us ruthless.'

'Perhaps you're right,' she said sadly. 'You understand him better than I do. He cannot bear weakness in me or Isabel. I hope this little one is strong for him.'

She placed her hand on her stomach. The hot skin was stretched as taut as a drum. The pale green silk of her dress had been gathered under her bust with the intention that it would drape gracefully over the stomach, obscuring or at least minimizing it. In fact, the baby had grown so outlandishly in the weeks since the dress had been ordered that it now had the opposite effect. Beneath her petticoats she could feel the raised blister of her navel against the slippery fabric, and hoped such an intimate part of her couldn't be seen.

At that moment someone dropped a glass on the unforgiving stone of the terrace, where it shattered like ice in the syrupy air. Everyone turned to look; everyone except Elizabeth, who stared blindly at the grass at her feet. The sound of smashing glass – she knew it. And when she had heard it before it had been so much louder, so much nearer. Reaching out in her mind, she tried to catch the tail of the memory but it flicked away, returning to the shadows where it silently mocked her.

The colonel, turning back to her, must have seen that her triumph after the toast was fast ebbing away. 'You!' He gestured at one of the younger footmen, who was self-conscious in his best for the occasion, dark hair shiny with oil. 'Fetch Lady Stanton a chair. Not one of those!' he cried, when the boy ran for one of the hard chairs they had hired for the evening. 'A proper chair, with cushions. Bring one from the house.'

When he returned, a shout of laughter went up. He was dragging a gigantic Bath chair across the terrace, its castors squealing in protest. The gardener's boy, Ruck, ran to help him and they carried it over the grass to the waiting colonel.

'This is more like it,' he said, helping Elizabeth lower herself into it and then fetching her glass from a nearby table. She sighed theatrically with contentment for the benefit of the clusters of guests nearest to them, and they broke obediently into applause. In fact, it was blissful to be off her feet, the child inside her a still but leaden weight, like the movement of a stopped clock.

Another memory crept like a traitor into her mind and, unlike the shattering glass, this one lingered. In it, she wore a dress of peacock blue and Edith was brushing out her hair. Inside her was the tiny boy she had lost three years ago and he was moving, the watered silk of her dress rippling as he turned. Finally a third memory surfaced, from just a year ago, when she had woken with blood on her sheets and metal in the air, just three weeks after she'd found that she was with child again. *But it will be different this time*, she told herself now, as she struggled to banish the recollections.

Forcing herself to think of Isabel, whom she had borne with perfect ease, she didn't know what frightened her more: the possibility of a third miscarried baby or another attack of the prolonged and crushing melancholy that had followed Isabel's deceptively simple birth. She had taken to her bed after the miscarriages too, but that had been caused as much by grief – the sorrow any mother would have felt – as the inexplicable state that had gripped her after Isabel.

It was precisely the sort of feminine superstition that her faultlessly logical husband despised, but part of her was convinced – horribly so – that her destiny as a mother had already been written and would now only repeat itself. She would never bear a living son, while another baby daughter would take her down and down, back into the black depths. Perhaps it was sinful to think it but she didn't know which she dreaded more.

She looked across the lawn to Edward, who was holding court amid a small group of people she hardly knew, Adelaide among them. Lit by the dying sun in his beautiful suit, he looked as happy as she'd ever seen him. She envied him his mental strength; the way he took his fear and turned it into implacable resolve – the conviction that she carried his heir, and that everything would be well this time. Another lost son was unthinkable so he had, at least in his own head, made it so. She fancied she could almost see the determination roll off him in waves. If she was to fail again, she couldn't imagine him forgiving her.

Alice

I had felt a little apprehensive about going to bed on that second night and had made sure Mrs Jelphs fetched me a new light-bulb before I went up. The candlestick was still on my bedside table but it reminded me of my strange experience so I shut it back in the wardrobe. As it was, the night passed uneventfully. My dreams were a confusion of the glasshouse I had once seen on a visit to Kew and the striped emerald lawns my father tended at home, but I didn't wake, and nothing woke me.

When I gradually came to, it was still early enough for the air to feel chilly. I got dressed as quickly as I could, deciding from the angle of the sun that I had time for a walk before breakfast. The clock on the mantelpiece had stopped again.

Since I'd heard about Stanton House and its ignomini-ous fall, the old manor had lost some of its unsettling atmosphere. I felt intrigued and almost excited, as though a mystery had presented itself to be solved. Delving into the past was just the sort of distraction I needed to take me away from my own present.

There was a great deal more to the story of the Victor-ian baronet – not to mention his wife – and I felt compelled to seek it out. It was only a few more days until the weekend and then I thought I would walk up to the village and seek out Nan's Mr Morton. Gambling, drunkenness and prolific spending had surely been the causes of such a dramatic reversal in Sir Edward's fortunes, and Mr Morton sounded like the man to tell me about it in all its colourful detail. I couldn't imagine I would have to tread as carefully with him as with Mrs Jelphs.

The kitchen was deserted when I got there and, according to the clock above the large fireplace, it was still before seven. Outside, my footsteps on the gravel crunched loudly in the undisturbed morning air. I half tiptoed back to the path Ruck and I had come down a few days before, then struck off in the opposite direction. Soon I was under the canopy of the beech trees, where the sunlight was still too weak to penetrate. Apart from the odd flurry of birdsong, there wasn't a sound. Though I had missed the spectacle of the bluebells it was still beautiful. Just as it had said in the library book, the path meandered around ancient trees that long preceded any people.

I walked on and on and was just beginning to think I had made a mistake and missed a turning when the trees abruptly opened out, the path widening to a clearing. Ahead of me were the remains of two cottages. Low-slung and built on one level, both were now missing their roofs. One was more tumbledown than the other and, remembering Ruck's words, I saw it had offered itself up to the weeds. Just as he had said, the nettles were in rude health: thick and springy, each stem a finger's girth and covered with spines. As I got closer I recognized a clump of deadly nightshade growing among them. My father had shown me how to spot belladonna when I was small, and this was a beautiful specimen, though it was too early in the season for its berries to have darkened until they shone like beetles' backs.

I couldn't hear any birdsong now. It was eerily quiet in the clearing, a quiet that was somehow expectant, like a breath held in anticipation. I looked around, not knowing quite what I expected to see. All was still. There is something about empty, abandoned buildings that is melancholy in company but unnerving when you are alone. The cottages would have been bucolic in the estate's heyday: not any longer. The window glass had long since gone and one front door was missing, the other ajar. As I moved off in search of the forbidden glasshouse I heard a creak that I could have sworn was made by that old door, its blue paint half peeled off in long uneven ribbons to reveal silvery wood beneath. But there wasn't even the faintest whisper of wind that morning to move it so I forced myself to keep walking.

The glasshouse was only a little further on. It was empty of anything except half a dozen bare trestle tables and a good deal of smashed glass, which liberally littered the ground beneath.

'You've no business poking round here,' said a voice just behind me. I swung round, audibly gasping, and only just stopped myself screaming in fright. It was Ruck.

'Oh! I'm sorry, I –' I came to a breathless halt, aware that my face was red.

There was no dog in sight; he seemed to be alone. Even as close as I had been to him on the journey from the station it was difficult to guess his age. He could have been fifty or seventy, his skin roughened and deeply creased by the sun but his body trim.

'I wanted to stretch my legs,' I said eventually. 'I thought the exercise would be good for me. I didn't mean to intrude anywhere I wasn't supposed to . . .'

He stared back at me and I couldn't read his expression. He probably thought I was a little fool to be wandering around on my own in my condition. I wondered how much he knew of my story.

'You shouldn't be here,' he said shortly. 'It's not safe.'

'I know. Mrs Jelphs told me about the glasshouse last night and I suppose I couldn't resist coming to have a look. I wasn't going to go inside.'

His eyes narrowed further. 'What did she tell you about it?'

'Just that it was dangerous. That the glass was loose and I mustn't go in under any circumstances. She was very firm about it.'

'You ought to heed her. Here's not a nice place to be.'

'I wanted to see where Stanton House stood, if you can send me in the right direction,' I stammered. 'I know there's not much left but . . .'

He gestured reluctantly towards the remains of a long red-brick wall, its length breached in some places – presumably stealthily, over time – by the thick ivy that was also doing its best to overpower the glasshouse's rickety frame.

'Beyond there is where the house stood. That used to be the wall of the kitchen garden. You'll sometimes see the foundations in winter but you'd be lucky now. Might see some rubble.'

There was nothing to indicate that a great mansion had ever stood there.

'Mrs Jelphs told me it was only there for a few years. It's as if it never was.'

'The weeds get everything in the end. Them cottages

– the glasshouse too. There won't be any sign of them either soon enough.'

There was a silence. Ruck was staring towards the wall's remains.

'So you live over there?' I said eventually, gesturing vaguely, my voice slightly too loud in the stillness.

He nodded curtly. 'I'm about as far away from the manor as you can be, right up at the southern end of the valley in the woods.'

'Ruin Wood, Mrs Jelphs called it. I wondered where the name came from.'

'It's an old name. Older than Stanton House, though some would say the cap fits.' He coughed and spat over his shoulder. 'I'll be off then. You go careful now, girl. Do you know which path takes you back to the manor?'

I nodded dumbly and watched him go. He didn't look back and, though I didn't particularly want to be alone among the abandoned buildings, that was outweighed by my relief that the encounter was over. There was something about Ruck that put me on edge: he seemed to emanate disapproval at one moment and mock me the next. It's a strange truth that we often seek favour from the people we're not even sure we like. Ruck was one of those people, and I felt sure I would always stumble over my words and act idiotically in front of him.

The nettles, ivy and other weeds grew high among the ruined remains of the kitchen garden. I stepped around the thickest clumps gingerly, wishing I was wearing trousers. I could already feel the pinprick stings of the nettles through my stockings. Further on, I bent to pick a dock leaf, even though my father had always said their soothing power was an old wives' tale. It was then I realized I was standing right above part of the vanished house's foundations.

There was some loose rubble close to my feet and I picked a few pieces up. They were uniformly grey, just as Mrs Jelphs had said. It was a cold colour, almost dirty-looking, quite different from the buttery stone everywhere else. I understood why the locals hadn't approved.

I glanced about but there was no sign of Ruck. It was odd, though: I still didn't feel as though I was completely by myself. A flutter of movement on the periphery of my vision made me drop one of the stones I held, which landed with a dull thud on the dry, packed earth. It was a barn owl, and as I watched, it took flight from the apex of the glasshouse's decaying roof.

As it flew over me it made its shrieking cry and I remembered how in old folklore it had been thought of as a harbinger of doom and killed for it. The cry echoed discordantly around me as the bird flew out of sight. The acoustics were peculiar here in the steepest part of the valley and I wondered if I was standing close to where Mrs Jelphs had once sat, watching the party.

I had the notion then that if I stayed a moment longer I would somehow summon it all back to life: the glasses clinking, the hum of the crowd and Elizabeth Stanton drawing everyone to her, like moons in orbit. In that moment it did not seem a romantic idea but a threatening one, the fabric of time suddenly straining at its seams.

As I turned to go, the sky darkened like a spreading bruise and a gust of wind charged through the combe, sending the old beeches into a frenzy of movement. The air filled with the sound of new spring leaves rustling, the noise building from a shimmer to such a roar that I put my hands to my ears. The glasshouse began to shake a little, or so it seemed to me, and I thought I heard a loose shard fall and smash. A tinge of menace coloured the air and I knew, as instinctively as anything I have ever felt, that the place wanted me gone. I didn't hesitate then. I ran.

This scene has become a recurring dream that I experience whenever I'm anxious. The hissing of the leaves, the shattering of the glass, and the barn owl's scream return to me in the night and they are just as they were that day. I've sometimes wondered if the reason it has stayed so fresh in my mind is because I've barely spoken of it in detail to anyone, never worn it out and dissipated its power through the retelling. I've never even written it down until now – my diary of that summer is oddly selective, as though I was writing with the knowledge that someone was reading over my shoulder. The worst of the dream version is that my legs turn to lead. I try to flee but I haven't the strength to move my limbs. I stand like a helpless statue, hands over my ears, until I will myself to wake up, my heart hammering and my pillow damp with sweat.

In reality I could and did run, and I ran faster than I had done since I was a girl, though much more awkwardly, of course. Stupidly, I didn't think to run in the direction I had seen Ruck go; I made for the path I had taken through the woods. Among the trees the noise of the wind was louder and I kept one ear covered, my other hand clamped to my belly. Old, dry branches groaned, and a few broke off, crashing to the ground close to me. As I ran I saw a flash of movement and colour to my right, but when I slowed to look there was nothing but the thick ranks of trees and the very last of the year's bluebells in a solitary cluster. I didn't stop again.

I arrived back in the kitchen garden out of breath and tearful. I was aware I might easily have taken a wrong turn in the state I was in, and my relief at glimpsing the manor through the trees had made a sob rise and fill my throat. I stopped to catch my breath and registered that whatever I had sensed had gone, the air becalmed, the threat – if that was what it had been – ebbed away.

If I had expected anyone to be in the kitchen as I went through the door, it was Nan. Instead, standing over the range, there was a man, too tall and nonchalant to be confused with Ruck. He turned at the disturbance and regarded me with amused detachment. His eyes, lit by the morning sky behind him, were an unusual pale blue. After a few moments of silence, when I couldn't think of anything to say, he raised his eyebrows.

'You must be our mysterious house guest,' he said, over his shoulder. He clearly hadn't spent his boyhood running about with the farm hands: his accent belonged to a type of man I had come across before, in the secret pubs James had taken me to. Languid and comfortable in his skin, he barely bothered to open his mouth to enunciate. 'You're up with the lark, aren't you? I've just driven up from London. Haven't been to bed yet – I always seem to leave getting here till the last minute.'

When I remained silent, wondering what he meant, as well as what I must look like, he started whistling and went to the dresser to get another cup.

'You do take tea, I presume?'

'Oh. Yes, please.'

'Why don't you sit down while I get it? You're a bit green around the gills.'

I was glad to do as I was told, my legs shaking now that I had stopped, and racked my brains to work out who he was. He was in a dinner suit, though his tie had gone and his shirt was unbuttoned at the collar. Then I remembered a few references Mrs Jelphs had made.

'You're Thomas Stanton,' I said, my voice wobbling slightly. Beneath the table my knees still trembled with the exertion of running, as well as the growing embarrassment of an unexpected encounter with one of the family.

'That's right,' he said, with a smirk. 'Who did you think I was? The odd-job man?'

His fair hair was all over the place and a vivid image came into my head of him driving through the night in a fast little motor-car, the roof down all the way. As if reading my thoughts, he put a hand to his head, ruffled his hair and yawned enormously.

'Did Mrs J not tell you about me, the heir to all you survey?' He smiled sardonically, gesturing around the kitchen. 'I suppose she's more concerned with the ghosts of old. I was only ever intended to be the spare, you know. My older brother Henry was the real heir, the first-born son and all that.' He stopped abruptly. After a pause he turned to pick up the teapot.

'Did he . . . ?' I began tentatively, as he sat heavily next to me.

'Die in the war? Actually, no. He didn't get that far. He died in the summer of 'fourteen.' He stopped again and suddenly looked exhausted.

The only thing I could think to ask was how his brother had died but the expression on his face warned me off it. Eventually, with a visible effort, he continued: 'I don't know why I'm telling you this, and I doubt you're old enough to remember it, but it was sweltering – at least, here it was. All we did that summer was wait for news from Europe and try to stay tolerably cool.'

I thought about myself at that time: a little girl at the seaside with my parents, the grey stripe of sea visible beyond the promenade from our boarding-house's window. How strange that events had conspired to bring me to the kitchen he had known all his life – and such a different life from mine. He poured me a cup of strong tea and added milk and sugar without asking if I took them, which brought me back to the present. He seemed to read my mind again.

'You look as if you need it sweet.' He leant back in the wooden chair, his legs folded lazily in front of him, hands clasped behind his head, and smiled properly for the first time. It gave his face a completely different aspect: open and kind, his eyes sparkling.

'Apparently Mother was quite taken with your story when she got the letter about it. I think she imagines you to be some sort of fragile creature but I'm not so sure about that, now that I've seen you.'

I blushed and looked down into my teacup. He sat up straight then. 'I'm sorry. That was an insensitive thing to say. It's not a story to you, of course. I know you weren't long married when it happened. What a ghastly situation.' His cheeks were now as hot as mine.

'It's quite all right,' I said quietly. I didn't want to talk about it any more than he did; after all, he had hit the nail precisely on the head – it was nothing but a story. 'I'm very grateful to be allowed to come here,' I finished in a rush.

'Well, someone might as well be living in the old place,' he replied. 'Apart from Mrs Jelphs, it mostly stands empty. I come back a few times a year, when I have to, to catch up on estate business for my father. He thinks it's good for me to learn the ropes so that when it's my turn I won't bankrupt the estate in a month.' He took a noisy gulp of tea. 'As for you, I wasn't quite sure why you'd ended up here rather than stayed in London. Mother mentioned you in passing on the telephone when I said I was coming down but she only told me the bare bones. I mean, it's a bit rotten sending you away after what happened, isn't it?' He got up and rooted in a cupboard for the biscuit tin. 'God, stale gingernuts. Where's Nan when you need her?'

I cleared my throat awkwardly. I hadn't even introduced myself. 'I'm Alice. I should've said before but . . .'

'But you haven't been able to get a word in edgeways. How do you do, Alice?' He leant over and held out his hand.

I shook it, and it felt warm and dry. I wondered if mine was clammy after my dash from the glasshouse and wiped it surreptitiously on my skirt. 'So what am I to call you if you're to be a baronet one day?' I smiled weakly.

'Call me Tom. All my friends do. Only Mother and Mrs J insist on calling me Thomas. Besides, I think the baronetcy was more or less bought back in the 1600s. James the First needed some ready money to keep the Irish quiet, as I recall.' He bit into another stale biscuit. 'So, for how long do we have the pleasure?'

'Well, I shall have the baby here,' I felt my cheeks heating again, 'and then I'll go back to London.'

'How long is it until you . . . ? Well, you know,' he said, raising his eyebrows again.

I smiled gamely back. 'I've a few months to go yet.'

'So there's no chance of me being called on to perform any heroics, then. I'll be here for a few weeks and out for much of the time, perhaps you'll be glad to hear. I've got to spend some fearfully dull days with our estate manager over in Stroud, and Mother has also extracted a solemn promise from me that I will call on all the local families. Sorry, my manners are appalling.'

He held out the biscuit tin but I declined. Instead, he poured the last of the tea into my cup. It was stewed and he grimaced.

'I'll make some more,' he said. 'And while I do it you can tell me why you came in with your hair all tangled, looking as though you'd seen a ghost.'

He reached towards me and I flinched as his hand went to my hair.

'Don't worry, I was only retrieving this.' He put a piece of twig on the table.

I ran my fingers through my hair in case anything else was lodged in it, wrenching painfully through the knots at the ends. 'Sorry, I just . . .'

He didn't say anything but his eyes were full of amusement. I took a nervous sip of tea and put the cup back down too hard. Taking up the twig again, he began stripping the bark off it. When he spoke, it was much more quietly than before.

'You know, something about the way you came in

before, white as a sheet, your hair dishevelled and as if you'd been somewhere quite far away, reminded me of my brother. I don't talk about him much but you don't forget. He used to sleepwalk sometimes. The first time he was found curled up in here by the range, sleeping on the mat, like a puppy, having eaten most of a cold roast chicken from the larder. The second time, he thought the boot room was the lav and relieved himself in my father's wellington boots.'

He smiled sadly at the memory. 'It was the best couple of months of my childhood. For once it was Henry who'd been bad while the incorrigible Thomas behaved like an angel. If he did it after that, he kept quiet about it.'

'I've never done it,' I said. 'Where I grew up in London, I'd have been mown down by a bus. No, I just went for a walk and well . . . something happened, something strange.'

'What do you mean?'

'I can't explain it without sounding foolish. It was nothing, really. A barn owl flew over and screeched and, well, it gave me such a fright. It was a horrible sound – I'd never heard it before.'

'I can see why that gave you a bit of a start,' said Tom. 'There's something about that sound that makes me go cold. Perhaps it's the same one that lives in the graveyard up in the village.' He jabbed his thumbnail into the exposed flesh of the twig.

'It wasn't just that. The wind got up and . . .'

'Oh, it comes and goes in this valley, something to do with the shape of the land. It's like a funnel. Look, it's as still as anything out there now.'

It was true. I had flung the kitchen door wide in my

hurry and it had stayed pushed back on its hinges. Through it I could see Mrs Jelphs's carefully tended herbs and flowers. They were unmoving, even the heavy plumes of the pink and lilac lupins that stood nearly three feet high.

I let out a shaky breath as I remembered it. 'I thought the trees were going to come down around me. Some of the branches . . .'

'Good job it was just this little one that got you, then,' he said, holding up the denuded twig with a smile. 'Listen, I know what you need.'

He crossed to another cupboard and brought out a dusty bottle of brandy. 'It's not the good stuff but it'll calm those nerves. I'll join you.'

He poured out two generous measures, swirling the amber liquid expertly into a couple of mismatched glasses.

To be polite, I took a sip of mine, and felt its fire dissolve the last of my fear. When I looked up, he had drunk all of his, and was pouring more.

'You probably think it's too early but, for me, it's actually very late.'

He sounded rather defensive so I smiled. 'It's your house and your brandy.'

'I'm not sure either of those statements is true,' he said, with a frown. 'The brandy belongs to Mrs Jelphs, for medicinal or culinary purposes, and as for the house, well, I'd rather think of it as my father's. I'm quite content to wait for that particular responsibility to land on my shoulders. Now, if you'll excuse me, I'm absolutely done in.'

He smiled before he left me alone in the kitchen but it was a preoccupied sort of smile and I wondered if he thought he had said too much, not only to someone he'd just met, but to someone his family had taken in as a favour.

I washed up the tea things and went back to my room to lie down for a little while. I didn't think Mrs Jelphs would mind if I rested for an hour or so and, besides, it was still very early. My mind wasn't on the glasshouse as I felt my body sink into the old mattress. The last image that crept into my mind as I drifted into a light, dreamless sleep was of Thomas Stanton, with his ruffled hair and sad eyes.

More tired than I'd realized, I slept away half the morning. By the time I had forced myself out of bed and crossed to the window, I saw that the shadows cast by the yew pylons at dawn had almost gone: the long dark fingers that had pointed towards the glasshouse and Stanton House's remains in the east now retracted. A grating sound by my leg made me put my hand into the pocket of my skirt: I'd brought some of Stanton House's rubble back with me. It felt cold and heavy in my hand and I was glad to relinquish it, putting the pieces on the dresser carefully, towards the back where they were almost out of sight.

When I got downstairs to the kitchen it was empty but the door to the little garden was ajar. Mrs Jelphs was outside tending her herbs and flowers, a wide-brimmed hat protecting her crêpe-paper skin from the sun.

'Good morning,' I said brightly.

She looked at me for a long moment, as if deciding something. 'Did I not tell you to stay away from the glasshouse?'

'I suppose Ruck must have told you,' I said, more

carelessly than I felt. 'I didn't go inside, I just went to have a look, and then . . . I won't be going back, don't worry about that.'

'I'm glad to hear it,' she said. 'There are plenty of other places to walk in the valley.'

She turned back to her gardening but I didn't want her to be angry with me, although that wasn't quite it: it was concern as much as anger that I'd disobeyed her.

'I met Thomas,' I said eventually, for something to say.

'I would have warned you he was coming but, as is the way with him, I didn't know myself until I got up and saw his motor-car.'

'He seems very nice,' I said and, to my horror, felt myself colour. Fortunately Mrs Jelphs was too busy with her flowers to notice.

'He is. He was quite naughty as a boy, I can tell you, but there's never been any malice in him. He can be a little thoughtless, but what young man isn't?'

'Is he up, then?' I asked lightly.

'Oh, yes. He never did need much sleep.'

'I suppose he's gone for a walk round the estate.'

'No, he went off in that little motor-car of his. He said something about visiting friends. I asked if he'd be back for dinner – he never seems to grasp that these things can't be produced out of thin air – and he said he might be, or he might stay away for the night and come back tomorrow. Away for the night!' She sighed. 'He's only just got here.'

To my annoyance, I felt disappointed and hoped it didn't show.

The baby wasn't much of a kicker but that day I could

173

feel him shift and turn inside me. It felt like the movement of restless, roiling water rather than a growing creature of flesh and blood. Out under the sun, it felt hotter than it had the previous day, and I stretched my arms out, waggling my fingers in the bright light. Just beyond the kitchen garden, I could see Ruck raking the gravel. I wandered over to the low wall, hoping to make friends with him after our exchange by the glasshouse. I didn't blame him for telling Mrs Jelphs about me going there: she had probably asked him to keep an eye on me in the grounds, where she was unable to check on me herself.

'Hotter today, isn't it?' I called. My voice, intended to sound cheery, rang out rather falsely in the still air.

He glanced up from his work but didn't come any closer. 'You might be right about that,' he said eventually. 'It's set fair for the rest of the week too.' He looked up into the cloudless, pale blue sky as if he could read some sign there.

'Is there a thermometer here?' I said.

There had been one at the boarding house where my parents and I had holidayed every August. Each morning after breakfast, my father and I always went to check it in a hopeful manner. Some fancy made me want to recreate this comforting ritual at Fiercombe. A combination of the valley's untouched and somehow mysterious beauty and what Mrs Jelphs had told me of its history had already convinced me that I wouldn't be quite the same person once the summer had gone. Fiercombe was caught in the weft and warp of time's net but, oddly, it was those mundane weeks on the south coast that seemed a hundred years ago as I attempted to hold an easy conversation with Ruck over the kitchen-garden wall.

There was a thermometer, old and sun-bleached, hanging on a nail gouged into the golden stone of the manor. Later I wrote the day's temperature down in my diary: sixty-nine degrees. I have the record still, in the little book that's tucked away on a high shelf in my bedroom, the numbers as fresh as when I wrote them.

The next days passed uneventfully. The baby was settled and content inside me and the weather mirrored him. There was no wind in the valley, and as time wore on, the unsettling episode by the glasshouse took on the surreal ambience of a dream. Only the rather desolate expression I occasionally caught on Mrs Jelphs's face when she looked at me ruffled my equanimity.

As for Tom, I saw him only once – and I suppose, if I'm honest, that also bothered me a little. He was coming down the stairs as I was about to start up them and I saw him first. I was about to say hello but his face was drawn and miserable. When he did notice me, he nodded and smiled, though it didn't reach his eyes. Rather humiliatingly, I stopped, expecting to talk to him, but he continued distractedly on, leaving me alone in the hallway beneath the mocking eyes of the alchemist. Later, Mrs Jelphs told me that something had come up and he had gone back to London for the time being. I realized that my first conversation with him had probably been uncharacteristic in its intimacy and felt a fool for having thought of him as a new friend.

I spent those quiet days polishing. I finished the cutlery sooner than expected and moved on to larger pieces: candelabra, salvers and tureens. I knew they would be tarnished again before they were used but I didn't mind. I invented histories for each piece as I rubbed and buffed them: a chilled soup prepared for a garden party in one enormous tureen; a packet of letters delivered at breakfast on a salver engraved with the now familiar Stanton S. I hadn't wanted to prise anything else out of Mrs Jelphs about the past, fearing it would stir up painful memories or invite her over-protectiveness as it had before, but Elizabeth was still in my mind: a figure I could see only from the back, however much I tried to summon her face in the old silver as I polished it.

This absorption was helpful when any thoughts of James hovered and threatened to land, not that I could always dismiss them. When one did occasionally steal up, stealthy and cunning, it still felt like a blow. Tom's small, unthinking snub hadn't helped, making me wonder if I was particularly inept with men – reading far too much into what they had probably meant to say quite casually. As for my thoughts about the baby, I simply tried not to have them. If I tried to picture my life once I had returned to London after the birth, I still couldn't – my imagination remaining stubbornly blank.

One evening after a supper when Mrs Jelphs had been at her most withdrawn and secretive, I decided to wander a little further down the path I had taken with her on my second day, alongside the stream. By the time I had helped wash up and slipped outside, before she could worry about where I was going, the twilight was deepening. The gloaming, I thought, the word coming back to me from a book I'd read years before. That indistinct point after the sun has slipped out of sight but before the darkness takes hold. I would have to be quick: I had already learnt that in the valley the black of night fell abruptly, like a candle suddenly snuffed.

The bank next to the stream was less boggy than it had been. The water still rushed on with the urgency I remembered but I was sure the level had gone down. I walked a little further and the proud little summerhouse came into view. I knew then why I had wanted to go that way.

I had come to the conclusion that Mrs Jelphs must have regretted speaking to me more freely on my first nights at the manor; certainly she had been doing her best to make up for it since. There was no reason to suppose so, but I thought the summerhouse might have featured somewhere in Elizabeth Stanton's story. It was the way Mrs Jelphs had gazed at it. I eased myself through the squeeze-belly stile, then went to it by a narrow path the stream must have flowed beneath. When I put my hand to the old iron door handle, I braced myself for the disappointment of it being locked. Instead, it swung silently inward, as though oiled regularly.

Inside it was much darker; the windows were set deep into the stone and not very large. When my eyes adjusted I saw I was standing in a room that took up the entirety of that floor. At one end, I could see a narrow spiral staircase ascending out of sight. There was nothing in that room at all so I decided to try upstairs, holding tightly to a thick rope that was fastened to the wall at intervals by brass rings. I paused to listen and, through the thick stone, I could only just make out the burble of the stream. Inside, it was deathly quiet.

The room on the next floor was empty too, though it smelt less like a damp church up there. I decided to carry on up to the top floor and stopped short when I reached the last step. This room was furnished, if spartanly. A rose-pink chaise longue stood in the middle. There were curtains in a similar fabric at the window, though they had been pulled right back so they couldn't be seen from outside. A small, covered stool was next to the chaise as though someone had placed it there yesterday, to rest their feet upon. I drew closer and the illusion of recent occupation dissolved a little. The upholstery was faded and water-stained in places, and dust had gathered in the folds of the fabric.

I sat down gingerly. The narrow window behind me faced west, allowing the last of the sun to bathe the little room in a warm glow. I looked around, drinking it all in properly.

On one wall hung a few framed pictures – two pretty country scenes and a stormy seascape that didn't match. There were other items dotted about, too: a jug and chipped bowl on a console table; a dozen or so small volumes lining a shelf hung at eye level; and a sprig of long-ago dried flowers pinned to the beam above me. They were grey and desiccated but I thought they might have been lavender once. I crossed to the shelf and saw that the books' spines had faded in the sun: scarlet bleached to palest pink, teal to robin's egg. I pulled out one at random and heard something fall down behind it as I did. It was another volume; this one smaller and bound in what would once have been fine calfskin. There was no title or author marked on the spine and the cut edges of the pages were speckled with damp and yellowed with age.

I took it with me to the chaise and held it up to catch the last of the day's light. I knew I couldn't stay long or I would be stranded in the dark but I felt unwilling to go until I'd looked inside. I turned one and then another page before I realized they were not blank but written on with what must have been a hard pencil, the writing faint and pale silver where it hadn't faded away completely. I peered more closely and eventually my eyes managed to pick up the thread, to distinguish the elaborate curls from the spiked down-strokes. I turned back to the beginning.

I have stolen away this afternoon to be here alone. My husband does not like me to come here, to the old manor – not when such a fine house, full of everything I should ever need or want, is just the other side of the Great Mead. He does not know about my secret room here in the old counting house – the summerhouse, as we know it now. If he did, I'm sure he would insist that it was closed up. I am so big with child now that I can barely squeeze up the stairs so perhaps he will soon have his way, and I will have to stay confined in the big grey house that he is so proud of.

I wonder if this child will be a boy, a son and heir for Edward. I haven't told him yet but I believe it to be a daughter, a daughter who will inherit his golden hair, his eyes of pale blue. I think he will not mind that too much this time; there is not much urgency in him yet. Only next time . . . Next time I must produce a son.

Yesterday I found the strangest thing in Edward's desk. I had run out of ink and instead of disturbing the servants for such a trifle I went to the library myself. I looked for a new bottle in the drawers and found instead a dozen or so journals of the kind that Edward likes to read. He prides himself on reading widely – boxes of pamphlets arrive here on every conceivable subject, from architecture to zoology, perhaps so no one in his London club can accuse him of being unsophisticated and provincial – so I didn't think anything of what seemed to be a new interest in medicine, not at first. But then I saw that each volume was concerned with a particular, narrow aspect of it: the asylum.

I haven't yet come to the strangest part – I feel reluctant even to write it down. Among the journals was a slim book, though quite expensively produced. Portraits of an Oxfordshire Asylum was the title stamped on the front. I imagined illustrations of a forbidding building, wards with rows of empty beds and bare cells, but I was quite wrong. Inside were perhaps twenty portrait photographs of the asylum's inmates, all of them women. They were accompanied by a short description of each woman's condition, her age and the circumstances in which she had found herself before admittance. Many of the portraits were set out in pairs, two of the same woman – one captured in the throes of madness, the other a neat, unremarkable portrait that might have been of anyone's daughter or mother. Some were quite unrecognizable after the madness had left them.

I pored over this book until it grew quite dark outside and I feared Edward would return and find me there. But there was one page I couldn't help turn to again before I left the library. A woman of my own age from a town on the border of Gloucestershire and Oxfordshire, not more than a day's travel from here. There was no second portrait of her: her only appearance in the book showing her in a desperate condition. Her hair was dirty, tangled and half hacked off at the front as though she had done it herself in a rage.

The expression in her eyes was not wild but empty, the overall effect one of desolation.

They had seated her next to a window through which you could see nothing but brick — presumably the walls of another of the asylum's buildings. The description next to it said her name was Emily and that she came from a good family, but that her neglect of her dress, particularly of her hair, had been the first signs of an insanity that had gradually worsened. It said that she had been there for two years already. I hope I am wrong but I believe the lack of any other picture indicates that, at least at the time of publication, Emily was not recovered. I wonder what she is doing now, some forty miles to the east. Is she still there? Perhaps she is dead.

In the introduction to the book, the author — a Dr Iain Logan — noted that the taking of the portraits was viewed by the women of the asylum as a great privilege and reward for good behaviour, a pleasure to be anticipated and savoured. He wrote as though they were wayward children, who needed only to be brushed and beribboned to forget their melancholia or ignore the voices in their minds. Can this really be so? To me they all looked sad, so dreadfully sad and gloomy and hopeless — even the most smartly turned out of them, a woman of sixty who wore a neat cap and a plain dress too big for her shrunken frame, a Bible in her hands as though she had been piously reading when the photographer had come upon her, except that the book had been placed in her hands the wrong way up.

I must leave this soon and return to the house. I just turned to look out of the window behind me and saw that the sun had sunk almost to the top of the valley's ridge, a great ball of crimson through which the tallest beeches are running their fingers. I will be missed if I do not hurry. Edward returned from London two days ago and is more proprietorial than I remember him, his hands on my belly to see if the child had grown even before he removed his coat.

He came to me last night but wouldn't touch me, even though I wanted him to. He said we might damage the child inside. Instead he made me lie above the sheets while he examined me, even pulling up my nightgown until it was around my waist so that he could better see my swollen stomach. I felt shame instead of desire then and wondered what medical books he had brought back with him from London. He said it must be a boy from the way it lies but I do not think so.

Edith says that . . .

But that was all I could see. The light had dimmed until I could no longer make anything out. I looked up and saw it had grown quite black in the recesses of the room, deep shadows hiding whatever might lurk there. I tried to quell the animal fear that swelled in me when I realized I had marooned myself, just as I had told myself I wouldn't. I had been afraid of the dark as a child and the old fear flooded through me then, shortening my breath and making my heart thud. I left the diary on the chaise and felt my way to the staircase, my hands flailing blindly for the rope.

Slowly I picked my way downstairs and out along the lane until I felt the cold iron of the stile. From there, it was easier, my hearing telling me where the spring was. When I came out from under the cover of the trees that lined the water's banks, I realized, with the glad rush of seeing an old friend, that the moon was riding high and bright. Compared to the underworld gloom of the summerhouse's stairs, my path through the Tudor garden and round to the kitchen door might as well have been in broad daylight, such was the contrast.

I jumped as I turned from fastening the door quietly behind me, my breathing ragged with relief. Mrs Jelphs stood there, her pallor stark against the gloom of her dress and the unlit kitchen behind her.

'Where have you been, Alice? I was very worried.'

Her voice shook, but with anger or fear I wasn't sure. I didn't think she could have seen me leave the summerhouse so it could only be fear. It looked as though the simple cause of her anxiety – something I was learning could be as easily tripped as a faulty circuit – was my being out alone in the dark. As oddly over-solicitous as she could be, and as hemmed in as that made me feel, I still didn't want her to be upset. Besides, I think I was already aware that there was a great deal more to it than simple concern for a girl she still barely knew; it didn't add up otherwise. No, the fear I had woken in Mrs Jelphs was an old one, just like my own fear of the dark. Why it had latched on to me, however, remained a mystery.

'I'm sorry, Mrs Jelphs,' I said, reaching forward to pat her arm awkwardly. 'Really I am. I just went for a little walk but then the night came down so suddenly. I'm sorry if you were worried.'

She stared at me so penetratingly that I had to look away. 'If you're sure you're all right, then I think I will go to bed,' she said eventually, her voice quite wrung dry.

'I've made you anxious and kept you from your rest,' I said, contrite, wishing I knew what memories in her mind were coalescing with the present. 'I won't do it again, not so late. I'm really very sorry.'

'No, no, it's quite all right,' she said absently. 'It's just that I mustn't . . . I worry, that's all.'

With a last, fearful look at me, she disappeared into the passage. The name in the diary came to me as I watched her retreating back: Edith. I hadn't taken it in immediately but of course the diary had been referring to Mrs Jelphs. A Mrs Jelphs four decades younger. An Edward had been mentioned too. My instinct about the summerhouse had been right: the diary was surely Elizabeth's. I pictured the pale silver handwriting, fading to nothing in the dying light. It had been altered by the pencil she had used but, yes, I thought it was probably the same hand I had seen on the note secreted in the sewing box.

I wondered if the little room had never been cleared because no one else had known about it. But, then, what had Mrs Jelphs said on our walk? That it had been something of a sanctuary or a refuge once upon a time? So *she* had known. Was it a shrine, then, to a mistress gone from the valley but never straying far from her thoughts? I didn't know, and I didn't dare ask and upset her further. Perhaps the diary would tell me.

That night, I dreamt not about Elizabeth but about James, waking in the first grey glimmers of dawn and feeling bereft when I remembered I couldn't see him again. I hadn't dreamt about him at all since my arrival in the valley and I'd thanked my subconscious mind for protecting me like that. He was just out of sight in the dream but I knew it was him and we were easy together as we walked through the Great Mead, where frost sparkled and crunched underfoot. There was a child with us, our child, though I couldn't see him properly in the glare from the low winter sun. It was one of those potent dreams that throws you, and on waking I tried hard to return to the glistening meadow, squeezing my eyes shut and pulling the blankets over my head – until finally I fell asleep properly and dreamt of nothing.

When I woke from my dreamless second sleep I knew it was hotter again. I sat up and pushed the covers away, feeling the sweat cool on my skin. I remembered the diary – what Elizabeth had said about being sure she was carrying a girl – and thought about my conviction that I was carrying a boy, which had only been strengthened by my dream.

I could have drifted back to sleep again, so soporific was the air, but I forced myself to get up, splashing water on my face until I felt awake: I didn't want to waste a free day. By the time I had finished my breakfast, taking my time, the temperature was seventy-one degrees. It was Sunday, another week gone. I had finished the polishing and Mrs Jelphs had been pleasantly surprised. In making it shine again, however pointlessly, I felt I had carved a small hollow for myself in the valley.

Outside, the sky was already a deep, flawless blue; the clarity of light was the painterly kind, raved about by artists summering on the shores of the Mediterranean. In Gloucestershire it seemed too intense.

'Isn't it lovely again?' Mrs Jelphs said to me, as I returned to the kitchen from checking the thermometer. She seemed quite recovered from the previous evening.

'It can't last much longer, surely?' I said.

While Mrs Jelphs was at church, I spent the morning reading a book, I forget what now, and trying to catch up with my diary, though I was still strangely reluctant to write it openly. I couldn't get comfortable wherever I sat; mindful of the glorious weather I had gone with a cushion to the formal garden, though I would have felt more rested inside, in the small parlour. I lay back as far as I dared on the rotten old bench facing the house, my book resting on my swollen stomach, the hot skin stretched tight across it.

. Over an early lunch, Mrs Jelphs asked me what I planned to do with my afternoon but I was deliberately vague. Something held me back from telling her I had decided to walk up to the village of Stanwick to pay a visit to Mr Morton. She was going out again herself anyway: to visit a friend in Painswick. Ruck would drop her off in the carriage before calling in on his sister's family a few villages away.

Once they had gone, I set off up the hill. Instead of taking the gentler, winding path Ruck had brought me down, I decided to go up the main lane to the village, which was more direct. It was also much steeper and I had underestimated it. I had always been slight, and light on my feet, but my every movement felt ungainly now, and after five minutes of walking I was sweating, a runnel of salt water inching down my spine. I wondered if the thin, pale cotton of my blouse would turn transparent. I kept going and tried not to think about having to arrive at Mr Morton's door in the state I imagined I was in.

The lane ended quite abruptly, around a turn in the road, and I was on level ground again. I caught my breath and took my first proper look at the village green. Ruck and I had bypassed it when we had driven from the railway station. It sloped upwards from the road, with a row of cottages behind it. Set further back was the church; I could see the tower, its clock with golden hands and, below it, a gorgeously painted sundial of a type peculiar to this part of the world.

The only splash of bright, artificial colour among the greens of the trees and bushes and the ochre of the stone was the pillar-box, an ornate 'VR' raised in the ironwork, and the adjoining telephone box. The place was deserted and I wondered if I'd made a mistake in paying a surprise visit on a Sunday.

I'd entirely given up with my own watch but the church clock told me it was almost three. Lunch should be finished, I reasoned, and any service at the church had been over for hours. I found Mr Morton's cottage easily. Nan had told me, after some casual questioning, that it was just past the post office but before the pub, with wisteria around the door. She had understated this last detail. The wisteria hung in heavy hanks, covering much of the front façade with its decadent mauve-blue foliage.

The front door stood open, a dull brass umbrella stand against it, though there was no wind to slam it shut. Against the bright sunlight it looked dark within. I thought about knocking but called out instead, my voice loud in the apparently deserted village. After a pause with no reply, I tried again. 'Hello? Mr Morton, are you there?'

I heard a door open and shut and then a figure came into view. He was probably a little overweight, his well-pressed shirt stretching over a paunch, but at his substantial height he carried it well. Despite the heat of the day, he was wearing tweed trousers and seemed quite comfortable. His clothes mirrored the colours of the countryside around him, a sort of unconscious camouflage. Like the scarlet pillar-box on the green, only his florid cheeks clashed.

I liked him immediately. He brought to mind the sort of uncle I had read about in the books I had loved as a child: fearfully clever yet patient and protective.

'Oh, hello! It's Mr Morton, isn't it? I hope you don't mind me turning up unannounced.'

'Why would I?' he said, in mock surprise. 'It's not often an old duffer like me gets any visitors. And do call me Hugh. Please, come in.'

He stood back to let me pass, his large frame only slightly bent by age. I stepped into the dark coolness of the hall. As my eyes adjusted I saw that, just as Nan had said, there were books everywhere, piled up on a wooden pew and along shelves that had been sandwiched between the tops of doors and the ceiling.

He ushered me into a large, beamed sitting room and gestured towards the most comfortable chair. There were yet more books in there, lining shelves that flanked the enormous fireplace. It was the kind that was big enough to climb into, and sit off to the side to poke at the embers without being scorched. The furniture was a hotch-potch of periods, colours, fabrics and materials – angular, simply varnished new furniture alongside good antique pieces. Some were dark and rustic, rough-hewn, while others were much more delicate, French-polished and inlaid.

My mother would have said the place lacked a woman's touch, which meant, I suppose, that everything had been chosen for its function, rather than its ability to chime and harmonize with anything else. But I liked it as much as its owner and, almost as soon as I sank down into the faded moss-green plush of the armchair, I felt sleepy and content. Although I hadn't been aware of it, I didn't often feel like that at the bottom of the valley. There, I was taut, strung too tight and on guard for much of the time, never quite able to shake off the sense that I was being watched.

It wasn't until I had drunk half the glass of water Mr Morton had brought me that I remembered he didn't know who I was or what I might want.

'You must think I'm very rude,' I said, smiling, and suspecting that he didn't. 'My name's Alice.'

I was so becalmed in that sunlit room, feeling the water slide down through me, cooling my insides, that I had begun absentmindedly stroking the mound of my stomach. The baby had been moving, not kicking but churning, as I had laboured up the hill. Now he was still, as soothed as I.

Mr Morton glanced at my hand and then away, embarrassed.

'I think the baby is as glad that I'm sitting down as I am,' I said, hoping to put him at ease.

His eyes twinkled. 'And does he or she have a name yet?'

'No, not yet. Though I'm sure it's a boy so that narrows it down.'

Mr Morton was the first person I'd admitted my conviction to and, as I did, I felt something approaching possessiveness for the tiny being inside me. He was beginning to become a person to me. My heart sank.

'It certainly will narrow it down,' he said. 'By about half, I would say. So, what brings you and Master Some-one to see me, then? It must have been quite a walk up from Fiercombe in this heat.'

So he did know who I was. He must have registered my sharp look because he chuckled to himself. 'Little escapes us here in the village, even me. We so rarely have anyone new arrive beyond the day-trippers who come to see the bluebells and the odd American hoping to poke around inside the manor. We never have the pleasure of any new blood. Certainly no one who stays for longer than an afternoon.'

He went out to refill my glass and brought back a plate of shortbread biscuits with it. 'You'll have heard about me from Nan, no doubt. Her mother is the saving of me. Without her I would probably starve to death and have to be buried in a dirty shirt.'

I laughed. 'Yes, it was Nan.'

'And how are you getting along with Mrs Jelphs?'

'She's very kind and I'm very grateful to her – I just wish she didn't worry about me quite so much. I don't know what sort of trouble she thinks I can possibly get myself into here but sometimes I catch myself creeping about so I don't make her anxious – and even as a pathetic act of rebellion. I suppose that's one reason why I wanted to come up to the village and see you.'

'I can guess the other.' He smiled. 'I'm no longer a bet-ting man but if you've come to me then it's because you'd like to know a bit more about these parts. And Mrs Jelphs is not one for gossip, regardless of the fact that all the interesting gossip is ancient history by now.'

'She talked to me a little when I first arrived – about how it was when she first came to be lady's maid. But since then . . . It's as though she feels she's said too much and is making up for it. To be honest, I can't tell what she's thinking most of the time. Sometimes she watches me like a hawk, at others she'll close off and I might as well be thin air. I feel like I put my foot in it either way – going for walks too late in the evening one minute and asking too many questions the next.'

He smiled again. 'Our paths rarely cross but from what I remember she had a similar effect on me. You mustn't take it personally. You're very young still – so much is in front of you – but there comes a point when you know that you've had your best times. It sounds terribly depressing, doesn't it?'

'It does a bit, yes,' I said. I thought of James and the only full day we had ever spent together. We had gone to Kensington Gardens and, later, I had conceived the child I now carried.

'What I mean is that I'm an old man now and quite content with my lot,' continued Mr Morton. 'I've had more than my fair share of excitement and now I'm quite happy to read my books and sit here thinking about what I've done, and with whom,' he twinkled once again, 'and indulge in a bit of harmless gossip at the post office of a morning. Now Mrs Jelphs is a different kettle of fish. She'd lived her life – or she felt she'd lived her life, the best of it – by the time she was, what, twenty-two, twenty-three?'

'But that's such a waste.'

'Yes, of course. You and I wouldn't have let that happen

to us. But Mrs Jelphs is one of those old-fashioned types you used to see in service. They're not even a dying breed now. They're a virtually extinct one. Those who lived for and through the people they served. When that's gone – the house sold, the fortune lost, the line died out – they haven't anything left. The Fiercombe estate, what's left of it, is the love of Edith Jelphs's life.'

We sat quietly for a time and the mechanism of a grandfather clock in the corner of the room shunted and clunked into life, chiming once for the half-hour. Distantly I registered that Mr Morton was able to keep time up here in the village.

'The little bit Mrs Jelphs did tell me about the past was fascinating,' I said. 'Despite not wanting to talk about her, she obviously adored Elizabeth Stanton.'

'By all accounts everyone loved Elizabeth Stanton. She was one of nature's true charmers. It wasn't affected, though, and it wasn't reserved just for the sophisticated types who came down from London either. You know how in old photographs everyone looks as though they've just been given some dreadful news?'

I nodded, and took one of the shortbread biscuits.

'It was the exposure time, of course. No one could hold a smile for long – a real smile, that is, not some rictus grin – so they ended up looking much too serious. Now, things had improved somewhat by the 1880s and 90s but I've seen photographs – just a few, mind – of Elizabeth Stanton and in every one she was blurred because she couldn't seem to help moving, even after a short time. You'd think she hadn't wanted to be photographed at all.

'There was one portrait of her, apparently taken at

some expense by a well-regarded photographer, in which you can see her features properly. It was a very good photograph technically, the image pin-sharp, but artistically it was declared a failure. Her husband Edward Stanton, who paid for it, is supposed to have exclaimed, "There is nothing of her in it so I will not hang it." Too serious and sombre for his liking, you see. I saw it once, tucked away in a minor bedroom, still unframed. I thought it extremely beautiful: not so much sombre as wistful. I've not seen it since. Perhaps it was lost or perhaps Mrs Jelphs has squirrelled it away somewhere.'

He stood and walked over to a cabinet with glass-fronted doors. From the pocket of his tweed trousers he plucked a tiny key and turned it in the lock. 'I don't know why I keep it locked. Not too many antiquarian-book thieves around these parts, but I keep my most precious volumes in here – precious both in terms of sentimental and monetary value. Ah! Here it is.'

Bound in dark green leather, the gold-embossed title was rather unprepossessing: *The Aristocratic Families of Gloucestershire.*

'I don't suppose this is the book that has the photograph of Stanton House in it?' I asked.

'That's right. How did you know?'

'Mrs Jelphs mentioned it in a more unguarded moment. She said it would be out of print now.'

'And so it probably is.' He lowered himself carefully into the armchair opposite mine, tucking his long legs underneath. Eventually he found the right page. 'And here is the very picture, though it's not particularly good quality. It was taken in the midst of winter, when the sun only gets a glimpse over the escarpment for a couple of hours during the shortest days.'

It occurred to me that it was the longest day soon: the summer solstice. Midsummer's Eve. I'd always liked the sound of it, an enchanted evening when anything might happen.

Mr Morton had been holding the book out towards me, his thumb keeping the place. I apologized for daydreaming and took it carefully from him.

The photograph was not so poor that you couldn't say with certainty that Stanton House had been a forbidding place. Though the image was black-and-white, you knew that the stones of its walls were grey, a light-leaching grey, like a rain-filled sky. It was large and sprawling in design, not the square, symmetrical shape I'd imagined but a high-Victorian house with deep bay windows on the ground floor and Gothic Revival flourishes about the roofs and chimneys. Of course, it had never got old enough for its lines to soften and smudge but I had the feeling that, had it been allowed to stand, it would look the same today: impervious to both the weather and time.

'Bit of a monstrosity, isn't it?' said Mr Morton.

'Mrs Jelphs said that the locals hated it from the beginning.'

'Yes, and who could blame them? The old manor, built by their forebears, was allowed to go to rack and ruin, while Edward Stanton brought in stone from miles away, often hiring labour from elsewhere to build it. It was viewed as a dreadful snub, a real insult.

'It came at a bad time, too, when some of the bigger woollen mills hereabouts had just closed. There wasn't much money around so the building of such a house in the county at such unnecessary and showy cost was considered rather vulgar. Any rift could have been healed when Sir Edward's younger brother inherited the title and revived the manor house with his young family but Sir Charles is a private man. He chose not to employ a large staff and has never encouraged people to wander the old paths. There were to be no more parties like those held in the days of Stanton House.'

There, feeling so safe in the sitting room, I asked the question I had been avoiding, because of my strange experience.

'Have you been there? To where Stanton House was, to where the glasshouse still is?'

He caught the hesitancy in my voice and searched my face curiously. 'Yes, I have walked there on occasion. I had a dog until last year – my faithful old Sammy. He was an excellent excuse to take some decent exercise. We'd go down the bluebell paths and I'd let him choose which way across the valley from there. He loved the Great Mead – the long grass was teeming with rabbits. We only went to the eastern end of the valley a few times.'

'Why was that?' I knew I sounded strained but I kept on. 'I would have thought you'd find that part of the estate the most interesting.'

He sipped his tea thoughtfully, then picked up a piece of sugar-dusted shortbread before setting it down again. 'I didn't like it there, if truth be told, and nor did Sammy. He was a bit of a barker when he got excited, which was most of the time on a walk, but you wouldn't hear a peep out of him there. He kept close to me, ears pricked – there was even the odd growl. So while I have been there, and poked dutifully around in the nettles so I can hold my head up as the area's only historian, I was glad to get back up here to Stanwick.'

He laughed ruefully and took an enormous bite of biscuit, chewing and swallowing it with gusto, as though he hadn't already eaten most of the plateful.

'I'm glad you felt that way,' I said, feeling a rush of relief at his admission. 'I got a bit of a fright there myself the other day. I was half wondering if I hadn't just imagined the whole thing.'

He kept quiet, looking at me intently so I would explain. I told it in a jumble so I wouldn't stop for feeling silly, the sensations the experience had produced made raw again now that I was telling it for the first time since I had burst in on Tom in the kitchen. I had written nothing but a single line in my diary about it: 'strange weather'.

When I'd finished he nodded, his eyes on the luxuriant grass of the village green, visible beyond the window. He looked as if he was going to say something, but when he didn't and the silence stretched out, I let my head fall back against the chair. Just then, a tiny foot nudged at the glass I was resting on my stomach. I kneaded it, not quite believing I was touching the nub of a heel, already formed.

'I don't believe in ghosts,' I said, after a time. 'It's not that. It's nothing so . . . obvious. Besides, Nan has already told me about Margaret of Anjou stalking the hallways in her fur-trimmed gown.'

He smiled. 'I wouldn't worry about her. The house has been completely reconfigured since those days, with corridors and rooms in different places.'

'Perhaps she just walks through the walls then,' I said, 'leaving a trail of floral perfume.'

He laughed and took another bite of biscuit, apparently swallowing it whole. 'She certainly passed this way, and there is some evidence to show that she and her armies broke their journey here too, but her status as Fiercombe's resident ghost is no doubt one of Edward Stanton's inventions. He was nearly as good a raconteur as I am. In the early days after he had taken over the estate, he was said to encourage guests to come up with colourful tales to tell around the fire in the dead of winter. I think he thought the house – his costly and painstakingly crafted Victorian pile – would not be complete without a local ghost story or two.'

'Did you know him personally?' I said.

'Not well but, yes, I knew him. I went to a few of his and Elizabeth's famous gatherings. He was a good deal older than me – perhaps twelve or thirteen years – and she must have been about my age, a few years older perhaps. I didn't live here then but came with my friend whose family had a place over near Cheltenham.

'I remember the last one – not least because it was the last time Elizabeth was seen in public. There was quite a to-do about the occasion because there hadn't been anything so big and grand for a few years. She and Edward attended the social events they were required to, titled as they were, and held the odd dinner party, but it was all rather subdued. As a result, I don't think anyone passed up that last invitation. I know William and I were most intrigued to go. We'd been allocated a room to share but we didn't get to bed at all. We left at first light, feeling rather the worse for wear.'

'Mrs Jelphs told me something about it,' I said. 'She said that she had found a special place to watch it all from a distance.'

'Well, that party – like those before it – was quite something to behold. The last one was in particular for me, and I thought I'd seen it all, having spent the previous few years living in London with a rich old aunt, who'd let me run wild. It was near the beginning of that period that I met Edward Stanton, at some card game that took place at his club, where my friend William was also a member. Stanton had just got married and was utterly besotted with his new bride. And who could blame him? She was a wonderful creature.

'I only went to two or perhaps three of their parties in those early days and then a long time seemed to go by before they threw the last one. Elizabeth was expecting her second child. I think it was late summer – it must have been: the garden was ripe, almost alive with it. You half expected the roses to start bobbing in time to the string quartet they'd got up from Bath for the night. No, wait, I'm quite wrong about the month – it was Midsummer's Eve, of course it was. But we'd had days of rain and everything had been washed clean and was plump with rainwater. The valley looked as lush as a jungle.

'She was huge with child. I can see her now quite clearly, sitting in an enormous Bath chair heaped with cushions that someone had dragged outside for her. She was glorious among all those insipid girls, younger than her and as pale as milk. Not to mention the bovine county matrons who'd come to gawp. None of the men could take their eyes off Elizabeth. She was luminous, and with that great mass of dark hair coiled up on top of her head. Someone was fanning her and she was laughing, saying how decadent it was and that it would be a shame not to have such treatment once the baby came.'

His face had taken on the faraway look I'd come to associate with Mrs Jelphs and, not wanting to break into his reverie, I looked back down at the book I'd propped up between the glass and my stomach. Beneath the picture of Stanton House there was a smaller photograph of Fiercombe. The caption read: 'Fiercombe Manor, presumed to have been taken around 1900. Stanton House already demolished.'

As Mrs Jelphs had told me, the manor's façade was quite overwhelmed by the giant yew pylons, while the ivy that was now restricted to the kitchen garden's wall had been allowed to climb unchecked, choking the casement windows and creeping up over the roof to work loose a number of the tiles.

'We're lucky to have that photograph – people didn't go about taking pictures of old tumbledown buildings then, only the new ones they were proud of. Fiercombe Manor is one of those houses people have always been fascinated by, however. There is something enchanting and mysterious about it, even when it's in the sort of sorry condition you see here. Perhaps that even adds to the allure. You glimpse places like it sometimes, usually from a train window. Lonely houses tucked into the countryside, almost hidden in the folds of the hills. You wonder who lives in them, what's happened in their history.' He smiled. 'Or, at least, I do.'

I nodded eagerly. 'You're right. If walls could talk . . .'

'Indeed, and wouldn't it be fascinating to know what Fiercombe's old stones would have to say? Stanton House's too, if it still stood.'

He put his hand out for the book, turned the page, then handed it back to me. 'Now, have a look at that and you'll see what I mean about Elizabeth Stanton.'

It was a small family portrait. At the heart of it was a man in his middle thirties who undoubtedly had a look of Tom about him. He wasn't smiling, of course, but his face – despite having been captured four decades earlier and reduced by the photograph to an arrangement of light and dark – somehow radiated pride and a fierce sort of happiness. Next to him, so close that their hips touched, was a woman. Her figure was curvaceous compared to what I was used to in London, her waist impossibly narrow, no doubt whittled down by whalebone stays. Sure enough, just as Mr Morton had said, her face was tantalizingly blurred because she had turned it away at the last moment.

Around the couple was an assortment of ageing relatives and servants. They were grouped at the end of the formal garden furthest from the house, the shadows of the yews falling across their feet. Beneath it, in cursive ink and just legible, was written, 'A picnic at the Old Manor, 1893'. I closed the book and let my head rest again on the back of the chair, my mind full of pictures from the past.

'That was the summer I was first here,' said Mr Morton. 'If someone had told me then that I'd still be here well into the next century, I'd never have believed them.'

Just then, the grandfather clock roused itself to strike

four and I jumped at the intrusion, the book sliding to the floor. He stood before I could reach for it, but as he picked it up I saw that it had fallen open at the gloomy picture of Stanton House. There were more questions I wanted to ask but my host seemed tired, the skin under his eyes so thin it looked blue.

Promising to return soon, I thanked him and made my way back across the green. I looked back before I turned off for the lane that would take me down into the valley and he was still at his door, one hand raised. He was a way off so I couldn't be sure but I thought his expression was a little grim.

Elizabeth

From her luxurious perch in the Bath chair, Elizabeth felt like a queen. The champagne had served its purpose: she could almost feel the bubbles coursing through her bloodstream, the alcohol seeping into her bones, leaving her languorous and pleasantly empty-headed. The creeping doubts and twists of anxiety that had become such constant companions in these late days of her pregnancy had scattered, carried off by the soft breeze that stole through the valley. She smiled with the relief of it and tipped her head back to look at the stars that were being lit one by one, distant sparks in a sky deepening from east to west; from Prussian blue to the delicate green of her silk dress.

'People always think sunsets are pink and orange,' she said, to no one in particular. She had not been left alone for a moment in the previous hour. An unending procession of guests had come to pay their respects and no one had, like Mrs Bell, mentioned her illness. Perhaps they had heard what she had said to the old busybody and heeded it. Or perhaps the aura of calm contentment she felt miraculously radiating from her, the tantalizing proximity she felt to simple happiness, had rendered them unable to hurt her.

'You're absolutely right, of course,' said an eager voice. Her eyes reluctantly moved away from the stars to Hugh Morton. 'I liked painting at school,' he continued, 'and our art master said just what you have. "Use your eyes, boys. Look up and use your eyes. Painting a sunset is not just an excuse to get out the carmine."' He chuckled at the memory and she laughed with him.

'I'm Lady Stanton,' she said. 'My name is Elizabeth.'

'Yes, I know,' he replied. 'Everyone here knows who you are.'

A slight tremor passed through her but she drank some more champagne and the sensation steadied and dissolved. 'I suppose they ought to know me, if I am the one to have invited them here – along with my husband, of course.'

'Well, yes,' he said. 'But I meant that you are famous for being so beautiful.'

He swallowed nervously, and even over the chatter around them, and the lilting music floating over from the gazebo, she heard it.

'You're kind to say so. I think everyone knows me because of my little brushes with madness.' She instructed herself to stop talking.

'I – I don't know anything of that. But if it were so, well, it's common enough, isn't it? An aunt of mine is said to be mad. She was always my favourite when we were children. She talked to us as though we were real people.'

She turned to look at him properly, this man – not much more than a boy – who was so kind. Her back muscles twinged with the movement and she winced.

He jumped up from the chair next to hers. 'Are you quite well, Lady Stanton? Is there anything I can fetch for you?'

She smiled to reassure him. 'Do you know? I would

love something to eat. I haven't touched a thing since lunch and all this champagne has gone to my head. I shall tell you all my secrets if I'm not careful.'

He grinned, straightened and saluted her. 'Straight away, my lady.'

Before she could say another word he had rushed towards the marquee, now a shimmering ghost ship in the near-dark.

'Who was that you were talking to?' Edward had appeared out of the gloom and she started.

'Oh, Edward, it's you. It was Hugh Morton, a friend of William . . . I can't remember his name.' She saw her husband's face as he sat down heavily. 'Oh, darling, he's just a boy.'

'He's in love with you, of course. He'll go upstairs later and think of you while he's in my sheets.' The drink had also loosened his tongue; it was rare for him not to dissemble when he was jealous.

'Edward! I very much doubt anyone is going to imagine such a thing when I am almost half the size of Stanton House.'

As she spoke, he was running his hand gently down her spine. When he got to the base, he massaged the tender muscles at either side. Without her normal corsets, she could feel his fingers quite distinctly. She moaned involuntarily and he leant closer, kissing her along her collarbone, his fingers kneading her flesh all the while.

'Edward, people will see,' she whispered, but the deepening twilight had become night, sending people closer to the music and the marquee, where torches had been lit. They were quite alone.

She knew he had had other women. Not Adelaide March, not yet, probably not ever – she was too vapid for Edward's taste. But others, surely. He spent whole weeks at a time in London, staying at his club. The lure of a card game was greater for him than a woman, she also knew, but she couldn't believe he hadn't gone elsewhere. When he did come to her, she let him, but it was not like it had been before Isabel was born. He seemed afraid that he would break her now. As for her, the part of her that could not forgive his treatment of her made her as un-responsive as a doll. She thought he knew why she only tolerated him but they never discussed it. To discuss it would be to admit it and his pride wouldn't allow him to do that.

'Beth,' he muttered in her ear, his voice thick with lust. He smelt of hair oil and smoke, which mixed cloyingly with the rich scents of the garden. Part of her wanted to push him away but there was a vestige of desire in her too, a remnant of feeling from the first months of their court-ship to which the sounds of the party, Hugh's simple admiration and the champagne took her hurtling back. In those days their mutual infatuation had been enough to ward off everything else.

'Darling, we will be a proper family again when our son is born. It will be a new beginning for us all,' Edward said softly.

The tiny flame of desire inside her went out. 'Are we not a proper family now, then?' The words were out before she could bite them back, as she usually did. That was also the work of the champagne.

Edward leant back and looked into her eyes. He was

flushed, his expression anguished. 'Of course we are. I didn't mean that we weren't.'

She was torn between encouraging him to talk as he almost never did – about the darkest times in their marriage – and allowing some devilment in her to anger him into walking away. Though she knew it helped no one, least of all herself, she had harboured feelings of resentment and betrayal towards Edward for almost half a decade, and sometimes it was all she could do not to unlock the box and let those feelings out.

She forced herself to reach up and stroke his hair and, after a moment, he rested his head heavily against her breast. Through the dark she saw a lean figure spot them and stop, hesitate, then turn on his heel. Her new friend, Hugh. For a moment she wished with all her heart that she was Adelaide's age again; a time in her life when men had expected nothing from her but a smile or a dance, a time when she had been able at the end of an evening like this one to return to the sanctuary of her father's home.

'The man who wins our girl will be fortunate indeed,' her father had often said to her mother. It would never have occurred to Elizabeth, by then growing impatient with the safe, predictable cadences of her life in Bristol, that her future husband would one day feel differently.

But it did no good to think like that. She couldn't go back to her charmed girlhood. She was married and she was a mother. She turned to her husband, who she sensed was close to tears. She had seen Edward cry only once before, when she had lost their son – the only lost baby he knew of.

'Edward, what is it? I thought you were happy. I'm sorry I spoke sharply.'

He was silent for a minute and she saw that he was gathering himself, swallowing the emotion that had taken him, too, by surprise. 'I am happy,' he finally forced out. 'So very happy. I cannot think what has come over me.'

'Perhaps tonight has reminded you, as it has reminded me, of the last time we hosted such a large occasion,' she said softly, though what she had really been reminded of that night were those little deaths inside her. Those, and the series of elusive memories that she could not unlock but that recalled, she suspected, whatever had driven Edward from her.

'We have held lots of dinners and gatherings,' he said.

'Yes, but not like this. Not like we did before Isabel was born.'

He sighed. 'No . . . well, perhaps not on this scale.'

'We have gone – or you have gone alone – to many more balls and dinner parties than we have hosted.'

'Very well, Elizabeth, you are right. What more would you have me say on it?' A plaintive note had crept into his voice.

'Nothing,' she said. 'Except that I can't help but be reminded of that last occasion. It is so much the same and yet so very different. We have a daughter now,' she took a deep breath, 'and we have the years in between, and the times that were so very hard for us both.'

'Please let us not dwell on those now,' he said. 'Not when we are so happy, and when the evening has been such a success. If we must talk of it, and I do not think that it will do us any good, let us do so tomorrow.'

'I'm sorry, Edward, but I think we must talk of it tonight. I do not usually feel brave enough to do so. I must speak now.'

He sighed heavily. She could feel the tension in his body, and how much he wanted to rejoin the throng on the lawn.

'What is it, then?' He looked at her closely. 'You are well, are you not? There is nothing wrong with the child?' Anxiety laced the last words.

'No, all is well with the child. You can see from the size of me how healthy the child is.'

'Are you sure? Because I don't think I could –' He stopped.

'You don't think what, Edward?'

He looked down. 'Oh, must I say it? You surely know what I mean. I don't think I could bear it to happen again.'

'*You* could not bear it to happen.' Her voice was cold but she couldn't help it.

'Elizabeth, you twist my words. I could not bear it to happen to you again. I could not bear it for you, and I could not bear it for me. Is that not understandable? It is not only you who has suffered.'

She breathed in and out before she spoke. Her heart was racing again, anger and fear simmering just below the surface. She knew she mustn't let them out if she wanted him to listen. 'That is true,' she said carefully. 'We have both suffered. Isabel too.'

Edward took out his handkerchief and blew his nose.

'After Isabel, I watched you descend into some darkness of your own making and I thought nothing could ever be so terrible,' he said. 'But then, when our son . . .'

He hesitated and she could sense his effort not to weep. 'When our son was lost, it was even worse. I couldn't possibly risk losing you as well as him, do you see that?'

'But you hadn't lost me, Edward. After the miscarriage it wasn't the same as after Isabel. It broke my heart that he died. I mourned for our son, just as you did. But I was myself, I told you that repeatedly. I was not . . . ill.' She dropped her voice on the last word.

'How was I to know whether I could believe that?' said Edward, not looking at her now, but across the lawn towards the house, where light glowed in almost every downstairs window. 'I could not take the risk. It's not as though I sent you away again. You were allowed to stay here, with Dr Logan treating you and a nurse paid to watch you as well. You begged not to go back to the private hospital and I let you have your way. You were cared for here instead.'

'Cared for?' she said, her voice rising. 'I was locked away in my rooms, unable to see my daughter for weeks. I was not allowed any food that I might have to chew. I was not allowed to walk in the garden or to read a book in case it over-stimulated my mind.' She thought of him – Dr Logan, the man Isabel had mentioned by another name only that afternoon – and remembered what else he had prescribed for her when the nurse was sent out and the door locked. She turned to her husband. 'Edward, there was nothing wrong with me but the natural grief I felt for my son. I was not insane. But, in a sense, that was the very worst of it: the thought that the cure prescribed for a madness I didn't have would eventually send me insane anyway.' She battled to lower her voice, but he still flinched at the words.

'I ask you again,' he said, after a pause. 'Why do you feel we must talk of this now, here, with all the people of the county just feet from us? It is perverse and I won't indulge you in it any longer.'

He stood to go but she caught his hand. 'Please, Edward. There is one thing I must ask you. Then I will say goodbye nicely to our guests and tell them I am exhausted and must retire for the sake of my health.'

Reluctantly he sat down again, though he would not look at her.

'What I need to ask you is what you might do if . . .'

'If what?' he spat.

'If the baby is lost or if . . .'

'Why would the baby be lost? You have only a few weeks to go and you are in perfect health – you said so yourself just moments ago. Even before the miscarriage you were sick, violently sick, and unable to eat. You grew so thin and pale that it was probably inevitable that the child would not survive. There was something wrong from the start. It is entirely different this time.'

'Yes, it is. But, Edward, I was not ill before I gave birth to Isabel. I was in excellent health then too – and so was she when she was born.'

'Ah, so we have got to the nub of it. You are afraid not of this child dying but of suffering from puerperal insanity once again.'

The words were so ugly. She hadn't heard them spoken aloud in a long time, though they often echoed in her head when she couldn't sleep. 'That is very unfair,' she half whispered. 'I am afraid of both. But, like you, I believe that this child must be healthy. It is so far along now. But that and all this' – she gestured at the gathering of people in front of them, the lit torches and the band and the laughter – 'so reminds me of when I was carrying Isabel. So, yes, I will admit it. I am afraid of losing myself again. And there is something else this time, too. I am also afraid of how you will feel about me if I bear us another daughter.'

He shook his head. 'Have I ever said I was disappointed that Isabel was not a boy? I love our daughter.'

'I know you do. But you have always talked of your wish for a son. You said as much to Adelaide March this evening. I know how important it is.'

'Well, of course. It is only natural for a man to want a son, who will take his name and inherit his title.'

'Edward, I don't seem able to say what I must say to you.' She wanted to sob with frustration. She was so unused to speaking to her husband honestly that she didn't know how to admit to the fears that never strayed far from her thoughts.

'It is time we returned to our guests,' he said, with forced indifference. 'We have been here, alone, long enough.'

'Just answer me this, then. If something should happen this time, do you promise that you will not send for Dr Logan? Do you promise that you will neither send me away nor banish me to my rooms and install that man, who will watch over me every second of the day and night? Who will force me to eat when I am not hungry. Who will insist that I am stripped naked and bathed by one of his odious nurses, who will treat me as though I were a child or an imbecile. I don't think I can bear that again. Don't you see? It only makes it worse.'

He finally looked at her, and when she saw how his jaw was set with determination, she felt cold all over. 'I cannot promise you anything of the sort,' he said. 'I will do what I think right, just as I have in the past, and always in your best interest, rather than my own. Do you think I wanted to send away my wife, and have half the county whisper about it? Do you think I wanted to have them discover, thanks to servant gossip, that the same doctor had to be sent for again, less than two years on? Do I want their pity? Of course not. I —'

'There was another miscarriage,' she broke in, her voice leaden. She couldn't quite believe the conversation they were having, the years of repressing the truth undone in mere minutes. It wasn't just the drink, or the liberating darkness — it was a remnant of her old spirit. That, and a sudden intuition that this was her last chance to appeal to him.

He had frozen at her words. 'What do you mean?'

'A little more than a year ago. I didn't tell you.'

'You didn't . . . But I don't understand.' Two spots of high colour appeared on his cheeks.

'It was lost almost as soon as I knew I was with child again. Two months, no more.'

'And you told no one of this?'

'No one but Edith.'

'Your lady's maid knew and I, your husband and the father of this child, did not?'

'She saw the blood on the sheet.'

He paled at the words; she could see it even in the gloom.

'Why do you think I did not tell you?' she continued sadly. 'Is it not clear to you now?'

She couldn't read his expression. It might have been horror, it might have been fear, it might even have been distaste – she couldn't tell.

Just then an elderly voice, slightly querulous, rang out into the night. 'Has anyone seen Sir Edward or Lady Stanton? We must leave shortly but we cannot go without thanking them.'

'It's the Fitzmorrises,' said Edward, quietly. 'You will stay here. Perhaps it would be as well if you went to bed. You have clearly over-exerted yourself.'

He strode away, leaving Elizabeth alone. The soft gauze the champagne had laid over her had been blown away by the words they'd exchanged. Though she was trembling with her own daring, she didn't regret them. They were the first truthful words they had spoken to each other for as long as she could remember and she felt lighter for them.

Without Edward's body next to her she realized that the last of the day's warmth had ebbed away. She felt weak with the need to rest. Before anyone else could come and talk to her, she got slowly to her feet and walked away across the lawn, leaving behind a party that had diminished but was still hours from drawing to a complete close.

The stars and nearly-new moon provided a surprising amount of light away from the torches and the part of the house that was open to guests and servants. Before she stepped through the unlocked double doors into the pitch-dark of the morning room she looked back at the scene. Perhaps it was superstition but, in that moment, she felt convinced she would never see its like again.

She waited until the hallway was empty before starting

up the stairs. The house felt like a warm bath after the cooling air of the garden, the carpet on the stairs deep and soft under her shoes, which had begun to pinch. She slipped them off and closed her eyes with relief, her toes sinking into the thick pile.

Instead of going along to her own rooms, she turned the other way at the top of the stairs, just as she had earlier. The large, light-filled nursery was a room she had chosen for Isabel herself. Edward had wanted to keep it for guests but she had insisted.

'Our child will be here with us every day,' she had said to him, in the coaxing tone she seemed later to have lost. 'A guest will stay, what, two or three nights and it is they who should enjoy these views and the best of the morning sun? I don't see the sense of that.' And she had got her way.

The nursery-maid slept in a smaller adjoining room and there was no sound coming from inside as Elizabeth put her ear to the door. It was not yet midnight so she was unlikely to be asleep. She was probably downstairs with the other servants, sneaking illicit sips of champagne and tucking into the poached salmon and slices of game terrine that the guests hadn't eaten.

Inside the nursery, Isabel's breathing was deep and regular, despite the hubbub of the party outside. The swell of its sound – a woman's abrupt shriek of laughter, a clash of glasses for a toast – was clearly audible through the window Isabel had opened as wide as it would go. Elizabeth imagined her little girl kneeling up in her nightgown and solemnly surveying the party from above. She wondered if Isabel had watched her, too. She would have been easy to find among the throng in her eau-de-Nil dress.

She smoothed the child's hair off her hot face. She could remember Isabel's first week in the world with pin-sharp clarity. The labour had been without complication: long and excruciating, certainly, but never dangerous. She remembered the shock she had felt after waking from her first exhausted sleep as a mother, seeing a tiny creature swaddled in white, its eyes screwed shut and a deep furrow between almost invisible brows.

'That's your daughter,' said Dr Frith, Edward's old family doctor. She was glad he'd said it because she couldn't quite believe she had produced such a miraculous thing.

'She's perfect,' he said. 'And don't worry, a boy will come along soon enough.'

It wasn't until a week after the birth that something had shifted inside her head, a cold iron bolt sliding into place. She had concealed it at first, claiming a delayed fatigue that forced her to stay in bed most of the day. The baby was brought in to her but she could no more rouse herself to comfort or feed Isabel than she could her feather bolster. In her mind the baby was no longer Isabel, she wasn't even a 'she': it was nothing to do with her.

Fathomless exhaustion turned to its opposite in the third week. She lay alone in the profound stillness of the hours before dawn, eyes open, unblinking and trained on the moon. If there was no moon she stared at a slight warp in one of the glass panes of the window. She came to think of those nights as stretched dough, and saw in her mind an image of Mrs Wentworth rolling a fat lump into a long, colourless snake, rolling and rolling, anointing it with flour all the while, until it was longer than the table was wide.

Then one day she found she couldn't bear to lie in one place for any length of time. She knew that if she did she would (and the phrase had suddenly rung true) go out of her mind. Of course the behaviour this created – the pacing, the tapping of a foot if she had to sit, the old nursery rhymes and poems recited in an urgent whisper – made it seem as if she was already mad. They did not understand that constant movement was the only thing keeping her from it.

She couldn't remember Edward in any of this. He must have been there; he must have been the one to call in a new doctor when Frith had presumably admitted defeat. She couldn't even remember the second one's name, the one before Dr Logan. He couldn't have lasted long.

Tonight, the party unspooling below, Isabel stirred in her sleep and muttered the tail-end of a sentence Elizabeth didn't quite catch. She leant closer and breathed in her daughter's scent. She had lost the milky fragrance of baby-hood but she still smelt absolutely clean. Not just her skin and hair, which would have been bathed earlier, but the whole of her, inside and out. She was still so new. The others, if they had survived, would be newer still. Elizabeth folded that thought away.

She hoped more than anything that Isabel couldn't remember her first year. She prayed – and it was the only thing she'd ever truly prayed for – that her daughter's first week in the world, when Elizabeth was still well, had been the most important one. That those precious days had rubbed out the ones that had come after.

Whatever it was that she hadn't been able to recall lately had happened during that awful time, she suspected, and it was something much more important than Edward's absence had been. It wasn't the feelings she had experienced then that she had forgotten – indeed, she remembered those so clearly that her stomach often lurched in fear that it was not just a vivid memory she was recalling but the madness itself, stealthily returned. The memory gap, the black well into which something enormous had fallen so deeply that she couldn't even hear the echo of its splash, was something else – something that had taken place outside her mind.

She rested her forehead on the pillow next to Isabel and strained to remember what it could have been. She was certain it had something to do with her daughter. She thought it must have been the reason that a letter had been written to Dr Logan, who had come, had his papers signed by her husband and taken her away. Perhaps it was also the reason she had been locked in her rooms two years later when she had been grieving for a lost child. Whatever it was, it had changed things for ever between Edward and her – even more than her illness had. Perhaps, if she could remember this event, the rift in their marriage might begin to heal. That, and the safe arrival of a baby boy who would grow up to inherit the Fiercombe estate.

Alice

Leaving Mr Morton's cottage and alone once more, I felt an inexplicable reluctance dragging in my belly as I descended towards Fiercombe. I hoped Mrs Jelphs would be back by the time I got there but the valley felt deserted, with nothing touched or moved since I'd left a few hours before. *If only Tom would come back*, I found myself thinking, then tutted aloud at my own silliness. Feeling soft towards Thomas Stanton was hardly any better than feeling wistful about James.

I thought of taking a nap, then remembered the summerhouse and its diary. As soon as I did, I felt a powerful pull and knew I would have to go. After seeing the photographs in Hugh Morton's book I felt as though Elizabeth had edged just a little closer to me, her presence in the valley more tangible than it had been.

The room when I got there was exactly as I had left it in the dark and I wondered if anyone knew about it. Anyone still here, anyway. I turned back to the front of the little book and skimmed over the entry I had read before. What followed was a shopping list of sorts and then a competent but incomplete sketch of the view through the narrow window behind me. I kept turning pages at random but stopped when a longer entry jumped out at me. Unusually, it had been written in ink.

The season has changed in a single day and I feel sharper for it. More returned to myself after weeks of soporific weather that made one fight not to simply lie down and doze the day away. Outside I can smell woodsmoke and rotting leaves, and this little room is colder than I can remember it ever being.

Edward came to me last night. It was the first time in weeks but still I was unaccountably nervous. He wore a determined expression but there was something in his eyes that caused me to think he could be wounded, and that made me kinder to him. If only he would allow me to see these chinks in his armour more often perhaps I would be more willing to become the soft, pliant wife he wishes I was. It was over quickly but he was easier with me afterwards and we even laughed together over something he had overheard one of the maids say.

After he had returned to his own rooms, I lay awake until the valley was entirely silent, the fountain switched off and the last servant retired. I opened the curtains, which are so heavy and long that no light can ever penetrate them, and the moonlight was bright and cold, a refreshing beam through the turbid air – the very dregs of the summer's heat. I thought that if I kept very still, not only my physical body, but my mind also, I might be more able to conceive a child. I put my hand – my left hand, the one that wears the gold band that once belonged to Edward's mother – on my stomach, and tried to keep the fearful thoughts from filling me as they do.

To quiet my mind, I made myself imagine a tap turning off until the last drop had fallen and that did soothe me, at least for half an hour or so. Of course, I don't know yet if it worked. It has been almost a year now since I was last with child. I'm sure Edward has been aware of that fact just as I have been, and today's sudden

*plunge into autumn will have brought it into sharper relief. Our
little girl will turn one next week. I know she must have a brother
before long.*

There was no date but suddenly there was a little girl of a
year old. Elizabeth had been right about carrying a girl. I
turned to the next entry, realizing that time passed unevenly in the diary, with whole months frustratingly lost.
Not that she had written it to be read, of course; quite the
opposite. Guilt stabbed me then, as I recalled the feeling
that I was being watched in the manor, that eyes other
than mine might have read my private thoughts. It didn't
stop me reading on, though, as I had with the note in the
sewing box. I couldn't help it.

*I have come again to the little summerhouse. My pencil is still lost
and I forgot to bring another so I must write in ink once more. I
wonder if someone has been here and moved things. But who would
think to? Who knows that an old chaise longue was once stored
here and then forgotten, abandoned in the topmost room? No one
has seen me bring over some of my books, and a couple of small
pictures filched from the walls of my rooms. I am so careful when I
come.*

*And I felt I must come or I would scream at the servants to leave
me be. It was Ivy today. I came upon her because it was so icy in the
yellow parlour that I missed my wrap and went upstairs to fetch it.
It is bitterly cold here in the valley, the sky iron grey — weather that
has always made me despondent, but so much more so in this
sequestered place.*

*When I got to my rooms, I thought I could hear some noises
within and presumed it was Edith. In fact I discovered Ivy who, of*

course, had no business to be there at that hour. I caught her at my dressing-table, rooting around in one of the small drawers. My brushes and combs had been moved and, no doubt, tested. I asked her what she was doing but she only stammered something unintelligible and went off in tears.

I rang for Edith, when I know it should have been Mrs Thornbury, now that she is housekeeper, Mrs Drummond having left, but I couldn't bear it somehow, not today. Edith believes the whole thing to be nothing more ominous than a housemaid having developed some sort of fascination with me; that she simply wished to touch my things. It is true that she seems harmless enough: a village girl who is not yet fifteen and whose great-aunt worked for the Stantons at the old manor for years.

Even so, I can't help but wonder if Edward has asked her to watch me. I confided as much to Edith and she gave me a peculiar look before she could stop herself. She does not know my husband as I do, though. And yet . . . I look at it again with a more dispassionate eye and see nothing but a village child playing at being a lady between blacking grates and sweeping ashes.

Perhaps I have simply grown delusional from being so closeted away: kept in because Edward believes it too cold or too wet or too icy for me to walk freely when I must conceive another child and have already taken so long to do so. I think it a fine irony that it is this perpetual quiet and inactivity that will send me mad rather than some hidden defect in my mind.

If I was to tell Edward my fears about Ivy today – and, thank the Lord, I cannot because he is away in London – he would start talking about rest cures again. Truly, I can think of nothing worse. I was right not to bring Mrs Thornbury's attention to it – she would have taken Edward aside on his return and told him in hushed tones, her face all concern when, really, she would have been thrilling

*with her prized gossip, hardly able to wait to go downstairs and tell
the other servants, shaking her head for poor Sir Edward, whose
wife causes him so much worry. 'Such a shame,' she would have
said, 'and her not even able to give him a son as compensation.'*

*I must try to be calm. My courses did not come yesterday and that
is why I am so unsettled by this trifling thing. I cannot feel the low
ache that usually signals them and it makes me hope . . . Could it
be? I have counted the days and, if it is true that I am with child,
then it will be safe to tell Edward at Christmas. What a gift that
would be for him. I would be left alone then, untouchable once more,
and my little girl too. My father was not like Edward — he loved me
for my own sake. With Edward it is as if the simple adoration he
wants to feel for our daughter is thwarted by her lack of a brother,
making her an object of resentment instead.*

I was tired after my walk up to Stanwick so I must have
dozed a little then. The next thing I was aware of was the
soughing of the wind in the trees outside, a rhythmic
sound that should have sent me back to sleep but instead
– in that strange little summerhouse, a room so redolent
of someone else – made me more alert. The light had
faded while I'd slept. The afternoon had gone and if I
didn't go back to the manor soon I would have to make the
walk in the dark again. Besides, I was hungry and, as Mrs
Jelphs so often reminded me, I needed to eat for the baby.

I stood for a minute at the window that faced west, out
across the overgrown meadow that lay on the other side
of Fiery Lane, and saw that the light was retreating fast
from the valley floor, as though it wanted to turn its back
on the place. As I carefully descended the twisting stone
steps, my eyes on my feet in the gloom, I hummed a song

my father had liked and which I associated with him going out to the shed at the bottom of our narrow strip of lawn. I would hear his low voice through my open bedroom window, curling up through the balmy air of a summer evening, like the fragrant pipe tobacco he sometimes smoked. There would be a dog barking a few gardens down and my mother would have the wireless on. That world didn't just seem far away to me there, alone in the depths of Fiercombe's valley, it felt like a scene from another life. Still, the familiar tune was a comfort as I stepped back inside that creaking old hulk of a house. It remained empty; I could feel it.

I ate standing up in the kitchen, two clumsily sawed slices of bread spread with jam. I didn't want it and each mouthful, soft and cloying, sticking to my teeth, threatened to come up as soon as I'd forced it down my throat. But I knew I should have it so I chewed doggedly on, sipping water from the tap to help it down.

At the very edge of my hearing a high-pitched whine started up – barely discernible but unmistakably there once I'd registered it. I wished it would stop before it gave me a headache but it kept on, setting my teeth on edge. The sweetness of the jam had gone from my mouth and it now tasted coldly of metal. I was pushing my finger around inside it to see if I'd bitten my tongue and drawn blood when I heard some other sound, beyond the whine. I gripped the knife I still held in my other hand and turned off the tap. As a final drip of water fell, it came again. A whisking, swishing sound that made my heart stammer in my chest and the baby – a beat later – kick so hard on my full bladder so that I couldn't help but let go, feeling the warmth soak through my underwear and turn cold on my inner thighs.

I stood for a time, my head still but my eyes darting back and forth, scanning for movement. Even as I waited, it seemed to get darker outside. I knew with total certainty in that moment that I was the only living thing there, not just in the house, which I'd already sensed, but in the whole valley. Ruck was not in the barn tidying his tools for the day and Mrs Jelphs was not tending her flowers in the last of the light.

A whole minute passed but I could hear nothing. All the while, waiting for it to come again, my brain was dismantling each element of the sound, then putting it back together to make something recognizable. I thought I knew it then: the movement of skirts against the panels, the swish of heavy fabric brushing wood. Even as I thought it, I dismissed it. It's just the dark, I told myself. The dark has always played tricks on you.

In an appearance of bravery I didn't feel, I put the knife silently on the breadboard and crept out into the hall. A faint, sickly glimmer of light showed at the end, where the passageway opened out into the high entrance hall. It faded as I made my way towards it, and by the time I had got there, there was nothing to see.

At a soft creak my head snapped round towards the front door. Through the gaps around the old, warped wood, I could see a narrow slice of the western sky, which was carrying off the last of the day's sun. In the dark hall, it seemed to lick around the gaps, like flames. I didn't want to be there any longer, however irrational I knew I was being. I hurried upstairs, gripping my belly, to what I hoped would be the sanctuary of my room and belongings.

I sat on the bed for a long time, my senses jangling, my breathing rapid and shallow. For the sake of the baby I tried to calm down but deliberately slowing my breathing made me feel as though I was suffocating. As unattractive as I had found the notion before, I now knelt up to loosen the bed curtains from their threadbare moorings. There were no moths this time and I was grateful for that. Soon I was enclosed on all sides by the dense brocade, my heartbeat audible in the confined space.

I lay back, tucking myself under the blankets, and immediately began to sweat but that seemed a small price to pay for feeling a bit safer. Finally, I fell into a fitful sleep.

In it, I dreamt I woke on hearing a rustle followed by a silvery tinkle of laughter. The damp bedclothes I'd wrapped myself in felt icy against my skin, a watery shroud. I pulled them off me, ready to get up if I needed to, and watched my stomach – poking up through the soaked white cotton of my nightdress – ripple and jump as the baby roiled around, much larger than he was in reality.

Outside I looked up to see that the last of the light had finally slunk away, quickly and craftily, so that I was abandoned in the complete darkness. That was when some movement caught my eye: a glimpse of paleness that gradually took shape.

I saw her hair first, a white shimmer that took shape around a little face whose features sharpened as I watched. Where there had been nothing, there was now a figure in the corner of my room, her outline not quite finished and her feet lost beneath the floorboards, leaving just the tops of her buttoned boots visible. In the dream, I scrambled to sit up, and when I looked again she was much closer, just behind the bedpost. She stared at me levelly but with no expression, her eyes shining like mercury and quite empty. One of her small hands stole around the post and something about it, the little fingers gripping the oak, made me rear back, certain she was about to heave herself on to the bed, feeling innately that she wanted to be close to me.

As I recoiled she seemed to fade slightly, her edges fizzling, the strange glow she emanated diminishing. Something approaching an emotion passed across her features then, but what it was I couldn't tell until I felt a wave of clammy hopelessness wash through me. It was such an awful feeling, so far beyond the limits of mere sadness and melancholy, that for a moment it swept away my fear. I watched her retreat and move off around the room, her little head bent so that her bright cap of silky hair swung forward to cloak everything but the tip of her snub nose.

I believe she moved right through the closed door but it's difficult to say for sure: by the time she reached it she had almost faded to nothing, her features dissolving as I watched into a shapeless aura of cold light. As the last of her went, now no more than a breath in winter air, I felt the sadness disperse and leave me, as though I'd been dragged ashore and wrung dry of it.

I understood I was dreaming then and woke myself up with a horrible start, desperate to escape the most powerful dream I had ever experienced. I still have the memory of that feeling the little girl left me with; unlike the pain of childbirth it refuses to be forgotten.

I thought of going outside and up the bluebell paths to take refuge with Mr Morton. But any frisson I had felt spark in the air of my dream had gone and I was oddly calm. I switched on the lamp and reached under the pillow for my diary. Instead my hand closed around the little velveteen hare I had forgotten about. The words I'd read in Elizabeth's diary entered my head unbidden: 'I believe it's a daughter' and then 'our little girl will turn one next week'.

Once again I must have fallen asleep sitting up. I woke stiff and muddled until the dream flooded back in its entirety. It felt quite unlike the usual sort of dream, where holes in a strange narrative expand before the whole thing falls to ash even as you try to play it again, dry paper held over a flame. I knew I wouldn't go back to sleep, though it was barely dawn, the light, when I pulled back the curtain, a pearlescent grey, with only the slightest blush colouring the eastern sky. The valley still slumbered on.

I went downstairs and hurried along to the kitchen, remembering the accident I'd had and hoping that no one had yet returned. They had not and thankfully everything was just as I'd left it. I mopped the floor twice and put the breadboard and knife back in their places. All the while I hummed as I had the previous evening, deliberately clattering about so I could attribute any noise to myself. I knew I had worked myself up over nothing more than a creaky old house and a ghostly dream but both were still fresh in my mind and I was unable to loosen the tension inside me.

When the kitchen was tidy, I went to the small parlour and played patience for an interminable couple of hours, using a pack of cards Mrs Jelphs had dug out the previous week. Questions wormed their way into my thoughts even as I shuffled and arranged the cards in neat columns. Why had I dreamt so vividly of a little girl? Who had the velveteen hare belonged to? And the question that had lurked in my mind since the very beginning: what had happened here? I thought about going back to the summerhouse and the diary in which the answers to those questions might lie, but I didn't feel quite up to it.

Finally I heard the kitchen door close and hurried back there. Nan jumped when she saw me framed in the doorway. 'Oh, Alice, you scared me! I didn't expect anyone to be up so early. Here, you're looking peaky.'

'I'm all right, Nan. I just had the strangest dream. I can't seem to shake the feeling I had in it.'

'I have those sometimes,' she said sympathetically. 'I had one once about the boy who lives next door but one. I don't even like him much but in this dream I felt as though I loved him. For two whole days I couldn't work out how I felt about him. It was the funniest thing.'

I laughed weakly and watched her go about her tasks in the kitchen, my mind soon wandering back to the vision of the little girl.

'You're brave spending the night here alone,' she said, as she filled the kettle, the water echoing noisily in the battered old thing. She turned. 'You did get the message, didn't you, about Mrs Jelphs's bad back?'

'No. I didn't know where she was. Is she all right?'

'I'll strangle that Will Kimber when I see him. He was supposed to run down here and tell you. Mrs Jelphs put her back out and had to stay. Ruck stayed on for some supper there, and then apparently he went for a pint in the pub. He never normally gets the chance. Were you scared?'

I managed a smile. 'Not really. It was just the dream that unsettled me. I'm glad it's morning, though.'

As Nan grinned at me before turning to put the kettle on the range, I pictured again the little girl – surely Elizabeth's little girl as my sleeping mind had imagined her. The hold of the dream should have been diminishing but it had left me more intrigued than ever, the threads of Fiercombe's past binding me tighter and tighter.

It was quiet for a time after that, the weeks accumulating gradually, sliding past in an easy routine of work, meals and sleep. Blessedly dreamless sleep. I thought of going to the summerhouse more than a few times but I was busy helping Mrs Jelphs in the day. By evening I was generally exhausted.

Three times I heaved myself up to the village: once with Mrs Jelphs to meet the midwife, a broad, kind-faced country woman who, to my profound relief, had nothing about her of the abortionist, and twice to visit Mr Morton. On those last occasions, I returned to the manor to find Mrs Jelphs sitting pensively in her usual armchair, as though she had been waiting anxiously for my return. I knew she disapproved of me leaving the boundaries of Fiercombe but she never said anything, except for the odd oblique comment about taking good care of myself 'for the child's sake'. I made sure I took the gentler of the bluebell paths, as well as my time to climb it. I didn't know what else I could do to assuage her anxieties, short of never leaving the manor.

Besides, without those pathetic little bids for freedom, I knew the sense I occasionally had of being a prisoner in the valley would begin to overwhelm me. I can't really describe the exact sensation, only the certainty I felt that I had to get out every now and then, as though I was a sea creature obliged to swim to the surface to breathe. I suppose it was a feeling of oppression; one that was only heightened by a watchful Mrs Jelphs and the pregnancy chemicals that were flooding through me.

At Mr Morton's – I didn't yet feel I could call him Hugh, though he repeatedly asked me to – I felt closest to my old self. It didn't occur to me that he might mind my spontaneous visits. He told me about his family, especially his wife, who had died fifteen years earlier. She was buried in Stanwick's churchyard, in a tranquil corner overlooking the next valley. They had never had children and I thought it was a shame: he would have made a wonderful father.

He always asked me how I was getting on at Fiercombe but it was nice to be away so I steered the conversation towards other subjects. I was no less intrigued by Elizabeth and the valley's past but I had become possessive of them. The diary was my secret and it had offered me a different, more intimate view of Elizabeth that Hugh Morton couldn't possibly have known about. As much as I liked him, I didn't want to share it and was scared I would if we talked as we had that first afternoon. He went along with this reticence until the end of my third afternoon call, when he caught me gently by my arm at the door.

'Are you all right down there, Alice?' he said. 'You seem rather distracted.'

Of course I didn't answer his question quite truthfully. Good old British reserve had me smiling gamely and teasing him for worrying unnecessarily about me. What else could I say? That I sensed a kind of melancholy down there in that secret and secretive valley? That I thought sometimes it might be infectious? I couldn't bear to have him look at me as Mrs Jelphs did occasionally, almost as if I was doomed.

His concern must have undone something in me, though, because once I had begun my descent into the twilit valley, the trees pressing in and closing over me, I felt my eyes fill with tears. It didn't strike me that I was simply lonely. Dora still hadn't written and I was starting to think she never would. Tom hadn't reappeared either and I thought I would never see him again.

Meanwhile the baby – apparently oblivious to any turmoil or anxiety I might be feeling – seemed to thrive and, just as the mercury continued to climb steadily, he seemed to grow a little more each day until I showed in all my clothes, even those that had been quite loose when I arrived. I worked diligently at every task Mrs Jelphs gave me, from patching old curtains to rinsing hundreds of pieces of china, and I knew she was pleased with me. I opened my diary one night and was shocked to realize it was August.

Something peculiar happens when you set out to recount the past. You begin with the obvious, the easy to explain – in my case, my burgeoning pregnancy and the incredible weather. I have never known a summer like it, not before or since. Each morning I drew back the curtains and searched the sky above the escarpment for a single cloud or the welcome veil of haze. It was always in vain. The sky by late morning had always deepened to a hard china blue that arched pitilessly over us until the relief of sunset.

Those are the sort of simple observations my diary

records in such English style: my health and the weather. But as I write now, smaller details trickle in and demand to be recorded. It is as though the memory is a series of interconnecting rooms, each leading to the next, less-visited one, if only you'll try the door.

I remember Tom's eventual return to Fiercombe in exquisite detail. As much detail as I can still remember of the day James and I spent in Kensington Gardens – and the pivotal evening that followed when I had let a man take me to bed for the first time. Usually, when you find yourself attracted to someone, everything else obligingly slides out of focus. Not on those two occasions. While one took place in the city and the other in the countryside, they have been filed away in the same compartment of my memory. Not because the events were similar, but because the sensation was the same: the knowledge that I was about to jump, despite being unsure whether I should.

I'd woken late that day after another series of vivid, unsettling dreams, some of them about Elizabeth – or, rather, the shadowy figure with the long, dark hair I always imagined – and others about James. In one, a person I knew was James had the face of Tom.

I had planned to walk up the bluebell path to see Mr Morton again but Nan said that he had gone to stay with his niece in Cornwall for a week. I felt irrationally jealous of this woman I had never met, imagining an ordered life in a pretty cottage high on the cliffs, the rhythmic crash of the sea far below and supper laid out on a table that had been brought into the garden for the summer. She wouldn't be carrying a child its father didn't know about.

After Nan had gone for the day and knowing that Mrs Jelphs had said she would be spending the morning in Painswick, I decided that I could risk having a quick breakfast in my nightdress before giving in to the now-ever-present pull of the diary in the summerhouse. I splashed my face with water, grimaced at my hair, which was tangled and wavy after another sweltering night, and wandered down the stairs, clasping the hot, swollen skin of my growing stomach.

In the tranquillity of the empty kitchen, my mind swung from James to Elizabeth and back again. The baby was restless that morning, his every twist inside me a reminder of the mistake I had made. Not that it had felt like a mistake: at the time it had felt like love.

It was the only time I had ever seen him at the week-end. His wife was safely away at her sister's in Norfolk and I had told my mother I was going shopping, then dancing with Dora. I hadn't been convinced he would turn up, but when I came out of the Underground at Piccadilly Circus into the overcast afternoon he was waiting for me.

At first we weren't sure what to do or where to go, our routine taken away from us by all the hours that stretched ahead, unplanned. In the end, he hailed a cab and we went west to Hyde Park. He had the idea of taking a lit-tle rowing boat out on to the Serpentine but it was much too early in the year. Instead, as a sort of joke for getting the season wrong, he bought me an ice in the cafe after-wards. When dusk fell, rosy light diffused by tissue-paper cloud high above the city, we crossed the Long Water to sit on a bench in a deserted corner of Kensington Gardens. I was lightheaded from having eaten nothing but the ice all day. I must have been cold too, though I didn't notice.

'Your eyes change all the time,' he said, when we had been sitting there quietly for a while.

'My eyes? What do you mean?'

'The colour. They're grey when the weather is and bluer when the sun's out. Now they look almost violet.'

I felt my cheeks turn pink with pleasure from the compliment.

'You know I've fallen in love with you,' he said softly.

I nervously laid my hand on top of his and he lifted it to his lips to kiss the back. 'I don't think I do know. At least, I can't quite believe it yet.'

'You'll have to when we marry,' he said.

I was lost in this memory – utterly transported to London – when the sound of an engine brought me out of my reverie. It had to be Tom, back at last, and the coincidence of his arrival just as I had been indulging in wistful reminiscence about James seemed significant. I was so slow in surfacing fully from the past that I only remembered I was still in my nightdress as the kitchen door opened. It was too late to bolt.

'Hello,' I said sheepishly.

He looked up from putting his bag down, his face clearing as he registered my presence. 'Oh, Alice, it's you.'

Taking in my nightdress, he straightened and regarded me wryly. 'Not getting dressed today, then? I suppose it is rather too hot to bother.'

I was wondering how I could get up from the table and leave the room without exposing more of myself when he laughed. 'Don't fear, I'll leave you in peace. I need to change and then I thought of going for a walk. Do you want to join me? I don't insist on a change of clothes, though you may be more comfortable.'

'Well, I usually go for walks in my nightdress but perhaps I will go and find some shoes, at least,' I managed to say.

He laughed again. 'Jolly good. I'll see you back here in ten minutes.'

Once we were more suitably dressed, we left the manor and made our way past the churchyard and out on to Fiery Lane. He was heading for the overgrown meadow I had seen from the window of the little summerhouse. There was a stile to get into it, virtually out of sight behind a hedge of overgrown hawthorn, that I would never have noticed. He helped me over and squeezed my hand lightly before letting it drop. I hadn't held a man's hand since James.

'I didn't think you'd be up to a three-mile route march to the other end of the valley,' he said, and I was touched that he'd been so considerate. 'Besides, it's a lovely spot. I used to come here often, albeit with a bow and arrow or a catapult in those days. I always forget how lovely it is.'

It was a meadow as depicted in a children's story: small and square and sloping, apparently ignored by the grown-up world. Strongholds of wildflowers had sprung up among the long grasses and in the bottom corner stood a venerable old oak, the far reaches of its lowest branches growing close to the ground. I could just make out the tinkling chimes of moving water where a spring surfaced nearby.

I looked back at Tom but he was deep in thought, his face younger but also sadder than I had yet seen it. I knew without asking that he was thinking about his brother – they had obviously come here together as boys. He hadn't told me how Henry had died but, for no good reason, I had assumed it had happened elsewhere – a deadly outbreak of influenza in the school san or something along those lines. Now I wondered.

As with Mrs Jelphs and what had happened to Elizabeth, I couldn't possibly ask. Tom would tell me if he wanted to.

We wandered slowly around the perimeter until we reached the spring, where it was cooler. The sunshine was remarkable for England – not only in its intensity but its unbroken appearance over so many days – but we'd grown accustomed to it, as people seem to grow accustomed to almost anything. Like those used to much more arid climes, we naturally sought out the shade, and found a pretty place to sit beneath the oak, resting against one of the low-slung branches.

We didn't say anything for a time, as if we had known each other much longer than we had and were comfortable thinking our own thoughts in each other's presence. When he did speak, I was on the verge of dozing.

'It's this place I should think of when my father tells me I must come back to sort out some estate matter or other. I would probably feel better about it then.'

I blinked and pushed myself up a little. 'Don't you like it here? You're so lucky to have all this.'

It was the wrong thing to say and his face darkened. 'Oh, yes, aren't I the lucky one?'

'I just mean that it's so lovely. There is so much freedom in all this space. At home, I can reach the end of the garden in twenty paces. That's all I meant.'

'Freedom has nothing to do with how many acres you own,' he said.

'Perhaps they help a little, though,' I said, as gently as I could. It was awful that he had lost his brother but surely he understood how privileged he was.

He didn't say anything, instead wrenching up daisies and dandelions and picking them apart. I laid my hand over his to stop him, marvelling at my own bravery as I did so. Perhaps it was because I could see the boy in him there, in the little meadow he had spent his childhood playing in.

'It's not easy, you know,' he said eventually, the words pushed out as though they were painful to say.

'What's not easy?' He hadn't moved his hand.

'Living with the past.' His voice was so low that I bent towards him to catch the words.

'What happened to Henry, you mean?'

He pulled his hand away and leant back against the branch, his gaze towards the house, its chimneys just visible above the yews and holly.

'This isn't the way it was supposed to be,' he said. 'Henry should be here, running this place, and he would have been, too – not just when he was made to come but all year round. He loved the manor. He loved the whole valley. His children would have been running about in here now, just like he and I did. I don't belong here any more – I belong in my club in London, halfway down a bottle of Scotch.'

I cast around for something to say that wouldn't make it worse. What I really wanted to do was to brush away the lock of his hair that kept falling into his eyes, but I didn't dare. I thought about what had happened to Henry and how hard it must have been for the little brother who had never been prepared to take on the estate when he grew up. He had lost his brother and gained a huge amount of responsibility in one stroke.

'Your father was the younger brother, wasn't he?' I asked tentatively.

He glanced at me and frowned. 'Yes. Why do you ask?'

'He wasn't supposed to inherit Fiercombe either, was he? His older brother Edward was.'

'What are you saying? That first-born sons are doomed in the valley?' His tone was dismissive.

'No, of course not. I just meant that your father never expected to inherit, but when he did, he managed it admirably. He saved the manor house, didn't he?'

Tom looked at me for a long moment and I realized how sorry I'd be if we were to fall out.

'I never thought of it like that,' he said eventually.

After that we were quite easy with each other, talking of this and that – silly things from our childhood and school, all the things new acquaintances talk of, rather than the serious subjects we had begun with.

On our way back to the house, I stopped abruptly, caught out by a twist of pain in my lower back. I sucked my breath through my teeth until it subsided and when I opened my eyes I found he was gently supporting me, one hand under my elbow and the other around my shoulders. 'Alice, what's wrong? Is it the child?'

'No, I'm all right. It was just a twinge in my back. He's getting bigger all the time – every day, it feels like – and I suppose it's taking its toll.'

'What was he like?' Tom said softly, as we started to walk again.

'Who?' I said, genuinely confused.

'Your husband.' He looked embarrassed. 'You don't have to say. If it's too hard for you.'

I hated lying but it would be even more dishonest to pretend I was too upset to say anything. 'His name was James.'

'How did you meet?'

'I met him in the office where I used to work. He was older than me.'

'You must have loved him a great deal.'

'Yes, I did,' I said simply.

We walked on in silence and I wondered whether Tom had noticed that I'd used the past tense. In truth, I couldn't tell any longer what my feelings for James were. Everything from that time was jumbled in my head. The clear recollection I'd had that morning in the kitchen was becoming a rarity, my previous existence in London retreating and blurring just as Fiercombe – past and now present, too – was coming to fill every corner of my thoughts.

'I'm going to carry on up to Stanwick,' said Tom, when we reached the kitchen garden. 'The White Rose will be open by the time I get there if I walk slowly enough. They've a pretty garden there. Have you been?'

I shook my head. 'Who would take me? Besides, I'm not sure Mrs Jelphs would approve of my visiting a pub in my condition.'

'Oh, never mind about her. She has a good heart, Mrs J, but she always was the most dreadful worrier. It was the same when Henry and I were boys. I'll take you up there some time. We can go in my MG to save your legs. Later this week, perhaps – once I've gone through the accounts in Stroud. I'll need another visit by then.'

I smiled and turned to go but he called after me. 'I'm

sorry if I was a bit of a misery earlier. In the meadow.' He stopped. 'I blame myself, you see.'

I turned to face him properly but he avoided my eye, looking off into the distance instead.

'For Henry, you mean? But how can you have been to blame?'

'I'm at it again,' he said, with a weak grin. 'Too morbid for words. Forget I said anything.'

'But –'

'Really, Alice. It's family business and I shouldn't be talking about it to a stranger. I'm not usually so loose-tongued, I can tell you.'

I flushed, hurt that he'd referred to me as a stranger.

'I didn't mean to be rude. It's just that we Stantons don't discuss the past. That way lies plenty of grief, you see. It should be on the coat of arms as our motto. Anyway, I'm off. Perhaps I'll see you later. I don't think I'll be here for dinner but you never know.'

He began to walk away, raising a hand without looking back.

I stayed there for a few minutes, breathing in the fragrant air of the kitchen garden. What had he meant about being to blame? Whatever it was, I thought my earlier instinct had been correct and that Henry had died here, in the valley. I looked around at the steep wooded inclines that had kept Fiercombe's inhabitants cut off from everything else for centuries and wondered where the answers lay. I had a momentary fancy that if I listened hard enough I would find out, but there was nothing to be heard except the whispering of the beech leaves.

Elizabeth

She thought it must be late when she woke the morning after the party but it had only just gone seven. The servants would be up, of course, but her part of the house was silent. Only a dozen or so guests had been invited to stay, those who were elderly and who had travelled furthest. With luck they would leave after breakfast, which she had asked Mrs Wentworth to make mountains of, in the hope that they wouldn't think of staying for lunch.

She levered herself carefully out of bed, holding her back as she stood. On her chair was the dress from the previous night, which she picked up. It felt cold and insubstantial as it rippled through her fingers like water. She brought it to her face and breathed it in, remembering the music, the voices and the moon. It smelt of fresh air.

She dressed comfortably and pulled an old shawl around her shoulders. Outside, under the lemon-coloured sky, Midsummer's Day was not yet warm. She left the house the way she had entered it the previous night, through the morning room's double doors. Despite her body's need for her to take her time it was not long before she was halfway across the Great Mead, the distinctive chimneystacks of the old manor coming into view.

The baby was as still as she – or perhaps he, after all – had been the day before. 'Come on, little one,' she murmured. 'I didn't mean that you should never move again.' And then, as if her entreaty had been heard, she felt something. Not a kick, nothing so definite, something closer to a flutter or a vibration inside her. She put a hand to her stomach and smiled. The embers of happiness she had felt glowing within her as she lay back in the Bath chair the previous evening might not, after all, have been entirely extinguished by the conversation with Edward that had followed. She still felt lighter for having been honest with him and she also remembered his words about her perfect health and realized that he was right. She did feel well. She looked well, too. That much had been obvious in the glances she had received all night.

The new day's sun cast a transformative light on matters. There was no reason to think that she would lose this baby if it was a boy, just as there was no reason to believe she would succumb to the blackness if it turned out to be a sister for Isabel. She had also survived the party she had secretly dreaded for weeks. She felt buoyant for it being in the past, with no disgrace of her making attached to it. She would find Edward after her walk and ask him to forget she had said anything. No, there was probably no need. Edward would be glad never to mention any of it again.

As she got closer to the old manor, she saw that the holly bushes that crowded the little summerhouse were full of birds. They trilled and bickered, flying in and out of the dense foliage in search of a better perch. She watched them for a time, and became aware that she was not thinking about anything in particular. Even the memory of Edward's threat to demolish the manor house couldn't blow her off course that morning. Though their exchange the previous evening had been painful, it had also been disarmingly honest, reminding her of a time when she had been able to ask for his help and he, for his part, had not abused that power. Besides, even Edward, great advocate of progress and rationality, must see that he couldn't destroy such a magical, tranquil place.

At the bank of the stream, she lowered herself so that her feet dangled over the side. After taking off her shoes and stockings, she reached out a swollen toe and dipped it in the water. It was so cold that it burnt like fire. Slowly, slowly, she tried again and this time it was just bearable. Soon she was able to rest the soles of both feet on the very surface of the water. When a breeze blew and lifted the water higher she sucked in her breath from the chill of it. It was blissful.

After a time, she dried them off and got carefully to her feet. Cutting past the summerhouse she had begun to use as a secret refuge just before Isabel was born, she reached Creephedge Lane, where she crossed the stream. She couldn't possibly get through the old squeeze-belly stile to reach the manor from that direction so she went round the long way, up to the chapel, past the graveyard and into the passage of rhododendrons. Edward had given the gardeners instructions not to tend the plants here, so far from Stanton House, but someone surely had done so. What should have been weed-choked and ragged was glorious, the scarlet and magenta flowers ablaze.

As if the thought had conjured him up, she saw a figure in the lane ahead of her and stopped short. Sensing her presence, he turned and she saw it was Joe Ruck. He was only young, surely no older than Edith, and he was holding a pair of long-handled secateurs. Further on she spotted a ladder. Her slight annoyance at being disturbed was tempered by the fact that he had made it so beautiful there.

He stared at her for a long moment, then touched his cap. She went towards him, the distance between them slightly too great to speak comfortably.

'Good morning, Ruck,' she said brightly, in the tone she found she always adopted with the younger staff. 'You're up and at your work early today.'

His already ruddy cheeks darkened. 'I'm not supposed to be 'ere,' he said, his accent almost impenetrable. 'The maister said to leave the manor gardens be.'

'I certainly won't be telling him,' she said, in a rush. 'You've made it lovely again.'

He scuffed at the ground with his heavy boots, painfully awkward.

The fragrance of the flowers was heady, the air seemingly thicker where they grew, and for a moment she wondered if she would faint. The thought of how awful that would be for poor Ruck kept her upright. 'Well, I shall be on my way and out of yours,' she said, as briskly as she could. She remembered. 'And thank you, Ruck, for your help with the Bath chair.'

She smiled and he lowered his eyes again.

When she looked back, he had resumed his inspection of his work. When the moment was right, she would suggest to Edward that he was made under-gardener, charged with bringing the manor's garden back to life. This morning she felt as though she could persuade Edward to do anything. She patted their unborn son. For the first time, she began to see him as Edward did, both as a boy and as the glue that would bind all of them together. She had done the right thing; in speaking her fears aloud, her tongue loosened by the champagne, she had dispelled their power.

She decided not to go inside the manor. The morning was too spectacular to miss. Besides, it was Isabel who loved to go exploring inside the old house. There was a game that they played there, invented by her daughter. Elizabeth was cast as the old witch, a terrifying harridan whose main pleasure in life was to chase the naughty Isabel, berating her as she did so. All Isabel's games were intricate, with many details that had to be attended to in the correct order. When the baby came Elizabeth vowed she would bring both of her children here. Soon enough Isabel would forget about the game she had played the previous day, the looming threat of the magician too.

When the two of them played the witch game, they always began among the yews, Elizabeth trying to catch Isabel, first at walking pace and then a little faster, until they were both running, out of breath, Isabel screaming in mingled delight and horror. Elizabeth understood that a little bit of her daughter believed the old witch was really there, lumbering after her between the overgrown flower-beds.

In the house they always had to visit the nursery, as it had once been. Isabel led the way through the dim passages to the small, narrow staircase that she preferred to take because it frightened her a little. It frightened Elizabeth, too, who had never liked the dark as a child and who had always wished for a sister to share her room.

The nursery, like many of the manor's rooms, was not quite empty of furniture. The appearance of unforeseen desertion – along with the warped oak floors and panelling – gave the place an air of the *Mary Celeste*. An old rocking horse gathered dust below the window, its white mane matted with it and, despite Elizabeth's warnings of dirt and sneezing fits, Isabel always insisted on petting it. She didn't ride it, as she did the new one bought for her in London by Edward, but handled it with the utmost care, whispering into its ear and pushing it gently so that it creaked back and forth.

Elizabeth took one of the bluebell paths back towards the house. She ambled slowly along, in no hurry to get back, wishing that Isabel was with her. She wouldn't tell her she had been to the manor: Isabel would only be hurt she hadn't been taken along. She wished her little girl had a thicker skin; that she could know to her marrow that she was loved and be content. Of course, it was partly Elizabeth's fault that she couldn't.

Just then she heard a cry behind her, triumphant but also close to tears. She turned and there was Isabel – the girl of her thoughts made flesh and blood – careering down the path from where Elizabeth had just come, her flaxen hair streaming out behind her.

'Mama!' she forced out, short of breath, as she rushed into her mother's legs. Her grip was surprisingly strong.

'Darling, where did you appear from? I was just thinking of you and then there you were. Something like it happened with Ruck, too. It's an enchanted morning.' She thought of the flutter in her belly and put her hand to it again.

'Why didn't you take me with you?' Isabel's face was mottled red and there were streaks of grass and mud on her dress, which Elizabeth saw was yesterday's. She must have dressed herself and slipped out past the careless nursery-maid.

'I didn't want to wake you. It was early when I left.' She stroked Isabel's tangled hair, unbrushed and loose.

'I wouldn't have minded what time it was,' said Isabel, reproachfully, but already she was forgetting the slight, and her fear that she would never find her mother, whose hand she now took. 'Where did you go? Did you go to the nursery?'

'I would never go there without you. I put my feet in the stream and then saw the rhododendrons – the pink and purple flowers near the churchyard – said hello to Ruck and –'

'I saw Ruck too, after I had gone to look in the chapel for you. I ran past him,' said Isabel. 'We went just the same way as each other, except that I was so far behind. I thought I might have got it wrong, that you hadn't gone out at all.'

'But you didn't get it wrong and you caught me in the end, didn't you? Let's walk together for the last part. We'll have a private breakfast before the guests come down, just you and I.'

Soon they were passing the lake that had been dug at the same time as the house was built. No one had thought to turn the fountain on yet. They walked around its perimeter, past the little folly that hid the pump, and Elizabeth glimpsed Stanton House. She waited for her breath to shorten, for her thoughts to start crowding in on top of each other, but nothing happened. This morning it was just a house. The mild, early sun lent it a benign air, the granite blocks sparkling, or so she imagined. A clock somewhere chimed eight. She had only been gone an hour.

Isabel led her to the front door and skittered across the tiles in the hallway.

'I will tell Mrs Wentworth that we want our breakfast now, just you and I,' she called.

Elizabeth put her finger to her lips. 'Don't wake our guests,' she whispered.

'You are back.' Edward had appeared at the door to the library. His tone was curt. It occurred to her that he was furious. But there was something else, too, in his white, set expression. She identified the emotion because she had seen the same look on Isabel's face, the daughter who so resembled him: he was frightened too. He wouldn't look at her; instead he gazed intently at Isabel. Elizabeth felt the old anxieties begin to twist inside her. The little girl hesitated, glancing from one parent to the other.

'Darling, go and tell Mrs Wentworth we are back from our walk,' Elizabeth said, her voice surprisingly calm to her own ears. 'See if she can find you a little something to eat.'

'But, Mama, you said that we would have a private breakfast . . .'

'I did, and so we shall. You tell her what you would like and I will have that too. Tell her we will have it in ten minutes. Something simple.'

Isabel skipped away, satisfied.

When she had disappeared down the back stairs,

Edward held the door open for Elizabeth and they went into the library. With the door shut it was unnervingly quiet in there, the books and Turkey rugs absorbing any sounds.

'Where have you been?'

'Edward, what is wrong? You are terribly pale.'

'Please answer my question.'

'I went for a walk.'

'And Isabel?'

'She must have left the house a little later. She didn't catch up with me until I was nearly back at the house. I will speak to her about going about on her own. Is that why you are angry?'

'You didn't take her?'

Elizabeth's mind raced to make sense of it. He must be angry because she had been going to the old house. 'Edward, I know the manor is not to your taste. But it's so pretty there. You should see the flowers. I saw Ruck and –'

'What are you talking about?' he interrupted. 'What has Ruck to do with any of this?'

She spread her hands, palms turned up to the ceiling. 'What has happened to make you so agitated? Is it what we talked of last night? Because if it is then I wanted to tell you that –'

He cut across her words. 'When the nursery-maid woke this morning, a little late, she found Isabel's bed empty. Next to the bed she found these.'

He held out something she didn't recognize for a moment. Her blank look seemed to infuriate him and he threw them so they landed at her feet: her shoes from last night, dyed to match her dress. They were a little water-stained at the toes and there was mud on one heel.

'I must have left them in there.'

'When?' he shouted.

She flinched. 'Last night. I went in to kiss Isabel good-night before I went to my own rooms. I had taken them off because my feet were swollen and they were rubbing. I must have forgotten them. Edward, please tell me what this is about.'

He shook his head. 'You really don't remember, do you? I've always thought that was a pretence of yours, to salve your own guilt.' He pushed out something like a laugh.

She felt herself go still and cold. She was standing in a bar of sunshine, the lines of the window's struts settling in a geometric pattern across her body, but she couldn't feel it.

'What do you mean?' she said, but the words came out as a hoarse whisper. *This is it*, a voice in her head told her. *This is the thing you haven't been able to remember.* With her husband's eyes on her, she racked her brain yet again for the elusive answer, the wisp of memory that she had tried to draw out and examine so many times. Her legs were trembling so much that she sat down in the nearest chair. He had looked at her as though – no, it couldn't be. And yet it was. Edward had looked at her as though she was a danger, not just to herself but to their daughter.

Alice

After our time in the meadow, I didn't see Tom for a couple of days. Though he'd said he probably wouldn't be at the manor for dinner, I was still disappointed when he wasn't, his motor-car gone again. It wasn't just that he was good company, or that his story intrigued me – though it did and, since our last conversation, nearly as much as Elizabeth's – it was more than that: I had found a friend.

It was foolish, of course. I was the ordinary girl who had been sent to the countryside for her health, and to have her child; he was the heir to an (albeit rather reduced) estate. In many ways, I was more Nan's equal but, as much as I liked her, I felt that Tom – despite the differences in our backgrounds – was a kindred spirit. I wondered if he thought the same about me and blushed at the very idea. Apart from anything else, I must have looked a sight in my nightdress when he saw me in the kitchen, my hair a tangle and my feet bare.

In truth, Tom was much of the reason that I was waking happier on each glorious morning than I had for months. One day, I decided to arrange my hair in a different way: pinning it up at the sides but leaving the back loose and long over my shoulders. My reflection in the mirror was an odd mixture. There were still smudges of tiredness under my eyes but my skin was a shade or two more golden than when I'd arrived and my hair seemed not only thicker and longer but wavier. There were even some roses in my cheeks. The baby inside me was moving only slightly and even my back was less stiff.

After spending the morning unpicking a tangle of old curtain tassels and cords, I wandered outside to check the thermometer.

'You're looking very well today, Alice,' remarked Mrs Jelphs, who was in the kitchen garden snipping chives in her meticulous way. 'A little tired, perhaps, but otherwise blooming. The baby must be thriving.'

She led me back inside and pointed out a cold chicken sandwich under a net to keep the flies off it. My mind went to the sleepwalking Henry eating chicken in the larder a quarter of a century earlier.

'Now, eat that before you do anything else. It's important for the baby that you eat.'

She said this to me at least once a day. I smiled my thanks and obediently drank a tall glass of milk, before helping myself to the sandwich. I tidied everything away, then decided to go to the summerhouse. I hadn't been for a while but I had been thinking about it all morning. It was almost as if it called to me some days, like a siren's song echoes across the sea to a lonely sailor.

'Thank you for the sandwich. I won't be too long,' I called to Mrs Jelphs, as I left the kitchen garden.

She put down her gardening scissors and peered at me anxiously, her gloved hand shielding her eyes against the sun. 'Where are you off to? It's really too warm to be walking.'

Rather cruelly, I pretended I hadn't heard and was just fastening the garden gate behind me when a shadow moved across my hand. 'You should heed her, you know.'

I recognized the dry creak of Ruck's voice and spun round to face him. He was an inch too close and I moved back until I was pressed against the gate. 'Oh, Ruck, I didn't see you there.'

'If you mus' go, don't go far. You should pay mind to heat like this.' He cleared his throat and I could hear the phlegm at the back of it. 'I reckon they was right about the midday sun.'

I looked questioningly at him. 'Mad dogs and English-women, is it now?' he said, and smiled grimly.

I could feel his eyes on me as I walked towards the passage of rhododendrons, conscious of my awkward gait now the child inside me was so much bigger. After that slightly unnerving confrontation, I had accidentally taken the longer route to the summerhouse and it was delicious to step inside its cool stone walls when I got there. It grew warmer as I climbed the stairs to the top but some of the room was still in shade.

I didn't know what to expect but the diary was exactly where I'd left it last. Evidently Mrs Jelphs, if indeed she came at all – an assumption that I was beginning to doubt – didn't come very often. Perhaps she felt it would be trespassing to go up there and I felt a prick of conscience at the thought.

Sitting down with a deep sigh of relief, I realized that Elizabeth would have done the same thing when she was big with her daughter.

Just as I took up the little volume again the summer-house door, which I'd left ajar so any whisper of breeze might find its way in, slammed shut with a crash that reverberated up through the walls to shake the floorboards. In my surprise I dropped the diary, which glanced off the footstool and fell open to the floor, pages splaying and spilling as the old spine broke.

Heart thudding, I scooped up half a dozen of the loose sheets but there were hardly any dates written in the faint pencil to help me. I would never be able to work out what order they had been written in. It was then it struck me that she might have used a pencil so she could erase her most private thoughts if she felt she needed to. Indeed, when I looked more closely, whole pages were half blank. When I held one up to the window to see better, I could just make out the indentations her pencil had made.

I collected all the sheets that had tumbled out and put them in a neat pile. I was furious with myself for being so careless but started to read anyway, drawn in as I always was. Perhaps I would be able to work out the order they had been written in as I went along.

The first entries were mostly concerned with social engagements and dresses. There were also frequent remarks about the servants, and Elizabeth's anxiety at running such a large household was evident – just as it had been in the entry about Ivy, the maid who had been going through the contents of her mistress's dressing-table.

In one entry, a parlour-maid had been caught stealing and Elizabeth had not known what the correct punishment should be. The housekeeper had said that the maid should be dismissed, without her wages or a character, and Elizabeth, though she thought it too harsh, had not had the nerve to say so, to her shame.

I read on until I reached a passage that recalled the portrait Hugh Morton had told me about. Perhaps it was not such a very great coincidence but it felt strange enough to me – hearing about it again but this time from its subject.

A photographer arrived today. Edward had come upon him last week in one of the villages, Painswick or Uley, I forget which, and engaged him to spend a day here. He has been commissioned not only to take our portraits but to capture the beauty of the estate's situation: in particular my husband's beloved Stanton House. Edward even said I might have a picture of the old manor taken, since the ones that were taken during my first year here have been misplaced, when my parents were alive and we had a picnic there, in the shade of the yews. I know this is a sop to me, for Edward knows very well how I dislike having my photograph taken. There is something intrusive and prurient about it that makes my flesh crawl. It surprises me that Edward will allow a strange man to study his wife so closely, fix his gaze upon her through that box, and bid her turn this way and that and to stay still for just another minute. Perhaps he will next buy his own camera and learn the skill of photography himself. Then I should be subjected to endless sittings, no doubt: no better than a prize animal at a county show.

I once read – Heaven knows where – that the Indians of America believe that the act of being photographed steals for ever a part of their soul. It is the sort of primitive belief that would be mocked by men of science (such as Edward fancies himself to be) but I think I understand that distrust well enough. To me, it is precisely an act of possessiveness. Edward would think it a fanciful notion, of course, but I find it resonates.

He has always watched me. I didn't attach much significance to it until we were well into the first year of our marriage. I suppose I noticed it – how could I not, such was its intensity? – but I didn't see anything amiss in it until later. Once I had, it was like an overlooked figure in the background of a gloomy painting that one day leaps out at you, never to hide again. Even now, when we have been married for nearly half a decade, he will not let me out of his sight for long when we are in a room full of people. Sometimes I think he wishes to control me as he does his staff or the workings of his estate; that he would like it if he could simply turn me off when he doesn't like what I have to say, like the fountain's pump. Last week we attended the Careys' ball at his insistence and I had sat down to rest in a quiet corner, just for a few moments. I could see him from where I was but he couldn't see me. His eyes were roving over the polished and dressed heads of the crowd before I could count to twenty.

There is a strange blend of emotion in the steely fire of those blue eyes of his. Love is certainly there, though perhaps I am mistaking it for desire. Sometimes I think it is all the same thing to a man when it comes to his wife, at least until she becomes nothing more than a sexless companion to him. Yet desire is not all I see in Edward's eyes: there is also frustration and contempt and even – for I don't think I imagine it – a little hate. Just a little.

I see it most when we are among other people, when we are forced together. If I am too quiet, he thinks I am rude. If I talk too much, I am craving attention, like the spoiled child he believes my indulgent parents made me. Never mind his own parents who, from what I have gleaned, saw fit to indulge his every whim and caprice. Perhaps that's another of our incompatibilities, understood too late: as children we grew so accustomed to being adored that we are incapable of adoring, each of us brimming with resentment that we go unappreciated, our lights hidden under the other's bushel.

I have just remembered something I haven't thought of in years.

An occasion when I enjoyed his gaze on me, when the thought of one day being alone with him made me feel faint. It was perhaps the second or third occasion we ever met, a sultry day at my uncle's house, a dozen of us gathered there for what reason I can't recall. Everyone was limp in the hot, windless air that lay heavy on us all. We sat in the garden, where tea had been laid out under the shade of the cedar, and where icing melted, sandwich paste congealed and vases of freshly cut flowers drooped disconsolately even as I watched them. Lifting my teacup to my lips was like moving it through treacle.

Edward sat down opposite me and was joined by an irascible old gentleman, whom my uncle perversely invited to everything, perhaps for his own amusement, and who immediately attempted to engage Edward in a discussion about a local boundary dispute. It was much too warm for such a dull subject and Edward was quite rude to the old man, virtually ignoring him and instead gazing at me.

I remember that I was wearing a white lawn dress with a high fluted neck and long sleeves that narrowed to tight cuffs, each fastened with a dozen covered buttons. I had regretted the choice as soon as I felt how warm the day was going to be and, once those blue eyes were on me, it was worse. I found myself growing unbearably hot. If I had been at home, I would have peeled off my stockings and rested my bare feet on the parched, brittle grass. But I was not. Even so, I decided I would have to remove my gloves and unbutton my sleeves or I would swoon.

I eased the first glove off as surreptitiously as I could but he watched me all the while, brushing away the hair that always fell into his eyes to see me the better, and making me wonder how I ever managed the task so easily. Finally they were off and I began to unfasten the cuff buttons of one sleeve, my fingers fumbling over them, one by one. It seemed to take hours. He continued to watch

me as I tried to eat a little, my cheeks aflame as I chewed and swal-
lowed, the perspiration prickling at my hairline.

Such a small thing, silly propriety aside. A man watches a
woman remove her gloves and unfasten the buttons of her sleeves.
But on such a day, in that fierce heat, the two of us quite cut off
from each other by those who surrounded us, my own mother and
father among them, I'm not sure I have ever felt so alive.

How is it that I had forgotten that until now?

I breathed out slowly, my cheeks hot: I had pictured
Edward as Tom while I read. I turned the page quickly
and let my eyes skim until another entry stopped my eye.
The handwriting was altered: larger and more childlike,
many of the letters printed. The pencil had been pressed
to the paper very hard.

When I came here before all was well. I was well. I knew she would
be a girl and I wrote it here and I was right. Not that he would
listen. 'He is my heir,' he would keep saying, though I knew he was
wrong. Then she came and he said it didn't matter and I believed
him then, a week ago. He hasn't said it again.

It is so very dark here tonight. The moon comes and goes so I
write half blind. I didn't dare fetch a lantern: one of the ser-
vants would have seen me. There is always one of them creeping
about, watching for me to do something I shouldn't, waiting for
me to be in a place I shouldn't be. I think I must have managed
before but now it is all so hard to remember. This child has
addled my brain, turned it to soup. Since her, I cannot think
straight.

Today I could not feed her. They brought her in but I felt my face
turn away. I feel as though black clouds are poised just above my

*head, heavy, pushing me down. I don't want to eat what they bring
me, all of it wet and over-salted, weak beef tea and tepid soups. It
makes me sick, though they said I must, for her. They did not say I
should eat for myself.*

*I was afraid when I crossed the Great Mead to come here. Out
in the middle of it, the moon went behind a cloud as it does again
now, leaving me in the oily blackness. I found I could hear everything out there, though, acutely and unlike I've ever heard anything
– the rustle and click of every creature in the earth under me and,
all around, the spun silk of spiders' webs tautening and humming. I looked for the green light of the glow-worms, friends in the
dark, but of course they have gone, just as summer has.*

*I thought I would feel safer here than I do in the house but it is
no good. It is myself I need to escape from and that is impossible.*

The tone was strange and melancholy. No, more than
that. Anxiety and dread seemed to leach out of every
word. It wasn't just the handwriting that was disordered:
her thoughts were too.

I didn't like to think it of Elizabeth, whom I now felt I
knew and was therefore protective of, but I wondered if
she had been . . . somewhat ill in her mind after her daughter's birth. I put my hand to my stomach. I had been
seduced by the idea of Elizabeth from my earliest days in
the valley but it had gone far beyond mere intrigue now.
There was a connection between us – a twisted rope of
silken threads stretching back through the years – and this
connection didn't exist only in my imagination. I knew it
because of the way Mrs Jelphs looked at me sometimes.
She recognized in me something she had once known in
Elizabeth. Then I wondered if the words I had just read

could somehow be infectious, bringing bad luck upon my own experience of having a baby.

I had heard of women who were no longer themselves in the immediate aftermath of a birth but I didn't think I had ever known any. An image of my mother came to the front of my mind then, and it was so vivid that it briefly swept away all thoughts of Elizabeth. I had always avoided questioning the difficulties my mother and I had always had in simply getting on. It had been so complicated with her – where it had never been with my father.

Sometimes I felt she disliked me; sometimes I could justify her behaviour as concern; other times she showed nothing more than indifference. None of this was new to me – indeed, it had been a source of fear and hurt through-out childhood, my skin apparently incapable of growing any thicker until I left school, when at last I became more able to put it into perspective. What struck me now, for the first time, was the way her mood had been dictated by what she called 'the curse'.

My mother regarded her monthly bleed as unhygienic and – perversely – unnatural. In contrast to some of the more sheltered girls I had gone to school with, who were blissfully (or so I thought) unaware of such things until they started their own monthlies, I had come to dread the onset of mine, so familiar was the sight of my whey-faced mother putting a steadying hand out to the sideboard or the table as a cramp gripped her.

Worse than that, though, were her outbursts in the week before she was due. She was sharp-tongued at the best of times, but my father and I learnt to avoid her then, when she was so spoiling for a fight that the least provocation would set her off, resulting in a bitter torrent of discontentment and regret at her life with us. When I was very young, my father had joked about us locking ourselves out of harm's way in his garden shed until her fury abated, but his voice always shook when he said it.

My own 'curse', when it did arrive, was nothing of the sort: not just irregular but light. I sometimes thought that was the result of such fervent wishing on my part never to get it at all. Later, I convinced myself it meant I would have trouble conceiving – one of the reasons alarm bells had gone off in my head so late when I did fall pregnant.

I had no idea if my mother's monthly anger and despondency could have been mirrored – and even amplified – by pregnancy or its aftermath. But it seemed to make sense to me there, in the silence of the summerhouse, the broken diary forgotten for the time being on my lap. Perhaps that had always been our trouble: I had made her ill when I was born and now I was for ever associated in her mind with a bleak chapter in her past. She had done her duty – I had always been fed, clothed and sent to school in a beautifully sewn uniform – but I wasn't sure she had ever really liked me.

At that bleak thought I began to cry, only stopping when I saw that the tears were soaking and rippling the pages of the diary. I sat there for a time, my mind not on Elizabeth for once, but my own past. Even though my mother had never been affectionate towards me I wished more than anything that she was with me so I could ask her if she had been brought low after my birth and if she could forgive me for it.

Eventually I forced myself to get up and put the diary back where I'd originally found it, tucked behind another book on the shelf. As soon as I stepped out into the sunshine my spirits lifted a little. Back at the kitchen garden, I saw that Mrs Jelphs had moved on to her beloved roses.

'Oh, good, you're back. I thought you'd be longer.' She turned to me properly and her face fell. 'Alice, dear. Whatever's wrong?'

My tears had dried but perhaps my eyes were red. I rubbed at them, then noticed I had pencil marks on my fingers. I must have looked like a grubby child after a tantrum and the thought made me smile sadly. 'I'm fine now, really. I just had a little cry over nothing.'

I thought she'd smile back and say something comforting and meaningless about pregnancy and its strong emotions, but she continued to stare until I had to look away.

'Has this happened before?' she said finally.

'The crying? No. To tell the truth, I just missed my mother for a moment.'

Her face cleared. 'Well, that's understandable. You're so far away from your family. You poor girl, I should have known. Listen, this may cheer you up: go and have a look in the small parlour. It completely slipped my mind before but Thomas left you something to look at, though I don't know why on earth he imagined you would be interested.'

He'd thought of me. Mrs Jelphs was right: I felt immediately more cheery. I put the diary entry and all thoughts of my mother firmly to the back of my mind.

It was on an occasional table next to the window-seat of the small parlour. A battered cardboard box with a lid

262

labelled in black ink by a spiky, rather messy hand: 'Thomas Stanton. Form I. Cranmer House'. And then, on one side, in capital letters and ringed falteringly in red ink, touchingly polite and earnest even as it was bossy, 'TOP SECRET. PLEASE KEEP OUT!'

I lifted the lid, ignoring the warning directed at some long-grown-up schoolboys. It looked a peculiar collection at first glance. On top were cigarette cards, some rudimentary watercolours that had crinkled as they dried, and a brittle oak leaf. As I lifted the box on to my lap, a loose, solitary marble rolled around at the bottom. They could have been the keepsakes of any boy of eleven or twelve.

I sifted through ink-splotched Latin prep and letters from home – Lady Stanton was not a very expressive mother by the sound of it – and wondered what he had meant me to find. Then I picked up a dog-eared copy of the *Boy's Own Paper* and a sheaf of photographs fell out, all different sizes, some mounted in cardboard frames. I moved everything to the sofa where it was more comfortable.

The first photograph was of the manor, taken from the edge of the formal garden. To me it looked exactly as it did now, except that the yew trees were taller. I calculated that if Tom had taken it when he was twelve or so, the image had been captured less than twenty years ago, a speck of time for a house like Fiercombe. I turned it over. The writing wasn't his. The F of Fiercombe was larger than the rest and written with a flourish – I would have guessed it was a woman's hand even if I hadn't known it was Elizabeth's. 'Fiercombe Manor, 1893. The day of the picnic', it read. I traced the words with my finger. I had put her to the back of my mind but here she was again.

The next pictures were newer and smaller, with no sense of composition. Presumably Tom had taken these during a winter in the valley – perhaps the camera had been a Christmas present. The place was transformed, the beech trees stripped of their leaves and heavy snow blanketing the Great Mead. In childish writing, each letter still carefully formed, he'd diligently labelled each one, 'Fiercome, 1911', the missing *b* squashed in later, in lighter ink.

There was one of a lopsided snowman, half a dozen of the manor from different angles – I noticed the yews were much smaller than in the previous picture – and one, taken by someone else, of two boys in mittens and woolly hats with their arms round each other. While Henry's features were different from Tom's – the older boy's nose a shade thinner, his eyes darker and slightly more close-set – the pair were unmistakably brothers. 'Me and idiotic Tommy playing in the snow' was scrawled on the back in a new hand. The boy who had written it had lived only a few more years.

The next set, distinguished by being slightly larger, had been taken in summer. All of them featured a lake. I had some dim recollection of Mrs Jelphs mentioning one when I had first come to Fiercombe but I had forgotten it until now. There was no sign of it on the estate that I had noticed. Could it have dried up? I could see the steep valley walls in the background of some of the pictures so it couldn't have been somewhere else entirely.

There was what seemed to be a small folly or eye-catcher in four of the pictures. Its oval window was dark in the bright sunlight that seemed to bleach those parts of each image that weren't in the shade. In two of these the lake was still and empty but in the third, taken from precisely the same angle, a boy now swam. His head was as sleek as a seal's, his arms and face pale in contrast to the dark water. It was the older of the two brothers, perhaps three or four years on. I turned it over and saw I was right. 'The first swim of the summer, 1914', the caption read. Just before war was declared, I thought. I realized the other, more personal, significance a beat later: it must have been taken just before Henry's death.

The next picture showed Tom in the foreground, pulling a face, each of his summer freckles a distinct point in his barely tanned face. Henry had written on the back of this one, too: 'Tommy larking about'. I lifted the next one. It showed Henry with another boy, their arms round each other's shoulders as Tom and Henry's had been in the snowy shots, the stranger drawing back his free arm in a fist as though he was about to punch Henry. From Henry's expression, this was all a huge joke. The other boy was leaner than Henry, with sinewy muscles under his brown skin. 'Me and Crawford' was scrawled on the back. A schoolboy friend who had come to stay in the holidays, I presumed.

The last picture had evidently been taken by Crawford and was of the two brothers, their damp heads touching. I thought of an hourglass, the sands running freely, gathering relentlessly in a pile at the bottom; time running out for Henry. I turned back to the first photograph, the one where Elizabeth had written on the back. Had time also been running short for her, when she'd written that strange entry in her diary?

I looked through the photographs again, then leant against the cushions to rest my back, trying to piece everything together. I suppose I must have drifted into a light doze, dreaming of Elizabeth as I so often did, but also of the boys and the dark expanse of the lake, because the roar of an engine brought me back into my own time. I sat up and yawned, the photographs scattering around me. The sound grew louder until I heard the crunch of loose stones and the squeal of brakes. I tipped everything back into the box and shoved the lid on.

Before I left the room, I checked my reflection in the mirror over the mantel, and ran my fingers through my hair. My eyes were the green of the beech leaves in the valley when the sun shone through them. I remembered how James had said they changed with my surroundings but thinking of him no longer hurt as it once had. My mind was too busy with other things.

Tom was in his shirtsleeves, the collar and two buttons below it open. There were still shadows under his eyes but they were probably always there. He raised his hand when he saw me, and slammed the door of his little motor-car with a bang. To my dismay, my heart had begun to beat harder at the sight of him.

It clearly wasn't quite the proper thing to do, but Mrs Jelphs decided that Tom and I would have supper together. I felt like a Victorian governess when she told me in a conspiratorial murmur: too high up the pecking order to eat with the servants and too low to eat with the family. Like a chaperone from the same era, she left us alone for no more than five minutes at a time but claimed not to be hungry herself. Afterwards, Tom suggested that the three of us repair to the small parlour for an after-dinner drink. He fetched Mrs Jelphs and me a sherry each and poured a generous slug of whisky for himself.

'How far did you get with that lot?' he said to me, when we were settled, nodding towards the cardboard box.

'Not that far, I'm afraid. I fell asleep. Thank you for leaving it out for me, though.'

I glanced at Mrs Jelphs but he didn't seem to mind her being there and hearing what was said.

'Did you find any of the photographs?'

He reached over to where I had left the box on the floor and pulled it towards him.

'Yes. You and your brother in the snow and then, later, by the lake.'

Mrs Jelphs looked up from her embroidery.

'It's all right, Mrs J. Alice knows about Henry. We've shared a few secrets, haven't we?' He turned to me and held my gaze until I had to look down.

'Has Mrs Jelphs told you the official Fiercombe ghost story, Alice?'

'There are no ghosts at Fiercombe,' Mrs Jelphs said tartly.

Tom raised his eyebrows at me.

We sat quietly for a while, me sipping my drink and Tom pouring himself another, until a small snore escaped from Mrs Jelphs: she'd nodded off.

'Was it Margaret of Anjou you meant before?' I murmured.

'Ah, so I can't be the one to tell you. Shame, I would've enjoyed that. I suppose you've been talking to Nan. She loves that story. If this house was grand and important enough to be written up in all the guidebooks, that would be the obligatory ghost story. It's got all the ingredients: a real historical figure, the tragedy of a dead son –' He stopped.

'I'm glad I didn't know about her on my first night here,' I said quickly, hoping to make him smile again. He looked up questioningly.

'Oh, I was woken up by some noise or other in the hall. But when I peeped out into the corridor . . .'

He leant forward, his face mock-serious. 'She was there, disappearing around the corner, her furs dragging behind her.'

I laughed. 'No, but I did think I smelt flowers. Of course I imagined it but it makes a nice adjunct to the story, doesn't it?'

'It does indeed. I had a bit of a vivid imagination myself as a boy.' He smiled ruefully. 'I used to scare myself by imagining I could be transported somewhere outside in the dark, far from the house. I used to think that if I pictured a place vividly enough I might accidentally wish myself there. Daft, really.'

'Where was the worst place you imagined ending up?'

'Oh, that's easy,' he said. 'The ruined glasshouse over in the eastern part of the valley. I had visions of myself trying to escape it and cutting my feet to shreds. I took to wearing slippers in bed for a while after I thought up that charming little scene. Have you been to that part of the estate?'

'Mrs Jelphs warned me never to but I stumbled upon it. It was the day I met you, in fact. Do you remember I told you about the strange wind?'

'I didn't know you'd been there,' he said. 'It's a lonely place.'

'I bumped into Ruck, actually. I don't think he was too pleased to see me.'

'That sounds about right. He was forever telling me off when I was young. He'd appear out of nowhere and give me this look.'

'I've had a few of those. Anyway, after he went off I had a bit more of a poke around. I'd asked him to show me where the foundations of Stanton House were, you see. Mrs Jelphs had told me a bit about it.'

'You did well there,' he said, nodding towards the sleeping housekeeper. 'She usually plays her cards very close to her chest. As for me, I know very little about the place – the usual Stanton reserve, you know.'

I dropped my voice again after the reminder of Mrs Jelphs's presence. 'I couldn't believe it when I heard about it. A great big mansion like that, disappeared as though it never was. When I was there, I was thinking about the people who'd lived there but were now gone.' I rolled my eyes. 'No wonder I scared myself.'

We lapsed into silence, though it was another of the easy silences I seemed to be able to have with him. I was thinking back to the photograph I'd seen of the house: black-and-white, taken some way off and very slightly blurred.

'Now, all this talk of my boyhood fears is absolutely secret, of course,' Tom said, after a time, 'but I used to imagine all sorts of murderers and ghouls visiting me in the night when I was growing up here. I never let on to my brother, of course. I had that blue room at the back of the house. Do you know it?'

I shook my head.

'It's always been a nursery of sorts, and when Henry

and I were small we shared it. It's quite a big room so we played in there, had our meals there as well. When Henry was ten he decided he was far too old and important to sleep with his annoying little brother so he moved into a room of his own.'

I remembered the key that had swung on its hook and the neat, handwritten label above it.

'I'd never liked being in there on my own much, even in the day, so you can imagine how I felt about sleeping alone. I didn't own up to it, but I don't remember many easy nights. I used to put the light on and read when it got too bad in the dark. I dragged the hearth rug over to the door to block off the worst of the light from leaking out and giving me away.'

I smiled, feeling the alcohol from the sherry seep pleasantly through me. 'I write lists when I can't sleep.'

He looked up from the box and grinned. 'Lists of what?'

'Anything. Counties, names, kings and queens, that sort of thing. But I used to read a lot as a child too. I'm quite the expert on Victorian children's fiction.'

'I'm afraid *Boy's Own* was more my level. Tales of derring-do, chaps swimming the Channel, disgraced boys regretting rustication after cheating, what to do if you caught a newt, that sort of thing. I never was much of a scholar.'

He glanced at the sleeping Mrs Jelphs. 'Did you enjoy leafing through the photographs? I thought they might amuse you.' He held up a sheaf of them. I couldn't read his expression.

'You must miss him,' I said carefully. 'Henry, I mean.'

'Of course. It would be unnatural not to.' His face had clouded.

'It must be hard for other reasons too,' I said.

'What do you mean?'

The words came out sharply and, knowing it, he bent to rummage in the box again.

'I don't know, suddenly being the heir – what we talked of in the meadow,' I said. 'But also being the only one. That in itself can be difficult sometimes, I know. You were the younger brother and I'm sure that was hard in its own way, with a brother like Henry, but then it was just you, and that turned out to be hard in a different way . . .'

My voice tailed off as his gaze met mine. He sighed. 'Yes, you're right. Women always are about these things. How is it you know?' He attempted a smile but it looked strained. Throwing the photographs and papers back into the box with studied carelessness, he leant back in his seat. 'It wasn't just that, though, that was hard to live with afterwards.'

'What do you mean?'

'Oh, Alice, you really wouldn't want to know the truth.' His mouth was almost a sneer. 'Besides, I'm not yet drunk enough to tell you all my secrets.'

After an embarrassed silence, during which he said nothing but stared miserably into the bottom of his glass, which was empty again, I got awkwardly to my feet, cross that I minded looking fat and ungainly. 'It's past my bed-time, I think,' I said. 'Thanks again for looking out the box for me. I loved seeing all the old photographs. Perhaps I'll see you tomorrow, after I've done my jobs for Mrs Jelphs.'

My cheeks burnt at the last: some compulsion to punish myself – and perhaps him too – by reminding him that I wasn't a house guest and he wasn't my host, let alone anything else.

As I got to the door, he stood and came towards me, one hand messing up his hair again. 'Listen, take no notice of me. I've no manners.'

Standing up made the room seem too small for the three of us and I cringed to think of Mrs Jelphs waking. He came closer still and reached out to gently tug a lock of my hair. It felt as intimate as if he'd kissed me.

I turned and half ran to the staircase. It was almost totally dark in the wood-panelled passage that led to my room but I barely noticed.

Once, I had held James in my mind almost constantly. Now he was growing fainter and fainter, even as his child inside me grew larger. Sitting up in bed, half listening for the sound of Tom coming upstairs to bed, I tried to make myself picture James instead. He now seemed the less dangerous of the two. For a second he flashed through my mind with perfect clarity: his dark hair gleaming with brilliantine and as beautifully neat as ever – he went to a barber's close to his office every other week to keep it like that. When I realized I was comparing it to Tom's too-long hair, the fair tips of which always got into his eyes, I cursed myself. Be careful, a voice said in my head, as clearly as if someone had spoken aloud.

What was I thinking? The only reason I had even met Tom was the terrible trouble my tender heart had got me into at home. I had fallen for a married man and that was foolhardy enough. To find myself drawn to another unsuitable man when I was expecting a child was dangerously stupid. Apart from anything else, this was a man who would one day inherit an estate and a title. I shook my head as if the movement could dislodge his presence there. I needed to forget any romantic notions I was beginning to harbour about Thomas Stanton.

My efforts to do just that meant I got a great deal done for Mrs Jelphs over the next few days. She had me darning and re-hemming old tablecloths and sheets, the latter worn so soft and fine that you could see through the cotton in places. I found that with her patient instruction – and without my mother looking for my next clumsy mistake – I wasn't nearly so bad at sewing as I'd always thought. It wasn't long before my mending became almost invisible. Meanwhile, the baby continued as still as the sultry weather. There was the occasional rolling sensation that I knew was him moving about but no kicking. The heat had apparently put him in a torpor, and that was perfectly understandable.

Though I listened for it, there was hardly any birdsong, the droning of bees drunk on nectar only a rare ripple in the treacly air. Everything in the valley seemed to have ground to a halt. Everything but the grass and the flowers and the trees, all of which seemed to grow more luxuriously verdant by the day. Even the old yew columns exuded a new vitality, one that was almost menacing. At night I imagined the new shoots worrying away at the mortar of the manor's golden stone, bony green fingers trying to find their way inside.

Tom was conspicuous by his absence again. He seemed to have an endless supply of friends and distant relatives he had to visit in the vicinity, not to mention the estate manager in Stroud he'd told me about. Sometimes I wondered if he was staying away because of me, the unsuitable young widow from London, but I told myself this was my own self-importance. After all, he was precisely the type to have dozens of friends and to spread himself thinly among them. I had an inkling that he thought he would be found wanting if he let anyone observe him too closely and for too long. In that sense, coupled with the oddly intense evening we'd spent, he probably was avoiding my company.

One afternoon, when my eyes had begun to ache from the close work of the darning, I caught sight of Tom's old box from school, which had been pushed under the table by the window. I was surprised that Mrs Jelphs hadn't spirited it away but it was pretty well hidden under there. I thought back to what he had said about the nursery, how it had been his room as a boy. That in turn reminded me of the key to it, and how I had wanted to reach out and pluck it off its hook.

It was quiet in the house and the kitchen was empty when I reached it. The door to the kitchen garden was open and I presumed Mrs Jelphs was outside somewhere. In the hidden cupboard the nursery key was hanging up just as it had been. Before anyone could see me, I took it down and slipped it into my pocket. Upstairs in my room I leant out of the window. In the garden below, sitting on an iron bench in the shade, I could see Mrs Jelphs. She was asleep, her chin resting on her chest and her pruning shears forgotten next to her.

I knew the nursery lay in a part of the upper floor I hadn't had reason to explore until now. The first door I tried was locked. I twisted the key both ways but it wouldn't turn. The next one unlocked on to a linen cupboard, stacked high with sheets and pillowcases, like those

I'd been darning. A narrow passageway took me up a few stairs to another couple of doors. The first room was small, a box room with nothing in it but a couple of old tea chests. At the second I paused. I could tell it took up a corner of the manor so it was unlikely to be some kind of storage room. Along with the box room, it was also fairly isolated from the rest of the upper floor.

When I first turned the key it wouldn't budge and I was surprised; I had been so sure it was the one. I twisted it back and forth until I thought I would snap the old metal and then, just as I was about to give up, I felt the mechanism relent. As soon as I saw the faded blue wallpaper dotted with red sailing boats above wood panelling I knew I'd been right. It looked to me as if nothing much had changed since Tom had spent the nights of his childhood there. The hearthrug he'd mentioned dragging over to block out his illicit reading light was by the fireplace. A single bed against the wall opposite was made up neatly, as though in readiness for the end of another boarding-school term. The only sign that the room was not in use was the dust that veiled the window and gathered in grey thickets under the bed.

There was a broad window-seat, like the one in the small parlour, but the only pieces of furniture, apart from the bed, were an ancient rocking horse and a chest of drawers that stood in one corner. It was painted cream and above it was a shelf of children's books. I went over and saw some old favourites from my own childhood. On top of the chest was a trio of battered tin soldiers in red jackets. Propped up between them was a miniature Union flag, now faded and frayed. An old-fashioned gramophone took up most of the chest's surface, the flower of its brass horn dull with dust.

I turned the wooden winding crank and dropped the needle on to the record that had been left on the turntable, who knew when? I hadn't expected it to work but the shellac disc began to spin quickly, though unevenly, undulating because it had warped. The sound of static came through after a couple of seconds. It wasn't a constant hiss but rose and died away again in volume, like the sea advancing and retreating on a beach. I put my ear to the horn and thought I heard distant voices or music that then fell away.

I let it continue to spin and looked about me again. The trio of tin soldiers were still facing the room in a dutiful line but the tiny Union flag had dropped to the floor. I knelt down awkwardly to pick it up and stood up too quickly. Dizzy, I sat down heavily on the nearby window-seat. The lumpy old cushion shifted under me and for a horrible second I thought I would fall to the floor.

When I got up to look I saw that, unlike the one down-stairs, this seat was not solid but hinged. I pulled the cushion off and lifted the lid. One set of the old brass hinges had broken completely, the metal corroded away.

Inside was a neatly folded blanket. Nothing remarkable: just a scratchy old tartan blanket of navy and dark green. It was low down in the cavity of the seat so I didn't expect much else to be in there but when I idly pulled at a corner, I discovered it was wrapped around something heavy.

Just then, the noise from the gramophone changed. The static now seemed to be punctuated by something more solidly rhythmic, the room filling with the sound. It was like a noise heard under water, amplified yet muffled. I knew what it reminded me of then: a heartbeat. Perhaps it was the enclosed space, the stale air and my dizziness, but I thought I could hear other patterns forming, the rushing and ebbing of sounds I couldn't make out.

I slammed the window-seat shut and ran to pull the needle off the turntable, the noise swerving and booming as I did so. My breathing was ragged in the abruptly silent room, my own heart rushing and stumbling. I looked around but there was nothing to see, everything in its place, although I found my mind going to the story of the toys that come to life when the children aren't looking.

The turntable came to a reluctant, creaking standstill as I rushed out, fumbling with the key to lock the door behind me, the iron stubborn again at first. As I hurried down the main staircase, I could feel the alchemist's eyes upon me and thought that if I turned I would see an amused smirk on his face at my foolish, overwrought imagination.

Mrs Jelphs came upon me as I was hanging the key back on its hook. I slammed the little door in the panelling in surprise, probably seeming more like a naughty child than a grown woman about to become a mother.

'My dear, you have lost all your colour again,' she said. 'What have you been doing?'

'Nothing,' I said stupidly.

'Were you looking for a particular key?'

Her tone was so patient, her words so deliberate, that I felt my nerves unfurl a little.

'Well, yes, I was. I mean, I've already found it. I thought I would have a look in the old nursery. Tom said I might. I hope you don't mind. I will go back to my sewing. It was just that my eyes were aching and I thought . . .'

I couldn't read her expression; it was so dim in the passage. 'Did you find anything of interest there?' she said eventually, her voice flat. 'There are some things that you can use when the baby comes but they're not kept there.'

'Apart from the dust, it doesn't look like it's changed since Tom was a boy,' I said, worried that she would turn cold on me, as she sometimes did.

'Ah, well. I suppose it ought to be cleared. I can't think now why it hasn't been.' She was battling to keep her voice light but it was obvious there was something she wasn't telling me.

'Tom said it's always been a nursery,' I said carefully.

Her eyes were the darkest I'd seen them. 'Yes, that's true. Even when there hasn't been a child to fill it.' With some effort, she smiled. 'I will make us some tea,' she said, her tone now carefully cheerful. 'There's nothing a cup of tea won't solve.'

I wanted so much to ask her about Elizabeth – Henry too – but again felt I couldn't, not just because I had learnt to tread lightly when it came to the past, or because I was English and therefore unaccustomed to prying, but because I understood that it was human instinct to guard one's secrets. After all, I did it with my own.

I hoped Tom would be back in time for dinner that night but, as darkness cloaked the valley floor and I still hadn't heard the throaty sound of his motor-car's engine, I gave up. I already missed his presence when he was away more than I would ever have admitted to any-one.

I wouldn't let Mrs Jelphs prepare me a hot supper that night and instead got myself a cold plate of this and that: some ham and cheese, a pickle, a tomato and some of Nan's homemade bread, which was only just going hard around the edges.

'It's quiet without him here, don't you find?' said Mrs Jelphs. She'd come in while I was eating alone at the table in the kitchen.

'I hadn't really thought about it,' I lied. Everything was easier when Tom was there. Even the sense that my every movement was noted by Mrs Jelphs – and Ruck – seemed to dissipate in his presence.

'I've always found it hard when any of the family go away,' she said. 'They always do and it never gets any easier.'

I didn't know what to say to that. It's probably why I asked what I did next: some silly worry that the conver-sation shouldn't falter or turn towards me and my health. 'Was there ever a little girl here?'

I hadn't known I was going to say it until I did, and I felt my cheeks redden. The food I'd just eaten churned in my stomach. I looked down at my plate and poked at the crumbs with the tip of my finger.

'Why do you ask?' she said, after a pause too long for it to be natural.

To anyone else she would have seemed composed, apparently only politely interested. I took a breath. 'I don't mean recently.'

She picked up my empty plate and took it to the sink.

Clearly she didn't want me to see her face. 'As I told you before, there have been people here for centuries, I'm sure some little girls among them.'

'It's just that I found a toy.'

I didn't know what else to say. I could hardly blurt out that I had been to the summerhouse to read Elizabeth's diary. 'It's like new,' I hurried on, 'but you can tell it's very old.'

'It probably belonged to Tom or Henry when they were children. They would leave things in all sorts of unlikely places.'

'I think it's older than that.'

She looked at me quizzically. 'What is it? A doll?'

'A hare, a little velveteen hare. I thought it was a rabbit at first, but the hind legs are too long.'

Perhaps it was my imagination or a trick of the light – it was gloomy in the kitchen by afternoon – but I thought I saw Mrs Jelphs's shoulders stiffen.

'How strange. It could have belonged to the boys, of course. It doesn't sound like a little girl's plaything. Did you find it in the nursery?' I thought her voice quavered slightly.

'I found it in the chapel in the first week I was here. I meant to tell you but never got round to it. I thought then that it probably belonged to one of the children from the village but no one goes in there except you.'

She remained with her back to me, running the cloth over the plate, which was already clean. 'I've never seen anything like that,' she said tonelessly, as she turned and dried her hands with unnecessary deliberation. 'Now, I know it's not even eight o'clock but my back is so stiff today that I'll turn in early tonight. Do you mind?'

'Of course not. Mine is giving me some trouble too.'

I received a ghost of a smile. 'At least yours is for a good reason.'

I heard her footsteps retreat down the corridor, getting fainter until they disappeared, and leaving me alone with the sounds of the kitchen. The old water pipes whined and grumbled and the tap dripped until I got up and used a tea towel to tighten it.

I knew I wouldn't be able to resist going back to the nursery to discover what was wrapped up in the old blanket but Mrs Jelphs's peculiar reaction to my clumsy questioning made me return that night. I waited twenty minutes, or what I estimated was twenty minutes, then went to the cupboard and took down the nursery key again. Not wanting to wake Mrs Jelphs, I tiptoed towards the stairs, wincing at every protest from the oak boards. That was when I remembered the old staircase, the one Mrs Jelphs had warned me not to use. It was much further away from her room; I would be far less likely to disturb her if I went that way.

I went back along towards the small parlour to find it. I had never looked for it before. There was a lamp burning in the room I had spent so many hours in and it looked welcoming as I passed it. I thought for a moment of just going inside, closing the door and forgetting all about the past for a night but I couldn't seem to let it rest. At the end of the corridor was a dog-leg. Around that was another short corridor. I was gripping the key to the nursery so tightly that the metal almost cut into my flesh.

Finally I came to the foot of the old stairs, which were even narrower and darker than Mrs Jelphs had described.

The very dregs of the day's light filtered through a tall mullioned window to land in distorted diamond patterns at my feet. Its weak glow made the staircase a total void of blackness by comparison.

I climbed the stairs slowly, placing my feet firmly so I didn't stumble. They began to curve round towards the top, the treads narrowing on the inside of the bend. The baby had been kicking but now stopped moving, as if he knew I had to concentrate and be careful. There was no carpet runner and however softly I trod my steps were clearly audible. My heart thudded harder as it got darker. The top of the stairs brought me out beyond the nursery door, where it would have been obscured by another quirky angle of the manor's architecture. I listened, my hand on my belly, but there wasn't a sound. My feet took me towards the door.

The key turned easily this time. I inched open the door and crept inside. There was little light but I could make out the bulk of the gramophone on the chest of drawers and the outline of the bed. The light switch, when I tried it, didn't work, but there was a little illumination from the window so I went over and wiped off one of the panes with my arm. Off towards the west, the sky was draped in wisps of orange and pink chiffon, the navy blue of night slowly spreading to blot them out.

I lifted the window-seat slowly. The blanket was reduced to a dark lump in the gloom so I brought it out to unwrap it where there was a little more light. Inside the folds was a framed picture and I knew in the instant before I turned it over that it would be the sole photograph that properly showed the likeness of Elizabeth Stanton.

It was a sepia photograph, the edges fading into the pale background so that she looked like an oval cameo. She was certainly beautiful, though not in the way I had come to recognize beauty in the stars I'd seen at the pictures. Her face was soft, her huge eyes vulnerable. Perhaps that was why Edward Stanton had not wanted to hang it: not because there was nothing of her in it but because there was too much. Without the disguise of laughter and the concealment of social talk, she seemed fragile and ethereal – even with her mass of dark lustrous hair to anchor her.

There were three more items at the very bottom of the cavity. The first was a tiny blanket, wrapped in paper. It was the opposite of the heavy blanket the picture had been wrapped in. This was gossamer light and cloud soft. Edged in satin it would once have been as white as snow. A blanket for a new baby.

I reached for the second item, obscured by the shadows at the very bottom of the recess. It was black and covered with a thick layer of dust. As I got hold of it, long-dried earth fell off in brittle chunks more grey than brown. I turned it over. A child's buttoned boot. Not polished and supple like those I'd seen in my dream but like a relic from a museum, wrecked by time, the sole curling and cracked, the leather stiff. It fitted comfortably in my hand but I dropped it back into its hiding place as if it burnt me. Leaving the last item, a sliver of cardboard no more than six inches across, I put everything back as quickly as I could and closed the lid. My heart was thudding painfully and, more than anything, I wanted to be shut safely in the small parlour, the warm lamplight pooling on my skin.

I hurried to the top of the old staircase but then, as I took the bend that would lead to the straight flight of steps and the ground floor, I looked for the window's misshapen diamonds to guide me from below. They seemed wrong in that moment, though I can't rightly say why, and their distortion made me dizzy. I lost my footing and cried out in fright, desperately flinging out my hand to grab at the banister. I couldn't get hold of it, though, my fingertips only skimming the wood. I seemed to stay suspended for a long second before I tumbled down. My last thought was for the baby inside me as I wrenched myself around in the air so that I would fall backwards.

When I came to I was at the bottom of the stairs on my back. I was still alone; my fall obviously hadn't woken Mrs Jelphs and that was of little surprise – the corridor back towards the part of the house where her bedroom was took so many twists and turns that the sound wouldn't have carried very far.

It was a miracle I hadn't broken my neck. I carefully pulled myself up to a sitting position, grimacing in pain at the bruises and wrenches in my muscles. I put my hand to my stomach but there was no movement. I didn't feel any acute pain there that I could distinguish from everything else, but I did think I could detect the beginnings of a low-slung ache. When I got to my feet, gripping the banister with all my might this time, and the weight of the baby shifted down, I felt a slight dragging sensation that I hadn't experienced for nearly eight months.

I felt too shocked to cry, or go and face Mrs Jelphs. Misery descended to cloak my sore shoulders, like a damp blanket. Very, very slowly I pulled myself up the main staircase and limped to the lavatory near my room. I expected to see blood but there was none. I knew it would come, though. In my room, I peeled my clothes off and left them in a pile, crawling into bed and pulling the dusty old curtains around me to shut out the approaching day.

I slept until noon and woke feeling numb. I checked my underwear for blood again but there was still nothing. When I got downstairs, Nan had been and gone but she or Mrs Jelphs had left me some slices of ham and a potato salad under a cloth. I felt sick at the thought of eating anything. The door to the kitchen garden stood open and I could smell the herbs and flowers as clearly as if I was out there among them. Dimly, I registered that the delphiniums were out for a second bloom; those that grew closest to the door seemed to be peeping in at me on their long stems, their intensely blue flowers a perfect match for the sky above. In a daze, I went out to look at them properly. I hadn't been there long when Mrs Jelphs came through the gate, the basket on her arm indicating that she'd been up to Stanwick. I tried to make my face look normal.

'Ah, there you are,' she said, her eyes searching mine. 'I knocked when you didn't come down for breakfast but there was no answer. I went in to check you were all right but you were fast asleep behind those curtains and I couldn't bring myself to wake you. After all, you need to get as much sleep as possible while you can. And you've worked very hard recently.'

I was about to thank her and apologize when a tear

rolled down my cheek and into my mouth. I was as surprised as she was but then her concerned expression made my face crumple.

'Alice, whatever's the matter?' She led me back into the kitchen and sat me down.

I put my hands up over my face and cried – really sobbed, like a child – until I was spent and hiccuping. 'I think the baby has died,' I said, swallowing so I wouldn't set myself off again.

Mrs Jelphs gasped and visibly paled. She sat down heavily in the chair next to me. 'What on earth makes you say that? Have you . . . has there been a miscarriage?' Her voice came out high and strangled.

'No, but he . . . it hasn't moved since yesterday.'

I couldn't bring myself to tell her about the fall. Her relief at my white lie took ten years off her face.

'My dear, you've said yourself that the baby moves sometimes more than others. Only the other week you said how lovely it had been that he had stopped kicking.'

'Yes but this is different. It aches there, as though my monthlies have arrived.'

She had warned me not to use the old stairs. I had had no reason to be there, especially in the dark. I suddenly remembered the key to the nursery. I couldn't remember where it was, or even if I had locked up after me. But there was another reason I couldn't tell her the truth: she was so pleased there was no solid reason for me to be worried about the baby that I didn't want to provide her with one – because that would make it more real for me, too.

She wouldn't hear of me going back to my jobs that afternoon.

'You need some fresh air, my girl,' she said firmly, so I let her fuss around me, the numbness returned after my bout of crying. 'And I'm sending Ruck for the doctor immediately.'

'Oh, no, Mrs Jelphs, I don't need a doctor. I'm sorry I made a fuss.' I couldn't bear the idea of a man I'd never met confirming that I had killed the baby inside me because of a foolish fixation with the past.

She hesitated. 'I would feel much better if a doctor examined you.'

'Please, Mrs Jelphs. I know I will feel much better if I just lie quietly.' I battled to keep the misery out of my voice.

'Very well,' she said reluctantly. 'But the minute you feel any different, you must tell me and we'll fetch him immediately.'

She arranged a rug and cushions around me on a shady patch of grass close to the stream, at the edge of the Great Mead.

'I sit here sometimes,' she said. 'It's a lovely peaceful spot. You stay here and doze in the sun. It'll do you the power of good.'

I did as I was told, lying back on the cushions and searching the sky for clouds that never appeared. The sound of the stream's clear, bright water was like something alive and purposeful, rushing through and over the pebbles that lay on the bottom, smooth and cold and unperturbed. I pretended I was one of them and made myself as still and unmoving as the baby. I can't have been there long when I slept again. I dreamt of Elizabeth Stanton, her expressive eyes not the shades of umber and cream the portrait photograph had rendered them but green flecked with gold.

In the dream she was in the summerhouse and when I woke I knew immediately that I would go there again. In the privacy of that little room I checked again for blood – there was still no sign of it – then sat carefully down with the diary. The entry I pulled out was on different paper, slightly smaller and squarer than the diary's leaves. I started reading and, as I began to understand its import, a horrible sense of inevitability stole over me.

I fear I am lost to the blackness again. Three mornings ago I glimpsed it: a slender thread of despair woven through my thoughts. The sunshine flooded in through the open curtains and my daughter peeped around the door to see if I was awake, clutching the little hare she won't be parted from. Even as I held out my arms to her I felt a wall start to go up between us, between me and the rest of the world, brick by invisible brick.

Today I am afraid that the wall has got higher, that the black-edged thoughts seem to be crowding in faster. Each one is a drop of black ink fallen on a clean blotter. No, that is not right. It is more than that for each thought spreads and marbles, running into the next. Like ink into a bowl of cream. Drip, drip, until every thought is tinged with bleak despair.

I know I am exhausted but I won't rest. I can't eat and took only a few mouthfuls of dinner tonight. Mercifully, Edward didn't notice because only a single lamp was lit and my plate was in shadow. Mrs Wentworth will have seen, though, and perhaps she will speak to the housekeeper, who may well speak to my husband. Mrs Wentworth, as wide as she is tall, does not take kindly to any food returned uneaten to her domain. She regards it as a personal slight but I could not force another morsel down, my stomach filled with dread, dread filling the space that the baby had occupied until last week.

It's very late now and everyone else in the valley slumbers on. I am writing this on a sheet of paper because my diary is hidden in the summerhouse and I feel I must write and write until my hand is stiff and sore, in order to ward off the gloomy thoughts; as though setting everything down in its proper order will bring some order to my mind. I must remember that I got well again after my daughter was born, and that I will be well again this time too. That is, if I am ill at all. It is impossible to tell if it is the feeling returned or if I imagine it. Perhaps it is all my own invention, so strong is my fear of the fear I remember so vividly. But perhaps they are one and the same, and the result identical.

Edith has been in to see me often these past days, her face drawn with worry. I think only she has noticed that something is awry in me — after all, she is the only person who knows when my courses come each month and therefore when they are missed. It won't be long until Edward notices. I must eat everything on my plate tomorrow or he will be told. Of course, he wouldn't need to be told anything if he had known about this child's short existence. He would have seen it for himself by now. I am glad — and it is the only thing I can find any gladness for today — that I waited to tell him about the child growing inside me. Another boy. I'm sure it was a boy. A third failure.

I closed the diary, not wanting to glimpse another word, my life apparently turning into a morbid echo of Elizabeth's. It wasn't just the reference to a miscarriage, though that was bad enough: it was the widening gap between Elizabeth and her daughter — just like the breach between my mother and me that I was starting to think had occurred many years before. The mention of the hare had also sent a shiver through me. Only the previous day I had asked Mrs Jelphs who it had belonged to. Now I knew for certain. It was another tangible bond to connect Elizabeth's time and mine, and I thought again of the silken tether that seemed to pull me back towards her.

I sat on the old chaise for a long while, clutching the diary. My fascination with Elizabeth had not lessened but I felt afraid of the contents of it. In my anxious state, exhausted and battered by my fall, I felt as though the past was reaching out to claim me. Its grip on the valley had never felt more tenacious, like invisible ropes winding slowly around my ankles until they were ready to pull me back in time.

It was these dark thoughts that were reverberating around the stone walls of the summerhouse when I felt it, deep inside me. It was only a small movement, more of a fluttering, but it was enough. I realized that, for the first time since I'd known I was pregnant, I was uncomplicatedly glad. The baby hadn't died and I wept again.

When I had calmed down, I put the diary aside and went over to the little window behind the chaise. Pushing it back as far as it would go, I found I was smiling. Whatever darkness I had felt draw close had, at least for the time being, melted back into the shadows.

Dusk was approaching and, despite the lingering heat of the day, someone somewhere had lit a bonfire. The sharp, melancholy scent curled through the valley, freighted with memories of summer evenings past. I breathed in deep draughts of the air, the heady perfumes of the valley rising to mingle with the smoke. My sadness for Elizabeth was still there but my fear about my own baby, so suddenly alleviated, made me put her aside as I had her diary – and my mother and a little girl who had once owned a small velveteen hare.

I went carefully down the stairs and pushed back the door I'd left ajar only to collide with Ruck. I let out a small scream and fought the urge to hurry away.

If I had similarly startled him, he didn't show it, only frowning as he peered around me to the empty room behind.

'What's brought you here, then?' he said sharply. 'Mrs Jelphs know you come here, does she?'

'I – I don't know why I came,' I stammered. 'I was curious, I suppose. Mrs Jelphs pointed the summerhouse out to me on my first full day here and . . .'

'You's an inquisitive one, in't you, creeping about? No good will come of it.'

I flushed. 'I'm sorry. I should have asked. I'll tell Mrs Jelphs when I get back.'

He shook his head violently, the furrows of his brow deepening. 'Oh no you won't! You leave her out of it if her don' know already. It'll be a kindness to keep it quiet, if you get my meaning.'

I thought I did and nodded, too embarrassed to look him in the eye.

'It's supposed to be closed up,' he continued more softly, as if to himself. 'I could have swore it were locked.'

He looked up abruptly and I got the feeling he'd temporarily forgotten I was there.

'Well, back you go now, to the manor,' he said, more gently, making me wonder if, like Mrs Jelphs, it was concern that made him so brusque with me, not dislike. 'Her'll be wondering where you've got to. And don't forget them blankets you've left behind. I saw 'em down there and thought you'd tumbled in the stream.'

'Oh, yes. Yes, I will. Thank you, Ruck. And I'm sorry.'

But he was already heading back up Fiery Lane. I breathed out slowly and reminded myself that the baby hadn't been lost. I felt the relief bubbling inside me again and I had forgotten Ruck by the time I reached my room.

Tearing off my stale clothes, I put on a yellow dress that I had bought two sizes too big in the weeks before I had come to Fiercombe. Mrs Jelphs had helped me alter it and in the spotted mirror of the wardrobe I thought I looked quite nice. I tied my hair back with a yellow ribbon but then pulled it out again. I looked like a schoolgirl. I fingered a lock of my hair and thought how thick it felt, the back of my neck hot and damp under it. On a whim, I decided to pin it all up, though it was not a style I had ever worn. When it was finished I looked different and realized, with a lurch, that I'd unwittingly copied the style I'd seen in the photograph of Elizabeth. It suited me, though, and it felt cooler, so I left it as it was.

There was no one in the kitchen and, not wanting to sit in the gloom during my favourite time of the day, I decided to go for a short walk before dinner. I felt too full of gratitude to sit still. I was on my way back, having just passed the chapel, when I saw Ruck again. He was standing in the lane that ran from the graveyard towards the back of the manor. The late rhododendrons blazed there on both sides. Somehow they were still at their blowsy best, in every shade of magenta, crimson and pink.

'Hello again, Ruck,' I said levelly, no longer so cowed now I thought I understood his motives better.

He flinched and turned awkwardly to face me, raising his arm against the sun that was sinking slowly behind me. His rheumy eyes searched my face for a long moment. 'Didn't know you then, miss,' he said finally.

I wondered if my hair had confused him. 'I'm sorry if I made you jump,' I said, unable to resist the slight barb; he was forever making me jump. He didn't answer.

We walked slowly down the lane together in the direction of the house. The perfume swirling around us was intense.

'The flowers smell beautiful here,' I said, to make conversation. I wasn't sure I meant it: the fragrance was heady and made my head spin.

'It's the pale ones what smell strongest,' he replied. 'Them bright ones hardly smell 'tall.'

When we reached the end of the lane, Ruck stopped and turned to look back. The bushes rose high on both sides to meet a sky that was turning a soft shade of apricot.

'I can't recall the last time I saw 'em out like this, and so late,' he said, as much to himself as to me. He shook his head. 'It's too hot for 'em and too late in the year yet here they is, in all their glory.'

'They're not like this every summer?'

He shook his head again, more vigorously this time. 'I was a young lad in his prime when they was last like this. I thought never to see it again.'

He stumped off then, presumably to return to his cottage close to Ruin Wood, and left me alone in the lane. I stayed where I was for a time, watching the sky deepen to an orange that clashed with all the pink and purple. Compared to Ruck and my father, I knew little about flowers and plants, but enough to understand that it didn't make sense. It hadn't rained for weeks.

Mrs Jelphs was in the kitchen when I got there. I saw her eyes take in my hair.

'You look . . . Well, you look better now,' she said in the end. 'Perhaps you were right about not calling out the doctor. I must say, you have some real colour in your cheeks.'

'I know the baby's all right now, so you really mustn't worry. It was just a false alarm. I felt something about half an hour ago. It was hardly anything, just a flutter, but I'm so relieved.' I smiled shyly at her.

Mrs Jelphs's face cleared and she put a hand to her heart. 'Oh, I'm so glad. I've been worrying about you all afternoon but I didn't like to interfere too much.'

'Thank you for looking after me earlier. It did me good by the stream, you were right. I'm starving now, though. I haven't eaten a thing all day. Do you need some help?'

She was preparing a salad. Thick slices of cold beef had already been fanned out on a plate. 'It's nothing much. I thought it would be too warm for a cooked dinner.' She gestured towards the door. 'Tom is back – did you hear him? Why don't you go and tell him it will be ready in a few minutes?'

My heart leapt. I hadn't even heard his arrival – he had probably come back when I was hidden inside the thick walls of the summerhouse. When I got outside he was leaning up against his car and smoking a cigarette. He mock-saluted when he caught sight of me. 'Good evening, Alice. Do you want one?' He held a battered packet out towards me.

I shook my head.

'That's a pretty dress.' He looked back out towards the Great Mead, where the grass had turned purple in the fading light. I was glad it would conceal the colour of my warm cheeks.

'Thank you,' I said, as carelessly as I could manage. 'Mrs Jelphs helped me let it out in some places and take it in in others so I didn't look quite so ridiculous in it.'

'I can't imagine you looking ridiculous in anything,' he said.

In my self-consciousness I put my hand out to touch the hot bonnet of his little motor-car. We stood in silence together for a minute – I hadn't felt so awake in months. A pair of tiny bats swooped low and fast over us and we watched them until they disappeared. I thought then for the first time that I loved the valley; that I didn't want to be anywhere else.

'Here, what's happened to your arm?' he said, breaking into my thoughts as he reached out and got hold of my wrist.

At his touch I started, then twisted round to see what he meant. A dark bruise bloomed upwards from my elbow. I knew I had a livid purple mark on one of my thighs, thankfully covered by my dress, but I hadn't noticed this one. I hadn't planned to tell anyone about the fall but now I'd felt the baby's flutter it didn't seem to matter.

'Actually, I tripped on the stairs. I'm all right, though. I thought . . . Well, the baby's all right too.'

'You don't have much luck, do you? Poor old thing.'

He was still holding my wrist.

'I'm just clumsy. Don't tell Mrs Jelphs, will you? She'll only worry.'

He was looking at me properly now, his eyes searching my face. 'That's all it was, a fall?'

'Yes, of course. What else? That I threw myself down them? Hardly.'

He smiled uncertainly and flicked ash on to the gravel.

'Come on,' I said. 'Let's go in and have some supper. That's what I came out to tell you.'

Now he smiled more openly. 'Did you wait for me?'

'Not intentionally, I'm afraid. I wasn't hungry all day but now I'm ravenous. Mrs Jelphs is putting some things out.'

I walked towards the house. When I looked back to see if he was following, I saw that he hadn't moved. Instead, he was watching me.

Elizabeth

Elizabeth and Edward sat at opposite ends of the library without speaking, a lingering vibration in the air that had so recently rung with his anger. After almost half an hour had passed, he got up abruptly and strode from the room. Elizabeth scarcely noticed. Instead, her mind whirred on – travelling back through time in her memory until she found something that might have caused Edward's distress and fury. She knew he wouldn't tell her: he hated to talk of that time. Whatever it had been, it must have been significant to cause such an extreme reaction.

She marked off the aspects of it that must have combined so dramatically in his head on that gentle morning. Their conversation last night, perhaps. Isabel gone from the nursery, certainly. She, Elizabeth, also disappeared. And the most curious aspect: her shoes left behind in Isabel's room. It was the last, apparently innocuous, detail that seemed to have disturbed him most. After all, she had been for many walks with Isabel.

A clear series of possibilities glided to the front of her thoughts. What if the nursery-maid hadn't checked Isabel last night because it was late and she had been drinking? What if, finding her charge gone that morning, and seeing the discarded shoes that may have also chimed in her memory, she had gone to Edward and admitted that she had not seen Isabel since putting her to bed the night before?

In the muffled stillness of the library, Elizabeth struggled to remember. The child inside her was quiet again and for a time she forgot the constant discomfort of his heft at the front of her. Her left foot, turned in under the right at an awkward angle, had gone to sleep, but she barely noticed that either. Fragments of memory were flitting through her mind. They came so fast, bats across a darkening sky, that she hadn't yet been able to grasp one and examine it.

She began again. She could remember Isabel's birth and the easy week that followed it. She could also, with a suppressed shudder, remember the arrival of Dr Logan and his nurse, the jaundiced-looking Mrs Blackiston. She could remember that, although she had kept her eyes tightly closed when they left the valley, she could feel the ground beneath them slope upwards. She sensed the strain on the horses as the weight of the carriage tried to pull them all back down towards Stanton House.

So, what of the days before? A blurred picture flashed through her mind again but this time it brought with it a smell. In the library she sniffed the air but could detect only leather, beeswax and paper seamed with dust. It came again and she didn't try to chase it this time. It hovered and settled. She saw reflections, she smelt something rich, almost sweet but not. A moon like last night's but not the same one, this one hung with ragged clouds. A baby's cry, tentative at first, then rising to a thin wail. Grit under her bare feet.

The sentence arrived fully formed. *I was in the glasshouse.*

She knew instantly that her mind wasn't playing tricks on her. The smell she couldn't quite identify was warm soil, stale air and ripening tomatoes. Almost sweet but not.

A sound shook her from her reverie. Isabel peeped around the library door.

'Mama, will you come and have breakfast now? Mrs Wentworth made our eggs a long time ago.'

'Do you know, my darling? I don't think I can. The baby has made me feel quite queasy. That's why I am sitting quietly in here.'

Isabel's face fell. 'Shall I fetch you something, Mama?'

'No, my sweet. I think what I need is a little more air. I felt wonderful when we were walking in the garden.'

'Shall I come?'

Her small face was hopeful but Elizabeth shook her head. 'You must eat your eggs. Go along, now. I won't be very long. Later, when our guests have left, you and I shall do something together. Would that be nice?'

The little girl nodded slowly, weighing up whether this was better than the breakfast. 'Can we take our sketch-books somewhere?' she said, her head on one side.

'Yes, that's a good idea,' said Elizabeth. 'We can sit on the terrace, in the sun.'

'And may we have tea there afterwards, just you and me?' Isabel wheedled.

Elizabeth smiled. 'You are driving a hard bargain, Isabel Stanton. Off you go now. We shall see about tea.'

When the little girl's light steps had died away, Elizabeth sat a moment more, gathering herself. She was sure now that something had happened in the glasshouse, something that had been enough to make Edward send her to the asylum. A comfortable sort of asylum, to be sure, a place for ladies of substantial means and high rank, but still a place for the mad and unwanted.

In some ways, it hadn't been so different from Stanton House. She had been given her own room, which was small but quite comfortably furnished, and little more was expected of her during waking hours than that she lie there quietly. It was better for hysterics to be prone as much as possible, Dr Logan had said, without anything that might over-excite their minds. Perhaps when she had improved she could take a turn in the garden or compose a letter to be sent home. She was fed nursery food for the first weeks: milky and scarcely warm, nothing that didn't slide easily down her throat.

It was at night that the illusion of civility lifted and the crying and shrieking began. Their doors were locked from the outside, the mechanisms kept oiled so that the sound of each key turning was less intrusive; less like the screech and clang of the prison's nightly round.

She got to her feet and left the library, retracing her route across the terrace and through the Italian garden. At the steps to the lake she paused. The shadow of the folly reached a third of the way across it; it was still quite early. One of the gardeners would be along to turn the fountain on shortly. When it was on, the water could be heard from the house: its hiss when the wind was blowing across the valley floor, its heavy patter when the air was still. It was also audible from the terrace, from the croquet lawn on the other side of the house, and from the paths buried deep among the beeches. So it could certainly be heard from the glasshouse, even with the door closed.

She thought hard. There was no sound like that in the

memory fragments she had managed to salvage; only the crying. The fountain was turned off late: Edward liked it on when he went for a walk before he retired, which was never before midnight. She could see the moon quite clearly in what she had recalled. Whatever had happened must have done so in the coldest, emptiest hours of the night.

This morning there was no one in the glasshouse or the kitchen garden that adjoined it. She stepped inside and breathed in the smell that had come back to her in the library. It was even richer and headier than she remembered and, with the door shut, the atmosphere was close. None of the glass panels in the roof was open. She remembered the mechanism that one of the gardeners had once pointed out to her. He had been proud of it and had wanted to show her how ingenious it was. She looked for the pole that connected to its mate in the roof and it was there, propped in one corner where it was supposed to be. She was hot now, beads of sweat at her brow and under her dress.

It was as she began turning the handles of the pole as she had been shown, one hand over the other, the large pane above her starting to lift, that it came back to her. The physical motion had allowed the rest of the memory to slide into place. She let the pole swing free and sat down heavily, her skirts spread out around her in the dust and soil. There was a bench behind her and she rested her aching back against it, her hands clasping the mound of her belly. She wanted to cry but the tears wouldn't come higher than her chest, where they swelled into a painful wall.

Now she remembered, she remembered it all.

It had happened at the beginning of the fourth week after the birth. She had been in the midst of one of the everlasting nights that had come to punctuate her formless, anxiety-sown days. When the solution to everything had occurred to her, she had felt a sense of imminent relief that was close to excitement. It seemed such an obvious answer once she had thought of it.

She waited until the gilt clock struck three, then quietly put on a thick wool dress that she had had made up for winter walks but had barely worn because it made her itch. It hardly needed to stretch over her still-swollen stomach but then she couldn't remember the last thing she had eaten.

At the top of the stairs she hesitated. There was no noise coming from the direction of the nursery but she had an urge to go in and see the tiny thing that had somehow unravelled her.

Inside the nursery for which she had chosen everything so carefully – when she had been a quite different person – the moonlight shone coldly through the uncurtained window. She could see the silhouette of the cot clearly but, as she started over to it, her shoes sounded so loudly on the polished boards that she stopped and pulled them off.

The baby had already started to wake when she got to it. A pale beam of moonlight had moved to lie across its face. Strangely fascinated, Elizabeth watched it fuss for a few seconds, its tiny hands curled into fists, its regular breathing becoming worried huffs and gasps. When it cried out, just once, she reared back in fright. If the nursery-maid woke, she would ask questions and Elizabeth would be taken back to her room. The next morning Edward would be told that his wife had been wandering through the house at night, like a wraith.

The baby squawked again, louder and more insistent than before. Without thinking, Elizabeth rested a hand on its stomach. 'Hush now,' she whispered, wondering where the words had come from. The baby's eyes opened wide, fixing on Elizabeth's in response and, for half a minute, they gazed at each other. Then it screwed up its face and began to cry in earnest. Elizabeth understood then that she had no choice, if she wanted to carry out her plan, but to pick up the baby, wrap it in a blanket and leave the nursery.

The baby stopped crying as soon as she held it to her, its snuffling breath loud in her ear as it calmed. It felt surprisingly solid and heavy for such a small thing; the word *dense* came into her mind. Muscle, bone, fat and blood all densely packed together.

Out in the hallway she listened to see if the noise had woken anyone but it was deathly silent. The front door – she couldn't think clearly of another way out – opened obligingly quietly and then she was out and under the sky. She looked for stars but there was too much cloud. It was a true autumnal night: tinged with woodsmoke and heavy with damp that made it feel colder than it was.

Something about the steps and the sunken garden between her and the lake discomfited her when she got there. She found she couldn't go any further. Instead she turned right, hurrying towards the stout walls of the kitchen garden. The baby against her shoulder had fallen asleep or was close to it, its breathing soft and rhythmic.

In the kitchen garden she stepped on a sharp pebble, burying her face in the baby's blanket to stifle her gasp of pain. Looking down, she saw that she wore no shoes but couldn't remember why, or if she had put any on in the first place. She had nearly reached the line of bushes that screened the kitchen garden's walls from the lake when it occurred to her anew that she was carrying a baby. She was looking around, wondering where to put it, when her eye was drawn by the moon reflected over and over in the smooth panes of the glasshouse.

It seemed like the perfect solution. She would leave the child there while she went on to the lake, alone. It would be warm enough, and they would find it easily in the morning when they started to look. A little crying if it woke early would not hurt it.

Quite decided, she went in, closed the door and placed an empty crate on a bench where it would be seen. Putting the baby inside, she arranged the blanket under and around it, feeling towards it as someone unsentimental might feel towards a rescued animal: concerned in a dutiful but not personal way.

Then a draught tickled her neck. Looking behind her she saw that the door was still shut but then she felt it again, cool fingers reaching down the back of her woollen dress. She looked up. One of the larger glass panels had been raised and left open. Somewhere in the fug of her mind she remembered how to close it and fetched the pole, slotting it into the mechanism above and beginning to turn the handles. Creaking slightly, it began to lower into place.

Hearing the baby begin to fuss again in its sleep, she felt suddenly desperate to have it done and started twisting faster. High above her something came loose and the pane suddenly crashed into position, shattering as it did into large shards that landed all around her. The child in response began to cry, thinly at first and then with great, wrenching sobs. There was no blood on it, she checked that – it had just been frightened by the terrible noise, which had rent the night's peace and left it in tatters. She knew that it had likely been heard up at the house.

It was then that she became aware of a stinging sensation in her feet, and looked down to see her already ruined stockings soaked with blood. All around her were small, jagged pieces of glass that reflected the moon in miniature. Frozen with indecision she sat down in the dirt, wondering if the alarm had been raised in the house yet, and whether Edward – always a heavy sleeper – had been roused and was in that instant blearily pulling on his boots.

The image of the lake that she had carried in her mind from her bedroom to the nursery to the glasshouse still tantalized. Her longing to slide under its surface into the murky silence was still powerful. She had chosen her thick dress because it would have saturated, then dragged her deeper. But it was too late now. By the time she had summoned the energy to leave the glasshouse and get to the lake, they would have reached her.

Her fingers found the piece of glass quite unconsciously. It was a good size in her hand, as though it had been snapped off the larger piece for the very purpose. She rubbed at one of its edges with her forefinger and watched the blood rise and spill out of the clean cut. There was little pain.

As the baby cried on, she squeezed her palm into a fist around the glass. That hurt more. When she opened her hand, it was dark with blood, the glass smeared with it. She wiped it off on her dress and then impulsively pulled up her skirts and laid the sharpest point of it against the white, tender skin of her thigh, above the line of her stockings. Making a small, deep cut into the flesh she watched as the blood began to run, faster and more freely, pooling between her legs. Something in its movement reminded her of the stream near the manor.

It was just as she began to feel cold – the draught from the broken pane stronger than before – that they burst in. It was the cries that had guided them to that part of the grounds; under the cover of night they wouldn't have been able to see the baby tucked into the crate or the woman slumped on the ground in a mess of blood, soil and glass.

What none of them had understood, and what she hadn't seemed able to say, was that she had meant the baby no harm, that she had forgotten it was there – the noise of its crying not connected in her mind to a child – and that she had meant only to end herself.

Alice

Tom was quiet as we ate and I thought he'd probably done enough socializing for the time being. After we'd finished and moved into the small parlour, Mrs Jelphs said she would make a pot of coffee and went out, leaving us on our own. At first neither of us spoke, though I think I found that more awkward than he did. He seemed deep in thought; I was fiddling nervously with my dress, pulling the hem down so it covered more of my legs, which I'd left bare in the heat.

'Did you get any further with the box?' he said, just when I'd begun to think no one would ever speak again. I glanced over to where it was. It was just as it had been when it had inspired me to go and explore in the nursery.

'No. I've been working so hard for Mrs Jelphs that I've hardly had the time.'

I thought about telling him where I'd been but didn't know what he would think. I had some vague worry that I would be encroaching too much on the memory of his brother.

He raised an eyebrow. 'There's no obligation. I just thought you might have.'

'No.'

The silence yawned and gaped once again. It was a relief when Mrs Jelphs came in with the coffee, in which both of us took an inordinate interest. We made small-talk for nearly an hour before Mrs Jelphs reluctantly excused herself and retired to her room.

I was at first nervous to be left alone with him again, this time in case he swiftly made his own excuses. But he made no move to get up, simply staring into the empty hearth. I'd never seen it lit and just the thought of it made my skin prickle with perspiration. Both the small side casements had been opened as wide as the old iron allowed but there were no cooling breezes. Any air that did curl in carried the heavy, golden scent of honeysuckle.

'Have you had a pleasant few days?' I said after a time. Any lingering awkwardness was dissolving in the soporific air and I felt almost sleepy.

He looked up as though he'd forgotten I was there. 'Oh, yes. Thank you. I always forget quite how many people I have to call in on but, then, I probably only come back twice a year.'

'Do some of them live in London as well, like you do?'

I had an image of him charming the daughters of all the best county families – girls with long legs who had grown up playing croquet and riding their own horses. Girls who had grown up to be glossy and accomplished.

'Not really. There are a few but most of them are people my parents mixed with when we were boys. As they're here even less than I am, it falls to me to visit and hear the latest news – who's married whom and so forth.'

'It sounds . . . nice,' I said lamely.

'If by "nice" you mean pretty dull then, yes, it is. But it keeps Mother happy. She likes to hear how everyone is ageing in her absence.'

'The worse the better, I presume.'

He laughed. 'Spot on.'

'Do your parents spend all their time in France now?'

'More or less. They come back to England only if there's some business Father has to deal with in person, and Mother rarely leaves London then. Most of their affairs can be dealt with via the post, or by me.'

'It seems a shame that they won't see it this summer, when everything is so lush and gorgeous.'

'Mother prefers the Riviera. Have you been?'

I shook my head. I felt foolishly flattered that he thought I might have.

'It's very beautiful and very . . . ordered. They have quite a small place, back from the sea near Grasse, where they make the famous scents. The house is almost new, with modern bathrooms and all the rest of it. Not like this old pile in its enchanted valley.'

As if what he said had roused it, the carriage clock on the mantel came to life, its ticking loud and slightly irregular.

'I expect you've long given up wearing a watch by now,' he said, glancing towards the clock, which said erroneously that it was almost two.

I glanced down at my bare wrist. I'd had a white mark where the sun had tanned the rest of my arm but it had caught up without my noticing. I couldn't remember when I'd last worn my watch. 'It's a funny thing down here, the time,' I said. 'I wondered if it was something to do with the magnetism in the rock but I didn't dare try out that theory on Ruck.'

'Probably wise. I'm not the one to ask – the sciences were more Henry's thing. Time never really mattered here,

309

growing up. You woke early and went out. You came in to eat when the gong went. In between we were out on the estate and did as we pleased.'

'The two of you must have had wonderful summers here,' I ventured.

'We did. What more could boys ask for than an entire valley to run wild in? We used to pretend we'd been shipwrecked and washed ashore somewhere deserted and exotic.'

'I used to love those make-believe games,' I said. 'I didn't have the run of a place like this but I did well enough with a couple of old sheets tied to the bedposts so they made a den.'

I thought of Dora and me as girls and felt a distant pang of something like homesickness. She still hadn't written; perhaps it was a case of out of sight, out of mind.

'We were lucky to be always outside,' he continued. 'Mother didn't want us making a racket in the house so out we would go, until dusk or hunger struck, whichever came first.'

He reached for the box. On top were the small square photographs we'd been looking at before, of the boys by the lake. He leafed through them, then tossed them back.

'I think I want a drink,' he said. 'Do you want a drop of this in your coffee?' He brought over a silver tray upon which was a decanter half full of whisky and a couple of crystal tumblers.

I declined, and watched as he poured himself a generous measure. Taking a couple of gulps, he topped up his glass before sinking back into the armchair.

'Do you want to know how he died?' he said abruptly,

just when I'd resigned myself to another long lapse in the conversation.

'Only if you want to tell me,' I said, my heart thudding faster.

'I'm not exactly fond of talking about it,' he said, voice thick with emotion. His glass was empty again and he paused to refill it, clinking the heavy crystal of the decanter against it as he did so. 'But, these days, all I seem to talk about is the weather, other people's aches and pains and what passes for scandal in the county. It's all nonsense.'

I remained quiet, not wanting to interrupt him.

'It happened near the end of the school holidays. Probably a blessing, that. I would have gone out of my mind otherwise. I was packed off to a cousin's house straight after the funeral and Michaelmas term began a few weeks later. War had been declared in August so no one at school was very interested in Henry. Almost immediately it felt as though it had happened in another time. There we were at war and his had been such an ordinary sort of death. Later, when my classmates' brothers started to die out there, I became almost ashamed of it, of how mundane it sounded.'

He looked up to see if I was shocked but I just nodded at him to go on.

'We got into a routine quickly that last summer: me, Henry and another boy from his form who'd come to stay, Julian Crawford. His people lived in Kenya and someone was ill, I forget who, his sister or his mother, so he was to stay with us all summer. He was a few months younger than Henry but seemed older. Henry was a little in awe of him and it got on my nerves.

'On the first afternoon – the "first swim of the

summer" in the photograph – we had been roaming around, taking pictures of trees, trying to be artistic. We had our bathing suits with us but wanted to get really hot and bothered before going in, to enjoy it all the more. "You really have to savour the first one," Henry always said. Eventually we gave in and headed for the lake.'

He paused to pour another few fingers of whisky, and I wondered how much he drank every day to remain as sober as he seemed.

'When we got there, Crawford went ahead and dived in before Henry and I had even stripped off. It was stupid but I was furious. The water had been perfectly still and dark and I had wanted Henry and me to go in and break the surface first. It was our lake, and over the years it had become a bit of a ceremony for me. It sounds ridiculous now, I know, but I was so furious that I even picked up a stick to throw at Crawford. I suppose I just wanted my brother to myself. The holidays were all I had – he didn't speak to me at school, you see.'

'What – not at all?'

'Older boys never spoke to their younger brothers. It just wasn't done. If he ever had to he'd call me "Stanton".'

I smiled, hoping to lighten the atmosphere. 'Ah, the vagaries of English public schools,' I said.

'Mock all you like, but it was that sort of discipline that built the Empire,' he said drily, though his eyes were still troubled.

'So, did you hit Crawford with the stick?'

'No, and if Henry hadn't intervened I expect it would have been me who came off worst. Crawford was thin but sinewy. He had muscles in his arms like steel cables.

'Anyway, Henry took the stick off me before I had a chance to throw it and told me to stop being an ass. He did it quite gently, though. He knew why I was being like that, though he would never have embarrassed me by saying so.

'From that day on we fell into a rhythm. They always let me tag along. We'd swim and then lie on the grass to dry off till we were too hot again. The weather was like it is now. Well, perhaps not quite as hot, but almost.

'At the end of July, war broke out on the Continent and from then on we were just waiting for England to join in. The waiting charged the atmosphere somehow. We couldn't imagine it not happening but we couldn't imagine anything changing in the valley either. We all felt some kind of heightened awareness. I began a diary – I don't think it's in the box, I must have lost it and I was no diarist. I wanted that time set down, though.'

'Written down as proof,' I said, thinking of Elizabeth's pencil marks, rubbed out in places.

'Yes, I think that was it. The spell seemed unbreakable but at the same time it was inevitable that it would be broken.'

'And then Henry,' I said softly.

'And then Henry.' He stopped.

'You don't have to tell me,' I said.

'I know I don't. But I felt lighter the other day, after we'd been to the meadow. I'm never allowed to mention Henry in front of my parents. No one has ever forbidden it as such – it goes without saying. Mrs Jelphs doesn't like it being mentioned either. I suppose they think it's better locked away and therefore . . . contained. But it's not. It's worse. He's with me all the time. I dream about him every night – I dream about what happened every night, again and again, as though someone's put it on a loop in my head. Do you remember we talked about ghosts last time we were here?'

I nodded. In the soft light, he was as grey and exhausted-looking as I'd seen him yet.

'Well, all that talk of Margaret of Anjou and her ilk is nonsense, of course – the ermine-tipped gown and the wafting scents, the headless horsemen and the hovering spectres on the stairs. That's not what a true haunting is. The real ghosts are the ones that take up residence in your mind, and that's what Henry had done in mine until I came back this time. It had been getting worse over the last few years – I think because the time when I will inherit is getting closer. It had got to be that the only way I could get to sleep at night was to drink myself into a stupor.'

He ran his finger around the rim of his tumbler until the crystal let out a low, sonorous hum.

'It's always been worst here. After that summer, I jumped at any chance to stay with school friends rather than come home at the end of each term. Now I have to take care of things for my father, I can't escape it.

'I always drive too fast on the way here from London. I always seem to set off at night, at the eleventh hour, putting the damned duty off until the last possible moment. I can't count how many times I've come within inches of wrapping myself around a tree in a pitch-dark lane. I flirt with it, I suppose. Death, I mean. I picture the end as a sort of black blanket of peace. Sometimes I can't think of anything more appealing.'

He half smiled at me.

'But then I came back this time and found myself

mentioning him here and there to you – and even to Mrs Jelphs. After the first time I just kept doing it, as a sort of test. And nothing happened. Well, nothing terrible. One night I didn't dream at all.

'My mother believes that never coming to Fiercombe – never even catching sight of the word written down – will eventually damp down the grief. But she's wrong. It won't. I have to live with what I did that day – what I didn't do – but it doesn't help anyone to pretend that Henry never existed. He deserves more than that.'

He sat back in his chair and a great sigh escaped him. The sharp lines of his face softened a little.

'Tell me what happened,' I said softly.

'Yes, I'm still skirting around it, aren't I? Where were we?'

'The war had broken out.'

'Ah, yes. So, it wasn't the war that changed everything, after all, not for me. It was well into August when it happened. It was just an ordinary day, like all the others. I suppose they always are.

'We'd got up early – before breakfast – but it was already hot, sweltering, so Henry and I had gone to the lake already changed into our bathing things. Crawford was still asleep – we'd left him snoring on his camp bed in Henry's room and I was full of glee that I'd got my brother to myself for once.

'Henry was in the water and I was taking photographs on the Box Brownie we shared. In fact, it was Henry's, but he always let me borrow it. I remember I was trying to capture the way the sun was dappling the water. Mother had told me off for wasting film so I was trying to ration myself, getting the angle just so before actually pressing the shutter.

'When I noticed the shadow falling across the lake, I saw it like that, through the viewfinder. It was distorted by the moving water but looked like a figure to me. I glanced up at the bank opposite, half expecting to see Crawford standing there. But there was nobody. "Did you see anyone?" I called to Henry, but he didn't hear me. He was right out in the middle of the lake, treading water and then diving down to see how long he could stay under. He'd broken his own record most days that summer, though perhaps that was because he was generally doing the counting himself, in his head.

'I took a photograph of him like that then, his dark head and back bobbing clear of the water's surface. The shadow was there again but I didn't take much notice because I'd suddenly thought of a trick he had played on me the previous summer. We'd both forgotten it. I put down the camera and ran round the lake to the folly. It was in there that the pump for the fountain was hidden, out of sight. It was a big thing and hardly used since we had lived in the valley. I hadn't been able to turn it by myself the year before and I wasn't sure I could this time.

'Inside the folly it was cold. Not just cool from the shade but cold and dank, like a cave deep underground. It smelt strange too, sort of sharp and green. Like mildew but somehow . . . alive. The pump handle was at the back, covered with cobwebs. I didn't much like spiders so I jabbed at the webs with my foot. I felt ticklish all over then and thought I felt something fluttering across the skin of my shoulder-blades. I don't know why I didn't run out – my hackles were up. I was determined to do it, though. I wanted to be the one to play the old trick – and do it before Crawford got there.

'I threw my weight against the handle as hard as I could

and of course it wouldn't shift. I wrenched at it uselessly, my hands on the freezing metal growing purple with the strain and cold. Quite suddenly it came loose, all in a rush, so that I crashed down on to my knees and scraped them.

'I almost fell out through the door in my rush to get back into the sunshine and there it was, a great jet of rusty water. It sounds morbid but it was precisely the colour of old blood. The force of it grew as I watched until it arced over almost the whole lake. It was then that I noticed Henry was still holding his breath. I couldn't believe he hadn't come up when he felt the water on his back. I stood and watched it pelt him, rivulets of reddish water staining his skin.

'It should've run clear but it didn't. I remember I looked up at the sky and it was as though it was twilight, not morning. It was such a strange colour – I can still see it now. The sun had gone and it was yellow and purple, like a bruise. I don't know how long I stood there, as if in some sort of trance, looking up at the sky and the water of the fountain against it like a simpleton.

'I didn't even hear Crawford arrive, though apparently he shouted at me, called my name again and again. It was like the sound had been turned off in the whole valley. By the time I noticed him he had already taken off his clothes and was running towards the water. He dragged Henry out. He tried to revive him but it was too late.'

Tom fell quiet and looked away from me, his face hidden in shadow.

'I'm so sorry,' I said eventually. 'How strange, though.'

'What's strange?' he said sharply.

I coloured, wishing I had thought before speaking. 'Well, everything,' I said. 'The sky and the shadow. And –'

'I was a cowardly sort of child, Alice. I told you already how I hated that nursery. The strange sky was a brewing storm. The rain started just as my father arrived at the lake to see his elder son drowned on the bank. As for what I saw through the camera, well, you must have heard of the child who is scared of his own shadow. That was me, in this case quite literally.'

He laughed bitterly and picked up his glass. 'The simple fact is that I stood there like a fool while my brother drowned. Do you think Crawford would have been afraid of spiders in the folly, or of the sun going in? No, of course he wouldn't. He didn't hesitate for a moment.'

I reached out my hand and squeezed his arm. I thought he'd shake me off but he didn't and we sat like that for a time.

'There's something left of it all, isn't there? I've always thought so,' I said quietly, not knowing if it would anger him further.

'What do you mean?'

'The past. It's here still, in a way. I mean, I didn't know Henry or anyone else who was here once, but I can feel them sometimes. Like you said before, it's not that they're ghosts. For me, it's more of an echo through time.'

I was thinking about Elizabeth's diary. My eye strayed to the sewing box. I could just make out the ornate E in the low light.

Neither of us spoke for a while. Tom let his head fall back against one of Mrs Jelphs's embroidered antimacassars and closed his eyes. When he spoke again, his tone was lighter than it had been and I hoped it was because he'd been able to tell someone about Henry.

'Tell me what you've been doing,' he said. 'We've been listening to my voice for far too long.'

All I could think of was the nursery, and my fall after the second visit to it.

'Well, I . . . went for a walk and saw the rhododendrons earlier,' I said after a pause.

He rolled his eyes. 'We'd better stop the presses for that.'

I laughed. 'You did ask.'

'What did you mean before, when you said the past was still here?'

The sewing box was still visible in the corner of my eye. 'I suppose I've got rather caught up in the history of the valley. That's all.'

'Margaret of Anjou, you mean? Sorry, I didn't mean to ruin the story earlier. It is a good one and it's possible, even probable, that she did come through here on the way to Tewkesbury.'

I nodded. 'Yes. Hugh Morton told me.'

'I didn't realize you knew him. He's a good sort, Hugh. I haven't seen him for ages. The last time I did, he was walking along one of the bluebell paths with his dog. Can't think when that was.'

I smiled. 'Sammy – that was the dog. He died last year and I don't think Mr Morton has wanted to replace him.'

'So what other tales did Hugh tell you about Fiercombe, then?'

'Well, he showed me a book that had a few old photographs in it. They had been taken at the turn of the century.'

Tom looked thoughtful. 'Just before my father's tenure. I know so little about any of that.'

I pushed my hair behind my ears. I wanted to be honest with him, as he had been, so painfully, with me. 'Listen, Tom, I hope you don't mind but I went and explored the old nursery yesterday. I just got the urge to and I'd seen the key hanging up when Mrs Jelphs showed me where they're kept.'

'Ah, the nursery. Scene of my childhood nights, not all of them happy, as you know. I haven't been inside it for years. Is anything still there?'

That was when I remembered. 'Oh! I forgot all about it.'

'What do you mean?'

'I found some things in the window-seat. A picture and . . . Well, there was something I didn't manage to look at.'

'There was nothing of any interest in there when I used that room. I think Mrs J kept spare blankets inside, something of that sort. As I say, I never go in there now. I sleep at the other end of the house these days, now that it's up to me.'

'I think it's more or less untouched from your day. Although it's strange – it's not dusted or anything and the door is kept locked.'

He frowned. 'That's not like Mrs Jelphs at all. So what's left?'

'An old gramophone and some odds and ends. It's as though it's been preserved in aspic. Actually, I went there twice yesterday.'

I could see he was intrigued, even slightly amused. I took a breath. 'The first time I found something in the window-seat but then, before I had a chance to look properly, I . . . well, I suppose I got a bit scared. I had put the gramophone on and ... Oh, it sounds ridiculous. Anyway, last night Mrs Jelphs's back was giving her a lot of trouble so she went to bed early. I knew then that I had to go back, look again.

'It was nearly dark by that time and the light wouldn't come on so I had to wipe off some of the dust on the window to let the last of the day in. It felt a bit sinister in there so I went through what was in the window-seat quite quickly. I didn't look at the last thing I came to at all, thinking it was just a bit of cardboard. I wonder now if it was another photograph.'

'Another photograph?'

'Yes. The first thing I found, wrapped in a blanket, was a sepia photograph of Elizabeth Stanton. I suppose she was your aunt. I never thought of it before.'

It was odd that she was connected to the present like that, her marriage bonds tying her to the man who looked at me now. It made her seem closer than ever.

'Hugh Morton told me that there was only ever one photograph of her taken that didn't turn out blurred or spoilt in some way,' I continued. 'He said that Edward Stanton – your uncle – hadn't liked it so it had never been hung but Hugh had seen it once and thought it must still be hidden away somewhere. She was very beautiful.'

'That's about the only thing I know about her,' said Tom. 'Ropes and ropes of dark hair apparently, like a Spanish gypsy. And great big eyes, like yours. She was famous for them.'

I coloured at the implied compliment but managed to continue: 'I forgot about the other photograph, though,

321

if that's what it even was. You see, it was after that that I stupidly tripped and fell and then it –'

'Wait a minute. That was when you fell?'

'Yes. It was dark and the stairs are steep and I just lost my balance. Listen, please don't tell Mrs Jelphs because she warned me off them but ... well, I was on the old stairs. The narrow ones at this end of the house. I know it was silly of me.'

'It was. There's no light at all on that staircase. I never used it as a boy. I didn't like it. You might have broken your neck, Alice. Are you sure the child is all right?'

'Yes.' I swallowed at the memory of how I'd felt and, as if the baby heard, I felt him flutter again. I put my hand on my stomach. 'I had a horrible day. I convinced myself that I was going to lose him.'

'Him? I noticed you said that before.'

I shrugged. 'Ever since I've really thought of the baby, he's been a boy.'

'Well, I'm glad you've only got a few bruises to show for your tumble.' He picked up his whisky, then put it down again. 'So what do you think the other photograph was of, if it even is a photograph?'

'Perhaps another of Elizabeth that no one else knows about.'

As I said it, an image of the ruined little boot came back to me with total clarity. There was something about it that I hadn't liked. I hadn't even wanted to touch it.

'Tom, do you mind if I have a sip of your whisky? I think I would like some after all.'

He passed me the tumbler. The amber liquid scorched its way down my throat and pooled warmly in my stomach.

I took a deep breath. 'Shall we go and have a look?' I said quietly. 'Will you come with me?'

He hesitated. 'Well, I suppose we could. But we'll make sure there's some light on the situation this time.'

He picked up one of the oil lamps Mrs Jelphs always lit in case the electricity failed and turned it up as high as it would go.

It was dark in the hallway and the lamp made it seem darker. When we got to the foot of the old staircase the light shining in through the leaded window was cold and faint. There was no moon and the diamond patterns on the floor were hard to make out. I rubbed my arms but the gooseflesh that had risen on them remained. Tom went straight towards the stairs but I hung back.

'Come on,' he said. 'Let's get this over with. Did you lock it again?'

I shook my head. I still couldn't think what I'd done with the key. 'Tom, can we go back to the sitting room?' I said urgently. 'I don't think I want to go any more. I feel like I might faint.'

He took my arm and led me back to the sitting room. 'You've gone pale,' he said softly. For a moment I thought he was going to stroke my cheek. Instead, he shifted the heavy lamp to his other hand. 'You stay here and I'll go and get this blasted photograph.'

He was off before I had time to say anything. I hadn't warned him about the boot or the poor little blanket, yellowed with age.

He was back within a couple of minutes, pleased that he'd used the stairs he had disliked as a boy. I thought he must have wanted to prove something to himself in going that way, as well as to the nursery.

'I found this at the top of the stairs.' He showed me the key. 'You must have dropped it when you lost your balance. I'll put it back later, before Mrs J misses it.' He set the lamp on the table and then sat down. 'You were right about Elizabeth,' he said, smiling sadly. 'What a beauty she was. There was some other stuff in there but it didn't look like much. I got this, though, as instructed.' He held up the rectangle of stiff cardboard I could see now was a sort of envelope. He sat down and opened it, bringing it close to his face to study it.

'What is it?' I said, leaning forward to look.

He pulled back a little so I couldn't see it. 'You were right, it is another photograph.'

'Is it of Elizabeth again? Let me see.'

He paused before handing it over, then took a gulp of whisky.

It was old – I could tell that from its brittle feel.

Although I had only imagined her, dreamt of her, I felt sure it was the daughter to whom Elizabeth had given birth, the little girl who had owned the velveteen hare. I suppose I had thought of her often since the dream I'd had of her, weeks earlier.

As Elizabeth had predicted in her diary, she had been fair, not dark like her mother. In the photograph, her silvery hair had been brushed until it gleamed, then fastened low at the side of her head with a dark ribbon. Dressed in white, someone had tied a sash around her waist that matched the ribbon in her hair. She was sitting in a broad, high-backed armchair that dwarfed her little frame, half a dozen stiffly plump cushions around her. It was difficult to see in such a small photograph – it was perhaps only four inches long by three across – but her eyes looked strange to me. Not empty, as I had seen them in the dream, but hard, almost flat.

I handed back the picture. There was something peculiar about it that made me not want to touch it. The overall effect was anything but childlike. I looked up at Tom. 'Do you know who she is?'

'No idea. Perhaps she lived at Stanton House. It's about the right period. I've no idea how this got into the nursery, though. As I said before, I don't know much about any of the family history, even the more recent stuff. Especially that. I don't even know what happened to Elizabeth.

'I know only a little more about my uncle, and that I found out from Henry before he died. Lord knows where he got it from. Apparently Edward Stanton rattled through most of the family money in a decade – not that there was such an enormous fortune to begin with, frankly. My poor father didn't just inherit a virtually empty coffer, he was also saddled with his brother's debts. From what hearsay I picked up from my own brother, Edward died in London after leaving the valley for the last time.'

I was leaning forward in my seat so that the baby was pressing painfully against my ribs. I hadn't even noticed.

'I'm not sure if they had any children,' Tom continued. 'In truth, I suppose I had rather assumed they hadn't – at least none who survived beyond childhood. But perhaps this little one was Elizabeth's, though she doesn't look much like her, and she died young. There was certainly no surviving son or my father wouldn't have inherited and that's the one thing I do know: the estate passed to him a few years before I was born. I suspect my uncle had indulged in a good deal of gambling and drinking to incur such debts.'

He paused and looked wryly at the glass in front of him. 'My mother and father must know all this, of course, but they would never talk about it. Even before Henry, that sort of talk would have been dismissed as superstition and gossip: old ghosts and needless raking up of the past when the thing was to go forward, not hark back. Of course, since 1914 there's a different reason why we can't be reminded of what went before. My mother would leave the room if I raised the subject. It made her unwell. She was the one who insisted that the lake was filled in after Henry drowned. She said it should have been done long ago. It took the men three days. There's still a great gouge in the ground at the back of the beech woods where they took the earth from to fill it.'

I didn't know what to say and found my eye drawn back towards the photograph of the little girl. I was trying to remember exactly what Elizabeth had written about her daughter when Tom spoke again. His voice was gentle. 'What are you thinking about, Alice? You looked then as though you were a long way off.'

I gazed at him blankly. 'Yes, I suppose I was. Perhaps it's something to do with him' – I placed my hand on my stomach – 'but I can't stop thinking about what happened to Elizabeth. I think that picture is of her child. Perhaps she took after her father in colouring. You're fair.'

Something held me back from telling him about the diary in the summerhouse. Just as with Hugh Morton, I felt as though Elizabeth was my secret and I was reluctant to share her.

He watched me for a while as he sipped his drink.

'What is it?' I said finally.

'You never mention him at all.'

'Who?'

He reddened slightly. 'Your husband. I'm sorry, I shouldn't intrude on your grief again. I should know that better than most. It's the only time you look guarded, though – it was the same when we were walking back from the meadow and I asked then. I'm sorry, though.'

I swallowed, suddenly alert. 'It's all right. I . . . We hadn't known each other very long when we were married. It sounds very callous but I don't think of him much. I can barely imagine my life in London now.'

I hated lying to him even more than I did to Mrs Jelphs, although the last of it was true. It dawned on me then with complete certainty that I wasn't in love with James any more. It had simply stopped. I made myself picture him but his image had lost any potency.

Tom was looking at me intently, as though he was deciding something. Then he put down his glass, took my hand and pressed it to his lips. We looked at each other for a long moment, his mouth hot against my cool hand, until I found myself pulling away. 'What is it?' he said. 'What's the matter?'

His tone had sharpened but his eyes were vulnerable. That made me hesitate and in the lull he reached forward. I thought he was going to kiss me on the mouth but something made him pause and, in the new lull, I found myself talking. 'We can't,' I said crossly, because I wanted him to. 'Mrs Jelphs might come in.'

'Very well,' he said quietly.

Awkwardly, we both got to our feet. I turned away to face the window, my mind as well as my heart racing with what had just happened. The darkness outside was complete and I could see both of us clearly reflected in the window, our outlines distorted by the old glass. He was standing behind me and I couldn't tell if he was looking at me in the window or not. I was watching him. I was about to say something, attempt to laugh the whole episode off, when he turned and walked towards the door. Too proud to move, I watched him go.

'I'll leave you in peace then, Alice. I'm sorry if I've offended you.'

I couldn't stop myself turning then but he'd already gone, and this time there was no sound as he made his way along the dark hall towards the staircase.

I felt close to tears after he had left me there. I was angry with him for wrong-footing me and I was angry with myself for my own desire, which had sidled up and pulled me under, like a retreating wave. I waited a while, pretending that I was calming myself when in fact I was hoping he might come back. He didn't.

When I got to bed, it took me a long time to fall asleep and, when I did drift away, my dreams were full of Tom and the lake and his brother – the latter a curiously flat, two-dimensional figure that my mind had pieced together from the photographs I'd seen. The little girl – her strange likeness alone on the table downstairs – didn't appear in those dreams, and for that, at least, I was grateful.

Elizabeth

In the potent air of the glasshouse, Elizabeth was still remembering – not just what had until that morning been a void in her memory but other times in her past that she habitually hid from herself.

She had spent almost three months in the costly confinement of Dr Logan's private asylum after Isabel's birth. That autumn had been lost to her altogether but then, quite suddenly, she was allowed home in time for Christmas. She presumed Dr Logan had seen some sign in her that signalled her complete recovery. She herself wasn't at all certain. She didn't believe and trust in anything then, not even the conclusions and instincts of her own mind. Especially those.

Edward had had the staff go to an enormous amount of effort. A huge tree had been placed and decorated in the hallway, each branch laden with gold-leafed fruit and nuts, slender tapers and tiny painstaking replicas of Stanton House's furniture – from the drawing room's convex mirror to the grandfather clock. Sprigs of holly studded with blood-red berries had been tucked behind the gilt frames of every one of the Stanton family portraits that lined the main staircase – the dour countenances that Edward believed lent the new house an air of permanence made a little less stern by their gaudy adornment.

As she came in through the door, afraid that the tears

would come and Edward would think she had not been cured after all, she detected the scent of cloves and cinnamon. Underneath the spice, more subtly, was the comforting waft of a baking cake, warming orange peel and vanilla, rising from Mrs Wentworth's domain. It was a fitting aroma for her return, redolent of home and hearth and family, but she found herself wondering if it was just a façade behind which there was nothing, no better than a circus tent's illusion bought for a penny.

High above them, unnoticed by Elizabeth at first, was a kissing bough that had been suspended from the chandelier. The mistletoe, its berries gleaming like pearls, was entwined with ivy – a strangely rustic contrast to the faceted crystal confection it hung from.

'Will you let me have a kiss, then?' said Edward, as the last servant melted away. 'To mark your return to us.'

Hesitantly, she nodded and went to him, tilting her face up as his arms encircled her waist. The embrace was awkward, though, all that had happened since their last kiss making them strangers. She was just raising her hand to his cheek so that they might try again when a small cough made them spring apart. It was the nursery-maid – a girl who, in Elizabeth's absence, seemed to have grown in confidence. Once barely able to raise her eyes to meet those of anyone who addressed her, she now met her mistress's gaze with bold curiosity. Elizabeth dimly remembered that the ancient nanny – the same nanny who had once looked after Edward and his brother Charles – had been retired, her eyesight having failed her. This girl must have taken over sole responsibility for the nursery.

'Where is my child?' Elizabeth said eagerly. The maternal instinct she had briefly lost while in the grip of despair had returned with renewed strength. She had dreamt of Isabel every night in the asylum, not only her tiny unformed face but her delicious scent.

'Miss Isabel is asleep and should not be woken,' the maid replied. 'She has had a cold these past days and it wouldn't do for her to be downstairs where it's draughty.'

Elizabeth knew she should say that she would see her own child when she pleased but Edward might side against her. That would be too mortifying in front of the young nursery-maid with the newly impertinent gaze. 'Of course no one must wake her if she's asleep,' she said in the end. 'I will see her later.' Her voice sounded meek, insubstantial.

The girl bobbed cursorily and made for the stairs.

Once she had gone, Edward turned to Elizabeth. 'So, do you like it?'

'Do I like what?' she said, suddenly feeling far away. No one at the asylum had demanded answers of her. It was a strange sensation to have her opinions sought again.

'The house,' he said, a nick of irritation in his voice. 'Everyone has made such an effort.'

His words made her feel as though the entire household, led by her husband, was on the other side of some unbridgeable chasm. She was outside, tapping on the window and imploring them to let her in, but no one could see her there. She tried to quell the thought as soon as it surfaced in her mind, and painted a weak smile on her face. 'Edward, it's beautiful. You shouldn't have gone to so much trouble.'

'Nonsense. You are home and everything will be well

again now. It has been the most distressing time but we must put it behind us. For Isabel's sake, even more than our own. Fortunately she is probably too young to remember.'

'Edward.'

He waved his hand, as if warding off a persistent fly. 'Let us not talk of it, not tonight.'

'But –'

'No, wait. Perhaps we should never talk of it. Perhaps it is better like that. I don't believe in raking over past ills. Nothing can be done about it now. You are yourself once more, Isabel thrives, and barely a soul outside the valley knows what happened. It is already forgotten. Look, I have a present for you. Why don't you open it now, early, while we are alone? It better says what I am trying to.'

It was a box, and for a terrible moment she thought it was a medicine chest that, if she lifted the lid, would be crammed with a dozen bottles of tonics and tablets designed to blunt the edges of her darker thoughts. But when she did she saw it was only a sewing case, the padded satin that lined the underside of the lid the same blue as the Stanton eyes.

'Did you see the engraving on top?'

The mirror shine of the brass plate in the candlelight had obscured it. She looked again and traced her own initial with a finger. Only then did she notice the Latin inscription. *Post tenebras, lux.*

'Do you understand?' he said.

'After darkness, light,' she said slowly, mechanically.

'Yes, my darling. We mustn't look back.'

He had smiled then and she had done her best to return it.

And that was how they had gone on for the next year or so, Edward coming to her bed a couple of times a month until she had discovered that she was with child once again. There had never been any question of her taking measures not to have more children. While Isabel had been enough for her, Edward wanted a whole brood.

Dr Logan's opinion was that Elizabeth's physical health was unlikely to be jeopardized by another birth. In fact, as he had pointed out in a letter Elizabeth found in Edward's desk, there was no reason to presume that each pregnancy would have the same deleterious effect on her mental health. The chances were possibly increased, especially if the patient was naturally inclined to introspection, but not inevitable.

And he had been right in believing that she might be spared the next time, though he was apparently unable to recognize that she had been when, after her second pregnancy had failed, Edward prematurely summoned him again. On the contrary, Dr Logan examined her for no more than five minutes before declaring that she was suffering from puerperal insanity again. She was too distraught to argue, afraid that whatever she said would be turned against her and offered up as further proof of her madness. Later she wondered if it had been Edward's money that had precluded an accurate diagnosis, or her own cursed charms. Whichever it was, a decision had been swiftly made behind the library door. She had not been consulted. Dr Logan was to return with a nurse in a day or so and this time he would stay at Stanton House until she was better.

Elizabeth had never discovered how much it cost

Edward to lure the doctor away from his duties at the private asylum. He seemed willing enough, though, and had returned to the valley by the next evening. She heard his arrival – the tumult of the approaching carriage and the slam of the great oak door as he was admitted – and put her hand flat to the glass of her bedroom window. There was a little low-lying mist that night but she could make out the point where ridge met sky, beyond which lay the rest of the world, impossibly distant.

At first, Dr Logan's ministrations took much the same form as they had at the asylum. The nurse was not Mrs Blackiston this time but a younger, though no less severe, woman whose eyes, hair and puckered mouth were all peculiarly colourless, as though she had rejected anything more vivid as vanity. She was a constant and ever-vigilant presence in Elizabeth's room during the early days of confinement – proving herself particularly hawk-eyed when her patient sought even the mildest form of diversion. Edith, of course, was banished from attending her mistress; Elizabeth had no idea if she had been dismissed altogether.

Gradually, as the days became a week and then a second, Dr Logan began to dismiss the nurse on errands or to get fresh air for her own health. Elizabeth watched this unfold with dread, understanding that she would soon be alone with him. Sure enough, one morning brought the asylum carriage, which had come to take the nurse back to that dismal place. Behind the bedroom door that they thought muffled their voices, Elizabeth heard the doctor tell Edward that the nurse's return was unavoidable after an outbreak of influenza had laid low much of the asylum staff. He, Dr Logan, would remain and assume sole responsibility for Lady Stanton.

During her time at the asylum Elizabeth had taken scant notice of the doctor's physical appearance. It had not signified then. Now she found herself aware of his every feature and all repelled her. Aside from his pale, fluttering, clammy hands, he wore a patchy moustache of ginger that did not match his tea-coloured hair. His teeth, though straight enough, had about them an unfortunate grey tinge that put Elizabeth in mind of the grave.

He never went so far as to kiss her on the mouth, let alone force himself upon her, though the unspoken threat of the latter hung, like a suspended blade, over her bed. What he did was more insidious and much more difficult to protest against.

It had begun innocuously enough: his tremulous but persistent hands holding hers while she lay prone under the sheets, his soft monotone reiterating her infirmity of mind and feminine frailty. Only her total submission to his proven method of rest cure would set her on the slow road to recovery and eventual release, he said.

One day he brought the palm of her hand to his wet lips, his eyes closed in a sort of ecstasy of healing or bald desire, she couldn't tell which. As he finally drew away, she felt the flick of his tongue. The next day he stroked her arm for an hour or more, peeling back the sleeve of her nightgown, inch by terrible inch, until the pale flesh of her entire inner arm was exposed. She didn't see how his fingers shook as they traced a line up and down because she turned her face to the window, but she felt it well enough.

After these episodes, she felt desperate enough to try to reason with him.

'Dr Logan,' she said, as calmly as she could one day, careful to keep her voice low. 'I am grateful for your treatment and believe it to be working already. Do I not appear different to you? Surely you can see that I am not as I was during my stay at the asylum.'

He smiled indulgently at her. 'Lady Stanton, I am flattered by your confidence in my treatment but you must know that, despite my experience in treating hundreds of women like yourself, no two individuals have yet displayed identical symptoms. Maladies of the female mind take many forms, each more cunning and adept at deceit and trickery than the last. I have learnt – I don't mind admitting to my cost on occasion – that even the most sincere declaration of sanity is more usually symptomatic of its dark opposite.'

She felt something in her break then and began to escape the days by retreating into sleep, waking only at night, when the doctor had retired to his own room. What she contemplated in those silent hours, after pulling back the curtains and watching the moonlight turn everything to dull, unpolished pewter, she didn't want to think about ever again.

One night, when she had taken up her usual station at the window, the glinting eye of the lake visible beyond the black lawn, something pale and gliding made her heart beat loudly in her chest. For an instant she thought it was a ghost but it was one of the servants, a young boy she couldn't identify from her upstairs window, his pale shirt giving the appearance of something floating and unearthly.

Though she didn't recognize him, she knew he had seen her, too, for he stopped and tipped his face up towards her. Perhaps, like her, he thought he had witnessed something spectral. And perhaps he had, she thought, as she caught sight of what he must have seen in her dressing-table mirrors: an apparition of loose hair and hollow eyes clad in the filmy glow of a white nightgown.

After five weeks, Dr Logan deemed her cured. When he informed her of this, naturally after Edward had been told, she nodded mutely, unable to meet his eyes in case he saw the anger that simmered there. It was not worth risking a confrontation with the doctor about his sham diagnosis, not when he seemed to wield so much influence over her husband – who could at any time put pen to paper and consign her to another spell in the asylum. Not that it had been better in her own home – she thought it had probably been worse. She had heard Isabel at the door a few times before the nursery-maid had dragged her away, and the subsequent guilt had wrapped itself around Elizabeth, like a dank shroud.

After Dr Logan had gone, she and Edward had retreated back into distance and politeness and, when she had later mourned another lost child, he hadn't even noticed her silence or the shadows that circled her eyes again.

Now, sitting on the hard floor of the glasshouse, Elizabeth reflected that it was quite astounding how far that sort of habitual restraint could take you. Until that morning's revelation in the library, of course. How strange that such a little thing, such an innocent thing as leaving behind her shoes in her child's nursery, could unpick all the steadfast work she and Edward had done to draw a veil over past events. All it had taken was the tug of a memory and, like a loose thread, the sum of it had been unwound into nothing.

Dr Logan's stay and, before that, the Christmas after her release from his asylum both seemed a lifetime ago – but, then, so did the previous night's party. She remembered how she had lounged in the Bath chair out on the lawn and under the sky – so different from the close atmosphere of the glasshouse. She found it hard to believe she had done that less than twelve hours before.

The glasshouse felt very different from the night when she had broken the panel in the roof, the fragments falling around her and a tiny Isabel. The sky above was now a soft blue and – yes – she could hear the fountain stutter into life. Someone had turned it on. It felt peaceful; what had happened in this very spot had not stained it. She tested her mind, very gently, by remembering how she had wished then that she could vanish under the surface of the lake, but it was just a second-hand memory, without even a shadow of any inclination to do it. At the thought she felt nothing but fear – not only for herself, but for Isabel and her unborn child.

As if he could hear her, a sharp pain lit up the underside of her abdomen and she gasped aloud. Suddenly the glasshouse felt airless and, when no more pain came, she got slowly, gingerly, to her feet. She had three weeks yet to go so it could not be that, could it? No. It was probably just the strain of his weight and the awkwardness of her position on the floor.

She walked slowly back towards the house, her arm underneath her stomach as if to support the child inside her. She moved as though another flutter might come but the baby was as still again as he had been yesterday. Anxiety about that, and the thought of returning to the house and Edward, flooded her and she began breathlessly to hum a tune – something Edith was always singing – to distract herself. She stopped to snap off the dead head of a rose and wondered if a little gardening would make her feel better. Being outdoors often did. It was much warmer now, though, the sun quite fierce, and she decided that she must fetch her wide-brimmed hat if she was going to stay outside.

Edith had been in to tidy her rooms and Elizabeth allowed herself to sit a moment on the bed. The windows had been opened and she could hear the fountain from here too. It was a soothing sound and she considered lying back and going to sleep. She was just about to take off her shoes and do just that – for half an hour or so – when Edward appeared at the doorway. He hesitated, apparently unsure whether to cross the threshold.

'I looked for you,' he said eventually, 'but you'd gone.'

'Come in, Edward.' She gestured for him to sit on a small velvet chair next to her dressing-table. His legs were too long for it and he soon got up again, perhaps feeling himself to be at a disadvantage in it.

'You might like to know that our guests have left,' he said.

She clapped a hand to her mouth. 'I forgot about them. I – I went to the . . .'

'It's no matter,' he said shortly. 'They were fed and now they have gone. I said you were exhausted after last night and couldn't be disturbed. No one noticed anything was amiss.'

'Thank you.'

'Where did you go?'

She paused, then looked up at him fearfully. 'I went to the glasshouse.'

His countenance darkened immediately. 'So you do remember?'

'Oh, Edward, I do now, but never before this morning.' Her voice was strangled and louder than she had meant it to be.

He strode over to the door and closed it. 'For God's sake, lower your voice. One of the servants will hear you.'

'I'm sorry,' she whispered.

He came closer but remained standing. 'Do you understand now why I had to send for Dr Logan the first time? Both times, in fact?' he asked.

She was staring now at her clasped hands but she could feel his gaze intently upon her. 'I would never have hurt Isabel,' she said.

'Elizabeth, if you say that, I cannot think you have recalled the episode accurately.'

'No, I remember everything. It has all come back. But what I couldn't say to you at the time – my thoughts were too disordered – was that I only took the baby, I only took *Isabel*, because if I'd left her in the nursery she would have carried on crying and woken the nursery-maid. And she would have wondered what I was doing in the middle of the night and –'

'There were shards of glass in the folds of her blanket.'

'She was not injured, Edward. Not a hair on her head.

Even in my – even though I was not myself – I made sure of that.'

He sat down heavily in the small chair, as if too fatigued to mind any longer that it was too low for him. 'I never dreamt, when we married, that something like this should happen. That there would be such a blight on our marriage.'

At this, she thought she might cry, from a strong blend of frustration and sadness, and so fixed her gaze on the nearest window. If she hadn't delayed she might have been out in the garden by now, her hat on and the pruning scissors in her hand.

She dragged in her breath shakily. 'I am sorry I have given you cause to regret marrying me,' she said. 'But you must believe me when I say that if there had been any-thing I might have done to stay well after Isabel's birth, I wouldn't have hesitated. It wasn't me, Edward, it was something quite apart from me.'

He sighed. 'Yes, I have read on the subject. Who has not, in the last ten years? The melancholy or mania that can follow the birth of a child. Even precede it in some cases. It seems that there is scarcely a village in the land that does not contain a new mother who has been similarly afflicted. Even in Stanwick and Painswick, it is practically an epidemic. There are many husbands, rich and poor, who have been in fear of their children's lives. I had no choice.' He hung his head.

'I asked you a question last night. Do you remember?' she said.

He didn't reply so she continued, 'I asked you what you would do if it happened again, if I were to become . . . unsound, unbalanced in my mind again.'

'Yes,' he said, with great weariness.

'You said that you would do as you see fit. But I don't know what that means. I don't know if it means that I will have to go away again, or if I will be locked away in my own home. I must know, so that I can prepare for it. I think you might give me that.'

'I do not understand why you persist in this black way of thinking,' he shouted, his voice breaking on the last syllable. 'Your very prophecies of doom make their fulfilment more likely.'

He stood again and began to pace in front of the fireplace.

She watched him, feeling detached from yet another frank conversation with her husband. How strange that two should come in such quick succession. Or not: perhaps the dam had been breached and this was how it would be between them now. Perhaps it would be no worse than the silences.

'Edward, I must ring for Edith and ask her to bring me some food and perhaps a tonic. I feel quite faint.'

He crossed to her and picked up one of her hands. She thought he might hold it to his cheek but he turned it over and pinched the wrist hard between his thumb and middle finger.

'Your pulse is far too rapid,' he said, after half a minute. 'Try to calm yourself, for the child's sake.'

She nodded meekly.

'Did it occur to you to eat something before you set off across the Great Mead this morning?'

She looked down, afraid to anger him further. In fact, she hadn't touched a thing since the previous day. 'No,' she admitted. 'Isabel and I were going to have breakfast but then you wanted to see me in the library and –'

'Please do not blame me for your inability to look after yourself. You know very well that you have a marked tendency to hysteria, yet you rush about without sustenance just a few weeks before you are due to give birth. I have been far too indulgent with you. I always have been. I should have insisted that your confinement began weeks ago, with bed rest and none of this . . . wandering about. Well, I shall do so now and you will not try to persuade me otherwise.'

During this speech he had grown quite red in the face.

'Edward, you are right. I have not been as careful as I should have been. But please, please do not bid me to stay in my bed with that man watching me. You know how I . . . You know.' A great shuddering sob escaped her, taking her by surprise.

At this he dropped her hand, which he had distractedly been holding all the while. 'Elizabeth, you must calm yourself. I say again, you must think of the child. I can only hope that a son will take after . . .' He stopped and coloured.

She looked up at him, the tears drying on her face. 'That a son will take after you rather than his mother? Is that what you were going to say?'

He raised his chin defiantly. 'I am not to be vilified for speaking of what is both true and desirable. Surely you, as his mother, would not wish any inherited affliction on your child, especially the taint of madness.'

'The taint of madness? Edward, you speak of me, your wife, your Elizabeth, as a kind of malign influence.'

'Is it not true?' he said, his voice rising again to a shout, full of mingled anger and fear. 'Is it not true that your mother's cousin was mad? That your mother herself was given to attacks of nerves and other – hysterical maladies? I do not blame you for it, but it is there nonetheless, a hereditary stain passed from woman to woman, down the female line. Isabel –'

'What of Isabel?' she said sharply.

He sighed and rubbed at his hair until it stood up in tufts at the back. 'You know I love our daughter. I have been her sole parent during your illnesses and I have done my duty by her. But she is so much like you. Her hair, the shade of her eyes – they deceive no one. She is your daughter to her very marrow. She is not robust, like I was at her age. She is fearful, fearful already, a tiny child.'

A noise then – something falling or being knocked over – made them both start.

'What was that?' said Edward. 'Is someone at the door?' He strode over and wrenched it back but the landing was empty.

'It is nothing,' said Elizabeth. 'Perhaps something fell off one of the shelves in my dressing room.' Her mind was going over the words she suspected he had always wanted to say. Even so, it had wounded her, hearing them spoken aloud.

Perhaps grateful for the interruption, the slight loosening of the brittle tension in the room, Edward continued to look for the source of the noise, peering out of the window, then crossing to the hidden door of the dressing room, wallpapered to match the rest of the room. Inside hung Elizabeth's dresses, with shelves below and above them for slippers, boots and hats in their smart, cylindrical boxes.

As he turned the handle and pulled the door towards him, a rush of movement exploded through the gap. It was Isabel, who had evidently been there all along. She liked to play inside sometimes, among the lace and the raw silk, the taffeta and the muslin, all of it infused with the fading scent of her mother.

'Isabel! Come back at once!' shouted Edward, as the little girl ran out of the bedroom. 'Isabel!'

She had appeared, then vanished again so quickly that it was almost as if she had never been there, the shining, rippling silk of her hair the only glimpse Elizabeth had caught of her. She knew where her child would run to, though, and she would not tell her husband.

'That child,' he exclaimed, his face redder still, 'has been spying on us.'

'She is not yet five,' Elizabeth replied curtly. 'She probably fell asleep in there and then was too afraid to show herself.'

He was not listening. 'I will go to Stanwick,' he said, almost to himself. 'I said I would call on the colonel today or tomorrow.'

His tone was terse; she knew he was suddenly desperate to leave the valley. Perhaps he thought that one day, if only he rode away far and hard enough, he would return to a different sort of wife – someone who would ask nothing of him but that she be at his side. 'I will be back late this afternoon, so I shall not want luncheon. Make sure that you eat some and remember what I said.'

'But, Edward, before you go, you must tell me. You have not answered my question.'

'I must not do anything,' he replied coldly, his face now impassive.

He is just like his name and just like his house, she thought. Stanton: place of stone.

'Elizabeth, are you even listening to me? I said, you are my wife and you will do as I have asked. Do not let me find out that you have gone against my express wishes.'

As he left, full of righteous indignation, she wondered what he would tell the colonel and what the colonel would say in return. She had faith that the old man would defend her, even if Edward didn't want to listen to what he said.

She decided to watch the clock on her mantel for twenty minutes, the amount of time she calculated it would take Edward to change into his riding clothes and call for his horse to be saddled up and brought round. After that, it would be only a matter of minutes before he had sped down the gravel drive and up through the beech woods to come out on to Fiery Lane. From there it was less than a mile up to the village that perched on the ridge of the combe.

As the time crawled by, she retraced the steps of her and Edward's conversation, hearing it anew as Isabel would have heard it. She thought of her little girl, hidden in the dressing room and hearing the ugly words Edward had uttered about her mother's family – madness, hysteria and inherited affliction – and thanked God that Isabel was too young to understand them. She would have understood enough, though. A sensitive child, she would not have needed to know the precise definition of the words to comprehend the fear and contempt in her father's voice as he spoke them.

Elizabeth's own father would never have said such things, and Edward knew it. The contrast between the two men, during the half-dozen occasions she had been able to observe them together, was marked. She had noticed it most on the day they had all picnicked by the manor. Edward strode about, complaining first about the spot the servants had chosen to lay out the rugs and then about the contents of the basket.

'What does it signify what we eat on a day like this?' her father had said affably, unaware of how irritating his son-in-law would find his remark. 'I'd be content with an apple and a slice of cheese.'

It was during the same stay that her mother had fallen prey to an attack of the nerves Edward had just alluded to. One of the reasons she hadn't seen her parents in their final years as much as she would have liked was her mother's fear of travelling long distances by carriage. (Another was Edward's reluctance to let his wife go and stay with them.)

The evening before they were due to depart for Bristol, her mother grew agitated, unable to touch a morsel of her dinner and clutching Elizabeth as if she would never see her again before she retired to bed. Elizabeth sensed Edward's barely contained impatience with this behaviour but her father remained oblivious to it, more concerned with reassuring his wife.

'How am I ever to live up to such a paragon?' Edward

asked, the next day, as he and Elizabeth stood waving at her parents' carriage as it disappeared out of sight. They had just watched the old man place his wife in it as if she were made of glass.

'It's not that he's a saint,' Elizabeth said calmly, though the sarcasm in his voice had made her want to strike him. 'He likes to protect her.'

It was true. To her father, her mother's delicate temperament was part of her femininity. It wasn't frightening to him or irritating. A broken thing was something to be mended, not tossed away.

In her bedroom, her eyes on the clock, Elizabeth put a hand to her swollen abdomen in a bid to calm herself. How quickly the hope she had found on her walk to the manor had dissipated. Her heart was palpitating now, a rippling of uncertainty in her chest as the rhythm of the beat was briefly lost. She could not lose this child. She could not be ill again either: she wouldn't survive it, she was sure of that – despite whatever Dr Logan had persuaded Edward about her basic resilience. Her heart's rhythm faltered again as she remembered what Edward had said last night: that she was even more afraid of the insanity returning than the death of her baby. She wondered if it were true.

Her mind rushed on. If the child was a girl, there was a strong possibility that she would succumb to the darkness as she had after Isabel's birth. And, of course, with the birth of a second girl, there would also be Edward's terrible disappointment to contend with. If he got his wish and she managed to bear him a healthy boy, a sturdy little heir in his father's image, who would grow up to inherit the Fiercombe estate, things might be different. The madness would leave her in peace if she managed that – surely it would. *But what if it did not?* a small voice in her head muttered. *What if this boy died too?* And what if this time she descended so far into the blackness that she couldn't find her way out again?

Alice

In the mirror, the morning after Tom and I had fallen out, I poked at my unruly hair, which had curled defiantly into thick, tangled ringlets at the ends. My eyes were dark with shadows. I tried to pin it up again but I couldn't do it so I tried to tie it back with the ribbon instead. My fingers were thickened and clumsy, though, and I yanked it out in a sudden fury, dropping it to the floor and stamping on it like a child. It lay there after I'd finished my foolish tantrum, a lemon-yellow snake of satin on the polished boards. Without washing I put on some clothes and crept down the stairs silently, my shoes in my hand.

I needn't have bothered being so stealthy. When I got outside Tom's car had already gone; the gravel where the tyres had turned too fast flung up, revealing scored mud beneath. In a concentrated repeat of an earlier morning, I felt bereft and relieved at once.

For the rest of the day, I found my thoughts drifting between the mystery of the little girl, Henry's death at the lake, the photograph of Elizabeth and the tension that existed between Tom and me – a narrow, tensile cord, like the one I felt connecting me to Elizabeth. In both cases they now pulled harder than ever.

That I had only a month to wait for the baby's arrival was not something I chose to dwell on, an avoidance made easier by the fact that he wasn't yet huge, but tucked neatly inside the depths of me. The gladness I'd felt after thinking I'd lost him had confused me more than I dared think about. The chain of events that would swing into motion after his arrival were also too much for me to contemplate calmly. I knew I had to give him up but I simply could not bring myself to consider it for more than a stomach-lurching second. Instead, my thoughts were like those tiny insects that flit and dart so haphazardly through the air, apparently without purpose.

Tom was the easiest to think of; there was something haunting and melancholy about Elizabeth and the little girl, whose fates I had now come to think of as linked in some way. So it was thoughts of Tom I indulged myself with for the next day or so, looking at the manor with new eyes, seeing it not just as a house brimming with centuries of secrets – secrets sewn into the faded tapestries and slipped down the cracks in the floorboards – but as his childhood home. The top of the forbidding newel post in the hallway was now shiny from his small hand turning on it as he reached the bottom of the stairs on summer mornings, chasing after Henry into each new day. The lovely views of the becalmed valley through every window were now views he had stopped short at the sight of too.

That feeling of being lit from inside again was disconcerting; an excitement I'd almost forgotten. It was also frightening, as it had been with James, but I was surer of myself this time. I had absolutely no reason to be yet a warm coal of certainty had settled inside me. In short, I didn't believe he simply wanted the novelty of seducing an expectant mother. When he came back, I vowed, I would be the one to extend an olive branch. After all, he had trusted me with so much the last evening we had spent together.

When he didn't come back that first night, or the second, I had to tell the wounded part of myself that he had dozens of friends who would entreat him to stay and that he would agree, with the unthinking, well-bred courtesy of his type. I also knew, though, that I'd hurt his pride and that he stayed away because of that, the proof of his minding something of a comfort.

A night or two later, after Mrs Jelphs had gone to bed, I returned to Tom's cardboard box to go through it all again, ostensibly to see if I'd missed anything intriguing, but more to touch his things in silly schoolgirl fashion. On top was a sheet of creamy writing paper folded in two.

I opened it with trembling hands. The top was embossed with the Stanton coat of arms and beneath it were a couple of lines written with a fountain pen whose scratchy nib must have been worn in by another hand. '*To my new friend Alice,*' it read. '*Sorry about our little misunderstanding, though I did warn you I had bad manners. I will be back on Friday and I hope we will have another of our interesting talks. TS*'

I smiled to myself and read it a few more times. I hadn't offended him too badly after all; my instincts had been right. I was nervous at the thought of seeing him, and I couldn't imagine what he was thinking about me, but my overwhelming feeling was gladness. The baby turned and wheeled and it felt to me, in my rather giddy mood, as though he approved.

The next morning was so hot that I woke in a sweat.

The sheets were tangled around me and damp to the touch and I had kicked the blankets to the floor. In the bathroom I ran the cold tap over the insides of my wrists, but it took a couple of minutes for the water to run cooler than tepid. I sponged myself all over but by the time I was dry new beads of sweat were forming at my hairline and under my arms. A runnel had trickled down between my heavier breasts before I'd even finished dressing.

Downstairs, Nan looked as though she might pass out from the heat in the kitchen. Her cheeks were crimson and strands of hair dark with perspiration had escaped her bun and plastered themselves to her neck. 'Oh, Alice, I'm miserable in this heat,' she cried. 'I've opened the door as wide as it will go and there's not a breath of wind to be had.'

I poured myself a glass of milk but it was warm and tasted off so I tipped it away down the sink. The sour, cloying taste lingered in my mouth.

'Nothing'll keep in this weather.' Nan sighed, fanning herself with a cloth. 'That milk was fresh this morning.'

I went out to look at the thermometer. Stepping out of the shade of the kitchen felt like walking into a wall of heat. The mercury said the temperature was already up in the mid-eighties and yet it was only just past nine. I wandered back inside.

'Do you think it's ever going to break?' I asked Nan, who had collapsed into a chair.

'I hope so. I'm going to have to jump in the stream if it carries on.'

I laughed. 'Why don't we? It'll be delicious. Where's Mrs Jelphs got to?'

Nan looked at me mischievously. 'She's gone to Pains-wick and said she'd be a while. Can we?'

'Yes, come on!' I held out my hand and we set off across the gravel.

'Where's you two off to, then?' Ruck had appeared out of nowhere, as was his wont. Despite the heat he was in his usual cap and thick wool trousers, his only concession to the weather his rolled-up shirtsleeves. His arms were burnt a dark, brick-red brown.

I glanced at Nan and saw she was too close to laughing to speak. 'Good morning, Ruck,' I said. 'We're just off to put our feet in the stream and cool down. It was my idea. We'll be back to work soon.'

He said nothing to that but, as we went on our way, I looked back and saw that he was still watching us. Watching me, I thought.

'He has this habit of popping up when I least expect it,' said Nan. 'He always gives me a turn.' She giggled.

The water was shockingly, deliciously cold as it swirled around our bare feet. Within a minute we felt normal again. I lifted my hair off my neck in the hope of finding a breeze but there was none.

'Come here,' said Nan. 'I'll do it.'

I shifted up the bank towards her. 'You've got enough hair for both of us here,' she said admiringly. She twisted it round and fastened it with pins from her own. She blew on the back of my neck, giggling. It was blissful.

'So,' she said, when we were lying back in the grass, our feet still dangling in the water, my hands resting on the hot dome of my stomach. 'Are you going to tell me, then?'

'Tell you what?' I said, not understanding.

'About Thomas Stanton.'

I turned my head to look at her. 'What about him?'

'Do you think he's handsome?'

I pretended to consider it, looking up at the flawless blue sky as if an answer might materialize there. Nan poked my nearest foot with hers.

'He's quite nice,' I said.

'Quite nice? He's a bit more than that.'

I laughed. 'He'll be back tomorrow night. Perhaps you'll catch a glimpse of him the morning after.'

She sighed. 'I don't come in on Saturdays, do I? How do you know anyway? He's hopeless about arrangements, never tells anyone where he's going and when he'll be back.'

I couldn't help myself, I smiled. 'He mentioned it in a note he left me.'

She sat up at that. 'A note! What – like a love letter?'

'No, of course not. We're friends, nothing more.'

I remembered how he had kissed my hand and knew Nan wouldn't think that was the behaviour of friends. But 'friend' was what he had called me in his note. And surely that was all we could be; even without the matter of my baby, we came from different worlds, he and I. There might not have been a huge amount of money left in the family but it was still an old, distinguished one. I had to remember that.

'I wouldn't be surprised if it was a love letter,' continued Nan, in a dreamy tone. 'He's ever such a flirt. All the girls round here are in love with him. He's the most eligible man in Gloucestershire.'

My feet were cold right through to the marrow so I

pushed myself up and away from the water. 'I expect Lady Stanton has someone waiting in the wings for when he's ready to settle down,' I said, trying to keep my voice casual.

'Oh, yes, a few of them, I shouldn't wonder. There was a distant cousin from Bath for a while, but Thomas wasn't interested. Pots of money but not pretty enough for his liking, I reckon. Then there's Caroline Summerhill and she's pretty enough for anyone. Well, pretty's not really the word for her. She's more beautiful, I would say.'

'Have you seen her?' I wanted the conversation to be over and cursed myself for being such a fool about a man who was not only unsuitable but intended elsewhere.

'Yes,' said Nan, brightly. 'She came just before Christmas last year. Sir Charles and Lady Stanton were here for once and Miss Summerhill and her family came for tea on Christmas Eve. You should have seen the amount of dusting and sprucing we had to do and they were only here for a couple of hours.' She rolled her eyes dramatically.

'What did she look like, this Caroline?'

Nan screwed her nose up to think. 'Everything about her was pale. She looked like she'd never seen the sun. There wasn't a mark on her skin, not a single freckle. It was like they say in old books, like porcelain. A porcelain complexion. She had blonde hair that had been waved but it hadn't been coloured – you could tell that by the roots. She was a real lady, the way she held her cup and sat up so straight in her chair.'

I must've looked disappointed because Nan nudged me. 'To be honest, he didn't seem that taken with her. She scarcely said two words. And when I say beautiful, really she was more like a china doll. It wasn't like she was a real person.'

'You're sweet to say it, Nan, but I don't care one way or the other. Tom's become a sort of friend to me. We've talked a little, that's all. Besides, look at me.' I laid my hand on my swollen abdomen.

'Oh, that wouldn't worry Thomas. He's always been the rebellious sort. He was nearly expelled from school when he was fifteen for sneaking out with a friend and going to a pub. Not that they would serve him, of course – he still looked like a schoolboy. Sir Charles had to beg to keep him there. I think they only let him stay because of what had happened to his brother. I don't think Thomas cares what people think.'

'It's not just about that, Nan, and you know it. We come from entirely different backgrounds.'

'But you're clever and you had a good job, didn't you? You're not like me either,' she said, knowing what she meant but at a loss to explain it.

Again, I felt like an old-fashioned governess: neither one thing nor the other; no Mrs Jelphs but hardly an Elizabeth Stanton either.

Nan helped me up and we walked slowly back to the manor, keeping in the shade where we could. Once she had gone, I finished my own duties, then wandered around aimlessly, unable to settle in the airless house but uncomfortably hot sitting outside. In truth, I was restless because I was nervous about seeing Tom the next day. I really didn't want to lose my head again, not like I had with James.

Mrs Jelphs was still not back from Painswick and I suddenly had the idea to visit Mr Morton, who would surely be back from Cornwall. Judging by the sun's position it had only just gone four o'clock. It seemed an age since I'd seen him and the distraction from thoughts of Tom would do me good. If I walked very slowly and rested along the way, the journey would not be too much for me. Besides, I was too stubborn to admit that I was becoming trapped down in the valley by my ever-growing bulk.

I caught sight of Ruck just before I got to where the easiest of the paths began. He was standing in the lane where I'd stood with him before. Even knowing he could turn at any moment and catch me there I couldn't help observing him. He was gazing again at the rhododendrons' almost menacing beauty, apparently unable to tear himself away. His shoulders were hunched in what I took to be confusion, and he seemed more shrunken and decrepit than I'd seen him before.

The heat was a tangible force pressing in at me from all angles. Even under the shade of the beech trees, once I'd started on the path, there was little respite. The dappling effect of the leaves left me dizzy and off-balance and I had to rest half a dozen times, breathing heavily. The air smelt of rotting flowers. I wondered if I had turned a little mad in attempting such a walk, or whether I just needed to escape the somehow denser atmosphere of the valley.

When I finally got to Mr Morton's house I was even more dishevelled than I had been on my other visits. He answered the door almost immediately, as I was still trying to smooth down my hair, which was damp with sweat.

'Ah, Alice, it's you. I'm so glad.'

'Uninvited as usual,' I said sheepishly. 'And even more unkempt.'

'Nonsense, come in. Are you quite all right? Surely you didn't walk here.'

'I like to walk. It makes me feel like I'm still the same person, somehow.'

He ushered me into the same sitting room we had sat in during my other visits. Just as then, I felt myself relax as I sank into the armchair.

'Did you have a nice holiday?' I said, when he returned from the kitchen with two tall glasses of ginger beer. A wafer-thin slice of lemon bobbed on the surface of each. It looked like heaven.

'Staying with my niece in Cornwall, you mean? Oh, yes. I like it down there. I love being by the sea. I thought I would end up there in my dotage but I've never been able to bring myself to leave this place. I don't know why it is that I'm so attached to this part of the world but I am.'

'You could go and live near your niece tomorrow. I'm sure she'd be glad to have you close by.'

'No, I couldn't, not really. I'm tied to this little corner of the world now.'

We sat sipping our drinks companionably. The cool liquid was refreshing as it went down.

'I was hoping you'd call,' he said suddenly. 'I found a few things that might interest you. Some I had filed away and forgotten about, one item I bought.'

'I hope you didn't spend any money on me.'

'My dear, it was hardly a king's ransom. Besides, I was intrigued myself.'

I felt my interest light, like dry kindling. During my last

visits we had steered away from discussing the valley's history by some unspoken mutual consent but I sensed that it would be different today. I felt I was up to it too. I needed to hear it. I suppose it was another reason I had struggled up the hill in the blazing heat.

He went over to a bureau in the corner, where he riffled through a pile of papers that had been gathered into a cardboard folder. From where I was sitting, I could see that some were brittle and yellowed. Then he pulled out a pamphlet in pristine condition and handed it over. It was an auction catalogue dated February 1899.

'I thought you might find this interesting, as someone who has heard a little about Stanton House.'

Attached with a paperclip to the front was a photograph I hadn't seen before. Taken far closer to the house than the image in Mr Morton's book, it showed in black-and-white the house at its newly completed best. An impossibly tall ladder had been placed against the façade and up it was an estate worker. Presumably this was in the days when there were dozens of them. It looked as though he was replacing a roof tile. I put it aside to look at the catalogue, which was unmistakably of the period, with its bold black script, the name of Stanton House dwarfed only by that of the auctioneers.

I leafed through the pages. As Mrs Jelphs had told me, it seemed there had been nothing too good – or too insignificant – to omit from the sale. Copper piping, wood panelling, brass door-handles: it was all there, along with items that spoke more poignantly of circumstances brutally altered. Things that had once been chosen and loved, that had added up to a comfortable, privileged existence:

an engraved silver-backed hairbrush, a mahogany and baize card table, a child's rocking horse.

'We haven't talked much about the Stanton family lately,' I said finally.

'I suppose that's true.'

'Thomas Stanton has been back,' I said, eyes lowered so I didn't give anything away.

'Yes, I heard. Quite literally, in fact. I've heard him zipping about in that lovely little motor of his.'

'He told me about his brother Henry. What happened at the lake.'

'Ah. That was a tragedy, though I didn't know the boy well. His and Thomas's father, Charles Stanton, is not like his older brother Edward was at all. He's always kept himself – and his family – to himself. They lived a quiet life down there and now, of course, he and Lady Stanton are hardly there at all.'

'She doesn't like it here.'

'She was from London, like you, and I think she would have been more suited to living there instead. It was always too quiet for her here, but I think she loved her husband and, of course, her boys. Henry was said to be her favourite. After his accident, there was nothing left for her to love about Fiercombe.'

'I remember Ruck telling me on my very first day here that she had got "notions" about things, I think he said. That she didn't sleep well.'

Mr Morton shook his head sadly. 'After Henry died, she became convinced the valley was . . . ill-fated in some way.'

'She thought it was unlucky,' I said softly.

'I suppose so. This is only what I've heard. Though it's true that Henry is not buried in Fiercombe's graveyard, which you might say speaks volumes. He was laid to rest up here, in Stanwick, at his mother's insistence. You can imagine how much talk that generated.

'But there have always been stories about Fiercombe. Its isolation, the very steepness of the valley, how it's cut off in winter when it snows. You know about Margaret of Anjou, of course, but there was another Stanton ancestor, a much earlier one than Edward, sixteenth century, I believe, who was said to be an alchemist.'

'Mrs Jelphs mentioned him. His portrait hangs on the stairs. I've no idea why anyone would want it up. It's a horrible thing.'

'And he was a horrible man, by all accounts. It's said that he pushed his wife down the stairs in a fit of pique. She broke her neck. Differing versions of the story have her paralysed or dead. His temper was legendary, and ruthless. There was barely a servant in the county who would work for him.'

Without thinking, my hand went to the bruise that Tom had spotted on my arm. It was fading slowly, purple to jaundiced yellow. 'There was a little girl once.' The words slipped out before I thought about it.

'Do you mean at Stanton House?' He turned over the auction pamphlet that I'd laid on the table between us. 'Yes, there was. Isabel.'

Hearing her name for the first time made me feel cold. I put down my glass and flexed my fingers.

'I suppose it would have been her rocking horse that was sold off in the auction,' he said.

I remembered a rocking horse a school friend of mine had owned when we were five or six. It was a battered old thing of dented tin with a tangled mane of red wool but I had envied her its ownership with a passion. We would take endless turns until her mother shouted up the stairs that she couldn't stand the creaking a minute longer.

'It's interesting you should ask about Isabel,' Mr Morton went on, bringing me back to myself. 'The other item I remembered I had is indirectly connected to her. It concerns her mother. Her mother being Elizabeth, of course.'

I had been reaching for my glass again but I froze.

He looked at me strangely. 'Really, Alice, I think you've overdone it coming up here on foot. You've gone a peculiar colour. Listen, you're not about to have . . . I mean, it's too early for . . .'

The sight of him worrying that I might give birth on his lovely old rugs took my mind off Isabel. I smiled as reassuringly as I could and took a deep breath. 'There's no chance of that, Mr Morton. I've a month to go yet.'

'Thank God. But I wish you would call me Hugh,' he said.

I laughed. 'I'm sorry I gave you a start. It's just that I saw a strange photograph of a little girl and I think it's of Isabel. I didn't know her name until you said it. I've wondered again and again what happened to her. To Elizabeth, too. Isabel especially has been lost somehow.'

He shook his head. 'No one really knows what happened to either of them. Of course, the few people who were left at Stanton House presumably knew but up here, in the village, gossip was rife yet nothing was confirmed. A doctor was seen going down into the valley not long after the last party I attended there but his carriage swept through Stanwick without stopping. No one knew him anyway – he was from Oxford, I believe. I always got the feeling that something had been hushed up and there was a lot of talk about money – or, rather, Edward Stanton's sudden lack of it.

'Really, it was the oddest thing. There was that one last, glorious party I went to, on Midsummer's Eve, and everything seemed well enough then. Edward was clearly in love with Elizabeth, she was healthy and with child – not Isabel, she was a little girl by then, four or five, I'm no good at children's ages – and the estate appeared to be thriving. That must have been 1897 – no, 1898. Some days later – no more than a week – the doctor was seen arriving. No one saw him leave but perhaps it was in the dead of night. An old itinerant who always stopped at the pub here on his travels claimed that he saw a white carriage go down there around that time, in the first glimmers of dawn, but I'm not sure his word could be relied on by anyone.'

'A white carriage?' I said.

'White carriages were sometimes used instead of black when a small child or baby died.'

'Do you think Elizabeth lost her second child?'

'I have no way of knowing, I'm afraid. By 1900, everything had gone. All that was left for Charles Stanton to inherit was the old manor and the land.'

'But someone must know what happened to them?'

'Many people think they know. There are a multitude of theories, each more fantastic than the last.' He sighed. 'Elizabeth was such a lovely woman, glowing with health when I saw her for the last time. We talked about sunsets . . .' He tailed off, his eyes sad.

I sat enthralled, my mind racing through the possibilities.

'So do you have your own theory about what happened to them?' I felt rude for intruding on his thoughts but I couldn't believe a mother, daughter and tiny baby could have vanished from history so easily. 'I mean, do you think they survived? Perhaps they were whisked away in the middle of the night.'

'As I said, there are many stories. Some say that Elizabeth died in childbirth and that Isabel simply pined away, dying of a broken heart at the loss of her mother, to whom she was uncommonly close for those times. Elizabeth was ill after Isabel's birth, you know – well, we shall come to that shortly – and it meant that the little girl had always clung to her. Others spoke to some of the staff who were dismissed during that strange week, and swear that the new baby, delivered slightly prematurely, caught scarlet fever from the nursery-maid and died. Isabel and Elizabeth were spirited off to London before she could catch it, with Sir Edward – who certainly left Fiercombe for good within weeks of that last party – following. It was all rather hazy and conflicting. Of course, that has simply added to the mystery over the years.'

'But do you think what the servants said was true: that Elizabeth and Isabel went to London?'

He sighed. 'Well, it's always been a fancy of mine that they had a happy ending, despite the debts and the probable death of the second child. What is known is that Edward drank himself to death within a year and the last of the money was spent settling his affairs by poor Charles. This included gambling debts and unpaid bills for the work on Stanton House that Edward had delayed payment on. Charles was lucky that the old manor house was spared.

'I have liked to believe that, even if her mother didn't survive into old age, the little girl was all right, that she was scooped up by a benevolent relative and taken far away, to somewhere exotic like India, to grow up as lovely as her mother. That was my hope, for what it's worth. Do I believe it any more?' He spread his hands, not needing to answer his own question. 'After all, wouldn't she have come back by now? Sir Charles would have taken her in, I'm sure.'

His words reminded me of one of my favourite books as a child, *The Little Princess*. I thought of Isabel's long journey to India to start a new life, the reverse of Sara Crewe's.

'She didn't look like Elizabeth, though,' I said. 'None of the gypsy curls and flashing eyes. Her hair was silver blonde. She took after Edward in that.'

Hugh sighed. 'Perhaps she did. Poor little mite.'

'Mrs Jelphs didn't tell me about Isabel. I asked her about a little girl because I found a toy – a little hare – but she evaded my question.'

'Can you blame her? She is one of a handful of people who were there at the very end – and is still there now. In fact, she might well be the only person left alive who knows precisely what went on down there during those weeks.'

'She and Ruck,' I said.

I don't know how long we sat there, both of us far away in the valley's past, but then Hugh got up and went back to the bureau. 'I said I had something else for you. I remembered it the other night, out of the blue. An antiques dealer friend of mine came across a desk in a sale a few years ago. It was an enormous thing with all sorts of drawers and compartments and had apparently belonged to a doctor. My friend thought it quite ugly but a local businessman had enquired after such a desk – specifically wanting something big and dark and Victorian, I suppose for the gravitas. This was just the thing and my friend got it cheaply enough.

'When it was delivered to his shop and he had a proper look at it, he discovered that one of the drawers – a sort of secret compartment for private papers – had been missed when the desk was emptied. Much to the surprise of my friend, he realized that a previous owner – a Dr Frith – had lived in this house at the time he'd written the notes found inside. The address was there, printed at the top of each sheet.

'The next time we met he brought them out. He said they were probably of little interest but he'd liked the coincidence. The doctor had died years before and he didn't see the harm in it, particularly as he hadn't noticed anything confidential in the pile.

'I did in fact buy this house off an old doctor who, if I remember rightly, was going to retire to the coast of Dorset for his lungs. I hadn't given him a thought in decades. I didn't look at the papers properly until later. I remember settling down in here with them that evening, thinking I had got hold of the mundane musings of a country doctor. I liked the fact that I would be reading them some thirty-odd years after they had been written, quite possibly in the same room. Most of it was trivia, old prescriptions and reminders to order various pieces of equipment. But there, among the rest, was something more interesting. When I sat down to read it never occurred to me that I might see a name I knew but it leapt off the page almost immediately: Elizabeth Stanton.'

He seemed to hesitate, as though he'd changed his mind about showing me. I saw him glance briefly at my protruding stomach.

'Please, I'd like to see them since you went to the trouble of digging them out,' I said, holding out my hand.

Rather reluctantly he handed over the pile of brittle papers, all covered with faded black ink. It was the kind of antiquated writing that looks beautiful but is actually very difficult to read; a slanted cursive only easily intelligible to the writer. 'Doctors' handwriting has always been impossible to read, it seems,' he said quietly. He swallowed the last of his drink and looked thoughtfully out of the window.

There, at the top of the paper, was the printed name and address. It was an odd thought: that those sheets had been written in the last century in the house I was sitting in, and had somehow found their way back.

Just then there was a sharp rap at the door. Hugh raised his eyebrows at me as he got to his feet. I began to scan the first page, my eyes managing to decipher the odd word. One was 'mania'. Another was 'hysteric'. I heard the door open.

'Mrs Jelphs, what a pleasant surprise.' It was said loudly enough for it to have been for my benefit.

I got to my feet awkwardly, wincing at the strain on my lower back. After what I'd heard, I couldn't let Mrs Jelphs know I'd been nosing around in what was also her own past. Without thinking, I took the dozen or so sheets of paper and stuffed them into the band of my skirt, pulling my blouse over them. The old paper had thinned and dried with time and I could hear it protest and crackle as I moved awkwardly towards the sitting-room door. Mrs Jelphs met me at the threshold.

'Alice, I've been so worried. I looked for you everywhere when I returned from Painswick. We even called at Nan's to ask if she knew where you might be. I've said it before but you really shouldn't be walking up any hills in your condition. What were you thinking?'

Her tone was shorter than I'd heard it before, her blue eyes dark with mingled frustration and anxiety.

'I – I'm perfectly all right,' I stammered. 'I suppose I just wanted some exercise and then I, well, I bumped into Mr Morton by chance.'

I stood as still as I could so the papers didn't rustle against my hot skin. I was glad Hugh had turned over the auction catalogue on the table, the bold typography out of sight.

'Yes, that's right,' he said. 'We met on the green. I insisted that she come back for a cold drink.'

'That's very kind of you, Mr Morton, but Alice shouldn't be over-exerting herself. She shouldn't be leaving the valley at all.' She looked back at me. 'You'll need to rest this afternoon. Ruck brought me up in the carriage so you won't have to walk down.'

I saw she was trembling.

'Mrs Jelphs, can I offer you and Mr Ruck a glass of ginger beer before you go?' said Mr Morton.

'Thank you but no, we must get Alice back where she belongs.'

'Right you are.' He looked at me and I managed a wan smile for him.

I didn't trust myself to say a word to Mrs Jelphs or Ruck as we descended back into the valley's arms. I sat between them like a prisoner on her way to the gallows. I think Mrs Jelphs imagined I was sulking, like a little girl whose game had been broken up by the call to bed, but my head was full of scratchy black script, my mind's eye running again and again over the unsettling words I'd seen.

There was a chance that Elizabeth had died when she had her second child. It was possible the child had died too, or instead of her. In a few short weeks, I would be giving birth in the valley.

And Isabel: what of her? Despite Hugh's notion and the rumours that she had been taken to London, I had an instinct that something darker had happened. Perhaps it was my mood, and my own fear, but my mind kept going back to Henry's early death in the valley. Had Tom's mother been right and the valley was ill-fated somehow? What of my child, due in just a few short weeks? What of me? I thought again of the words I'd seen and Elizabeth's diary entry.

As the carriage wove down the steep path, the wheels finding the ruts in the dry earth as if it drove itself, I heard the wind stir. I looked up through the layers of beech leaves that crowded over us, and watched them shift and shiver. Mrs Jelphs and Ruck stared straight ahead, apparently oblivious to it.

I put my hand to my belly and felt the papers there. The heat from my skin had dampened them so they felt plastered to the mound. I didn't like those unflinching words pressing against the baby and wished I could pull them out and let them flutter down to fall under the wheels. Mrs Jelphs glanced sideways at me.

'Why do you do it, Alice?' she said, and her voice was curiously flat. 'We're just trying to look after you while we wait for the baby to come. You can't be in your right mind going up that hill in this heat. What if I had been too late?'

'Too late for what?' I said, but she didn't reply.

We were nearly at the bottom of the path, the manor's pale stone glimmering from behind its dark concealment of holly and yew. As soon as we came to a stop I climbed down clumsily without waiting for Ruck to help me, and heard Mrs Jelphs sigh.

'Thank you for collecting me,' I called over my shoulder, as I hurried awkwardly towards the kitchen door, a note of defiance creeping into my voice. 'But you really needn't have. There's absolutely nothing wrong with me.'

As soon as I reached my room and closed the door I tore off my blouse, letting it fall to the floor. I peeled the old papers off as carefully as I could bear to in my desire to be rid of them and then spread them out on the bed to dry. None was torn but the ink had blurred in places. I crossed the room to wash my hands but caught sight of my reflection in the wardrobe glass and stopped dead. Some of the dark ink had been imprinted on my skin. It made me want to step out of it like a snake.

As I stared at my reflection, a lock of hair fell forward and lay like a loosened spring against my shoulder. In the sunlight that surged unremittingly into the room, I could see embers in the dark brown that was the colour of freshly turned earth. I thought of the confusion swimming in Ruck's eyes when we had met on the path flanked by rhododendrons. He hadn't known it was me.

Outside, the wind – an uncanny, murmuring sort of wind – began to build until I thought that if I dared to cross to the window I would see the Great Mead filled with all the people who had ever been there. The casements I'd pushed back that morning began to rattle very slightly, as though a pocket of pressure deep underground was being released. I believed that if I turned there would be someone behind me.

I stood immobile with my eyes shut for a long minute, concentrating on breathing in and out, in and out, so that I didn't fall. I told myself that I was overwrought after all that Hugh Morton had told me and because the existence of the doctor's notes on the bed seemed to chime with some of what I'd read in Elizabeth's diary – and what I'd been wondering about my mother.

When I opened my eyes I realized that the wind had died down a little. I glanced at my reflection again. My stomach looked horrible, a swirl of blurred ink. The baby began to move and twist inside me, which finally galvanized me into action. I went to the jug, poured water into the bowl and began wiping off the mess with my flannel, the water turning grey.

When I was clean I didn't fetch a towel but let the water on my skin be dried by the warm wind that sporadically barged through the open windows, only to die off again. Outside, I could see the yews moving reluctantly back and forth in the turbulent air. They reminded me of the furled parasols you see by the seaside at the end of the season, when the weather is turning and the crowds have gone. They creaked as they moved.

I went over to the bed and made sure the papers were in the correct order. They had dried but now rippled, like a book left next to the bath. I propped up the pillows so I would be comfortable and began to read. It was hard going at first but after a few minutes my eyes adjusted to the unfamiliar handwriting and began to decipher it automatically. Some of it was lost, smudged and blurred and gone for good, but I could make out most of it.

The Private Observations of a Country Physician Regarding Serious Cases of Puerperal Insanity, its Consequences and Cures
By Dr Robert A. Frith
Stanwick, Gloucestershire, 1894

As we are all surely aware, severe disturbances of the mind are not only more common among women, but women of childbearing age. Those suffering from puerperal insanity, whether taking the form of a suffocating and gloomy melancholia or absolute insanity, are not rare cases. Indeed, it would not be unreasonable to suppose that, in the course of the last century, these conditions have become as good as contagious, spread by the influence of lurid newspaper accounts of infanticide and misguided health manuals.

In decades past, physicians would have treated women suffering such flights from reason in a markedly different way. There is ample evidence, dreadful to relate, of women being sent to asylums where they were treated like animals. Some would be chained to their beds; others plied with leeches; still more sent further into the blackness by close proximity to the truly deranged. A dim view is now taken of such treatment. It is understood that women who, after giving birth, and occasionally before it, seem to display signs of advanced hysteria and madness, must be treated lightly, carefully and with sympathy, their delusions remaining unquestioned so as not to disturb their weakened minds still further. This extends even to those who, without constant supervision, would do harm to themselves or to their infants.

It is now more widely understood that alarming changes in behaviour are merely symptoms of the malady, not the true character of the sufferer rising to the surface. This usually temporary loss of wits leaves little or no memory of it behind, at least for the afflicted. I have seen with my own eyes women raving and wild-eyed one week and quite calm and restored the next. There is no remnant of the mania that has blown through them and most are recovered completely within a few months.

Of the two types of puerperal insanity, the melancholic variety seems to be the more insidious, hovering like a spectre for many months, sometimes years. It is this type that is least likely to be cured and most likely to return. Mania, while distressing in the extreme for the loved ones of the sufferer, with women of previously excellent character observed shouting, stamping, screaming, swearing and otherwise lost to a state of high phrenzy, is eminently curable. Of course, either path is a painful one for all concerned, particularly at a time that should be marked with joy.

From my own observations, puerperal insanity — as well as the related conditions of insanity during pregnancy and insanity brought on by problems with lactation — is as likely to afflict the woman of high as low rank. That is not to say their treatments should be similar. While a woman of very poor means will gain much from a month's sanctuary in an asylum, where she will likely be better fed and rested than at home, a place of respite rather than cruel exile, a woman of better breeding is better cared for at home. If she must be separated from her loved ones, the private asylum must be carefully chosen, so as not to make the most damaging kind of lingering melancholia a more likely, and permanent, outcome.

Case Study
I have been the family physician of the Stanton family, of Fiercombe Manor and more recently Stanton House, for many years. As a much younger man I helped safely deliver Sir Edward (as he would become) and his brother. The tradition had continued and in the autumn of 1893 I was called to attend the first labour of Sir Edward's wife, Lady Elizabeth Stanton. She gave birth to a baby girl, and while Sir Edward was perhaps a little disappointed not to have a son, the child was healthy and Lady Stanton seemed exhausted but overjoyed.

A week or so later I was called again to the house and found its mistress quite altered. The contrast was stark – a calm, radiant happiness replaced by someone at first coldly unresponsive and later increasingly agitated and disturbed. She would – or could – not sleep and refused all food. The child she showed absolutely no interest in, which is common in these cases. I would go further: she did not seem to recognize or acknowledge any kind of personal connection to the infant at all. This was different in the extreme to another case that I shall presently come to, of a woman of comparatively poor means, residing in Painswick.

I last attended Lady Stanton about three weeks after the birth and was helpless to halt or even alleviate her symptoms, which only worsened. She seemed, even as I watched, to turn inwards upon herself. Her lips moved constantly in silent prayer or song, the words only occasionally audible above her shallow breathing. I have found that relatively little can be done to effect a quick cure in these cases; complete rest and a withdrawal of circumstances that might over-stimulate the patient's fragile mind and worsen the hysteria that has already taken hold are doubtless the best (and perhaps only) remedies. In some cases resembling this one, I have found that light purgatives and nutritious tonics offer some relief, though not in this instance.

My private belief in this case was that Sir Edward's distress at and frustration with his wife's condition — something born of fear but that showed itself in anger — served only to heighten and prolong it. Though Lady Stanton seemed entirely oblivious to what was around her, I felt sure she could sense what I can only describe as the vibrations of the air in that house, which was an increasingly unhappy one. I confided to Sir Edward as I left Fiercombe Valley for the last time — though I was not to know it was the last time until I received a note asking me not to call again and enclosing a cheque to pay my bill — that it might be less injurious to Lady Stanton if she was to be sent away, perhaps to the house of a trusted family member, until she was quite recovered. I still fervently believe that the close, stifling atmosphere of Stanton House only hindered Lady Stanton's progress, producing in her a kind of claustrophobia. This, in my opinion, simply augmented her insanity, which soon progressed from a clouded and rather vacant disposition to something closer to mania, culminating in her attempts to harm herself and her child.

In fact, a subsequent doctor from outside the county advised a similar method of cure, though I believe — through hearsay only, sadly my ties with the Stanton family are severed completely — that it was an institution she was taken to, by a third physician, rather *than the peaceful, familiar place I would have recommended for her. Still, it is said that it cured her. Certainly she survives. Not much is heard of Sir Edward and particularly Lady Stanton, these days, indicating that she has not entirely recovered her previous spirits, but she was able to return before Christmas last year, having come through her ordeal. It is said in the village that she is belatedly close to her small daughter.*

Whether Lady Stanton would suffer similarly if she were to have another child is not easy to predict. If I were asked, though it is with great sadness that I know I shall not be, I would say that taking into account all her circumstances — her husband's tendency to anxious anger, the underlying need for an heir, as well as what must be a natural, ingrained tendency of her mind to be so afflicted — that she would likely be wrenched under again. I hope I am wrong in that.

Wrenched under. In that generally factual account of what must have been a significant medical case for Frith, the phrase had a raw power. I wondered if it had also had prescience. I put the sheaf of papers down and thought about how the man who had written them had been here, in this same valley, visiting her when she was still alive.

I had been too engrossed in my reading to notice but the wind had grown fiercer, the unsecured casements juddering back and forth in the old frames. I got up carefully, my arm supporting the baby's weight, and closed them firmly. Outside, the yew pylons continued to sway. I thought about going downstairs and apologizing to Mrs Jelphs for making her worry but I was drawn back to the rest of the papers on the bed.

Case Study

Above I made mention of an ordinary village woman from nearby Painswick. This was one of the more extreme cases of puerperal insanity I have attended, some years ago now, in 1876, though I am glad to say that the patient, whom I have been able to examine thoroughly many times since, made a complete recovery. Interestingly, and perhaps hopefully for those like Lady Stanton, this woman had given birth to two children uneventfully, with no evidence of mania or even a mild depression of spirits, either during the pregnancy or in the crucial days and weeks following both labours.

Janey Litten was struck down with a very serious case of puerperal mania two days after the birth of her third child – also her first daughter, though I believe the sex of the child to be neither here nor there in these cases.

I broke off reading and read the name again, feeling such a jolt of shock that the writing on the paper seemed to shift and tilt for a moment. Janey Litten. My grandmother's name. I thought of Hugh Morton's hesitancy before handing the papers over to me but knew that could only have been to do with my own impending labour and the circumstances surrounding Elizabeth's illness. The chance that he had connected me to someone named Litten, or had even read further than Elizabeth's case, was so slender as to be negligible. With a second jolt that made my heart hammer painfully in my chest, I realized that the child mentioned – the third child, the first daughter – was my mother.

I pieced together what I remembered of my mother's mother – which was not a clear picture but something closer to a melding of senses: the waft of her lavender scent, her cool hands over mine as she showed me how to rub slippery yellow butter into flour. I could still hear the soft timbre of her burred voice, though not the actual words she spoke, and I could still taste the toast she made for me and remember how the bread's edges blackened and frilled as I watched. As all this came back to me in a rush, I began to cry, an effect her memory had always had on me, like turning on a tap; a great welling of loss inside me.

I couldn't remember when I had last seen her, though I knew my mother had said I was too young to attend her funeral – as well as my grandfather's, which took place not long after. My uncles had moved away at some stage, to Bristol perhaps, I wasn't sure. I wished I could go to Painswick and search for her gravestone, and those of my grandfather and other Littens too.

One of my tears fell and spread on the papers I still held and blurred the word 'mania'. I was glad to see it marble into something unintelligible. I knew I should put them away – no, burn them – before I read on but, even as I resolved to do it, my eyes searched for the next sentence.

The infant girl, as in the case of Lady Stanton's child, was a healthy one and the family were at first relieved. Mrs Litten had endured the births of her two boys – both large babies – with fortitude but it was physically a blessing that this child was two pounds smaller, though no less hardy. 'That'll do for me now, Doctor,' I remember Mrs Litten saying to me.

As is still fairly common in the countryside, I had not attended the birth itself, only checked on the mother and child after, the local midwife being present for the duration of the labour. There are many who seek to banish these traditional practices but I cannot see harm in them and think this but a fashion, as all things are subject to, even medical theories, it seems. I have witnessed no rise in cases of puerperal insanity when a midwife has attended over a physician. In my opinion, the female mind is always vulnerable to disturbance when in confinement, and whether this turns to insanity is unexplainable, and some combination of many causes, from an inherited nervous tendency to an excess of unrelieved pain in the labour.

In the case of Janey Litten, I should mention that she had also suffered a miscarriage between her second and third confinements. This took place some six months into the pregnancy. I examined her myself after this and she was much saddened, but only to a degree one would expect, perhaps a little more withdrawn, and for longer than some — she was not herself for a year or more — but nothing I believed was untoward.

With the new infant, she was much changed from the third day. Her relief on having been able to carry the child to term seemed quickly to grow into a restless sort of excitement. She claimed she could hear things, whisperings and rustlings, and, after a week had passed, the symptoms clearly worsening, appeared to be lost in conversation with someone conjured up by her own, increasingly disturbed, mind. In this state, she was quite uncanny to observe: apparently listening intently and then erupting into laughter or exclaiming that she couldn't or mustn't, shaking her head in a highly agitated manner. Normally of a quiet, gentle disposition, she was utterly altered, and was heard to shout out often in what her husband called 'a most bawdy manner'. On one occasion, she was suspected to have bitten the *infant, and on two occasions was seen violently shaking her when she cried.*

John Litten was so much disturbed by his wife's behaviour that he asked that she go to the asylum at Wootton and would hear no arguments to the contrary. Such was his fear of her mania, and what he believed were her 'crafty' intentions to injure him and their children, that I felt it would do the family more harm than good for her to remain in the family home. She was well nourished enough but I reasoned that the rest an asylum could offer her outweighed the benefits of her staying close to her family. It is best if women like this do not receive visitors while they are confined in an asylum. Once there, they are much better cared for by trained nurses and physicians whom they are unfamiliar with.

Mrs Litten returned to the family home after a seven-month stay, after which time she was quite back to her usual peaceable demeanour, with little or no memory of what had passed. The infant, known as Maggie, also survived with no visibly lasting ill effects.

I stopped reading and let my head fall back against the oak headboard of the bed. The child inside me, now just weeks from being born, rose hugely above the sheets that I'd smoothed down that morning. I seemed to have got bigger in a single day and felt more ungainly by the hour, so there was no escaping the fact of my condition, let alone the physical discomfort that came with it. Now its imminence was freighted with extra significance.

I looked down at the old papers beside me on the bed. Along with a dozen other women, who meant nothing to me, they contained secret information not only about the elusive Elizabeth Stanton but my own grandmother. What would have made disturbing reading at any time was multiplied many times by the fact of my pregnancy. Put together with Fiercombe's seemingly tarnished history and the way Mrs Jelphs often looked at me, I really did feel doomed. However sensational that sounded, there was no other word that did justice to my feelings. Not only was I trapped in the disquieting atmosphere of the valley, already half wondering if my mind was being turned or haunted by it, but I was also becoming increasingly certain that I had inherited a predisposition to madness after giving birth.

Feeling a swell of panic rising inside me, I got to my feet and immediately caught sight of the pieces of Stanton House rubble that I had put in my pocket unthinkingly, all those weeks earlier. They were at the back of the dresser and had been obscured until now by a clutter of pins and combs and pencils. I picked them up, suddenly aware that I wanted to be outside, even if it meant being buffeted by the wind that had now found a finger-hold in the old casements and was whining to be let in. I stumbled through the door and down the stairs.

Mrs Jelphs wasn't in the kitchen when I got there. I hoped that she wouldn't go upstairs to look for me and see the papers I'd left strewn all over the bed. The door was rattling slightly in its frame as I opened it and I felt it almost sucked out of my grasp as I lifted the latch. I looked up but there were no distinct clouds; only a sky that was no longer celestially blue and clear but glowering, lowering to violet.

I hadn't consciously intended to go to the graveyard but that was where I found myself. I suppose I'd long meant to see who was buried there, but had never quite got round to going. It was deserted as usual, the cheek-pink blossom that should have fallen in May only now beginning to flutter to the grass as the wind tore through it.

I went from stone to stone with a feigned purposefulness but the panic didn't subside as I moved around; instead it only grew with the pitch of the wind. To me, every grave seemed to belong to a woman, though that couldn't have been the case. Some of them must have been old, too, but all I could see were women who had died when they were young – them and their tiny infants. I couldn't see Elizabeth, though, or Isabel. I went from stone to stone, my hair whipping around me and getting in my eyes, until I had inspected them all twice. Only a dozen were too old or too stained with lichen to read: those that were unevenly propped in a row against the walls of the chapel, like badly aligned teeth.

Then I saw it, so much bigger than the stones that my eyes had skimmed over it. Perhaps seven feet by four, it was a great hunk of stone set in its own corner of the graveyard away from the rest. Surrounded by metal rail-ings a foot high, the stone was grey and impervious to weather, its edges as sharp as the day the stonemason had cut it. A marble plaque confirmed what I would have guessed: that I had found the final resting place of Edward Stanton and his newborn son, also Edward.

As abruptly as I'd wanted to leave my room, I now wanted to leave the graveyard. I stumbled away down the lane, the rhododendrons bobbing wildly as the gusts thrust among them. The only place I could think to go was the summerhouse, but before I went inside, I stopped and took out the pieces of grey rubble I'd brought with me. I wanted to be rid of them. Raising my arm, I threw them into the stream, intending that they should be carried away by the fast-moving current. Instead they sank heavily to the bottom, incongruously jagged among the smooth pebbles.

It was like a tomb inside the summerhouse after the tearing, howling wind. I half ran up the stairs to get to the diary, though I don't know what I expected to find in it. If I'd hoped to find an entry about a new gown or a small kindness of Edward's – something that would reassure me, calm me – it wasn't to be. Unusually, the page I started reading was dated. Elizabeth had written in ink and it was blurred in places, just as the doctor's notes had been after I'd had them so close to my skin, then wept over them. The date was June 1898. Midsummer, I realized, remembering Hugh Morton's words.

So he is gone. A third child died inside me.

I won't come here again and write in this book. It does no good to set things down after all. It makes no difference; it wards nothing off.

My mind keeps straying to something I read once about the Jewish faith, the ritual they call shiva. It means seven in Hebrew: seven days of mourning for a loved one as close as a child or a parent. For a son. During this week, washing in anything but cold water is prohibited, jewellery is removed, mirrors are covered. The family gathers at the house where the death has occurred, finding solace in each other.

Here there is no one. The servants are silent or dismissed. Edward does not look at me. Edith's heart is broken. My parents are dead. Isabel has not said a word since she was carried back from the old manor's nursery.

Edward has written his letter, as I knew he would. Dr Logan will be here soon.

More than anything, I am just so very tired.

There it broke off, leaving the rest of the page blank.

I didn't want to read any more: I was afraid of what else I might find. I tucked the little book back into its hiding place and went down the stairs before I could change my mind and find myself irresistibly drawn back to Elizabeth's words.

Still not wanting to return to the manor, I veered off Fiery Lane and entered the tall grasses at the far end of the Great Mead. It was at that moment that the thunder began to roll in slowly from the west, like the approach of a huge army. I kept going, my feet catching all the while, until the first drops of rain stopped me in my tracks. I had not felt rain on me for months, and those months felt like years. I looked at my arm, where a heavy drop had splashed, and instinctively put it to my lips. It tasted like my tears had, when I'd thought about my grandmother.

Elizabeth

The long hand of the clock hesitated and relented, finally marking the twenty minutes she had made herself wait for Edward to leave the valley. She rose and felt a pain like the one in the glasshouse earlier, except that this one was stronger, a shudder deep within. It was more than a cramp: it was a clutching right in the depths of her, and she put her hand out to the cabinet next to the bed to brace against it.

It could not be the baby yet: it was too early. A little less than five years ago Isabel, reluctant to leave the dark, muffled sanctuary of her mother, as though she already had some intuition of what would happen, had arrived late. It flashed across Elizabeth's mind that this baby wasn't just early, there was something wrong, but with all her might, she flung the thought away. An image of Isabel took its place. She mustn't forget Isabel. She had to find her.

Crossing the Great Mead took far longer than when she had crossed it that morning. The tall meadow grass, thick and lustrous from the recent rain, seemed intent on tripping her. It was past midday now and the sun rode high, the early morning's gentle touch turned savage. After all that had passed between her and Edward, she had forgotten her hat. Absurdly, she thought about the freckles that would scatter across her cheeks and how, when she had returned to the house, she would ask Edith to go to the kitchens and squeeze a lemon, so that the pursed-mouth juice would fade them.

It was just as she felt shame for this vanity when Isabel was hiding somewhere, tear-streaked and frightened, that a new wave of pain gripped her. She wondered if she could continue and looked back towards the grey house beyond the lake and gardens. But she was fractionally closer to the old manor now: she could already hear the bright burble of the stream. If she could reach Isabel, she could rest in the shade of the yew parlour. Isabel could fetch one of the old rugs or coverlets that had been abandoned in the cupboards and chests of the manor, dust incrementally turning them to rags. They could sit quietly together until the strange spasms of pain had passed.

She would be glad to see Ruck now, she thought, as she retraced the steps she had made so lightly this morning. The undulations of pain were now such that she would no longer care about his embarrassment at seeing his mistress so exposed and unseemly. But he was nowhere: the passage of rhododendrons, when she finally reached it, lay deserted. The blooms tangled over her, their beauty altered to be almost monstrous, their scent in the hot air enough to make her stagger. It was only the thought of Isabel that stopped her lying down in the dirt and closing her eyes.

'Isabel!' she called. 'Bel, where are you? Please come out.' Her voice was weak, echoing feebly off the walls of the chapel as she passed it. She wouldn't look at the gravestones marking the Stanton women lying under the luxuriant grass, dead from consumption, from tropical diseases contracted in the Indies, from childbirth.

'Isabel, please!' she cried, trying to hurry faster towards the manor as the pain receded briefly.

There was no one in the Tudor garden, though she felt, as she had before here, a finger's brush on the bare skin of her neck as she stumbled over the shadow line drawn by the yews. She knew it was her own fancy, a feminine notion that she would never dream of telling Edward, though once she might have done, right at the beginning. Perhaps he would have been charmed then.

Some photographs had been taken here in those early days, when they had picnicked here. She had asked for another of the manor by itself, catching it unawares as it slumbered peacefully in the afternoon sunshine. She had been entranced by the ancient house from her first glimpse of its golden stone. Where was that picture now? She had looked for it many times.

The pain came again as she pushed back the silvered wood of the broad door and stepped inside. Even after the shade of the yew parlour, she was blinded by the dark of the house's interior. She waited as her eyes adjusted and the spasms lowered in pitch, noticing for the first time how the fabric of her dress was sewn too tightly under her arms, chafing and rotting. She could smell herself – not almond oil or violets or rosewater – but her own animal body, dark and sweet, sweat and blood. But it could not be blood, not yet.

'Isabel.' It was almost a whisper now.

A noise, a gentle creaking, spurred her on. She would be in the nursery. Elizabeth pulled herself up each stair, knowing her waters must have broken. She could feel her silk undergarments rubbing the tender, scarred skin of her inner thighs as she lifted each leg.

When she reached the doorway the little girl had her back to it, arms clamped around the neck of the beloved old rocking horse – so careworn compared to her new one, ordered from London. She rocked him gently like an elderly pet, and the soft creaks were strangely comforting to Elizabeth too.

When Isabel sensed a presence and turned, Elizabeth could see that the little girl's face was marked with trails of tears and grime. Shock entered her small face when she took in the sight of her mother, clutching the doorway as the pain reared up again to rage through her.

'Mama!' she cried, and rushed towards Elizabeth, who gave in to the spasm and went down on her knees. Somewhere in the midst of the boiling pain she had a clear thought, an instinct she had dreaded feeling again: knowledge that something was very wrong. She waited until the pain had eased enough to speak.

'My darling, you must listen to me carefully now,' she said, gripping the little girl's narrow wrist. 'You must be very brave. I know you will be, for me.'

'My father thinks I am not brave,' Isabel said, her voice high with terror.

'He is wrong about that, Bel. I know that you are as brave as anyone, as brave as a little lioness.

'Now, the baby is coming early. You must run as fast as you can and find your father. You must tell him where I am. Tell him to send one of the grooms for the doctor because the baby is coming too quickly. Do you understand, Bel?'

The little girl nodded as another wave of pain nearly toppled Elizabeth on to her side. She bit the inside of her cheek so she didn't scream and scare Isabel into senselessness. It lessened, just a little.

'Go now, my darling. Run the way you ran earlier. Do you remember, when you were looking for me?'

Isabel nodded again. 'Shall I go past the lake or through the kitchen garden, Mama?'

'Whichever you think is fastest. I know you will choose the right one. But go now, as fast as the wind. Just remember to tell your father: the baby is coming too fast.'

It was only as Isabel's footsteps faded into nothing that Elizabeth remembered Edward was gone from the valley, galloped away in anger and fear. She gave in and let herself collapse on to her side, barely registering the impact as her cheek met the dusty floorboards.

How much time had passed was unclear. She had been hurled in and out of consciousness, the pain so bad that she had prayed to die. Such agony could drive a woman out of her wits, she knew that. Whenever it descended a degree she had gratefully drifted away. She had felt herself floating along a dark river, a cavernous gloom above her instead of the sky. She thought it must be the River Styx, deep in the Underworld.

Something made her open her eyes. She looked up and saw the pale oval of Edith's face framed in the nursery doorway, her mouth a round O, her dark blue eyes black with fear. Behind her, gripping the maid's skirts with grimy fingers, was Isabel.

Elizabeth looked down and saw that she had stained

the bare boards with her blood. It was thick in places, clotting on the surface rather than sinking darkly into the wood. She couldn't rouse herself to move her skirts so they lay more modestly. The pain had dulled to a low but powerful ache, the rhythm of the waves that had rocked her still discernible. She might have been alone for minutes or days.

'Oh, my lady,' whispered Edith, finally moving forward as if released from a spell. 'The baby's come.'

Elizabeth couldn't hear anything after that, only the rustle of stiff skirts as Edith crouched beside her and a high keening sound that escaped from Isabel as she flitted from wall to wall, too disturbed to be still. Lying there, Elizabeth registered only the silence, the air cold and viscous and resolutely unpierced by the tentative, newborn cries that ought to have risen by then.

'He's dead, isn't he?'

She was unsure whether she had spoken aloud. There was no answer so she let go, feeling herself drift away again, away from the stench of the nursery and the horror etched into the faces that stared back at her.

Alice

From that first heavy drop on my arm, the rain seemed to pause, gather its strength and then throw itself down, like something from the tropics. In minutes I was soaked through, my blouse and skirt plastered to me, my hair streaming as though I'd just emerged from a river.

It was then that I felt it, a clench of pain in my abdomen that made me forget where I was for an instant, all my focus turned abruptly inward. This is it, I thought. This is the delayed result of my fall. I was losing the baby and I would do so alone in the Great Mead, as the earth beneath me was inexorably saturated with rain.

I looked back towards the gable of the manor, which I could just make out, a warm glimmer through the sheeting rain and beyond the dark holly bushes that seemed to crowd it from this angle. I didn't know what had drawn me to that still corner of the Great Mead but I didn't want to be there now.

I stumbled back towards the fork where Fiery and Creephedge Lanes converged, the pain gripping again and again. The parched, iron-hard earth was already turning to thick clay that sucked at my shoes until I gave up and left them behind. The tender tops of my feet looked very white as they sank again and again into the mud. When I got to the point where Fiery Lane began to slope upwards in earnest I saw it already transforming into a river of russet-brown water, made opaque by the churning mud. The old wheel ruts deepened and widened even as I watched, spellbound by the sight of it and the noise of the rain drumming on every leaf, not only glancing off the trees above but hammering down into the dense hedgerows on either side of me.

An agonizingly strong cramp brought me down on to all fours, the water shockingly cold as it swirled around my knees and up to my elbows, my stomach also submerged by a few inches. I realized that the volume of water couldn't be just from the rain, though it continued to tear down the steep slopes of the valley without pause. The stream must have broken its banks. I knew I needed to get away from the middle of the lane soon or I would be swept away. Slowly, inch by inch, I shifted myself sideways, like a crab, towards the green verge where the grass and cow parsley and buttercups were slicked with mud but not yet under water. There, I rolled on to my back and pulled myself awkwardly across until I was right up against the roots of the hedgerow, like a frightened animal trying to burrow away. Every inch of me was coated in the cloying mud and it seemed to press down on me, chilling me to my core. Then a stronger cramp seized me and I screamed aloud for the first time, the sound drowned by a mighty clap of thunder.

What passed then was an indeterminate period when I alternated between vivid dreams of Isabel and Elizabeth, their faces so clear it was as if I had always known them, and the grim reality of the lane. As each new shudder of pain lit me up, the lightning that cut jaggedly through the purple sky mirrored it. The thunder snarled and clashed simultaneously: the storm was directly over the valley.

Eventually it moved away a little, and some time after that, I felt a small hand stealing into mine, its flesh cold and wet and stiff but still comforting to me. I kept my eyes shut, hearing the hiss of the rain and knowing that I must be awake, but the pressure of the little fingers remained. I lay like that for a time but then I felt an overwhelming urge to see her and opened my eyes. My hand was empty but then, struggling down the flooded lane, I noticed two figures, bent over from the force of the rain and wind and looking about them. With my last shred of will I shouted out so they would see me, tucked away in my muddy den.

I must have fallen into unconsciousness because when I next opened my eyes I was in my own room. Through the fug of my pain, I saw Mrs Jelphs's face above me. She didn't look at me, and I dimly recognized that she was concentrating, a look of total, absorbed focus on her face. I had never seen anyone so determined. There was no one else there: she and I were alone.

It's difficult to recount the labour with any degree of accuracy. I couldn't tell if whole days were passing, as I bucked under the pain of the baby coming, or mere minutes. Whenever the agony briefly abated, I sank into some sort of floating state, where a jumble of images filed through my mind – my grandmother and Elizabeth in sepia, their faces blurred, the little girl with her strange, cold stare, Henry and Tom racing to dive into the lake.

The first clear thing I remember was the thin wail that went up after a long period when I thought the searing pain inside would kill me. When she'd cut the cord and wrapped the baby up, Mrs Jelphs placed him on top of me and I caught sight of her face, luminous and suffused with relief.

He was small but strong; my first sight of him his face screwed up in fury, his chest heaving up and down so he could cry out at the indignity of it all. When I saw that, I knew he was safe and let myself go, falling away into the depths of a sleep I didn't wake properly from for many hours.

When I did come to properly, I was clean and dressed in a cotton nightgown. The sky beyond my open windows was blue again, but a pale English blue scattered with soft white clouds. The breeze I could feel on my bare forearms was a cool breath, fresh and light.

The baby was nowhere to be seen but I knew he was nearby, taken to another room so I could rest. I didn't call out but enjoyed lying there peacefully, the lead weight of anxiety I'd learnt to live with for months entirely seeped away. I had survived and I knew I was myself in my mind. There was no curse on the valley, which felt, for the first time since I'd arrived, utterly benign.

I thought of calling to Mrs Jelphs and then it occurred to me that I could get up and go and find the baby myself. But, as if even the thought of it was too much for my battered body, my eyes closed and I let myself be pulled back into another healing sleep.

When I woke again, the sky was pearl grey through the half-open curtains and I realized I was witnessing the first glimmers of dawn. I'd slept right through the previous day and night. In contrast to the fug of the hours following the birth I felt completely alert, my mind as sharp as the cooler, crisper air.

I had spent months unable to think about the time after the pregnancy and now it had arrived, weeks before I was expecting it. I was amazed that things were much the same. Just as I felt I was still myself, so the dawn still lifted away the night – as it always had. And yet I had a son.

At the thought, I had an urge to see and touch him that was so strong I didn't even bother putting on my dressing-gown. I thought Mrs Jelphs must have put him in the old nursery but I wasn't sure I wanted him to stay there. I wanted him with me.

I stood in the dim light of the passage and listened. Eventually I heard a small sound that might have been a deep breath or perhaps a hushing. As I approached the nursery, I saw a faint light under the door and knew I'd been right.

She'd lit a solitary oil lamp, the flame softened by a deep yellow glass casing. The baby, if he'd woken at all, was asleep again in his cot, and Mrs Jelphs was sitting in a low nursing chair, her embroidery on her lap.

She smiled when she saw me and put her finger to her lips.

'How are you feeling now, Alice?' she said. 'I thought you should be allowed to sleep as long as you needed to and the doctor agreed with me. You barely woke when he came. He said you were fine, that both of you were fine.' She smiled again.

I crept towards the cot and looked in wonder at the tiny creature inside, his dark shock of fine brown hair and the miniature fist, curled and pushed up against a sharp little chin.

'Thank you for looking after us,' I said, turning to Mrs Jelphs. 'I don't know what I'd have done out there on the lane. Was it you who found me?'

'And Ruck too. He carried you here, out of the downpour.'

'Ruck?'

'Yes, he saw you leave the manor and when the storm rolled in he came to check you'd come back to the manor safely. That was when we realized you were missing. I know he's gruff but his heart is in the right place.'

Apparently, after carrying me back to the manor from the lane, he had somehow found his way out of the flooded valley in the torrential downpour on foot, in order to fetch a doctor.

'What about Tom?' I asked shyly. 'He must be back by now.'

Mrs Jelphs shook her head. 'He sent a telegram to say he'd be here next week – something important delayed him in London. He said he was sorry, too. Strange: he never normally worries.'

'Does he know about the baby arriving early?'

Mrs Jelphs looked surprised. 'No. I thought he would see you when he gets here.'

Of course there was no reason in her mind why he would need to know. Perhaps there was no reason at all.

For the first time I noticed how pretty the nursery looked. It wasn't just that everything was clean and fresh-smelling, the windows polished and the floor swept. It also felt different. The atmosphere that had charged the air had lifted, lightened.

'He won't wake for a few hours now, so why don't you go back to bed before you catch cold?' Mrs Jelphs said gently.

She led me back to my room and tucked the covers around me.

'Now that you've recovered your strength a little, I must write to your mother and tell her that the baby's arrived. Perhaps I shouldn't have waited until now,' she said, her face suddenly concerned.

My stomach turned over and I pushed myself up to a sitting position. 'Do you have to write to her? The baby isn't due for another few weeks and she always said that first babies are late.'

Mrs Jelphs was clearly perplexed. 'Well, surely you want her to know. I mean, you're more than welcome to stay on, of course – for as long as you need to – but you can't keep such happy news from your parents. He's their grandchild, don't forget.'

My mind raced. Once my mother knew, she would be on the first train to Gloucestershire and, once she was here, I knew that matters would be taken out of my hands. I wouldn't be able to argue against her carefully arranged plan and, before I knew it, we'd be on our way back to London to give away my son.

'Let me write to her,' I blurted. 'That's all I meant – that I wanted to do it myself. I'll write it now and Nan can post it later, after she's done her work for the day.'

'Well, of course you must write with your own news. I'll come up for it later. Make sure you get a little bit more sleep after you've done it.'

When she left me alone, I did write a letter to my parents, sealing its envelope with care. I just didn't mention that the baby had arrived.

Tom returned the next week, as he'd said he would, and my heart thudded when I heard first the motor-car and then his tread on the stair. It was still early and I hadn't yet got up and dressed, the baby in my arms as I sat up against the pillows in bed. He had just fed and was close to falling asleep, his eyes blinking sleepily open to look at me every now and then, their colour the newborn's rich, deep blue.

'I'm so sorry, Alice,' Tom said, as soon as he came through the door after knocking. 'Or, rather, congratulations. Mrs Jelphs has only just told me. Are you all right?'

He caught sight then of what was in my arms and leant in for a closer look. Then he gave me the most uncomplicated smile I'd ever received from him.

'He's a fine boy, isn't he? Well done, you clever thing.' He kissed my cheek and then brought a chair over to the side of the bed.

'Has he got a name yet?' he said, sitting down. 'I won't object if you call him Thomas, of course.'

I laughed. 'I thought of Joseph. It's Ruck's name, you know. He carried me in out of the storm when I went into labour, then fetched the doctor on foot in the rain. I don't know what would have happened if he hadn't been there. Mrs Jelphs too, of course.'

'I had no idea,' Tom said, shaking his head. 'Mrs Jelphs told me about the flooded stream and I've just seen for myself that Fiery Lane is half washed away. I had to leave the MG back up in the village. We didn't have a single drop of rain in London.'

'Well, all's well now,' I said. 'I still can't quite believe he's here.'

'He has a look of you, you know,' said Tom. 'The same defiant little chin and those big eyes. I wonder what colour they'll turn in the end.'

He reached forward and stroked the baby's head. 'Listen, I'm sorry about what happened last time we talked. I'd had too much to drink, as I so often do. Did you find my note?'

'Yes, and it cheered me up no end when I did.' I smiled at him. 'It was just a silly misunderstanding and you'd been through a great deal that night, recalling all that you had.'

I took a deep breath. 'Look, Tom, while we're clearing the air, I think it's your turn to hear a confession of mine.'

Tom pulled an exaggerated face. 'Gosh, what can this be?'

'No, honestly, please let me get it out or I'll lose my nerve. Mrs Jelphs doesn't know anything about this and I'm not sure why I'm telling you. Only . . . only, I suppose having the baby has put things into perspective for me and I don't want to lie to you any more.'

'Lie? What do you mean?'

'I'll tell you but, first, will you please promise not to tell Mrs Jelphs? She was my mother's friend once and I . . . Well, do you promise? You can tell her once I've gone if you want to.'

He frowned. 'I hardly know what I'm promising but, yes, all right. I'll keep quiet.'

'It's about the baby's father,' I said firmly. I was apprehensive but determined. 'Remember you said I never talked about him?'

'You don't have to tell me anything, Alice, really. I don't need to know what happened before.'

'I want to tell you the truth. You see, there wasn't a husband. My mother made him up.' I exhaled shakily.

He looked utterly confused. 'Made him up?'

I kept on, desperate to get it all out: 'There was a man, but we weren't married.'

He nodded slowly. 'So she said you were married to make it sound more respectable, because you hadn't got round to it before he was killed.' Something else occurred to him. 'And your wedding ring was there for the same reason?'

He glanced at my left hand but I'd taken it off weeks before, when my fingers had begun to swell around it.

I swallowed. 'The ring belonged to my grandmother. But you still don't understand. You see, the baby's father . . . well, he's not dead at all. He was already married to someone else, had been for years. I was so green and foolish that I believed him when he talked about getting a divorce. It was only once . . .' I tailed off, ashamed.

There was silence for a long minute and then he looked up at me. 'I said to you once, on the way back from the meadow, that you must have loved him a great deal and you said that you had. You used the past tense. I wondered about it afterwards but then put it down to his death. Do you still love him?'

'No, and that was one of the moments I began to realize it. Perhaps I never really did. It seems like a childish infatuation now. I suppose he took terrible advantage of me. He was that sort.'

'Does he know?'

'Not about the pregnancy or the birth. The last time I saw him I meant to tell him but knew there was no point. I couldn't bear to when it came to it. Aren't you shocked?'

He shrugged. 'No, not really. People do strange things when they're swept away by their feelings. He was married and older – if anyone's to blame it's him. And –' He broke off and I saw that he had reddened.

'Tom?'

'Well, I'm glad you're not in love with him,' he said gruffly. 'He doesn't deserve you. Or the child.'

I smiled and put out my hand to cover his. 'Thank you.'

'So, is the part about you going back to London to live with your parents still true?' he said. 'You know you can stay here as long as you like. I won't tell my parents any-thing, or Mrs Jelphs – though I think she would understand. She's very fond of you, you know.'

I looked down at the child in my arms and clutched him to me a little tighter. My mother would have read the letter by now – the letter that told her nothing. I couldn't keep her away indefinitely, though. Something stopped me telling Tom the whole truth then. I saw that what I was really ashamed of was not my love affair with a married man but my mother's plan to give away my child. What would he think of her? What would he think of me, for allowing that to happen? I wasn't sure he would be so understanding about that part of it, some-how.

'Yes,' I said heavily. 'My mother will come in a few

weeks, once I've completely recovered, and then we'll go home.'

'I'll miss you when you do,' he said. 'But perhaps I can take you out for dinner in London one night. The business that delayed me coming back last week means I'm going to have to stay down here much more than before, but I'll be in London sometimes.'

'Perhaps you could,' I said sadly, though I didn't think it would ever happen. London was a different world. There, our differences would seem so much more pronounced.

Just then Mrs Jelphs came in with a breakfast tray for me. Tom got up hurriedly and I snatched back my hand, which had still been on his.

'Ah, you're awake,' she said cheerfully. 'And how's this little one?'

She lifted the baby from me and Tom placed the tray on my lap. Suddenly she tutted.

'I've forgotten your letters! They're still on the kitchen table.'

'I'll go and fetch them,' said Tom.

'Letters, for me?' I said, when he'd gone.

'Three letters all in the same hand, and one from your mother – I recognized her handwriting. The other three were sent weeks ago but were overlooked at the post office. They didn't know the name and the address was wrong. Whoever it was must be persistent to have written three times.'

Dora. She had written after all. My heart lifted briefly until I remembered my mother's letter; my putting off of the inevitable.

'I hope you don't mind, dear,' Mrs Jelphs continued,

'but I sent my own letter to your mother while I was in the post office, once I'd seen that she'd got your letter and you'd been able to tell her about little Joseph's arrival yourself. I wanted to pass on my own congratulations, of course, but I also wanted to reassure her that we were looking after you properly.'

I found I couldn't quite catch my breath.

'What did you say?' I blurted, unable to keep the panic from my voice.

Mrs Jelphs looked at me oddly. 'Just what I said. I congratulated her on becoming a grandmother and said you were both doing well. I also said that she was welcome to stay a night – your father too – when they came to collect you, if that made their arrangements easier. It's a long journey. Thomas, I hope that's quite in order?'

He was back with the letters, which he put down on the bed next to me. 'Yes, yes, of course,' he said quietly.

When the two of them had left me to my breakfast – Tom departing rather reluctantly, I thought – I opened my mother's letter. Naturally it said nothing of the baby's birth because she had known nothing about it when she sat down to write her reply. She would almost certainly receive Mrs Jelphs's letter the next day and probably catch the train as early as the following morning. It was possible I had just a couple of days left at Fiercombe.

As if sensing my agitation, the baby, whom Mrs Jelphs had put down in a Moses basket by the window, began to fuss. I went over to him and put my little finger into his mouth to soothe him, thinking furiously all the while.

More than anything, I wanted to stay where I was. All the anxiety I had felt on the day I had gone into labour had fled with the arrival of Joseph. Any terror I had felt that I would take after my grandmother – perhaps my mother too – was now overshadowed utterly by the thought of giving away my child. I understood that women had done this out of dreadful necessity for centuries but I couldn't for the life of me imagine how they had borne it. I didn't think I would be able to. It would be the wrenching apart that sent me mad, if anything was going to – I felt sure of that.

But what could I do? I was back to where I had been before I left London for the countryside: trapped and utterly reliant on others. I didn't dare tell Tom and Mrs Jelphs the whole truth. I couldn't run away: I had no money. My father would never go against my mother. As for James, my instinct in the cafe that last time had been right: he would not want to know about it.

So I did nothing. I felt as if a seam of pure fear lay just beneath the surface of my skin, rippling and threatening, like lava, to break the surface. The only thing that eased the anxiety, just slightly, was being in Tom's presence so I spent as much of that day and the next with him as I could. He pushed Joseph in an ancient perambulator that had once belonged to him so we could take a sun-dappled walk through the beech woods, then spread a rug and sit by the stream when I tired. Only once did I allow myself to pretend that we were a family, Tom Joseph's father – it was too hard to return to reality.

The presence of the baby changed something between Tom and me, even during the anticipatory lull of those two days. Tom was no longer so proud and quick to take offence and I was less afraid to show my affection towards him. The attraction, that flinty charge between us, had not dimmed but changed. I saw that not only I but both of us were playing a child's make-believe game of a happy family: father, mother and baby, all living harmoniously in a place of almost fairy-tale beauty. Around us the birds sang, the breeze caressed and the stream burbled contentedly, and I couldn't imagine why I'd ever thought of the valley as melancholy. The threat was now beyond its steep sides and I wished for the first time that I could lower the blue sky, like a lid, sealing us off from the rest of the world.

A telegram from my mother arrived on the third day. By a quirk of Fate, she had missed Mrs Jelphs's letter for a day – my father having picked it up with his newspaper by mistake. The fact that she had gone to the expense of a telegram spoke volumes of her anger at my deception, though the message, which had to remain neutral enough for other eyes, said only that she would arrive at the station the following afternoon around two o'clock. She thanked Mrs Jelphs for her invitation to stay but said that we would return on the last train, which left Stonehouse at twenty past five. There would be time only for a polite cup of tea at Fiercombe, and I watched Mrs Jelphs frown in confusion as she realized it.

I lay awake for a long time that night, my exhaustion after the birth no match for the fear that juddered through me. I tried to calm myself when I was feeding Joseph, not wanting to transmit my feelings through my milk, but by the time he woke hungry for the third time – just as the dawn light revealed the first overcast sky I'd seen since the storm – I was restless enough to dress and take him downstairs.

We were in the small parlour when Tom came in, his eyes as smudged with tiredness as mine. Joseph had already fed and was quiet again.

'We didn't wake you, did we?' I said.

Tom shook his head. 'No, it was just one of my bad nights.'

'Were you thinking about Henry?'

'No, not him,' he said shortly.

We sat in silence for a few minutes until he spoke again. 'Is it too early for a drink?'

'Yes, it is,' I said. 'You drink far too much.'

My nerves were making me short-tempered but there was genuine concern for him too.

To my surprise, he laughed. 'No one has said that to me for years. My mother has long given up, says I won't be told.' He ruffled his hair in the way that had become so familiar to me. 'Don't you want to know what I was thinking about?'

I hoped he wasn't going to ask my advice about his father, or his inheritance, or something of that kind. I simply couldn't think about anything but my own fix in that moment.

'I was thinking about how much I didn't want you to go.'

It took me a moment to absorb his words and when I did I promptly burst into tears. At the sound, Joseph opened his eyes and peered at me in apparent astonishment. Tom came over to sit by me and pulled out a creased but clean handkerchief. 'I'm sorry, I just meant that –'

'There's something else you don't know,' I cut across his words. 'Something about Joseph that I couldn't tell you before because I couldn't bear to have you despise me.'

He nodded at me to go on, his face grave.

'When my mother made up the story that would allow me to come here, it wasn't just so I could . . . recuperate in the fresh air. It was because my pregnancy had to stay secret. My mother was horrified when she found out. I did well at school and then I got a good job, but she always wanted me to settle and marry. When I did what I did, with a married man, I ruined things for all of us, not just myself. Because there was never a husband, there can also never be a baby, do you see?'

I watched comprehension flood his face.

'So where . . . ?' he said.

'She decided that it would be better, more anonymous, to . . . arrange things in London. When we got back, we would give the baby to an orphanage straight away. I suppose it will be too late today, by the time we get back, so it will be tomorrow now.'

So I didn't disturb the baby again, I handed him to Tom and then put my head into my hands and wept, as quietly as I could. 'I don't know what to do,' I said, through the tears. 'All night I've been thinking about it – where I might go if I ran away before my mother gets here, how I could earn some money to keep us, but none of it works. It's impossible. There's no way out.'

He looked stricken rather than angry. 'Don't you have any other family you could go to? Or even give the baby to, for a time, have them adopt it so at least there would be a connection?'

'We've lost touch with my mother's wider family and

all my grandparents are dead. My father's sister lives in London but she couldn't possibly . . . Besides, my mother would never allow it, not so close to home. It's not like here, where you can hide away. She would be sure that someone would hear of it. She couldn't live with the shame.'

'What about you?' Tom said softly. 'Could you live with the shame?'

'I could, for him, but how would we live? I can't work if I have a baby, and if I can't work, there's no money.' I laughed bitterly. 'And who would marry a woman in my position? My mother would disown me if I disobeyed her, then Joseph and I would be entirely alone. I have no choice. It's as simple as that. I just haven't been able to admit it to myself until now.'

I had a fleeting thought of Elizabeth. Our circumstances had seemed so different and yet were not at root: both of us women, both of us mothers and both of us entrapped by those supposedly closest to us, unable to direct our own destinies.

Tom didn't say anything else. He got me some tea, and bread and butter, and simply sat with me until Nan arrived for her morning's work. When Mrs Jelphs came in and found us there, he distracted her from my red-rimmed eyes by talking about the flood damage. As he did, I held on to Joseph as tightly as I dared, studying every texture and line of his tiny body as if the memory would be some sort of compensation after he'd been taken away.

The weather didn't improve as the morning wore on towards afternoon, the sky a hard white hung with wisps of low cloud, like old smoke. Ruck left in the carriage at one o'clock and from then time seemed to accelerate, hurtling towards the hour of my mother's arrival. I hadn't even finished packing when I heard the carriage wheels on the gravel.

She was thinner than I remembered her – as if my predicament had whittled the flesh from her bones even as I had grown bigger with child. She didn't embrace me and, though I hadn't expected her to, I saw the scene through Mrs Jelphs's eyes and blushed at the absence of affection. Tom was nowhere to be seen and, in a way, I was glad of it – not quite able to imagine his and my mother's worlds colliding in Fiercombe's gloomy kitchen.

While Mrs Jelphs and my mother shared a pot of tea and reminisced in a rather forced manner in the small parlour, I excused myself to finish my packing. I left a sleeping Joseph with the two of them – not that my mother had done more than give him a cursory look before setting her jaw in the disapproving way I had seen so many times. Mrs Jelphs had surely noticed her lack of interest and I wondered what she had made of it.

In my room, I tried not to think about the fact that everything was the last time: the last time I would pull open the wardrobe door, the last time I would see myself in its foxed glass, the last time I would look out across the Great Mead, unfamiliarly shadowless under the dulled sky.

Outside on the gravel, my case and a bag of items pressed on me for the baby by Mrs Jelphs had been loaded into the carriage. I looked around but there was still no sign of Tom. I didn't blame him: the truth – the whole truth – was rather sordid as well as hopeless. I thought he probably didn't like goodbyes, either. Perhaps I would see him in London, as he had suggested. But perhaps I wouldn't.

Mrs Jelphs clasped me to her while Ruck waited to help me up into the carriage. My mother was already settled on the seat and making no effort to hide her impatience to leave.

'I will miss you – and the little one – so very much,' Mrs Jelphs whispered fiercely in my ear, and when I drew back I knew that she would go to her room and weep after we had left.

I looked around for Tom again and she must have seen my disappointment – though it was so much more than that – in my face.

'I don't know where he's got to,' she said anxiously. 'I know he'll be sorry to have missed you.'

'Alice,' said my mother sharply. 'I'm sure Mrs Jelphs has plenty to be getting on with today. Mr Ruck too.'

I climbed gingerly into the carriage, Ruck supporting me, and Mrs Jelphs handed up Joseph.

'Will you send me a picture now and then?' she said. 'You know you can bring him to see us whenever you like. Will you come next summer? We would be so glad to have you.'

'Yes, perhaps,' I said, biting the inside of my cheek so that I didn't cry. 'Thank you again for everything you've done. I'll never forget it.' My voice trembled.

Ruck lifted the reins and we moved off. I looked back and Mrs Jelphs was standing at the gate to the kitchen garden I'd first walked through at the beginning of the summer, wondering what the next months would bring. She raised her hand, her face a curious mix of emotions:

sadness, loneliness and even something that looked like relief, though I knew she was sad to see me leave. I clutched Joseph closer to me and felt my mother stiffen slightly as she noticed.

We rounded the corner of the manor, the gravel beneath us giving way to packed earth. Too soon we were passing the little churchyard, past the tomb of Edward Stanton and his baby son. Now I would never know what had really happened to Elizabeth and her daughter and I felt a pang that I was leaving them behind, as well as everything else. It was all too sudden and, as we reached the tunnel of storm-damaged but still lush rhododendron bushes, I had to fight the urge to clamber down from the carriage with Joseph and run.

It was as we came out from under those unchecked flowers that I saw him: a lone, lean figure who stepped out into the middle of the lane. Ruck slowed the horse to a stop.

'Who's this, then?' my mother said loudly enough for Tom to hear.

'I'm Thomas Stanton,' he said, as he reached us. His voice sounded confident and privileged in the quiet lane. 'You must be Alice's mother.'

He put up a hand and my mother shook it quickly. 'Pleased to meet you,' she said curtly. 'I hope Alice has thanked you for allowing her to stay here.'

'Oh, yes. In fact, she's made herself quite indispensable,' said Tom.

I blushed. 'Well, I've tried to be as much of a help to Mrs Jelphs as I could although in the last few weeks I –'

412

'Not just to Mrs Jelphs,' Tom interrupted. 'Mrs Eveleigh, I'm afraid I've rather taken advantage of Alice's skills as a typist while she's been here. I'm no good at correspondence and the like and, now that my father is abroad so much, most of the estate paperwork falls to me. Alice has been invaluable. In truth, she's become something of an unpaid secretary.'

I opened my mouth to speak, then closed it again. Tom had a curiously intense look about him and instinct told me to keep quiet.

'In fact, I've been mulling things over during the last day or so. If I'd known you were coming to fetch Alice and the baby so soon I would have been a bit quicker off the mark.' He brought out his cigarettes, lit one and looked thoughtfully at it.

'I'm glad she's made herself useful,' my mother said, with an impatient edge. 'I'm sure it was the least she could do. It's nice to meet you, Mr Stanton – is that what I call you? Unfortunately we really must be on our way if we're to catch our train.'

'Well, that's precisely what I wanted to talk to you about. I have an offer for Alice.'

My heart began to thud in my chest and the baby shifted in my arms as if he could feel it.

'An offer?' I said faintly. 'What do you mean?'

Tom smiled broadly. 'Well, to be precise, it's an offer of work. A few days here and there at first, of course, but later, when the child is older and I take on full responsibility for the estate, there will be rather more to do. Mrs Jelphs adores children so I'm sure she'll be keen to help you with little Joseph. Of course, you can continue to live in the house. Perhaps, eventually, we can tidy up one of the estate cottages for you.'

'She can't possibly stay here,' said my mother, sharply. 'She'll need to find work in London as soon as we get back. I'm afraid we need her contribution since her father lost one of his grounds-keeping jobs. Times are hard for some of us.'

'But surely she won't be going back to work yet. Not with such a young baby.'

My mother said nothing, her lips a thin line.

'And as for money, well, that presents no difficulty,' Tom continued blithely. 'I understand that I must match a London wage to secure a secretary as good as Alice. She'll get her bed and board here, of course, so I suppose she'll have rather more than she did before, some of which I'm sure she would send home.'

He raised his eyebrows at me.

'Oh, yes, I would,' I said dazedly.

'Besides,' continued Tom, 'it's viewed as rather irregular for a mother to go back to work at all, isn't it? In that sense it's different here at Fiercombe. We can do things our way – one of the few advantages of being so isolated. I assume you were planning to look after the child yourself, Mrs Eveleigh?'

'There'll be no need,' she began to say.

'Oh?'

I watched the colour rise on her cheekbones just as it always did on my own. 'I mean that Alice will bring up the child herself,' she said.

Tom seemed perplexed. 'But then, as I see it, things will be rather difficult. How can Alice take a job in an office, working Monday to Friday and quite probably Saturday mornings too, and care for her child at the same time? Do you think she will find an employer who will let her do her work with Joseph by her side, as I would?'

I glanced at my mother again, expecting to see fury. Instead she seemed strangely defeated.

'Alice has had a dreadful time, losing her husband so young,' said Tom. 'The doctor was right to prescribe rest in a new place. Perhaps her fresh start ought to become a bit more permanent. After all, she and the baby seem to be thriving here, no one could deny that.'

My mother turned to me and I made myself meet her eye. 'Is this what you want, Alice?' she said.

I nodded, my eyes filling with tears. 'I can't go back now. I just . . . can't. Mother, do you understand?'

She searched my face for a long time but then finally nodded once. 'Have it your way then, though I can't think what I'm going to tell your father.'

'I think he'll understand,' I said.

She pushed out a sort of laugh. 'Yes, he always was soft when it came to you.'

I looked at Tom. 'Do you mean it? Can we really stay?'

He smiled openly. 'It will be as much for my sake as yours, if you do. My father is about to start his retirement in earnest and I had no idea how much of the estate paperwork he still did.'

I could have cried again but managed to swallow the tears. 'I will, then. Thank you, Mr Stanton. You're very kind.'

'Not at all. Now, Mrs Eveleigh, you're very welcome to stay a night and catch the train tomorrow,' he said.

My mother shook her head. 'No, I must get back. Mr Eveleigh will worry otherwise.'

Tom lifted my things out of the carriage, then held out his arms for the baby. I had to lean over my mother as I passed him down and then, as I straightened again, I knocked her handbag, which fell into the footwell and spilt its contents.

'Oh, how clumsy of me,' I said, as I bent to pick it all up.

'Leave it now,' she said, but I'd already crouched down awkwardly for the spare handkerchiefs, keys, a folded train timetable, loose change and a cardboard envelope that reminded me of the photograph of the little girl I felt sure was Isabel.

My mother reached for it but it was too late, I'd already opened the flap. In many ways, it was like the Victorian photograph. A child had been positioned on a chair, cushions around her to prop her up and a ribbon tied in her hair. The only real differences were in the clothes and the expression on this little girl's face, which was open and eager, the eyes enormous and full of life.

'Is this . . . me?' I said wonderingly.

'Who else would it be?' my mother said sharply, as she took it from me.

Tom helped me down, then moved away with Joseph so I could say goodbye.

I reached up to clasp my mother's hand. 'It would have broken my heart,' I whispered. 'You do know that, don't you?'

She looked into the distance and I saw, with a shock, that she was holding back tears. 'I couldn't think of another way.'

'I know,' I said. 'But now there is one.'

'Yes,' she said. 'I know I've been hard on you. If I wanted to toughen you up it was only to protect you. There's so much of your father in you and I didn't want you to be hurt. That was all it ever was, Alice. I wanted you to be strong like me.'

'I am, though. Can't you see I am?'

She reached down to touch my cheek briefly.

I glanced towards Ruck, who had thoughtfully got down to adjust the horse's bit, and dropped my voice. 'Mother, did you want me?'

She turned to me with astonishment. 'Whatever do you mean?'

'When I was born, were you . . . unhappy?'

She looked down at the cardboard photograph, which she was still holding. 'Some women get that way. There was someone I knew once who had been ill with it, mad with it even, and I wondered a few times if I would be too. But it wasn't like that for me. With me, it was fear – not fear for my mind but fear that I'd lose you.

'I've never told your father this. I've never told anyone this before, but there was a baby before you, when we were first married. I began to bleed the very day I felt the quickening. Your father was at work and I was going to tell him I was having a child that evening. When I fell pregnant with you, I expected to lose you every day. I thought that terror would stop when you were born, but it didn't. I couldn't live like that, so fearful, and it would have done you no good either.'

'So you closed the door,' I said quietly.

She sighed. 'For both our sakes. Besides, you had your father to love you.'

I laid my hand on hers for a moment, withdrawing it before she could, but she hadn't moved, her hand still on the photograph of me.

'Mother, will you come and see us here, you and Father? If I send the fare?'

She glanced back towards the bundle in Tom's arms as though she was seeing it for the first time. 'I expect we might. He'll be glad, you know, that you've been able to keep him.'

'Are you glad?'

'I think you'll do a better job of being a mother than I ever have, Alice.'

'Oh, no, I didn't . . .'

'I mean it. You will, and I'm happy for it.'

I stood waving until the carriage had turned up Fiery Lane and my mother was out of sight. Then I turned back towards my child, and Tom.

Alice

July 1936

I didn't forget about Elizabeth during the three years that followed: she was always there; it was just that my own life was suddenly so full and then, in time, so content. Occasionally I caught sight of the sewing box and her face would swim into view, though not as I had seen it in the portrait that had been hidden in the manor's nursery but blurred, like the photograph Hugh Morton had shown me. I suppose I came to associate her with the uncertainty and anxiety that clouded my first summer in the valley, then with the wooden box that had belonged to her and finally with a box fashioned in my mind, into which I put her and Isabel.

There was one occasion when I might have been drawn back into their story but I chose not to go. My own future was only tentatively secured then, and I was still preoccupied with Joseph – Tom, too, of course.

It was almost summer again when I was nearly hooked for the second time by Elizabeth, a year on from my arrival in the valley. Hugh Morton had come to tea and the two of us, full of Mrs Jelphs's lemon and poppy seed cake, were sitting in a couple of deckchairs on the lawn just beyond the Tudor garden, the tinkling stream a little way off.

A few days earlier, Tom had discovered the photograph of Isabel that had been hidden in the nursery window-seat. We had never put it back and it had somehow found its way under the rug in the small parlour. He had seen a corner of it poking out and brought it to me when he realized what it was. Now I remembered it and wanted to show it to Hugh, though I was careful not to let Mrs Jelphs see it. Some instinct that had survived from the previous year told me it would upset her.

When I handed it to Hugh, he stared at it for a long minute without saying a word. When he did speak, he sounded sad. 'They were a rum bunch in those days.'

'What do you mean?' I said.

'I believe it's one of those mourning pictures. *Memento mori*. They took them as a last memento. In poorer families it was probably the only time they could spare the expense.'

I took the picture of Isabel back from Hugh and stared at it more closely. She was looking not quite at the camera but at some indistinct point in the distance. 'Surely not,' I said to Hugh. 'I've heard of those but thought they were taken with the children lying down surrounded by flowers, as if they were asleep.'

'Her eyes look odd, don't they?' he said.

I nodded slowly, aware for the first time of the wind that had begun to keen in the highest branches of the beech trees.

'Sometimes they would paint eyes on the closed lids. It's macabre, to say the least. They would prop them up in chairs as though they were still alive, like this poor little one. It's said that they sometimes used metal stands to keep them upright but I don't know how much truth there is in that.' He sighed. 'I wonder what did happen to her. This rather puts paid to my romantic notion of her disappearing abroad with a rich relative.'

That night I slept only fitfully, my dreams haunted by figures from the past as they hadn't been for many months. I woke with the old urge to go to the summerhouse and lose myself in Elizabeth's words, but then Joseph cried out for me and I decided to put her away in the box again. It was easy enough to avoid the path that ran along the stream to the little summerhouse and I no longer had to fight temptation to look in the window-seat of the old nursery: I had peered into it one night when Joseph couldn't settle only to find it empty.

Besides, any lingering questions about Elizabeth and Isabel had retreated as soon as my mother had left the valley without Joseph and me. I felt as though we had been saved. After she was safely on her way back to London, Tom sat Mrs Jelphs and me down in the small parlour and between us we thrashed out the finer details of the plan that Tom had scarcely managed to outline in his head before presenting it to my mother. Mrs Jelphs hadn't been able to hide her delight at not being parted from the baby, though I saw her steal a few curious glances at Tom and me as we talked.

'I had no idea there would be so much work for you to do, Thomas,' she said at one point. 'I didn't know your father was intending to step down so soon.'

'I'm not sure he was, in all honesty,' said Tom, with a smile. 'I wrote to him when I was in London. I said I was ready to take more on, if he was willing.'

'And was he?' I said, feeling Mrs Jelphs's questioning eyes on me again.

Tom laughed. 'Yes. In fact, he sounded rather pleased in his reply. He said it was about time I grew up and took the helm. I must say, I wasn't sure he would think me up to it.'

'Well, there you are,' I said.

When Mrs Jelphs went to prepare the supper, I asked the questions I hadn't been able to in front of her: whether he really needed my help, if he was sure he didn't mind me staying on, was he regretting the impulse to rescue us now that it was made real. There was only one question I didn't ask that night – a question that wouldn't be answered until deepest winter settled over the valley, the denuded trees and thick, blanketing snow oddly familiar from the photographs Henry and Tom had taken as boys.

One day, during the week before Christmas, we were outside in the Tudor garden: Tom, Joseph and I. Ruck had shovelled a path past flowerbeds turned to square pillows of brilliant white by the snow and we made our way carefully up to the highest terrace for the best view of the house. The weak wintry light was fading fast that afternoon. We turned to look back at the house and I thought how different it seemed from my first glimpse, months earlier, from the same vantage point. Fires and lamps had been lit in all the rooms and the light that spilt out glowed warmly against the snow that lay in thick shelves on the sills. Even the usually sombre yews had been made festive, the snow covering the dark foliage, like a layer of royal icing.

Tom swept the wooden bench clear and we sat down

to admire it all. All sound had been deadened by the snow-fall and the valley, always quiet, had been left profoundly silent. Whatever it was that had been growing between Tom and me since the summer now seemed enormous in the heavy air. I heard him swallow and turned to look at his profile. A spot of colour had appeared on his cheek.

'Alice,' he began.

'Yes?' I quavered. All through autumn and into winter we had talked in the small parlour and taken long walks in the valley, and through it all I had wondered if there could ever be anything between us. I had thought of his words about things being done in their own way at Fiercombe many, many times.

'Are you happy here?' he said.

'I don't think I've ever been happier,' I said honestly. 'Are you, Tom?'

'I never thought I would be again but I am, yes – for the first time since Henry and I were boys.'

'Boys taking photographs of the snow,' I said softly.

He smiled. 'Yes, since then.'

I shifted the baby on to my shoulder, then reached out to Tom with my free hand. 'I know I've said it before but . . .'

'You're not going to thank me for saving you from the workhouse again, are you?'

'You joke about it but I –'

'Alice, I did it as much for me as for you.'

I tutted. 'I wasn't the only girl in Gloucestershire who could type.'

'I'm not talking about your typing.'

'No?' I looked him in the eye. They were very blue, even in the dying light.

'No,' he said, and reached out to cup my face in his hands. The kiss, when it came, was light and sweet, and everything after it was just as simple. We were married just as the valley welcomed the first green shoots of spring.

Three months ago I gave birth to our daughter. The event brought none of the drama that had accompanied Joseph into the world: she arrived not early but a day late, the midwife and Mrs Jelphs in steady attendance, Tom just outside the room and the weather entirely unremarkable. During the new baby's first weeks I did wonder if the darkness that had come for my grandmother, and for Elizabeth, might be summoned by the arrival of a Stanton child in the valley – if I was somehow pushing my luck with this second baby, provoking something in Fiercombe's past and in my own blood. But as the days accumulated and nothing happened, I forgot to be afraid. I was well – that much was obvious when I looked in the mirror.

There was only one moment when I felt the cold finger of fear brush the nape of my neck and that was when I told Mrs Jelphs we had decided to name the baby Isabel. It was just a fleeting look, a flash of horror that briefly leached away the colour and ease from her face and so, later, when I went to the nursery to look at my tiny daughter's sleeping form and smoothed her silvery curls back off her forehead, I told myself it had been nothing more than a trick of the light.

In my heart I knew, though, that whatever I thought

had been switched off in the valley after Joseph's birth had only been turned down. It was still there, a heartbeat deep in the ancient earth beneath the Great Mead. It wasn't in my mind – I was perfectly well, I knew that to my very core – it was whatever had happened before. The past was clamouring to come in once again.

Elizabeth

She had dressed herself that morning, sending away her maid because she couldn't bear anyone to see her body or touch her with gentle, pitying fingers. The flesh of her stomach was still stretched but the taut mound the child had inhabited had a deflated, defeated look about it. She had been glad to cover it with the stiff black fabric they had made up into mourning for her. This was the first day she had found the strength to leave her bed and put it on.

Outside, the rain fell like stair rods. She opened the window to hear it better and thought she could discern in the hiss and clatter against grey stone and glass, the hoofs of the horses that had taken away the little coffin four days earlier. The sound mingled with the others in her head, which were becoming ever clearer, ever more pressing. The murmurs of the children who'd died inside her, the last only a week before, had been joined by another voice, belonging to an older woman, whose low, unhurried tones soothed her like a balm.

The rain had wrapped the valley floor in a grey cloak. She couldn't even see the lake: the world seemed to end at the top of the staircase that led down from the Italian gardens. Through the rain she thought she glimpsed the Styx's ferryman on the steps, waiting patiently for his next fare, but then she peered harder and he dissolved into nothing.

As she pinned up her hair as best she could, she avoided

looking into the glass. She thought that if she met her own gaze she would be distracted from what she had to do, from what the older woman had said would be best for everyone. The pins slid in easily, the coils of her hair complicit in her need to hurry. When she had finished, she hung an old shawl over the trio of mirrors, noticing her wedding band as she did so. She slipped it off and let it roll under the shawl's folds.

She didn't meet anyone on her way to the nursery. That's not luck, said the older woman. They're staying out of your way. They know what's got to be done.

The door was ajar. The heavy oak swung back silently, too new to have warped in the damp valley. The child was kneeling up on the ottoman, which she must have dragged from the end of her bed to the window, her small hands and nose pressed against it. The warmth of her skin and breath had made auras of mist on the glass.

'Isabel,' Elizabeth called. 'Come to me.'

The little girl rushed into her and she kissed the top of her head.

'Quiet now, little one,' she said, crouching painfully so their faces were level. 'All will be well soon.'

'Will you have to go away, Mama?' she whispered.

Elizabeth shook her head. 'No. I will always be here with you.'

Isabel smiled at that: a vestige of a happier self.

Don't be too long, said the voice in Elizabeth's head. You're taking too long.

'Isabel, you're so tired. Look at the shadows around your eyes.' She led the little girl over to her bed and pulled the coverlet over her. She stroked her hair until she fell asleep, her breathing heavy and regular. The door closed behind Elizabeth with a well-oiled click.

Isabel sat up when she was sure her mother had gone. She got out of bed and fetched her new button boots from their place under the desk. The leather was stiff, the buttons stoutly sewn to it, and her fingers wouldn't work quickly enough.

Her mother had not come out from behind her bedroom door – not since the men had carried her back to the house after the baby had come out of her dead and blue, choked on a rope that had got inside there somehow. Isabel had run as fast as she could but she had not been able to find her father anywhere. Not in his rooms or in the stables. By the time she had decided to tell Edith, who was always kind to her, and they had got back to the old nursery, it had been too late.

That morning she had gone to her mother's door, laying her hand flat on the thick wood that separated them. A noise behind her had made her jump and she had turned to see the nursery-maid who hated her.

'Come away now,' she had said, in a hard whisper. 'You mustn't disturb your mother. You've been told that.'

The maid had grasped her arm tightly and started to drag her up the corridor. Isabel dug the fingernails of her other hand into the rough skin of the maid's. The girl took a sharp breath. 'You've drawn blood, you wicked little thing,' she spat, her voice rising. 'Do as you please, then. Your precious mama will be gone soon anyway, without a thought of you. Dr Logan has been sent for again, just as he always is when she's raving mad.'

Isabel had run back to her room and shut the door, where she had sat still, thinking about the maid's warning, and about the magician's return.

The idea of being abandoned with the servants and her father sent white-hot spurts of terror through her. She had seen how her father looked at her. She knew the baby was dead and her mother ill because of her. He hadn't needed to say so.

When the boots were finally fastened she ran quickly out and down the stairs, as silent as a ghost. She knew where all the creaks were.

She looked around the hall, half expecting to see her father standing at the library door, but there was no sign of him. She wondered where the tiny coffin was. It must be there somewhere: she had seen it arrive a few days earlier in a white carriage.

She reached the front door, which had been left open by her mother – she knew it must have been her – and looked back. Still nobody had come to stop her.

She had run all around the formal gardens, the ones her father had ordered to look like a famous one far away, when she saw her mother. She had stopped on the final step that led to the lake.

Isabel briefly turned her face up to the rain. Instead of the upturned bowl of blue that had greeted her almost every day that summer, the sky seemed to have lowered until it sealed off the valley. It reminded her of how the larder ceiling had looked last winter when there had been so much rain. It had seemed to sag.

She glanced down and saw the rain running off her boots in urgent, shiny trails. The ribbon in her hair had drooped, one end dripping down her neck and under the collar of her dress. Below, her mother appeared to be listening to something, even nodding to herself as she took the last step.

Isabel followed closely but her mother still didn't hear her. The lake was full to the brim and would spill over into the grass of the Great Mead before long. Her mother bent and started gathering stones. The lake's bottom had been lined with rubble, Isabel's father had told her, to stop the water leaking away. Jagged pieces always seemed to find their way out, though, to be scattered around the edges. Isabel watched her mother, suddenly apprehensive about approaching her.

After a few minutes, the pockets of her dress were full. She stood up and brushed the masonry dust off her dress as Isabel stared, not understanding the game yet but straining to so that she could join in. She watched closely as her mother gazed out across the water. Her face and hands were pale against the black fabric of the new dress.

Then, still without looking back or noticing Isabel, she began to wade out into the lake, the stones in her skirts grating together as she moved.

Isabel found her voice. 'Mama, come back! Please, Mama. Wait for me.'

But she didn't seem to hear over the rain and whatever else she was listening to.

Isabel thought her chest would burst with panic. She glanced in the direction of the house, wondering whether she had time to run back for help. Through the downpour she could scarcely even see its grey stones. If she took too long, like last time, she knew her mother would be gone.

She seemed a long way out now. The lake was deep –

Isabel had been warned often not to get too close and fall in. Beyond the shallow edges that were beginning to flood, the bottom fell away steeply. Already she could see that her mother had tilted her chin up to keep the water out of her mouth. Her hair had come down and was swirling around her like weeds. The swell of the water turned her slowly around so that Isabel could see the side of her face. She did not seem frightened; she looked perfectly calm.

The thought that struck Isabel then did so with such force that her knees buckled slightly. *She is leaving me here so she can be with my little brother.* It felt like the truth. She cried out again but there was not a flicker of a response. Her mother's eyes were closed.

She thought about taking her boots off but they were so new that she didn't want to go without them. The water when she stepped into it was colder than she expected and her teeth began to chatter immediately. The mud and sodden grasses beneath her were treacherous and she slid further in without warning, taking down a sour gulp of the water as she did. Out of her depth, she thrashed around, reaching out to grasp at a clump of rushes that came away in her hand, useless.

Her dress and petticoats were dragging her down and she opened her eyes wide under the murky water for a terrifying instant, unidentified shadows tangling in her boots. With all her might she broke the surface of the water and shrieked out for her mother, who finally opened her eyes and turned to her child.

'Come, then,' she said and, not so far away after all, reached out and pulled Isabel to her.

Epilogue: Alice

The manor is quiet tonight, as I finish writing my account. It is such a very old house, a survivor of five or more centuries, and you can usually hear it settle and sigh after sunset on midsummer days like this one, the heat stealing out of its timbers and the damp creeping in to take its place. But tonight it waits patiently for me to finish. It was high time I set it all down – I have only been waiting till I knew the truth about them. The truth about Elizabeth and Isabel: the last piece of the puzzle that has haunted me from my first days in the valley.

It was Mrs Jelphs who gave me the answers and, in the end, it was just a little thing that finally made her expose the truth she had been shielding all these years. A little thing but also a fitting thing.

A few weeks ago, the two of us were sitting in the Tudor garden admiring the newly trimmed yew pylons. Mrs Jelphs's embroidery hoop was forgotten in her lap, as was my book in mine, and little Isabel was sound asleep in the old perambulator that had once transported Tom, and Henry before him. Joseph had been playing peacefully on the topmost terrace but now began to cry.

'What is it, darling?' I called, as I got to my feet and went to help him down the stone steps. 'What's happened?'

'My hare,' he said thickly, and held aloft the velveteen

toy he wouldn't be separated from. It was missing one of its black bead eyes.

I picked him up and went back to where he had been. It took a few minutes on my hands and knees but then I spied it, rolled into a cushion of moss, its polished surface glinting in the morning sun.

'Here it is, Joe!' I cried triumphantly. 'Mrs Jelphs will have it sewn back on for you in half a minute.'

He was already distracted by another toy so I took the bead over to her, watching her face close slightly as I handed it over with the little hare. Laying her embroidery aside she reached over to her sewing box and lifted the lid.

'Do you remember I asked you about that box the first day I was here?' I said.

She glanced up at me. 'I was sharp with you, wasn't I?'

I smiled. 'I'm sure I deserved it, being nosy.'

She shook her head. 'You weren't to know who she was to me.'

Her direct reference to Elizabeth surprised me, and I kept silent so that I didn't scare her off, just as I had learnt to do in my early days at Fiercombe.

'You gave me such a start saying her name, I remember that,' she continued. 'I hadn't heard it spoken aloud for so long. It hurt to talk of her but it was something of a relief too.' She brushed the soft nap of the little hare with her fingertip. 'She made this, you know. She wouldn't let me. She wanted to make it herself. For Isabel.' Glancing over at the pram, she smiled. 'For the first Isabel.'

Her openness was disarming and I found I couldn't keep quiet then.

'Mrs Jelphs, there's something I want to tell you. I shouldn't have done it, I had no business looking.'

She looked up from stroking the hare.

'On the day I arrived, when you left me in the small parlour, I didn't just look at the sewing box, I looked in it. The secret compartment – I'd seen one like it before so I knew how to open it. There was a flower inside, and a note to you. I'm afraid I read it. That was what made me ask over supper that evening – not the library book. I'm sorry.'

She didn't say anything but tucked a skein of silks deeper into the box to reveal the small brass button, which she pressed. The platform of satin shifted, just as it had for me three years earlier. She took out the note and I saw her eyes move over the words, though I'm sure she knew them by heart.

'I should have told you the truth about her – and Isabel too,' she said eventually, so quietly that I found myself leaning towards her. I held out my hand and, when she took it, her fingers were as soft and cool as I remembered them from that first day.

'I couldn't tell you – or anyone – because I've always blamed myself. I thought that if I never talked of it again then it wouldn't be quite so true, somehow. Only Ruck and I are left now of those who knew and we have never spoken of it. Never. People up in Stanwick wanted to know what had happened but we never said. It was none of their business.

'I remember the weather breaking on the day you gave birth to Joseph. Nearly three years ago now – how fast it's gone. I think the rain of the previous two months must

434

have fallen in a couple of hours. The rhododendrons bent their poor heads, some of them eventually snapping off under the force of it. The stream burst its banks and, what with the water running down off the escarpment, Fiery Lane soon turned into a river.

'When we found you there, and we nearly missed you because you'd hidden yourself almost inside the hedgerow, I thought it was happening all over again. I saw again, as if it was yesterday, Elizabeth on the banks of the lake, just after Ruck had pulled her out. Unlike you, she wasn't breathing.'

'Elizabeth drowned?' I saw her lovely face, the eyes closed, her long hair flowing around her.

Mrs Jelphs nodded, just once. 'They both did. We didn't find the child at first. No one knew she was missing. But then Ruck saw her little boot in the reeds at the edge. I kept it afterwards, though the sight of it broke my heart. Years later, when Thomas's parents had virtually moved away, I took it with the other things from my room and hid them in the nursery. It was a relief – just a tiny fraction of a relief – no longer to keep them so close. With the little boot was a portrait of Elizabeth that Edward Stanton had never liked, a blanket I had knitted for the new baby and a photograph of Isabel I could never look at.'

'I've seen it,' I said quietly. 'I found it all.'

She sighed. 'Well, you'll know, then. The photograph was taken at Dr Logan's suggestion, and what a morbid one too. He arrived a few hours after . . . after we found them. I like to think that I wouldn't have let him take Elizabeth away again, if she'd still been alive to take, but really, what could I have done? Instead I would have said nothing, just as I had the time before. I have always said nothing. Until now.'

'Where are they?' I said.

She looked down. 'Sir Edward was not thinking straight. At least, that's what I chose to believe. He had only buried his tiny son a few days before. Now, he had to bury the rest of his family. He was full of rage and there was no one to blame. I believe he was actually mad with grief, easily as ill as his wife had ever been. He sent Dr Logan away, then dismissed most of the staff. He sent them from the valley in the space of a few hours, telling them a month's pay would follow.

'By evening, there were no more than half a dozen of us left, it seemed. We stayed below stairs, none of us going to bed at all. I was completely numb with the shock of it. I'm sure we all were. Our mistress, little Isabel, both gone. Those who remained didn't intend to stay. Already there was talk of a curse in the valley. It's all a dreadful blur now.'

'I couldn't find them in the churchyard,' I said. 'I looked for them on the day I went into labour with Joseph, just as the storm was breaking. I've looked since but they are nowhere. I thought of asking you more than a few times but then . . . I just couldn't.'

Mrs Jelphs gripped my hand tighter. 'I should have told you. Not speaking up has never helped anyone here. Not just then, but in the years that followed, too. When Thomas lost his brother he was scarcely allowed to speak of him again. When you came, we – Ruck and I – thought we could keep you safe, not by warning you but by watching you.'

She bowed her head.

'Where are they?'

She dragged in her breath. 'They are buried in the Great Mead. The graves aren't marked. I don't know precisely where – it was done before we knew about it. Sir Edward said they had sinned. It . . . it wasn't an accident, you see. There were rocks found in her pockets – pieces of Stanton House used to weigh her down.' She shook her head. 'He said Elizabeth had sinned for taking Isabel's life as well as her own. I don't know how he thought a tiny girl had sinned but he partly blamed her for the baby's death. I know that much. It was written all over his face in those terrible days after the stillbirth.'

I closed my eyes and thought about the corner of the Great Mead I had found myself drawn towards on the day Joseph was born. They were there, I knew it. They had always been there.

Since that day, when Isabel's little hare helped to draw out her confession, Mrs Jelphs has been different, altered and lightened by the liberation of it. I see now that she hasn't always been so reserved and careful – that the naïve, cheerful Edith who came through in Elizabeth's diary had been locked away with all her secrets. Now that she can talk freely of Elizabeth, whose portrait has replaced the horrible oil of the alchemist, she is quite changed. She even looks different: younger and less brittle. She is Edith again.

I was glad of her confession, not only because I finally knew what had happened to Elizabeth but because of Isabel. At least a few people had remembered her mother, mourned her all this time, but Isabel had almost been forgotten. Now her name, handed down to my daughter, is spoken aloud in the manor again and it has made something in the atmosphere of the valley shift and realign.

Their stones were laid early this morning, the air still fresh, the sky already a vaulted ceiling of blue. The stonemason had suggested granite, saying it would weather better than the soft, pale golden stone I wanted, but I had shaken my head firmly. 'Not granite for them.'

They lie in a secluded and lovely corner of the Great Mead, where the wild flowers bloom first in summer and the jewels of frost linger longest in winter. Now that it is midsummer again, I will walk out there each evening and watch as the tiny lamps of a thousand glow-worms are lit, earthbound stars all around them.

Acknowledgements

Thanks to all my family and friends who have supported me during the writing (and guilt-ridden not-writing) of this book. Special thanks, however, must go to my mum, for being a stalwart champion and early reader, and to my husband, Darren, who suffered without complaint me writing every weekend as my deadline approached. I also want to thank my fellow Cheltenham writers – Hayley Hoskins, Helen Maslin, Amanda Reynolds and John Matheson – for their company and encouragement, and Jade Smith and Andy Bodle for being firm friends throughout. My dog Morris is also due some recognition: lying across my keyboard didn't help much, but keeping me warm on the colder days did.

I must also mention Owlpen Manor in Gloucestershire for inspiring the setting of Fiercombe. I first came across this beautiful, atmospheric place in 2007, when I was invited to stay in one of the estate cottages for a travel piece I was writing. A few years later, I found another excuse to go and Sir Nicholas Mander, who lives there with his family, was kind enough to show me around. Thank you for letting me borrow some local names, features and ghost stories.

Huge thanks also to the wonderful team at Michael Joseph: particularly Louise Moore for liking it in the first place; Maxine Hitchcock, Celine Kelly and Lydia Good for their editorial expertise and general loveliness; Jessica Jackson and Sarah Arratoon for their marketing and publicity wizardry; and Hazel Orme for a meticulous copyedit. Last but certainly not least, thank you to my agent Kate Burke (and Diane Banks before her) for excellent suggestions, pinning me down to a deadline and enabling me to make novel-writing my actual, real-life job.

Reading Group Questions

1. Did you find that you related to Alice or Elizabeth, and if so, in what ways?

2. Why do you think that Mrs Jelphs stays at Fiercombe Manor, even though she is so reluctant to remember the past?

3. Alice has a complicated relationship with her mother; in what ways is the theme of mothers and daughters significant throughout the novel?

4. Which part of Alice and Elizabeth's story shocked you the most?

5. Do you think more could have been done to help Elizabeth? Who was really responsible for her death?

6. Alice seems to bring life back to Fiercombe Manor, and vice versa. Do you think that the personalities of other characters in the novel were also shaped by their connection to the house and landscape?

7. What did you think of the ways in which the author dealt with 'female madness', pregnancy and attitudes to post-natal depression in both the 19th and 20th centuries? Did Alice's revelations of the treatment that Elizabeth received surprise you?

8. Do you think that the characters are victims of their own circumstances? Do you feel that there are particular victims and villains in the story?

9. History seems to repeat itself as Alice's story begins to echo Elizabeth's. What impact did these echoes of the past have on your reading of the novel?

10. Were you surprised at Alice's decision to stay at Fiercombe Manor? Do you think you would have made a different choice in her position?